A Nation Divided

VOLUME TWO
For Love of Country

ROBERT MARCUM

Covenant Communications, Inc.

Cover image: *Sailors Ancient Kit* © Irina Tischenko. *Gettysburg Battlefield* © Paul Giamou.

Cover design copyright © 2013 by Covenant Communications, Inc.

Published by Covenant Communications, Inc.
American Fork, Utah

Printed in Canada
First Printing: September 2013

19 18 17 16 15 14 13   10 9 8 7 6 5 4 3 2 1

ISBN 978-1-62108-560-7

To my wife, Janene, the love and strength of my life.

Chapter One

MATTHEW ALEXANDER FOLDED THE PAPER and put it aside. Filled with news about the South's boasts since the fall of Fort Sumter, it sickened him. His home state of Louisiana had sent a good share of its militia marching toward Virginia in order to "defend the integrity of the new Confederate States of America."

"Nothing new, I don't suppose."

Matthew looked over at Joe Polanski, his partner of two months in Allan Pinkerton's new government intelligence agency.

"Same old rhetoric," Matthew responded. "If Southern politicians keep this up, we'll do battle before the end of the week."

Polanski was a broad-shouldered little man of maybe five feet five inches if he wore thick-soled shoes. A bulldog of a man, Joe was the son of immigrants from eastern Europe. He'd been with Pinkerton since the agency was established, and he had the scars to prove it. His most recent encounter had been in Maryland a few months earlier when troops from Northern states had been ambushed by a mob. Sent by Pinkerton to assess the situation there, Joe had learned that the Plug Ugly organization planned to attack, and had tried to intervene. He'd been shot for his efforts. Fortunately the bullet had been deflected by his hard head, and he only lost the upper half of his left ear.

Matthew had been assigned to work with Polanski because Joe knew the ropes better than anyone else and Matthew didn't have a lot of time for training.

Matthew removed his pocket watch. Four a.m. "I suppose he's still sleeping?" Matthew asked.

"I am not sure the man takes the time," Polanski said.

Matthew looked out the window of the White House. It was dark, and there was nothing to see but a few dimly lit streetlamps. There were a dozen other Pinkerton's around the property, but none of them were moving about. Laying his head against the back of the padded bench and stretching out a bit, Matthew closed his eyes. Maybe he could get a little shut-eye before the president was up and ready to work.

But it wasn't to be. Polanski slept even less than President Lincoln.

"The boss will arrive in about fifteen minutes," Joe said.

Matthew lifted his bowler hat and eyed his partner expectantly, causing Joe to shrug. "I haven't the slightest notion what it's about. Pinkerton don't pass everything he does by me, though it would be a smart move."

Matthew smiled. He'd been on bodyguard duty since Lincoln left Springfield. The train had meandered through what seemed like a hundred cities, and they'd stopped at every one of them for the president to give his speeches. Then there had been the scare of assassination that had forced them to sneak Lincoln into Washington, a decision Lincoln had regretted ever since. Since then, Matthew and Polanski had been assigned to keep Lincoln from being shot by disgruntled Southerners looking for a quick overthrow of the federal government. Lincoln didn't like it much. He wasn't used to being followed around by watchdogs. Made him feel unsafe, he said.

Matthew put the bowler back over his eyes in hopes that that was all Polanski had to say. It wasn't.

"Any mail catch up to you yet?"

Matthew's family still thought he was at West Point, or the Academy, but Pinkerton had arranged to have mail and telegrams sent to a nearby hotel room—a room Matthew seldom used.

"Adam says I have that commission in the Louisiana militia if I want it," Matthew answered, not bothering to move his hat from his eyes. Adam was Matthew's only brother and an attorney who practiced in New Orleans until accepting a commission in the same regiment.

Polanski smiled. "He'll disown you when he finds out you're riding shotgun for Lincoln."

Matthew had resigned his commission at the Academy with everyone believing he was going back to Louisiana. He would eventually but not now—not until Pinkerton thought he was ready.

"It would be worse if he knew what Pinkerton had in mind for me," Matthew said.

"Yeah, he would have you shot. What's the latest from your sister?"

"Last I heard she was still in St. Louis but intending to come here to be close to her husband. That was two weeks ago. Haven't heard from her since." He lowered his bowler over his eyes again.

"They still think you're at West Point?" Polanski asked.

"Yeah." Pinkerton had asked Matthew to keep his whereabouts a secret. If he was going to go undercover in the South, even his own family had to believe he'd turned rebel.

At six feet with thick, dark brown hair around his ears, Matthew had piercing blue eyes, one of which was partially damaged by an accident at the Academy. Squared at the shoulders and thin in the hips, he had been known for both his mental and physical acuity. Boxing champion for two out of three years, he held the record for knockouts, accomplished more by quickness than by overwhelming strength. He usually wore no beard, but this morning he sported a day-old growth that was already beginning to bother him. He scratched at it.

"I saw your new brother-in-law the other day. Forgot to tell you. He and his St. Louis boys are a part of Cump Sherman's brigade."

Matthew only nodded. They had talked about Rand Hudson before. Polanski had met Ann's husband while doing work for Pinkerton along the new Missouri railroad line, which had been attacked by marauders for the money the trains carried. Polanski hadn't told him the details.

Everything Matthew had learned about Rand Hudson had been good. The man was of good character, a good businessman with plenty of money and a strong constitutionalist who was willing to fight for his beliefs. Most important to Matthew was that Ann had chosen Hudson. Ann was the best when it came to knowing good character.

"The brigade's heading south in the morning," Polanski added.

Matthew sat up, his bowler falling into his lap, forcing him to grab it before it went to the floor. "They're moving against Beauregard at Manassas? I thought McDowell said they weren't ready?" He had read that in the newspapers of all places. Washington was an open book when it came to the war. More leaks than a sieve. One had only to read the papers to know what the army was doing—who was ready and who wasn't, how large their forces were, and even what some of their plans were. But then it was the same in the South. If this war went on very long, Lincoln would have to put a stop to such talk and so would Jefferson Davis, the so-called president of the Confederacy. Wars couldn't be fought with their enemy knowing as much about their troop movements as they themselves did. Because things were so open, Matthew was actually shocked that he hadn't heard. "Who shut the papers up?"

Polanski nodded. "You can bet they know this morning. Probably be in the first edition. McDowell has more than thirty thousand men; Beauregard, about twenty." He shrugged. "Numbers would favor McDowell."

"You're forgetting Johnston's ten thousand," Matthew said. General Joseph E. Johnston had troops camped in the Shenandoah Valley, a four-day march or a half-day train ride west of Manassas Junction.

Polanski leaned forward. "I heard from Pinkerton that Patterson has been ordered to make sure Johnston doesn't leave the Shenandoah. If they can be held there . . ." He sat back. "Well, then McDowell should win the day."

"But if he doesn't hold them—"

"You're a pessimist by nature, ain't you, Matthew boy," Polanski smiled.

Matthew shrugged. "A realist. McDowell is fighting with untried men, most of whom are ninety-dayers and who won't look kindly on being killed just a few days shy of release. It's a near guarantee they'll run if things get tough." When Lincoln first called for troops, he asked for volunteers on the basis of ninety days. Most considered an all-out war unlikely and felt that within that time frame a settlement would be found and no troops needed. Matthew, Southern born and bred, knew they were wrong on two critical counts. First, they underestimated Southern resolve to leave the Union, and second, they overestimated the ability of any general to prepare men for war in such a short time. Most joined out of passionate patriotism, which was fine, but they considered it a lark and had no desire to actually fight a war let alone die in one.

But the call for immediate action had reached fever pitch in the North; the call seemed to be ignoring troop preparation and focusing on the insolence of the Southern government moving their capital to Richmond, Virginia, only a stone's throw away from Washington.

Northern radicals wanted to crush this insolence by taking the whole wretched Confederate government to prison. Matthew knew it wouldn't be that easy. "And Hudson is with Sherman's Brigade?"

Polanski nodded. "Hudson is a good man, Matt, a fighter, but he's deliberate and keeps his head. And his boys are well trained. Not like the others who spend most of their time lying about, drinking, and carousing around the city causing trouble. His three hundred are disciplined—ready for a fight."

"Too bad there aren't more like them. I would feel a lot more comfortable about how McDowell will fare if they were."

They heard the entrance door open and close, the muffled sound of voices. "That will be the boss," Polanski said as he stood. "Check on the president, and make sure everyone's at their post."

Matthew got up and went down the hall to Lincoln's bedroom, where two well-armed men sat near the door. They nodded as he passed them and continued to the stairwell at the far end. The two men there were wide awake, and he went back the way he'd come, passing by Lincoln's door again just as the president stepped out.

"Mr. President," Matthew said.

"Matthew. What's going on?" Lincoln knew every man by name. He was neither pretentious nor demanding and was more comfortable sitting about with regular citizens and telling stories than he was mincing with politicians or high society. He dreaded balls and hated political game playing. He would rather be at a turkey shoot.

"Mr. Pinkerton is coming up, sir."

Lincoln nodded. "I'll get dressed."

Matthew gave a slight smile and a nod as Lincoln disappeared. Lincoln was still in his pants and shirt, his suspenders hanging to his knees. Matthew supposed that getting "dressed" meant adding a coat and shoes.

Matthew waited for only a minute before Pinkerton and two others came into view, a servant leading them, lantern in hand. Matthew recognized the two men as Secretary of State William H. Seward and Secretary of War Simon Cameron. Matthew knocked on the door, and Lincoln opened it, stepped out, and greeted his guests before inviting the three inside.

The president's office was still under remodel, and Mrs. Lincoln slept in an adjoining room. In order to accommodate the inconveniences, Lincoln had requested that a desk of considerable size be moved into his own bedroom. This would not be the first meeting he had held there.

* * *

It was nearly an hour before the three men came out. Seward's face was flushed red, a look he seemed to get whenever things didn't go his way, and Cameron had an arrogant smile on his face, a look he always had when things did go his way.

Seward noticed the sun was up and took a deep breath before thanking Pinkerton for making the meeting happen and telling him they'd find their own way out. Pinkerton let them go then signaled for Matthew and Polanski to follow him to his small office on the first floor. Once there, Pinkerton closed the door and filled them in.

"Seward wanted to delay the attack on Beauregard's troops; Cameron wanted to move forward. You boys could tell who won the argument. Two or three days from now we will fight our first battle." He took a deep breath. "It won't be our last. McDowell isn't ready, and Seward knows it." He looked hard at Polanski. "If McDowell loses and Beauregard is smart, they'll come north and try to take the capitol. If the North wins and marches on Richmond, Southern suporters in Washington may take action against the president. Either way, you're to see that Lincoln goes nowhere without a full contingent of men protecting him. Is that understood?"

Polanski nodded.

Pinkerton shook his head, a bit frustrated. "The man does not see the danger to himself, and he doesn't want to be seen as a coward so he may want to go out. Try to prevent it, but if he does . . ."

"I'll see that he's safe, but this sounds like you're leaving the city."

"McDowell needs intelligence. He wants me along. Heaven knows why; we haven't got a system set up worth talking about." He looked at Matthew. "And that, Mr. Alexander, is why it is time you went south." He pulled a heavy envelope out of his desk drawer and handed it to Matthew. "There's a good deal of money in there. If you're to look like the Southern gentleman we intend you to be, you'll need it."

"Then the president agrees with my—"

"The president knows this will be a long war. That means we need someone behind Confederate lines who can find a way to keep us informed and can attend to a little skull doggery at the same time." He smiled mischievously. "There is one lady you might look up. Elizabeth Van Lew. Hates slavery and isn't shy about it. The press in Richmond has excoriated her for her views even though she's a very prominent lady. She might just be willing to help."

Matthew nodded. It was a big order, especially in getting information back to Washington fast enough to make a difference. He could only hope that Elizabeth Van Lew had some solutions.

"Be careful, my boy," Pinkerton went on. "I have learned to like you and do not wish to see your name in the obituaries of the Southern papers. If you feel in danger, run without hesitation."

"Thank you, sir. I appreciate your trust." He knew the conversation was over and stood, extending a hand. Pinkerton stood and took it. "I'll gather my belongings and be leaving, sir."

"Put on a good show then, and we'll see you when this bloody mess is over."

Matthew nodded and left the office, then the White House. At his hotel, he packed his personal items before going to the dining room to get a substantial breakfast while he waited for his train's departure.

As he sipped his last bit of coffee, he noticed two women conversing in a dark corner of the dining room. One of the women stood, handed the second a letter, and spoke, though Matthew couldn't hear what she said. When she seemed to be finished, she smiled lightly and then gave a loving pat to the younger woman's shoulder, causing her to look up. Her returned smile was less comfortable, even a bit confused, and she fondled the letter before finally putting in her handbag. The first woman walked away, and as she passed a nearby window, Matthew recognized her. He was tempted to follow but waited as the second woman also stood and placed coins on the table to cover the cost of the meal. He could see from her stride and stiff demeanor that she was upset. Matthew got to his feet, flipped several of his own coins onto the table, picked up his bag, and put on his hat before following. He arrived in the street just as the first woman closed the door of her conveyance and was gone.

The woman was Rose O'Neal Greenhow, who had publicly shown support for the Confederacy and was believed to be spying for them. Matthew had been assigned to watch Mrs. Greenhow's house on two occasions and had seen prominent members of the federal government go inside both times. The first had been Senator Henry Wilson of Massachusetts, the chairman of military affairs and a good source of information about federal troops if one could get him to talk. Pinkerton's concern that Greenhow had the "physical attributes" to get Wilson talking had come to the fore when Matthew told him of the senator's early and rather lengthy visit.

Matthew looked up and down the street and saw two men watching him, slight smiles on their faces. He tipped his hat, and the two men smiled in return as they boarded a carriage to follow after Mrs. Greenhow. Pinkerton's men were on duty.

Matthew looked quickly about and saw the second woman climbing into an open buggy across and down the street. He quickly strode along the walk on the opposite side. He could see that she was of average height and weight, had ample dark hair done up atop her head, and even from a distance, he could see she was young, pretty, and moved with determination. Matthew's concern was for the letter he'd seen pass between the two women. If Greenhow was sharing secrets with Southern leaders, and Pinkerton was sure she was, she would have couriers.

But his time was limited. He had a train to catch, and he couldn't follow her long. A sudden idea occurred to him, and he picked up his pace enough to get ahead of the woman's buggy without drawing her attention. He then veered across the street directly in its path, spooking the horse and causing it to rear upward. Out of the woman's sight, Matthew flopped to the ground as the horses hooves came to the earth at a safe distance to his right. He lay still, waiting as the woman calmed the horse and a crowd gathered around his inanimate body. He was turned over, hearing a concerned chatter all about him. He opened his eyes to the woman leaning down, the stiff, upset demeanor he'd seen earlier replaced by a real look of fear and concern. Feeling a bit guilty at his ruse but unable to turn back now, Matthew blinked, faked an adequate moan, and then tried to sit up as if in pain.

"Are you all right, mister?" came a question from a lad to his left.

"Yes, are you all right?" asked the young woman.

Matthew looked into her light green eyes, momentarily taken aback by their color, but he forced himself to shake it off and give an answer. "Yes . . . I . . . I think so." He sat up straight then winced a bit, touching the back of his neck. As he tried to get to his feet, another man helped the woman aid him. "Thank you," he said, giving a slight smile. "It was my fault. I was in a hurry, and . . ."

She stood, her demeanor immediately changing. "Yes, you were, and yes, it was," said the woman. "You frightened my horse, and—"

Matthew frowned. "And *you* lost control of him," he said with a false but convincing irritation.

"Why, I . . . I did no such thing. You . . ." He noted that her accent was just slightly Southern but Southern nevertheless. But then his own voice had a Southern lilt to it, though his years at the Academy had made it hardly distinguishable.

The crowd began to dissolve mumbling or chuckling, and Matthew forced a smile. "Yes, yes, you are quite right. As I said, it was my fault."

He leaned over to pick up his bag then winced as if in pain before straightening. "I was in a hurry to catch my train to Richmond. Not many go there these days, and if I miss this one . . . well, I hear there is to be a battle between here and there, and I doubt that anyone will get through once it begins."

The woman's eyes softened again. "I am afraid you are already too late. There are no trains going to Richmond today and possibly for some time to come." She paused.

"Unless I can catch one that goes to Gainesville."

"But that is a very long way. I suppose you could go by steamer. If you have the right passes—"

"I don't, nor do I have time and connections to get them. Gainesville is a roundabout way to be sure, but it *is* possible and I really must get there." He pulled his watch from his pocket. He could have gone by steamer. He did have the connections. But Pinkerton had set up this route for a reason. Johnston's Confederate army was south of Front Royal, and he wanted Matthew to see it.

She waved a hand in invitation. "Come along then. The least I can do is see that you get to the station without injury." She gave a humorous smile. "After all, it's obvious you're a bit clumsy, and to leave you to your own devices could be dangerous for someone else's life as well as your own." Of average height but thin of form, the woman was both beautiful and energetic. He noted her hands were not those of a city girl kept from work but belonged to one who worked the land. He found himself very intrigued.

He smiled. "Your concern is touching, Miss . . ."

"Atwater. Millicent Atwater. My friends call me Millie. I am also of Southern heritage. Alabama born and of Virginia since a child, but I went to school for several years in New York. And you?"

"Matthew Alexander, formerly of Louisiana but most recently of West Point."

"Ah, and you are returning to the South to join your brothers in battle?"

Matthew sensed some sarcasm as he climbed in the buggy and unwrapped the reins. "You don't agree with Southern views?"

"I don't agree that we should tear this country apart because we cannot come to accommodation over slavery. I believe President Lincoln will help us if we will but give him a chance. Trampling on the Constitution by secession is a fool's errand. If we used the funds that will surely be spent killing one another to purchase the freedom of the slaves, we could save this country millions of dollars, not to mention hundreds if not thousands of lives," Millicent said stiffly.

Matthew was mystified. Rose Greenhow was an adamant supporter of Southern rights, and Millicent Atwater had been at breakfast with her. He decided to dig a little deeper, considering his next words carefully even as he whipped the reins against the horse's rump and directed the thoroughbred into the flow of other carriages on the street. "Do you hold slaves, Miss Atwater?"

"There are slaves on our plantation, yes, but I intend to end it as soon as I return."

"And your parents agree with your decision?" They hit a bump, and she grabbed his arm for balance. When the carriage was settled again, she let go. He found himself wishing she hadn't.

"My father and mother were killed last year. Beauchapel is mine now."

Matthew felt the anguish in her words and was immediately sorry for his intended challenge of her position. "I'm sorry, Miss Atwater. How did you lose them?"

"A boiler blew up on the steamer they were taking from Richmond to Savannah." She paused a moment before going on. "It shouldn't have happened. The captain was racing another steamer and overheated his boilers. They say it was a horrible accident. Fifty other people were killed as well, but the captain and some of his crew escaped, went over the side once they saw what was going to happen. Cowards. And if I could get my hands on them, I would surely wring each and every neck."

Matthew sensed her anger and knew she might actually do it if given the chance. He had heard of such explosions; they usually happened when steamers were racing one another or trying to beat a schedule or another steamer to port to grab the business that waited.

"And why have you come to Washington?" he probed, still looking for answers about her meeting with Rose Greenhow.

"I traveled to England with my uncle, who had business there. We returned to New York only a few days ago then came to Washington so he could meet with some of his business associates before we go to Richmond. With this horrible talk of war, he was afraid it may be some time before he can return to Washington."

"It must have been a shock to find the country split in two," Matthew said.

"The English relish our divided condition. It's the news on each front page they publish, but to actually experience it—the anger and hate coming from both sides—yes, it is quite a shock." She paused again as if deciding whether she should go on. "When we left for England I still had great hope that the country would come to its senses, but after arriving here I find there is little hope at all."

"There's always hope, Miss Atwater," Matthew returned.

"Is there? I wish to believe you, Mr. Alexander, but my uncle's friends give me little. They want a fight because it's the only way that Lincoln will let the Southern states go."

"Then your uncle sympathizes with the Southern cause?"

"Very much so as do all his friends here. Just this morning I ate breakfast with a lady whom I have known for most of my life, and for the first time, I realized just how much even she supports the South. Why she continues to live here when she has such sympathies is a mystery to me. She should run off to Richmond or Mississippi if she loves their way of life so much. Instead, here she sits, right in the middle of Union power. Such hypocrisy is appalling."

She paused, grabbing the side of the carriage seat as Matthew had to pull back on the reins to keep from hitting a boy who dashed into the street. His mother quickly grabbed the child, paddled his overall-covered bottom, gave him a quick tongue lashing—more from her fear than for his foolishness—and pulled him back onto the boardwalk.

Matthew loosened the reins, and the gelding danced forward again. He was beginning to regret his assumption that Millicent Atwater was of the same cut as Rose Greenhow. Like him, she obviously was not an advocate of the Southern position, and it was a bit unfortunate that he had to deceive her. But there was no other choice that he could see. They were both going to Richmond, and if their paths crossed and she knew the truth, it could be quite disastrous for him.

"Forgive me, Mr. Alexander. I should not burden you with my frustrations, but for the life of me I cannot understand why so many— and obviously that includes you, Mr. Alexander—are set on leaving the Union over a question that could be resolved inside it." She tucked at her long hair, tied up on the back of her head, as if she were nervous that it might fall with the next jolt of the carriage. Matthew pulled back on the reins and slowed their movement so as to give her less concern.

"Possibly your uncle has tried to explain his reasons," Matthew said.

"Uncle Richard is an opportunist. He will side with whomever brings him the greatest advantage. His conversations deal more with money than politics."

"And is he your father's brother or your mother's?"

She looked at him, unsure of why it mattered. "My father's."

Matthew made note of the name. Before he left Washington, he would see that Pinkerton heard of it. If he were associated with Rose Greenhow, he would need to be watched.

"Where's your plantation, Miss Atwater? Forgive me, but what did you call it?" he asked.

"Beauchapel. It's along the James River east of Petersburg."

"I am sure it was difficult to be there after the loss of your parents."

"Actually, I haven't returned since their death. My uncle insisted I go with him to England instead. He said it would only depress me to be in my parents' house so soon. He was quite wrong. I miss it dearly and should never have let him talk me into leaving. But he was my legal guardian until my twenty-first birthday, so I really didn't have a great deal of choice, but I do regret it now."

"But now you're twenty-one and can make up your own mind."

"I will leave for Beauchapel in a few days. He's not happy that I refuse to wait for him, but it is time I take care of my own affairs and see to the safety of my property and servants."

"It's not easy to care for a plantation."

"I was my father's only child; I know Beauchapel like the back of my hand. He taught me which fields are best planted with tobacco and which are best planted with corn or other crops, how to rotate them, what bugs to watch for, and how to be rid of them. I have met those with whom my father did business and know which are honest and which are not. My father shared his books and records with me and had me keep them the last few years. I have every confidence that I can run Beauchapel."

Matthew admired her pluck but wondered if she'd considered how just the *possibility* of war would change everything. The North was already moving to blockade Southern ports and prevent free flow of goods as a warning. It would only get worse if the South remained intransigent. And, since Beauchapel used slaves, either war or peace would eventually bring it to an end. How did she intend to run her plantation then, especially if they had already started running away?

"You do have slaves, right, Miss Atwater?"

"Yes, but—"

"And if the South is not allowed to secede and they're forced to free their slaves, how do you expect to continue working your land?"

"First of all, Mr. Lincoln says that he will not put an end to slavery where it already exists, that—"

"And you believe him?"

"Yes, I do, but I also know that we must eventually end it, Mr. Alexander, and that is my second point. I intend to end it, regardless of whether others do or not. In fact I will do so as soon as I get home and take charge of my own affairs. Slavery cannot last. It is inhumane, and why you or anyone else would go to war to protect it is beyond understanding."

"And yet your father used it to build your fine plantation," Matthew responded, egging her on.

Millie didn't answer immediately. "Yes, but he intended to end it. In fact the papers were all drawn up before he and mother were killed. I simply intend to follow through with their wishes."

Matthew felt like a heel and didn't know what to say, so he said nothing. He was grateful that Millie continued.

"My father inherited the slaves when he bought the property. It's true, he continued to use them, but our slaves were never treated badly. In fact my parents provided good housing and kept them well clothed. Father swore that as soon as his debt was paid, he would end it and had even written careful instructions to that effect." She paused, struggling to keep her emotions in check. "My father's debtor was a friend in Charleston. He and mother had gone there to pay the final installment of the debt when they were killed. Since then my uncle has been taking care of my affairs, and I have not been able to fulfill my parents' wishes. I intend to do so as soon as I return."

"And you think your workers will stay? After all, freedom to go where they want—to leave the South, especially now . . ."

"They won't leave the farm if they know they can achieve a good life by helping me work it. I will pay them a fair wage—more than they could get here in the North—and share my profits with them. I also intend to give them a school and even help them buy property of their own someday."

Matthew listened as Millie continued to explain her intentions in more detail, her eyes lighting up with the prospect of her future.

"You see, it can be done and done very well," she said in summation.

"Yes, I suppose it can."

They came to a cross street filled with marching soldiers, and Matthew pulled back on the reins, bringing the horse to a standstill. The slap of boots on cobblestone and the sound of military bands mingled with the yells of enthusiastic bystanders. Matthew peered down the street in both directions. There were parading soldiers as far as he could see. To make matters worse, the street was lined with well-wishers who impeded even those on foot.

"This could go on forever," he said.

"The last of McDowell's forces. Rose says that they're headed for a rude awakening."

"Rose?"

"Rose Greenhow, a friend of my uncle's. I had breakfast with her this morning." Her countenance darkened. "She knows how I feel, and yet she went on and on about Southern superiority. She even talked about a visit she had with General Patterson, the federal general who is supposed to keep Johnston's army locked up in the Shenandoah Valley. He told her he didn't intend to fight, that if McDowell couldn't win on his own, he didn't deserve to be head of the army. Patterson called him a fool. I let her have it then, and though she didn't like it, she accepted my scolding, not because she felt she was wrong—Rose never thinks she's wrong—but because she needed my help."

Matthew felt sudden apprehension. "Your help?"

Millie nodded. "She asked me to deliver a letter for her."

Andrew gave a wan smile. "I see. So you are to be Mrs. Greenhow's courier."

Millie looked at him curiously. "That is a strange word to use. You talk as if—"

"Mrs. Greenhow is known for her Southern leanings, Miss Atwater. She would like nothing better than to send information to her friends in Richmond that would warn them of General McDowell's movements."

Millie stiffened, her eyes widening. "But she wouldn't involve me without my consent; she knows how I feel."

"Earlier you mentioned I could go south by steamer if I had the right passes. I assume that means you have such a pass?"

"Yes. Rose arranged it through Senator Wilson. I . . ."

Matthew hesitated. "And yet at present passes are impossible to get, and yours was obtained with the help of a man whose allegiances are questionable. Surely that should seem a bit strange to you." He shrugged.

"Miss Atwater, as a Southern gentleman, I am torn between your safety and what is obviously a letter intended to help the South. If you were caught with such a letter, it would be troublesome and a return to your beloved Beauchapel quite out of the question for some time. Possibly you should consider . . ."

She had removed the letter from her handbag and ripped it open before he could finish his statement. Inside was another envelope. With an angry gesture she quickly tore off one end and dumped the contents of the second envelope into her lap. It was addressed to a Mr. Pike.

"Do you know Mr. Pike?" Matthew asked.

She shook her head as she quickly scanned the letter. "It seems innocuous enough, but some of it hardly makes any sense at all."

Matthew pulled the carriage to the curb. "May I?" he asked.

She handed him the letter, concern etched in her face. Matthew scanned it. "My guess is that it's coded and that Mr. Pike has the key."

"But how can you be sure?"

"I can't, and if you're caught with it in your possession, it will mean little to authorities. As you say, it is innocuous and makes no sense at all. Mrs. Greenhow has masked any ability to discern her chicanery if she intended any. You will be quite safe." He paused. "Unless of course, federal authorities have intercepted her cypher. Of course that would be exceptionally good work on their part but not beyond their ability."

She looked at him then at the letter as if making a decision. Matthew could only hope she would make the right one. He knew no cypher had been discovered and that the letter would prove nothing of Mrs. Greenhow's duplicity, but he was confident it was coded and intended for Confederate authorities. It must be destroyed, but Millicent Atwater must take those steps; he could not. Not if he wished to remain a Southerner in her eyes.

Millie did not debate long, and Matthew was relieved as she ripped it into pieces and threw it into the street, where it was immediately scattered by wind and passing carriages. "As much as I know it must disappoint you, Mr. Alexander, I shan't take the chance."

Matthew gave a faint smile. "I assure you, Miss Atwater, that even in defense of Southern rights I do not condone the use of innocents. Such an effort is intolerable, and I intend to tell your friend so."

"Do not concern yourself, Mr. Alexander. I would just as soon she think her message has arrived. That way she will not send another."

Matthew laughed. "Yes, that is true."

"And if you have any honor you will not warn her against my wishes, Mr. Alexander. Do you understand me?"

"All right then. I will not speak to Mrs. Greenhow," he answered. But he did intend to send a message to Joe Polanski.

They finally arrived in the square outside the train depot. It was packed with carriages, wagons, and people rushing to catch one of several trains that would be departing from the large station, almost all of them going north or west. Matthew maneuvered the buggy into an opening along the curb, tied the reins to the carriage post, and climbed out.

"Good day to you, Mr. Alexander," she said with a smile.

"When will you go to Richmond?" he asked as he picked up his bag.

"In a few days."

"Then possibly we will see each other again."

She smiled. "Possibly, but I fear that our different politics . . . with you fighting for the secessionists view . . ."

"You assumed that; I didn't say it."

She looked both surprised and confused. "Then why are you going south?"

"To try and reduce the damage this horror will cause," he said. Forcing a smile, he picked up his bag from the back of the buggy. "I need to catch that train. Thanks for the ride."

Matthew watched her go. Once she was out of sight, he went to the depot, where there was a telegraph and message center. He quickly wrote down what he'd learned, sealed it in an envelope, and paid a messenger boy to deliver it to Joe Polanski. It encouraged a more diligent surveillance of Rose Greenhow.

*   *   *

Millicent slapped the reins against the horse's rump in frustration, and the carriage immediately bolted left, cutting off another and causing its driver to curse. She didn't notice, her thoughts elsewhere. It would do no good to consider Matthew Alexander as anything more than a momentary happenstance. She could no longer countenance slavery and would do everything she could to end it, if not in the South at least at Beauchapel, and obviously Mr. Alexander had other ideas about the institution.

And yet . . . She looked over her shoulder in the direction of the depot, which was no longer completely visible.

And yet she did hope she would see him again.

And that confused her even more.

*   *   *

The trip from St. Louis to Washington had been mostly uneventful for Randolph Hudson and his company. Such travel was new to his men, most of whom had never been farther away from their homes than they could travel in a day. They were enamored with the sight of Cincinnati and Baltimore, even though coming through the latter was a bit tense because of the large numbers of secessionists who had burned bridges and even torn up railroad track to slow down the movement of Union troops into Washington.

But they had finally arrived in the country's capital only to find the city in chaos with more troops arriving than there were places to house them. There were enough tents in the space between the capitol building and the Potomac River—a distance of nearly a mile—to make the area look like it was coated in canvas from one end to the other. Some had even pitched tents inside the new capitol building, which was still under construction.

Soldiers were being marched and drilled along nearly every street, while those off duty drifted about the city aimlessly. Saloons were filled to overflowing, with brawls breaking out as easily as chicken pox in an epidemic. They had received orders to march completely through the city and camp on the banks of the Potomac outside smaller Georgetown at Fort Corcoran. Irvin McDowell had been made commander of the army, and he assigned Rand's Missouri boys to General Daniel Tyler's First Division of the federal army.

Once encamped, Rand met with Tyler and was reintroduced to his brigade commander, Colonel William Tecumseh Sherman. Their division was put to work preparing battlements for the city of Washington; off duty, Rand drilled and pounded them into shape for what was to come. In the heat of summer, the work was grueling, made endurable only by regular dips in the cool waters of the Potomac. Rand was grateful they were kept busy. His boys were like most others, they enjoyed their pint and were just as quick to get in a brawl, but he kept them as chained to camp as he could without wearing them down. Rand quickly discovered that too many federal soldiers joining the army thought it a lark, a chance to kick up their heels and sleep in before they "marched south to teach the rebels a lesson in manhood." It made Rand cringe, and he and Hooker and Malone kept preaching to their men what the reality would be. Most listened; some didn't. Those that didn't received special attention from Hooker until they did. Hooker knew battle, and he knew that a good thumping now would pay off when the rebels started shooting at them.

Rand had known William "Cump" Sherman before the war. The redheaded, bright-eyed Sherman had a reputation for excellence in whatever he did and had served in Southern posts during the Second Seminole War in Florida. He left the army in 1853 and headed west. A few years later he'd ended up in Missouri after a near disastrous career as a banker and land speculator in California. He accepted a position as the president of the St. Louis Railroad. Rand had met him at a dinner party. After that their roads hadn't crossed again until Rand found his unit assigned to Sherman's brigade.

Sherman and Rand disagreed on the purpose of the war. Sherman thought it only about keeping the Union together and did not like talk about freedom for the slaves, but Sherman was a good tactician, decisive, and a fighter—all qualities Rand knew would be needed in war, and at present, Rand was more concerned about both the survival of his men and a quick victory than he was about Cump Sherman's political views. There was a better chance of both under Sherman.

He and Sherman had definitely butted heads on the reasons for the war, but Sherman had made the point that at the moment the *reason* didn't matter. "When our boys start to die by the hundreds, then the thousands, then we will see if Mr. Lincoln and the Northern politicians have the stomach for freeing the slaves. If they do, I will fight for it, but if they don't, then I will go back to Louisiana and be happy about it."

On the twenty-third of May, the citizens of Virginia voted for secession. Considered the same as a declaration of war against the Union, troops were ordered across the river into Virginia that same evening. Cump Sherman's division was the first to cross. More than thirty thousand strong, the army quickly spread out across the open ground of northern Virginia, occupying plantations and villages as both Confederate soldiers and Southern sympathizers acquiesced or fled. Since then, Rand and his men had been doing what every other unit had been called to do—building more fortifications and preparing to drive farther south to Richmond.

Ann had arrived in Washington shortly after Rand had left it. He had tried to discourage her, but she'd come anyway, found a house in Georgetown, and sent him the address. He longed to see her, and having her only ten miles away was a temptation, but by the time he received her letter, it was too late. Lincoln had ordered them south.

The endless line of infantry came to a slow stop, forcing Rand to raise a hand and halt his battalion.

Rand had been put in charge of the three companies he'd brought from Missouri. It took eight to ten companies to form a regiment, but Sherman gave them battalion status and promoted Rand to major. It was unusual, but Sherman said he didn't want to break up a good thing. Hooker, Malone, and Newton Daines had all been promoted to captain, and the three of them led companies A, B, and C. Each company captain had at least two sergeants to give direction to the hundred men under their command. So far it had worked out well.

Standing in his stirrups, Rand tried to peer through the thick dust to see what the hold up was this time. Foot soldiers deserted the road and removed heavy packs to find shade that would relieve the high humidity and rays of a blistering sun.

Isaac Hooker came up the line and reined in next to Rand. "At this pace we'll all die of old age a'fore we git anywhere's near Manassas. I say we get around these boys."

They had already been on the road for two days and had gone only fifteen miles, the roads choked by the sheer size of the army. Add to that broken wagons, horrible heat and humidity, and random fire from Confederate sharpshooters; their advance had become a crawl.

Hooker removed his wide-brimmed hat and used his hanky to wipe the band free of sweat before replacing the hat and hanky. "Never seen such heat," he added.

Isaac Hooker was a big man, and his horse matched his size, putting him a good six inches above Rand. His uniform jacket had been altered to fit more loosely around his shoulders and waist and was partially unbuttoned, revealing a white linen shirt, stained from the dust of the road. His wide belt held a holster for his .44 Colt repeating revolver and a scabbard for a knife as long as a man's forearm. His Sharps rifle was cradled in one arm, the reins of his dapple gray quarter horse held lightly in two fingers of the other hand. In training, Rand had watched Isaac ride the gray at full speed, using the rifle to hit one target a hundred feet away, then draw his pistol and hit three out of four others as he guided his horse with his legs to avoid half a dozen obstacles. The man had learned from his frontier years and was a fine horseman and a skilled fighter. Rand was glad he was here.

"Speed is everything, Rand. If we keep up this pace, Johnston will have more than enough time to free himself from Patterson," Isaac said in a worried tone.

Rand only nodded. General Patterson had been sent into the Shenandoah Valley to occupy Johnston's army of ten thousand so they couldn't come to the rescue of the troops at Manassas. But Patterson could only hold them so long, if he held them at all. Rand had not been impressed with Patterson's response to McDowell's orders. He was even more reluctant, more a foot dragger than McDowell, and Patterson's obvious jealousy of McDowell didn't help either. Rand wondered if he would engage Johnston at all, let alone hold him in the Shenandoah. It was indecisive, foot-dragging commanders that got men killed, even the most seasoned men. The thought gave Rand a chill, but he shoved it aside. He was not about to let Patterson's disease of will infect his own.

Malone appeared alongside the troops in front of them, the men cursing him as his horse stirred up the thick dust that had just begun to settle. They scattered and made a wide path as Malone rode through, seeming to enjoy their discomfort.

The tall, solid Malone fought in the Mexican-American War in the infantry and knew his business. His graying ponytail stuck out from under his officer's forage cap and hung to his shoulder blades, adding to the warning most men saw in his blue Irish eyes. As commander of Rand's C Company, he had handpicked a bunch of fellow Irishmen from the Irish slums known as the Kitchen before leaving St. Louis. They were mean brawlers but good shots and had not the least sign of yellow running up their back. Rand expected that they'd make the difference to the rest of the battalion. They did not cotton to cowardice, and if one of the men showed signs, he'd probably find himself hanging from a tree by his toes until they could skin him alive.

Malone reined up in front of Rand and Hooker and saluted. "Major," he said with a wide grin.

"Captain," Rand said, returning the salute.

There had been no saluting when they were training, but Sherman had witnessed this "lack of proper decorum" and insisted it change. It had, but even Sherman couldn't stop them from smiling about it.

Malone handed Rand an envelope. "From Sherman."

Rand opened it, quickly skimmed the instructions, then spoke while shoving the letter in his jacket pocket. "General McDowell has ordered us to the front. Any ideas how we can get there without further slowing down thirty thousand foot soldiers?"

Isaac grinned. "When Sherman sent my boys to look things over at Manassas a few days ago, we ran onto a game trail." He looked up the steep slope of the hill thickly covered with trees and underbrush. "Gettin' up to it will be the challenge, especially for those on foot." Sherman had asked Rand to provide a dozen men mounted as cavalry from the battalion. Rand had assigned Hooker to select the men, and Hooker had pulled together a sneaky bunch of hard-riding Missouri frontiersmen that had followed him into the army at the time they'd defended the arsenal at St. Louis. Sherman now used them as often as Rand did.

"Should be an openin' up ahead, maybe a quarter mile," Hooker said.

The troops in front of them were starting to wander even farther from the road, some looking for berries, others looking for a grassy place to stretch out under a shade tree. Rand just shook his head. He couldn't blame them. Why stay out in the heat when you had come to know you could wait half a day and still catch up.

"What's happening up the line?" Rand asked Malone, his voice tinged with frustration.

"There be a crossroad. Troops comin' in from the left o' us are jammin' it all up. Then there's a bridge. Team o' horses panicked, wrecked a wagon in the middle. They're still tryin' t' get it ou' o' the way," Malone said.

"Snails could move faster 'n this," Hooker said, spitting at a rock and hitting it directly in the middle.

Most of the foot soldiers directly in front of them were off the road, and Rand decided to get moving. "Captain Hooker, let 'em know we're coming through."

"Yes, sir, Major," Hooker replied, putting a spur to his horse's flanks. He was on them in a few strides and yelling at the top of his lungs while he waved his hat in the air. Rand knew there would be a few well-placed curses in his tirade. The men still in the road scattered, and Rand turned to Malone. "Wait for the wagons. Tell the drivers to keep on the road, and we'll find 'em later. Then you and Captain Daines fall in after the last of our battalion and make sure they keep up."

Malone saluted, and Rand raised his hand and called for his men to move forward at double time. They passed by men who had a few curses of their own to express, but his men kept their eyes forward and their minds on getting through the gauntlet. After only a few moments, Rand saw Hooker pull up, look up the side of the hill, then turn back and point that direction. Rand watched him start up the slope, where he seemed to disappear in thick trees. When Rand reached the trail, he saw how narrow it was. He wondered what Isaac was thinking but called for a single line and quickly followed. Samson, his black gelding, dug his hooves into the hillside and propeled them both upward between thick trees and scrub brush. There wasn't much of an opening and it was a steep climb, but he was quickly up to where the game trail meandered along the hillside. He turned into it and told Hooker to keep ahead as the men clamored up the trail. It was tough work in the hot sun, but Rand was gratified that most were making the climb without trouble. The first few were mounted and quickly passed Rand. When the first of the infantry came up, Rand moved ahead. The rest of the battalion reached the trail quickly and fell in behind, hardly winded. All those marches in the Virginia heat and humidity were paying off.

The trail meandered along the hillside for nearly half a mile then turned sharply down, where it came to small creek. Hooker stopped at the edge of it and then drove his horse into the water at a left angle to the trail. Rand watched as the other horsemen followed. It wasn't deep and would probably be welcomed by his men. He spurred his horse forward and leaped into the water. It splashed high enough that he got a good dousing and was grateful for the immediate relief. Looking over his shoulder, he saw the first of his foot soldiers jump into the water, grins on their faces. He figured they would need a few minutes to empty their boots when they were out of the water, but they would need a rest anyway and most carried a second set of socks.

Rand remembered this stream. The road they had been on would cross it via covered bridge a couple hundred yards down and just around the bend. On the southern side of the bridge, there was a large meadow and open farmland then a well-traveled road that would lead them to Centreville, not far from Manassas Junction itself, and Centreville was where Sherman wanted him.

As Rand reached the bridge, he turned south, and Samson launched up the bank and through a few trees into the meadow where Hooker and his small cavalry waited. The infantry followed a few minutes later, the men coming quickly up the bank. Some thought to fall out of ranks, but Malone was quick to remind them with a stern set of commands—mingled with an Irish threat or two—to keep formation until ordered to do otherwise.

Rand gave the order to fall out and told Malone and Hooker to give them a rest and a change of socks. It was then he saw the bridge. There were a few men on this side of it, but most of those who had already crossed had moved on toward Centreville. Rand saw a man with a captain's insignia on his uniform in seemingly casual talk with several other officers near the bridge. Rand spurred Samson to join them. As he rode up, the captain turned to face him then lost his casualness and gave a sharp salute. Rand returned it.

"Captain, what's the hold up here?" Rand asked firmly.

"Busted up wagon, sir," the man replied.

Rand looked into the darkness of the covered bridge, eyeing a wagon that seemed to be getting very little attention.

"The team broke, sir, ran off. We got men looking for them, but . . ."

Rand glanced at the half a dozen horses standing nearby and bit his lip. "Any horse will do. Just hook some ropes to that wagon and get it out of the way. You're holding up the remainder of your brigade *and* Colonel Sherman's. If they aren't moving in five minutes, I'll have your hide hanging from my saddle horn. Do you understand?"

The captain paled a bit. "Yes, sir." He ordered the others to get moving, and there was a sudden flurry of action. "Where's your commanding officer, Captain?"

The captain was trying to get on his mount as it danced in a circle but answered just the same. "Up ahead, sir. He left me in charge and—"

"Don't make him feel like he made a mistake. Get these men moving."

"Yes, sir." The captain was finally aboard and quickly ordered the others to follow. The hooves of their horses pounded on the wooden floor of the bridge as Rand turned Samson and returned to where his men waited.

"Seems you lit a fire under 'em," Hooker observed with a wry smile.

"Let's hope it doesn't go out anytime soon," Rand answered, his eyes on the last of his men coming out of the creek bed. He saw Daines and Malone follow and then quickly ride to the front of the line.

"They be all accounted for, Major," Malone said, his eyes on the bridge. "They should 'ave tha' wagon out o' the way b' now." He was about to spur his horse and take action when Rand spoke.

"Never mind, Captain. I took care of it."

"What be yer orders, sir?" Daines asked.

"Give the men a few minutes' rest." He gave Newton a slight smile. "How ya doin' Mr. Daines?"

Giving a side-glance in Hooker's direction, Newton answered with a bit of a red face. "I be fine, sir," Daines said with his Irish accent, but Rand could see the injury was still giving him a good deal of pain. Newton Daines had arrived in St. Louis by way of Ireland at about the same time Lincoln was elected. He'd helped Rand's sister, Lizzy, after she'd been thrown from her horse. Rand had hired him to work for Hudson shipping as a carpenter, and Daines had also gotten involved with their clandestine operation to help runaway slaves in Missouri. A more honorable man Rand did not know, nor did he have a better friend—along with Isaac Hooker and Brenden Malone, of course.

Daines's work in Missouri had helped free more than a hundred slaves and send them on their way to Canada. But in the process, he'd lost Mary, the only woman Newton had ever loved, to a vile Irishman bent on revenge.

Rand knew Newton wasn't past his loss, but that was not their immediate concern. Newton had been shot, and Isaac Hooker had done the shooting.

It made Rand smile to think about it. Isaac had been showing several of the men how to "fast draw" their revolvers, telling stories about gunfighters he'd run into while working for the army out of Dodge City. Rand had been watching from his tent and saw Daines join the group just as Isaac drew his revolver. Isaac was good once his pistol was drawn, but he was no gunfighter. He dropped the pistol, and it fired, grazing Newton across his buttocks and sending him to the ground writhing, one hand on the wound and the other in his mouth to keep himself from screaming.

Isaac stooped down, quickly turned Newton over, checked the wound, found it wasn't serious, then retrieved his revolver and slammed it back into his holster. "Tain't never shot no one quite like that before, but seems effective, don't it?"

Of course everyone busted out in laughter, and even Newton smiled as Isaac helped him to his feet and off to the infirmary. But at the moment, Newton wasn't smiling.

After a few more minutes, Rand could see that the wagon had been pulled from the bridge and that the rest of McDowell's army was about to get moving again. He did not want to wait.

"Mr. Malone, Mr. Daines, get them moving—double-time all the way to Centreville. Let's see if they can stand another sturdy march. Mr. Hooker, let's you and I go and see what the good general wants of us." With that he spurred his horse toward the road, and Malone and Daines ordered the men up and moving. Rand didn't need to look back. He knew they were already on the march.

He and Hooker traveled a mile before approaching more troops spread along both sides of the road, most sitting, their weapons causally set aside. Most were eating, and the conversation seemed more in keeping with a church social than troops headed for battle. They walked their horses to keep from stirring up more dust, noting several fires had been started, and coffee and food were already cooking over hot coals. Rand noticed one fire circled by a half dozen officers, their mounts tied and saddles removed as the men settled in for a meal. When they reached the front of what seemed to be an entire division, Rand saw the commanding officers' table set up under a tree and a dozen cannon caissons parked in a small meadow; teams of horses hobbled and grazing on what was left of summer grass. And yet it was only noon. Either the army had decided to take a vacation, or they were nearly to Centreville.

They arrived in Centreville a few minutes later and found McDowell's headquarters on the southern outskirts of the village. He had taken control of a farmhouse. Troops were encamped around the southern edge of the village and in its village square. He saw no one but soldiers and figured the citizens were either inside their homes or had already deserted them for safer ground. The odors of cooking food reached them as Rand and Hooker dismounted in front of the farmhouse. He saw some uninhabited meadow a hundred yards to the left and told Hooker to have the men rest there when they arrived, which he knew wouldn't be long. "Get them something to eat, but no fires. I have a feeling we won't be here long." Hooker gave a quick salute and a slight smile as Rand tied Samson to a makeshift line that was holding a dozen other horses. He passed a number of officers, saluting as needed, then entered the house to find McDowell's adjutant set up at a small table in the hallway. He could hear McDowell's voice in an adjoining room but couldn't make out the conversation. The adjutant looked up, saw who it was, and smiled.

"Major, welcome. The general would like you to come in immediately." He stood and pushed aside the sliding pocket door. McDowell stood at the window; another officer sat on the couch. Rand recognized the man as Colonel Dixon Stansbury Miles, a good fighter by all accounts but obviously unhappy at the moment.

"Major," McDowell said, forcing a smile. "You were near the middle of our movement, were you not?"

"Yes, sir, but it's slow moving. We had to go around, find another way past most of the division," Rand said.

"How long before the last can get here?"

"Hard to say, sir, but at our present rate, two days, minimum."

McDowell paced, thinking, his brow wrinkled with concern. "Too long," he muttered. "Much too long." He took a deep breath. "We have taken far too much time. General Tyler has moved a good portion of your regiment up to Bull Run and is about to engage the rebels and test their lines. Colonel Sherman has gone with him even though most of his division is still coming up to Centreville. He had me send for you. He says your men are ready, Major. I hope he's right." He looked at a map spread out on the table in front of him. "As soon as your men arrive, you will find Colonel Sherman. He will be here"—he pointed to the map—"just this side of Blackburn's Ford. He will give you your orders." He stood straight as if the interview was over, and Rand saluted.

"And Major." Rand had already partially turned to leave, so he turned back to face McDowell. "You have Isaac Hooker in your command. Colonel Sherman says he has men mounted who could do surveillance for us. Is that correct?"

"Yes, sir," Rand confirmed.

"Tonight, when things are settled and your battalion is relieved, I want you to send Mr. Hooker on reconnaissance. I need to know if Johnston has slipped away from Patterson. I fear that he has, but I must know for sure. Do you understand your orders, Major?"

"Yes, sir. Isaac, er, Captain Hooker will get you what you need, General."

McDowell nodded. "Yes, I know Isaac, and I trust you're right. The question is can he get it to us in time."

Rand saluted both men, turned on his heel, and left. Outside, he mounted. He saw Malone and Daines at the front of his men. They were double-timing it and probably thought their journey nearly at an end. He would soon disabuse those feelings.

As he settled into his saddle, Isaac joined him, a half a loaf of bread in one hand, his mouth full of what must have been the other half.

"We move out in fifteen minutes," Rand told Isaac.

Isaac chewed some more, then swallowed. "Then it's come time, has it?" Isaac responded as he shoved the rest of the bread inside his shirt.

"It has." Rand wrinkled his brow as the first of his men reached them, sweating and tired. He wondered if they could go another three miles at a similar pace.

"Gentlemen," Isaac shouted above the clatter of packs, rifles, and feet. "We are going to meet the rebels this day. Are you ready for it?"

With one loud acclaim Rand's concerns were put to rest. Isaac continued, "Get a quick drink then, and grab a little bread form the mess tent over yonder, and then back in line and eatin' on yer way. Let's not keep 'em waitin'."

The men needed no further instruction and were quickly at the well or the mess tent with a few wandering off in the woods to answer Mother Nature first.

Rand felt a mixture of excitement and fear in the pit of his stomach as he watched and listened to their exuberance. Though most of them did not realize it, this was no longer a game of cat and mouse, of waiting and firing at targets that didn't shoot back. This was war, and they would be right in the middle of it. He felt the hair stand up on the back of his neck. And they would rely on him for their safety.

He closed his eyes briefly as he touched the soft, deer-hide pouch hanging from his saddle horn. Ann had made the pouch for him before he left St. Louis. It held his small Bible and personal copy of the Book of Mormon. Getting down from Samson's saddle, Rand removed the pouch and tied up the reins around a tree branch before stepping into a bit of a thicket near the road. He needed a little preparation of his own.

* * *

Isaac watched Rand go, a worried look on his face. He'd promised Ann Hudson he'd look after her husband. His promise was about to be tested.

Isaac was not a religious man. He had been baptized as a child in the Baptist faith but to his recollection hadn't seen the inside of a church since he was old enough to disappear before meetings and take a licking for his absence afterward. But he did believe in God, and he did pray—even more so since discussions with Rand about God's place in the scheme of things. Isaac just wasn't sure God listened much, at least to him. He was a sinner, pure and simple. He'd been immoral in his younger years though completely true to his wife since their marriage. But worse still was that he'd killed men. None in anger, none that didn't ask for it or attack him first, but he'd killed just the same, and the worst part was he had even enjoyed it, at least in some cases. There were mean men, men who had slaughtered for pleasure. He'd put an end to them and enjoyed it. He knew it was wrong—knew it deep down—and because he knew it, he figured that while forgiveness might be real for others, it no longer existed for him. And that scared him. Death would bring hell, and he wasn't much excited about going to hell.

He shoved the thought aside. He was a lost soul, and no matter how many men he had to kill, he intended to see Rand Hudson return to his wife. Isaac intended to keep his promise. If in doing so he shook the hand of the devil, by morning he'd have at least one good thing to remember. Rand Hudson was still alive.

He mounted his horse, watching as Rand came out of the trees and hung his bag over his saddle horn again. When Rand was astride Samson, Isaac gave the order. And the battalion went to war.

Chapter Two

MOSE AND LYDIJAH BROWN WALKED into Georgetown's High Street. They didn't seem to garner any special attention until a man stepped out of the storefront and nearly collided with Mose.

"Hey, Nigra, watch where yer goin'."

Mose knew it was expected—even in the so-called free North—for blacks to show deference to whites; he lowered his head and gave a slight nod of apology before moving quickly on.

Over the years, Mose had grown thick skin in handling such affronts, but they still made him grind his teeth. Whites like the Hudsons had treated him as equal and made him feel of high worth, and when some ingrate prig like this one challenged his dignity, he wanted to grab them by the collar and toss them into the first hard and bruising object he could find.

Mose and Lydijah, now in their fifties, had worked for the Hudsons since Randolph and Lizzy were children. They'd served the siblings' parents before that. They were freedmen and chose to work for the Hudson family; in turn the Hudsons had paid them well and provided good housing. Mose had been a well-treated freedman so long that having to put up with such nonsense from whites grated at him.

A black man who had been standing nearby tipped his hat and spoke, looking them over before meeting Mose's eyes. "I can see you folks are new to Georgetown. Can I be of some service?" The man was well spoken, obviously educated, and dressed in a fine dark wool suit with a matching stovepipe hat.

"Thank you, suh," Mose said. "We're lookin' fo' 21 Washington Street. The home of Mr. and Mrs. Randolph Hudson."

"Well, I do not know the Hudsons, and I know most black folk in Washington Street, though there aren't many. Are the Hudsons . . . ?"

"Yes suh, they's white. Good folks from St. Louis. Mr. Hudson is with the army, and Mrs. Hudson—"

"Then he fights for all of us." The man smiled. "I am more than happy to give you directions. Just cross the canal there and go a block to Bridge Street. Turn right and go two blocks to Washington. Turn right again, and number twenty-one will be just a few houses up the street." He tipped his hat and was about to go on his way when he spoke again. "My name is Henry Thospe. I own a store along the docks—a dry goods store. When you have need of work, I might be able to help."

He bowed slightly and was about to turn away when Felix replied, "Thank you, suh, but we has worked for the Hudsons for most of our married lives. Don't suppose that be changin' anytime soon."

"Well then, the good Lord be with you," Thospe said, tipping his hat again. Thospe disappeared into the crowd, and Mose took Lydijah by the arm and started to follow his directions. They were both quiet. The long journey had taken its toll.

Mose began to notice the number of blacks they passed as they moved along High Street and across the canal, but that number quickly diminished as they walked north along Bridge Street, where the houses grew bigger and more impressive. Georgetown was no different than most cities it seemed—his people would have to earn their place; they would have to show they could do the same tasks just as well or even better than white folks before they'd be accepted. That's why he hoped Mr. Lincoln would let black folks into the fight if there was one. No sense demanding your freedom 'less you were willing to work for them just as hard as the white man.

They turned left on Bridge Street and ran smack dab into a long column of soldiers coming toward them. The walkways were filled with well-wishers shouting phrases filled with hostility toward the Southern rebels. Mose and Lydijah slipped behind the crowd and did their best to watch as hundreds of men, led by a brass and drum band, passed down the street toward the docks and then turned on Bridge and went south. It was a fine display of soldiers, their long rifle barrels glinting in the afternoon sun. Dressed in mostly blue uniforms, they looked like first class warriors as they stepped in time, their chins held high and proud.

"Wonder where dey's goin'," Lydijah said.

A white man of slight build overheard the words and turned to give an answer. "Off to join our troops down at Manassas Junction. Latecomers from up in New York State somewheres." He had a wide, prideful grin on his face. "Our boys will send them Southern rebs packin'. That's for sure." He turned back and shouted a "hurrah" and a "good luck, boys" at the soldiers.

"Come on," Mose said, taking Lydijah's arm again. "Miss Ann is probably frantic about where we is."

"Dat man is a foo'," Lydijah said. "Countin' his chickens afore they even hatch dat away brings nuthin' but bad luck." She quickly reached down and scooped up a small bit of dirt, throwing it over one shoulder and causing Mose to smile. Though she'd been a Mormon since Baker and Mary Hudson had first joined the faith, she came from a religious background of ancient African practices mingled with Christianity. Out of the mixture came a number of practices for warding off evil spirits and calling upon the dead to prevent harm. Throwing dirt over one's shoulder was used to ward off a possible whipping by an owner. Mose found it humorous that Lydijah used it here as if to ward off a whipping of the North by the South.

"'Taint gonna do no good," he said with a wry smile.

"'Taint gonna do no harm neither," she responded.

They arrived at number twenty-one just as the last of the soldiers passed by, the sound of their boots on the cobblestone quickly waning.

"This be the place," he said, relieved.

"Looks like a fine house," Lydijah remarked. "I sho' does hope Miss Ann is home. I is tired as I ever be."

Mose climbed the few steps, set down the bags he carried, and used the eagle-shaped brass knocker to rap on the door.

They heard stirring inside and then saw a familiar face at a curtained window to the left. The face lit up with joy then disappeared from the window. Seconds later the door was flung open, and Ann Hudson threw her arms around Mose's neck in a joyous hug.

"Oh Mose, how wonderful to finally have you here!" Ann said, stepping back to look him over then hugging him a second time. Mose's hair was graying, and he was round in all the normal places, but he was sturdy, a hard worker who'd cared for the Hudsons' farm and animals most of his days. But he was tired, and Ann could see it. "My, you must be exhausted." She grinned. "But then, of course you would be. It's a long trip."

"And you, Miss Ann." Mose smiled. "As usual you is lookin' mighty fine," Mose said with relief. The trip had been exhausting.

Ann turned to Lydijah and gave her a long hug. "Oh, Lydijah, I've missed you!" She stepped back. "But you look tired as well. Come, come, you must sit down." She led them toward the sitting room and saw that they were comfortable.

"Now chil', we is jus' fine," Lydijah said. "How is you feelin'? With a baby comin' an' all . . ."

Ann beamed. She had found out she was pregnant just before leaving St. Louis, and only Lydijah knew. From the look on Mose's face, Lydijah was still the only one who had known.

"You is expectin', Missy?" Mose threw a sharp look at Lydijah. "Why didn't yo' tell me, Liddy?"

"'Twern't my place t' tell yo' or no one else," Lydijah said adamantly. She turned back to Ann. "Now, how is you feelin'?"

"Sickness in the morning, but not nearly as much now as when I was aboard that horrible steamer. And those trains—they're even worse! But, I made it and am doing very well most of the time."

Ann had been in Washington almost a week now. She came by herself because her mother and Lydijah had both become ill at the last minute, but she couldn't wait. Rand had been gone for two months, and she wanted to get close enough to see him when he could get away from his command. Unfortunately, it hadn't worked out as she'd hoped. She still hadn't seen Rand.

She shook off the thought. "How are Mother and Lizzy?"

"Yo' momma got better quicker than I did. She a strong woman, Missy," Lydijah answered. "And she take over de house! Yes'm. Miss Lizzy doan have no worries 'bout dem things."

"Miss Elizabeth is doin' fine, Miss Ann," Mose chimed in. "De comp'ny jus' as strong as ever, an'—"

"An' she still bein' a fool 'bout chasin' into Missouri afta run'ways. 'Taint safe!" Lydijah protested. "Why, since de war break ou' dey's been a dozen battles. Black folk runnin' jus' to get away from bein' killed, an' white folks too, but Miss Lizzy, she keep goin' in! Scare me half to death wha' she doin'."

"Now, Lydijah," Mose said. "She got plenty men helpin', an'—"

"Still ain't safe," Lydijah insisted. "But, she headed fo' Florence, Nebraska, 'bout now. Takin' supplies t' Mr. Gates and de Saints. She doin' good in dat, and maybe it keep her outa trouble! Heaven knows dat woman needs a good man to keep her from doin' foolishness."

"She doin' our people a good thing, Liddy," Mose said firmly. "And don't you be sayin' otherwise now."

"Has she heard from Andrew?" Ann said in an attempt to change the subject.

"No ma'am, nothin' since he say he in Virginy somewheres. But dey say no mail goin' back North to South no more. Is dat right, Miss Ann?"

"Yes, I'm afraid it is." Ann stood. "You both look exhausted. I will prepare you something to eat while you unpack and take a bit of a nap." She turned toward the door. "Come, I'll show you to your quarters."

"Now, Missy, I ain't about t' be lettin' you do my work, no ma'am," Lydijah said. "'Specially since yo' is spectin' a chile. Now you go on upstairs to yo' room and—"

"Nonsense!" Ann interrupted. "You will rest. I am just fine, and it's nothing to prepare a meal. Mose, I have a boy taking care of the horses at the carriage house out back, but you need not worry on that account until you're ready. But keep the boy. His name is Maple Smidge; he's a freedman's son and needs the work."

"What kind o' name is dat?" Lydijah shook her head. "Maple ain't no name fo' a boy tryin' t' be a man."

"It seems the first thing his momma saw when she woke up with him lying on her belly was a bottle of maple syrup on the table. She figured it was an omen. He's a fine boy just the same," Ann said.

"Yes'm," Mose said as he picked up their suitcases. He would be glad to have help. He just hadn't been as able lately. It was hard catching his breath, and he got tired much easier. Just aging he guessed, but it relieved him that there was someone to do some of the work.

Ann led them to the back of the house, where she opened a door into a well-furnished suite of rooms that included an indoor bath and a separate bedroom and living space.

"Mah, mah, this is nice," Lydijah said. "Thank you, Missy." She gazed longingly at the large bed. She just needed to get her feet up, and it looked so comfortable!

"Now you get some rest. Dinner will be at five o'clock, and I don't want to see you before then," Ann told them.

"Will Mista Rand be comin'?" Lydijah asked.

"No, I am afraid not. His unit has gone south with the rest of the army," Ann replied with a bit of a pained look. She forced a smile. "But I'm sure he will return soon."

Lydijah had known Ann long enough to know that the young woman was not sure of those words. She had never seen a woman more in love than Ann Hudson was, and as she looked more closely, she could see darkening rings under Ann's eyes and the pale look of worry on her face.

"Dem Southern boys doan know wha' dey messin' with when they mess with Massa Rand," Lydijah offered. "He chase dem clear back to Mississip. Now doan you be worryin' none, Miss Ann. He be jus' fine. Jus' fine."

Ann gave a wan smile. "I'll see you at five o'clock." She paused. "I'm so glad you're here. I miss home terribly. I must hear all the news at dinner." She closed the door and left them alone.

Lydijah sat down, weary and concerned. "We's been in de house of Mr. Rand and Miss Lizzy since dey was jus' babes," she said. "All dem years my dream has bin about freedom fo' my people. 'Tis a dream I gave to Rand and Miss Lizzy when I bounced 'em on my knee, but now dat dis dream might cost dem deys life . . ." Her voice trailed off. "And now Miss Ann, and the baby . . ." She breathed deeply. "'Tis a hard thing we ask of dem, Mose. A hard thing."

Mose sat down next to her and put an arm around her shoulders. "The goo' Lard be watchin' out fo' 'im, Liddy, and fo' Miss Lizzy too."

Lydijah only nodded then lay her head on her husband's tired shoulder. "Elliott be wantin' t' go, yo' knows dat."

Mose nodded. Elliott was their only son, and he'd stayed behind in St. Louis with his wife and child. He was taking care of the Hudson place now—and of Miss Lizzy. He had spoken of fighting, of doing his part, but white folk weren't letting blacks serve in the army, at least not yet. But they would; Mose knew it. Whites couldn't see what this all meant to black folks. Freedom was on the line—their freedom—and they had to be let in the fight. If they weren't, white folk would still always consider them lesser, unable. Elliott would fight, and so would Mose if he had a chance, despite his age and weariness.

But right now it still wasn't about slavery and freedom for blacks for most folks. It was about holding the Union together, they said. But it would be. Mose knew it. The good Lord was sick of slavery, and He would end it—He had to end it.

"We do our part, Liddy. We has to."

Chapter Three

THE PARTY WAS CROWDED AND should have made Millie feel both adored and accepted. After all it was a celebration of her birthday, but instead, she felt very uncomfortable. Her Uncle Richard's guests were obviously all Southern sympathizers and were so caught up in belittling everything federal, especially President Lincoln, that she finally went out to the veranda for fresh air.

She had very much wanted to be out of Washington by now, but her uncle said that the promised papers that would give them safe passage had not arrived and wouldn't for several days. They had come the very next day, but still her uncle delayed, telling her that he had to attend to another matter. Then, the very eve of her departure, he had surprised her with this awful party—inviting his friends to celebrate her birthday even though she knew very few of them. Even if he was her uncle, Richard Atwater could be infuriating!

As she took a deep breath, Richard came onto the veranda, a young man beside him. Millie cringed. What on earth was *he* doing here?

"Millicent, look who has come all the way from Petersburg to surprise you."

Millie forced a smiled. "Why, Daniel Geery, I did not think even a team of the strongest horses would ever pull you out of your beloved Confederacy," she said.

Daniel Geery was a neighbor, a very rich neighbor. His father had owned and run the largest plantation in Virginia and the largest wholesale tobacco cartel in the East. Geery Tobacco Company sold more tobacco to European markets than all other wholesalers combined. And Daniel Geery had inherited it all after the sudden death of his father more than two years ago.

Since then Daniel had been trying to expand. He'd bought more land on both sides of the five thousand acres he already owned and had even made an offer to her father to buy Beauchapel. Her father had turned it down.

Geery smiled. "I was in New York, but your uncle and I had business, and he was kind enough to invite me to the party. I'm grateful he did; I wished to see you again."

"And what business would you have with my uncle?" she asked warily.

Richard seemed nervous, but Geery kept his eyes on Millie. "Your father and I . . . Well, I had asked him if I could court you, but with his unfortunate death, he never did reply. So as your uncle is your guardian, I came to discuss it with him. He has—"

"Mr. Geery, surely my uncle has told you that he is no longer my guardian. I will be returning to Beauchapel in a few days. You and a chaperone are quite welcome to call at that time because we are neighbors and I want to remain friends, but any interest beyond that . . ."

Geery gave a quick, hard look at Richard. "I apologize. Apparently I was misinformed." There was anger in his eyes, hard and mean. Daniel Geery had a reputation for a quick temper, and Richard was certainly going to become its target unless she tried to smooth Geery's feathers. Even then she was reluctant to do it, her uncle's actions over the last few days still irritating her.

"Well, forgive Uncle Richard. I'm sure he had only the best intentions."

Geery glared at Richard as if expecting him to speak. Finally her uncle cleared his throat and forced the words out. "Daniel has another matter, my dear, a possible transaction of business. Because you are leaving tomorrow, I thought tonight—"

Millie interrupted him but spoke directly to Geery. "Daniel, if this is another offer for the purchase of Beauchapel, you know it is still not for sale." She gave a small smile while forcing herself to put her arm through Geery's and guide him back to the party. "Now, no more talk of business. This is an evening of celebration. Uncle Richard, please be sure Mr. Geery gets introduced to everyone. We would not want your Northern secessionist supporters to miss meeting such a staunch advocate of Southern rights, would we?" She let go of Geery's arm. "I thank you for coming by and hope that you will enjoy yourself." With that she turned on her heel and tried her best to carry on a conversation with some guests she hardly knew or cared about. She wanted no more of Daniel Geery.

Geery was obviously furious. He grabbed hold of Richard's arm, pulling him toward Richard's portion of the suite. The door closed behind them, and Millie was sure that her uncle was getting a fresh taste of Daniel Geery's temper. Though she had tried to prevent it, she was beginning to think it might be good. Her uncle had no right to meddle in her financial affairs, let alone her personal ones, and he had obviously been doing both. This might effect a needed change.

Other guests diverted her attention, and the clock ticked painfully away until people began to depart. It was at the very moment that she closed the door behind the last two that Geery suddenly appeared directly behind her.

"Mr. Geery, what are you doing here this late? Everyone is gone, and—"

"I am afraid there has been some misunderstanding, Millicent." He moved closer, and Millie felt some apprehension.

"Misunderstanding?"

"Yes, your uncle has kept some things from you, and it's time you became aware of them." He moved closer, and she suddenly realized she was trapped between him and a table holding what remained of refreshments.

"What things?" she asked.

"Your uncle has incurred a great deal of debt, Miss Atwater, and he has used Beauchapel as collateral."

Millie felt panic creep up her spine, and it took every effort to keep from letting it overcome her. "He has no right to incur any sort of debt against Beauchapel. He—" She looked at her uncle's door. "Uncle Richard?"

Daniel smiled. "He thought it best that you and I discuss this matter alone. You will find my attorneys quite efficient, Millie—may I call you Millie? Of course I may. We're friends, neighbors, aren't we? Anyway, you'll find the agreements are quite legal." He stepped closer, forcing her to lean back over the edge of the table. He ran a finger lightly up her arm. She felt his hot breath on her cheek. "But there are ways for us to prevent such an end."

Millie felt a cake knife against her hand, grasped it, and brought it quickly up and against his throat, applying slight pressure. He tensed as she forced him away. She pushed harder, and he jerked back several steps, his hand going to his neck where his fingers encountered blood. He looked at her with flaming eyes. "Why, you—"

"Mr. Geery, if you wish to live, you will leave this suite instantly." She annunciated the words slowly.

Geery sneered. "If you wish to keep Beauchapel, Millie, you will reconsider our relationship."

"Go!" she said, taking a step toward him: the knife was long, sharp, and the blood already staining its tip was a reminder of the damage it could do. Geery swiped at his wound as he turned and marched angrily to the door. When he slammed it shut behind him, Millie dropped the knife, stumbled toward the chair, and fell into it before putting her head in her hands.

What had her uncle done that Geery felt he had such rights? Richard Atwater was wealthy in his own right, or at least she had thought so. Now . . . Now she wasn't so sure.

After a few moments, hands still shaking, she got up and locked the door, then she went to her own room and locked that door as well. The thought of her uncle being a part of this chilled her to the bone. Was she even safe here? How could he have left her alone with such a man as Geery? *Why* would he?

She paced as she waited. When she finally heard someone enter the suite, she wondered, hardly able to breathe, if Geery had returned. Surely the man would not, and he had no key, unless . . .

"Millie?" The voice was her uncle's and she relaxed a little, but she was still angry. So angry she could not bring herself to even speak to him.

"Now, Millicent, surely you understand that my leaving you alone with Mr. Geery was only so that you could get to know him. He wants very much—"

She had the door unlocked and open, and shoving her finger in his chest, she caused him to fall slightly backward. He stumbled over a chair and went to the floor. "How dare you even think of letting that—that vile lecher anywhere near me without protection!" She stood over him, her fists doubled, face red with anger. "Oooh!" she lifted her dress and kicked him in the foot, hard enough he grimaced and tried to scamper away.

"Now, Millie, Mr. Geery is a fine man and . . . and you misjudge him if—"

"A fine man? A fine man, you say?" She took another kick at him, but he pulled back. She swung with the other foot and made contact this time. She continued kicking until his back was against the wall. "He is a vile fool; that is what he is! And what have you done, Uncle? He spoke of your debt and the use of Beauchapel as—as some sort of collateral! Are you an even bigger fool than he is?!" She kicked at his leg again then stomped toward her room. Before entering it, she turned around and faced him, pointing firmly at the door. "Get out, Uncle. You cannot be trusted with my safety, and I will not have you staying in the same suite with me! Get another room if you can or sleep in the park, but if I see you again before morning, I swear I will shoot you."

He stood and was about to say something. "GO!" she screamed. "And leave your key!"

He removed the key from his pocket and tossed it in a chair, then he walked to the door and hesitated as if wanting to speak. But he thought better of it, opened the door, and left.

Millie locked the door again then threw herself into a chair, trying to calm down. The more she thought on what the possibilities were, the more angry, betrayed, and fearful she felt. *What had her uncle done?*

It was another hour before she felt strong enough to get up, dress in a nightshirt, and lay down on the bed to try to get at least a little sleep. Though she was exhausted, it didn't come easily, but she finally drifted into a listless sleep.

She awoke to a knock, struggling out of bed and cursing her uncle as she threw on a robe. She angrily flung open the door to find herself facing the maid. Mille asked the time and realized she would be late for her steamer if she didn't hurry.

"Have a bath run for me," she told the maid. "And have them bring the usual breakfast. Hurry now! I must not miss my steamer."

An hour later she was packed and had her luggage taken to a carriage. She made sure she had her papers before leaving the room and heading down to the lobby. As she hurried to leave, her uncle appeared and gently took her arm.

"You had no right to lock me out of my own suite." He forced a smile. "But I forgive you and—"

"Forgive me?" She realized her voice was loud and quickly quieted it as others in the lobby turned to look. "Forgive *me*? Uncle, you *are* a fool!"

"Mr. Geery is fine gentleman," he said stiffly. "You should count it a blessing that he has such interest." He paused. "I have done nothing of which your father would not approve. You are a woman and cannot run Beauchapel, nor should you. Mr. Geery would give you everything and see that Beauchapel thrives, just as your father would want it. He—"

"I understand your traditional thinking about a woman's place, Uncle, but I don't agree with it, and neither did my father. That's why he prepared the papers he did. He had faith in me and—"

"He was a fool, then." Her uncle stiffened. Seeing her reaction, he quickly flashed a smiled. "Now, Millie, if you will not consider Mr. Geery, possibly I should continue to run Beauchapel. After all, I alone know its present condition and—"

She jerked her arm free. "Uncle Richard, I will have nothing to do with Daniel Geery, and as far as business matters are concerned, you will no longer have *any* say about Beauchapel. It's obvious that you have done something either immoral or illegal concerning my property and affairs, and you are a fool if you think I will let it continue."

His face hardened. "I just as well tell you. I have taken some money from your accounts. Your care has been costly, and I—"

She felt sick inside as she interrupted him. "How much?" she asked with anger.

"Several thousand dollars, but I have it covered. Your property . . . you must understand, I have had a rough two years, and my debt—well, I had to make some decisions with regard to Beauchapel."

She felt the anger like bile in her throat. "Uncle, father left you land for your services concerning my care. Taking additional funds for your own use is nothing but thievery."

"Now see here . . . " He grabbed her arm again, and once more she pulled away.

"I will be leaving, and if I find any money missing from my accounts, I shall sue you for the entire amount! I swear it, Uncle." She started for the door, her stomach churning and her mind in turmoil. She had trusted him with everything and so had her parents. To find out he had been stealing from her was devastating. What damage had he done? She must know, and that meant getting to her bank in Richmond as soon as possible.

She was helped into the carriage and told the driver to hurry; she was late and could not miss her steamboat. As the carriage lurched into traffic, she sat back, closing her eyes against this nightmare, trying to calm her fears and her frustration. After only a moment the carriage slowed then stopped, and she looked out the window to a mob coming down the road, chanting something she couldn't understand and holding signs high above their heads declaring, "Let them go" and "No war." It was then she understood the words. They were shouting, "Lincoln's folly," over and over again. But they weren't the only ones shouting. Angry people were following them along the sidewalks shouting and shaking fists and clubs at them. Suddenly, several men ran into the protesting crowd, attacking. It quickly turned into a brawl, forcing the driver to turn down a side street to avoid the whole affair.

They rushed down the street and out of Washington toward the docks. She arrived to find the steamboat loading the last of the passengers, and she quickly jumped from the carriage, paid some stewards to board her luggage, and then rushed to the point where papers were being checked. She was still catching her breath when the soldier took her papers. She noticed that other soldiers had pulled two men aside and were in heated discussion, then the two stomped back toward the city, one of them throwing their apparently inadequate papers back toward the soldiers. She felt her breath catch as the one looking at hers lifted an eyebrow, glanced at her, then finally gave a wan smile.

"Miss Atwater, please come with me," he said.

Millie felt her stomach wrench. "But my ship. I cannot miss it. I—"

"It'll wait." He pointed to a small building nearby. "Please, this will only take a minute."

Disgruntled, unsure, she went in front of him. He opened the door, and she was ushered inside to find a stocky man in a bowler hat sitting in a chair, his feet up on the table. A woman stood near a window. When he saw Millie, he let his feet down and stood then took the papers the other man held. He looked at them while the soldier left the room.

"Miss Atwater. You had breakfast with Rose Greenhow a few days ago?" the man asked.

Her mouth went dry. "Yes, but how do you know what—"

"My name is Polanski, Joe Polanski. I'm with the new intelligence organization of the federal government. We've been watching Mrs. Greenhow. Our agent, a man posing as your waiter, said you received a letter from Mrs. Greenhow," Joe said. It was at least partially true.

Millie felt sick but knew it would do no good to lie. "Yes, that's true. It was for a friend in Richmond, a Mrs. Stephens. But there was another letter inside addressed to a Mr. Pike. It was obvious she had deceived me, and knowing Mrs. Greenhow's politics, I decided it would be folly to trust her so I destroyed it."

Joe smiled. "Did anyone witness its destruction?"

"Yes, a man to whom I was giving a ride to the train station, a Mr. Alexander. Matthew Alexander. He knew of Mrs. Greenhow and warned me it might be a coded letter."

"Is Mr. Alexander still in Washington?"

"No, he caught his train, Mr.—what did you say your name was?"

"Polanski. This is Mrs. Smith," he said nodding in the direction of the other woman, who turned to look at her. "She will need to search you and your luggage. Are you adverse to her doing so?"

"Of course, as anyone would be, but if it will satisfy your mind concerning the letter I was given, you are free to do so." This was all very annoying and even a bit frightening. What had Rose gotten her involved in?

Joe measured her then nodded to Mrs. Smith, who left. Millie got the distinct impression her name was *not* Smith, but she would search Millie's luggage. But Millie didn't care. She had nothing to hide. Still . . .

"Are you traveling to Richmond alone?"

"Yes, though my uncle is still here in Washington. He's been delayed by business, and I must return to take care of my plantation."

"His name?"

"Richard Atwater."

"Your uncle is also friends with Mrs. Greenhow?"

"Yes, a very good friend." She said it out of spite and anger. It was becoming very obvious both her uncle and Rose had tried to use her.

"Good enough that he would help her destroy the federal government?"

She didn't answer immediately. "My uncle is a fool and lacks the intelligence to be a good spy or agent or whatever you call such men, but he could be used by Mrs. Greenhow, yes."

Joe measured her before finally speaking. "Tell me what you can about Mrs. Greenhow and your uncle's relationship with her."

There was very little to tell, but Millie did what she could, sensing that Polanski's intent was just to buy time. Ten minutes later Mrs. Smith returned and gave him a slight nod. Polanski smiled at Millie. "Thank you, Miss Atwater." He handed her the papers. "You are free to board your steamer."

She took them, a bit unsure, but started for the door.

"Miss Atwater."

She turned back.

"If you ever see Mr. Alexander, you should thank him. If you had been carrying that letter, I would have arrested you."

Millie only nodded then left the building and walked to the steamer, her mind relieved but still unsettled. It had been a very strange conversation. But she pushed it aside as she boarded the steamer and the boarding ramp was quickly pulled up. She saw Polanski come out of the building, his bowler hat still in place, a large cigar between his teeth. She feared for her uncle. And then she smiled grimly. But it would serve him right.

Chapter Four

AFTER A GRUELING MARCH AT double time for three miles, Rand's battalion joined the rest of the regiment above Mitchell's Ford. They were immediately held in reserve to get their breath and prepare for battle. Rand saw General Tyler, Colonel Sherman, and others on a small knoll overlooking the river. Rand could see immediately that some of Tyler's division were already moving down to the river in an attempt to engage rebel forces that might be protecting it. A cannon boomed, then another, and finally a third. Rand watched as the balls whistled over the men's heads and across Bull Run, exploding in the trees on the far side. He pulled out his binoculars and quickly eyed the result.

"Don't see much in the way of opposition," Hooker said, squinting at the spot.

"They're there alright," Rand replied. He could see men scattering for deeper cover as the second and third ball landed. "Question is, how many."

"An' 'ow many be down there," Malone said, pointing farther down Bull Run where smoke settled atop the thick forest. Rand used his binoculars to inspect up and down the river.

Hooker also pointed. "There's another camp down there, where the run turns south." Everyone knew there were three good fords on Bull Run—Mitchell, Blackburn, and McLean—and all three had rebels prepared to defend them.

"That's Richardson's men, isn't it?" Hooker asked, looking at the federal troops moving at double time down the road toward the ford.

Rand felt the intensity himself as he looked carefully. He could see Israel Richardson at the front of several hundred soldiers. "That's him." He looked at his own exhausted, wide-eyed, and expectant battalion.

He saw Sherman speak to Tyler, then turn his horse and come toward them at a gallop. He pulled up in front of Rand. "Major, good to have you here," Sherman said. "Get your men under the cover of those trees over there. Get them ready for a fight. It looks like we're going to be in the thick of things sooner than we expected." Sherman and his aides rode off toward the rest of the regiment, and Rand knew the colonel would give instructions all along the line.

Rand, Hooker, and Malone turned back to their waiting battalion. Rand told his men to fall out and get in skirmish line of command, then he turned to Malone. "Captain, I want your company at our far right, nearest the crossing." Malone nodded and gave the order to his hundred, and they quickly spread out into the trees nearest the road. Rand noted that despite the grueling march, there was a new excitement among the men, a buzz about finally going into battle, especially among Malone's Irish, but he wondered how long it would take before the bravado shown around campfires for the last few months would disappear when confronted by the reality of suffering and death. The thought was disrupted by the distant sound of rebel cannons exploding along the ridge above them, searching for the Union artillery that was harassing rebel lines. As if tourists, some of the men were standing up straight watching the explosion of Union artillery shells in the far woods.

"Get yer bloody heads down!" Malone screamed at them. The men ducked and all went down as if attached to one another just as a rebel cannonball crashed into the trees around them. Rand felt the power of the explosion of dirt and broken limbs as they sprayed him and his mount. As much as he wanted to flee, he only gripped the reins tighter to keep Samson under control.

He glanced at Malone, who stood erect behind his men, his shoulders and hat covered with the spray of dirt.

"Captain, you might want to obey your own orders," Rand called.

Malone gave him a wry smile. "'Tisn't the way of a captain, Major. Can't see where the enemy be comin' from if I be layin' on me belly." He looked at Rand's horse. "Nah t' mention the fact tha' you ha' nah left yer own saddle fer cover. When ya do, mark me words, I'll be dashin' off right after ya."

Rand only smiled as he lifted his own binoculars to his eyes and scanned the far side of the river. He could see plumes of smoke on the far edge of the forest and figured that's where the rebel cannons were. It was a fair distance, and the Union artillery had a distinct advantage as they were high on the knoll and shooting downhill. He watched as Richardson's men spread out to the left and started through the trees down to the run. Seconds later the first crackle of infantry fire echoed up through the forest; a few pained cries told of hits. Anxiously, Rand glanced up at where Sherman and the others were now watching the scene alongside General Tyler. He figured it would only be minutes before they were ordered to add support; he turned Samson back to his men.

"Get ready boys! We'll be in it soon." He said it several times as he rode behind his line. Eyes widened, and there was a sudden flurry to check weapons as the cannon volleys continued to explode above and around them. It wasn't the first time Rand felt his gut wrench at the realization that much of what would come next would be his responsibility. He must see things clearly, control his fear, and strategize where his men would do the most good with the least amount of harm.

"Randolph, the men are in position," Hooker said as he rode up. "The trees run clear to the river and should give good cover when we advance."

Rand nodded. "Good." Their training would be put to the test now. They had taught the men how to move forward in order, how to fill in gaps, how to fight from cover, and to leapfrog forward, but in the confusion and heat of battle, men did not always remember.

"Hey, Major, when we gonna stop hidin' in these here woods?"

Rand turned to face the man with the impatient challenge and smiled. Farley Judkins was a country boy from Missouri who had walked to St. Louis when he heard about the Union enlistment at the arsenal. There was no better marksman in their battalion than Farley Judkins, not even Rand, and he'd proven a good leader as well. Rand had made him a sergeant.

The sound of pounding hooves caused Rand to turn around before he could answer Farley's question. Sherman's aide rode up.

"Major, you are to move forward and support Richardson's men. Test the rebels' strength east of the run, but do not cross, is that understood?" Rand nodded, and the messenger turned his horse and rode back up the hill.

"Sergeant Judkins, you have your answer. Captain Malone, get this bunch on their feet. Let's move."

Momentary confusion normal to such orders ensued as men rushed to line up and get moving; then they started through the trees and underbrush toward the river. Rand did not cotton to having them all line up like toy soldiers and advance in one strong line. In fact he'd taught them the contrary, telling them that sneaking about through the trees was not only manly but kept death from knocking at one's door a good deal longer than sitting in a line like ducks on a pond. He could see that his efforts paid off as his men advanced, sure but careful. Even though every one of them was filled with the same fear, the same sudden impulse to get out of it, their training and a little bit of bravado kept them moving in the right direction.

"We bust through now, get t' Manassas, an' take that junction . . ." Judkins said. "This could be over, Major." His broad smile revealed a missing tooth in the front left of tobacco-stained teeth. He spat juice at a tree with force, splattering it with brown goo as he turned resolutely toward the river.

"Major, if I were you I'd get down from that horse. You're a fine lookin' specimen up there, but you make a target the size of mountains," Hooker warned.

"Captain, keep your mind on your business." He kept Samson moving behind the line of men, ignoring Hooker's words.

Hooker bit his tongue but didn't stay silent for long. "Sir, yer battalion commander, an' you should stay back an' tell us what t' do if they create holes in our line. That's yer job, Major, not out here in front as ya are at present."

"Mr. Hooker, leading from behind is more for generals and colonels, not for majors. Now if you don't mind, you'll be keeping your mind on what's ahead instead of where I am in the line. Is that understood?"

Hooker's face reddened, and Rand immediately regretted the harshness of his tone.

"Yes, sir." Hooker turned and started back to his place in the line.

"Captain." Hooker turned back. "I appreciate your concern, and if you go and get yourself shot, I will not be forgiving you anytime soon so keep your head down."

Hooker smiled and nodded then went back to his place just a bit ahead of the rest of the line.

They were within a hundred feet of the river when a piece of bark snapped off overhead then another and another. Rand heard a cry from one of his soldiers and saw him go down. There was a brief hesitation by the entire line as they fully realized those were real balls and they were aimed to kill.

"Steady, men," Rand yelled as he readied his Sharps rifle. "Keep low, work tree to tree. Fire when you see a good target but not before. Don't give yourself away for nothing."

A modicum of calm and resolve seemed to be restored, and the men began moving through the trees again, this time more carefully as balls continued to zip about them, sawing off bits and pieces of thick underbrush. Hooker was right. It was time to dismount. He did so and slapped the reins around a tree limb, his eyes straight ahead as Malone moved fifty yards to the left, directly behind C Company, while Hooker moved behind A Company.

Rand followed Malone downhill listening to him give an Irish curse to anyone who was lagging back and telling them if they didn't want *him* to shoot them, they'd best get out front. Laggers suddenly picked up their pace, their eyes wide as they threw furtive glances at the tenacious Irishman whose reputation as a veteran of the Mexican War had preceded him.

"Boys, concentrate now. Look ahead. Get your rifles ready," Hooker said from behind his own men. "Ain't nothin' you ain't ready for. You're Missouri boys, and you be actin' like it now or I'll shoot you myself."

Rand felt his breath catch in his throat as he looked down the line and saw Daines in the line of B Company. Everyone was in place, everyone moving forward.

He saw one of the men slip behind a tree, catching his breath, unsure if he could move forward again. "Steady, Mr. Privett," Rand said, controlling his own fear. "Be cautious but keep moving. You honor is at stake as well as your life, and we need your help today."

Privett looked at him, fear in his eyes, but nodded, stepped out from the tree in a crouch, and kept forward. Rand knew all of them would be hard-pressed to control their fear now; even he had to force his feet to keep moving.

Rand heard the whistle of the cannonball before it exploded fifty feet down the line. Bark, stone, and lead shrapnel tore into several men, and a piece of wood as thick as a man's arm stuck itself into a tree near Hooker's head, though he hardly seemed to notice. Except for Hooker, Daines, Rand, and Malone, the line of men went down like they were chained together as another ball ripped through the trees. It landed near his and Hooker's horses with such force that Hooker's horse went down; Samson jerked back on his reins. Hooker's fought to get back to its feet, a sharp piece of wood stuck in his neck. Rand threw himself to the ground as a third ball blew past him, cutting a tree as big as a fence post in half. The top half fell hard on top of him. He struggled to get free of its branches, popped up, and found his men staring in his direction, their eyes wide and wondering.

"There it is boys: resurrection at its finest," Hooker yelled. The relief in his voice was tangible, and there were a few chuckles until another ball whistled overhead and landed at the edge of the woods, creating a crater the size of a woodshed.

"Up boys! Steady now! Ready to fire!" came the firm, emotionless words of Isaac Hooker. The men got up and moved forward again. They could see the open river, its waters shimmering in the afternoon sun, and rifles went up along the line. A man on Rand's left was hit and went down with a scream, then one to his right. Balls zipped past him, and he screamed the order to return fire. The volley was deafening as the entire line exploded. He felt the hard kick of his own Sharps, saw the bullet hit the movement he had targeted, heard the cries and screams all along the rebel line.

"Take cover!" Hooker screamed. As everyone went down, a return volley from the rebels mowed down tree limbs as if they had been cut with a scythe.

His men loaded quickly and returned fire. Rifles exploded all up and down the line on both sides of the run. Beauregard's force was ready.

And it was formidable.

After three shots and loading he looked down the line again. His men were holding. No panic. No running. Most were prostrate on the ground, behind trees, fallen or standing, and were firing methodically. He stood and quickly moved along behind the line, encouraging even as he loaded his Sharps breach loader for another shot. He found a wide tree, stood behind it, steadied the weapon, and fired again. The man next to him raised up and was hit, knocking him on his back, his eyes wide and staring. Rand shook off this sudden look at death, anger roiling in his stomach. He grabbed the man's loaded rifle, steadied, fired, and watched another man drop across the river; payment, life for life, he thought. Such was the horror of war.

He glanced around for Hooker as he tossed the rifle aside, picked up his own, and began reloading. He could not see his friend clearly any longer, the smoke from powder heavy in the forest. The smell mingled with the blood and sweat born of fear and adrenalin. Two more men between him and Hooker fell, and a third tried to help one get to cover. Just as he did a bullet ripped through him, and both fell to the ground, one dead, the other still holding his comrade. Rand sat down his weapon, grabbed the man, and lifted him back into a stand of trees. He was bleeding badly, and Rand ripped a piece of his shirt away and wrapped it tightly around the wounded man's upper arm even as he tried to keep track of the battle.

"Hold it tight, soldier," he said, trying to smile. "And keep your head down. You've done enough."

The man only nodded, his face pale with the pain. Rand kept low as the balls whistled overhead. He found his rifle just as the firing from the rebels seemed to stop almost at once. The smoke lay heavy across the water, making the far side hard to see. What had happened? Why—then he knew. They were coming. He glanced down the line. There was a gap.

He ran that direction, yelling to close ranks. At first, the men looked confused, but they rallied and quickly spread out the line, filling the gap the dead and wounded had created.

"Load, men! Load! Quickly now! They'll be comin'! Get ready for it!" he screamed. The men quickly did as they were told even as a yell of a hundred rebels resounded across the water and they blew out of the smoke like ghosts—coming straight at them.

"Let 'em have it, boys!" Hooker yelled from down the line.

Rand raised his weapon along with all the others and fired as the rebels plunged into the shallow waters. The volley from his men mowed them down, and the attack was over before it had begun. He thought of pushing forward now, of attacking the line across the run before the rebels tried to bring others, but Isaac's words rang out.

"Steady. Hold. Load quickly now!"

Rand remembered the order then. They were to hold, test the strength of the rebel line, but not to cross the run. Why, he didn't know, but he figured it out it in the next few seconds as another charge came before most of his men were even half loaded. A few fired; he fired, several rebs fell face down in the water, but more kept coming. Rand could see a few of his men about to panic, about to run as the rebs hit the shore only thirty feet away. He pulled at his saber, flung his rifle down, grabbed the butt of his revolver, and lifted it from its holster. The rebels were on enemy turf now and were finding it hard to get up the bank. It was now they could hit them.

"Get 'em, boys!" he yelled, even as he sprinted at the onslaught of rebels clawing up the bank. His men lifted with one movement and followed, knives drawn, rifles ready to be used as bludgeons. Malone's Irish hardnoses met the enemy first, hitting them like a battering ram against a half open door and slamming them back into the river. Rand rammed his saber home, shoved one rebel off, and fired at a second with his revolver, slamming the soldier back down to the bank of the river.

The yells, the screams from both sides were distant, muffled voices as Rand fired, sliced, and fought for his life. He felt the hot steel of a knife graze his shoulder. Turning, he slammed his pistol into the side of the attacker's skull, sending him to the ground like a fallen log. Suddenly the remaining rebels broke and ran back the way they had come. Rand heard screams for retreat from the other side and knew they had held their ground. But he looked up just in time to see rebels on the other bank preparing to fire.

"Down!" he shouted. He heard Isaac scream the same command, then Malone and Daines; he heard it reverberate all along the line, saw men dive for the shore, crawl up the bank, trying to scramble for anything that would protect them from the volley that was to come. Worried for his men, Rand froze then felt something slam into his back. He was driven to the ground just as the opposite shore exploded with the volley of hundreds of rifles. Balls ripped through the woods around them like a steel knife. Rand realized that he'd been knocked to the ground by a man. The man got to his feet and extended a hand. It was Hooker.

"Best if you don't stay up too long, Major," Hooker said.

Rand only nodded as he realized he would have been cut in half if he'd been up a second longer. He watched Hooker pick up his rifle and return to his own men.

"Load, boys, and be quick about it!" came the clear voice of Hooker.

Rand shook off the shock and grabbed his revolver, loading as quickly and calmly as he could. He would need it more than the rifle if the rebels tried to cross again. He felt the sweat drip down his forehead and into his eyes and wiped it away with the sleeve of his shirt. His hair was soaked, dirt and grime sticking to it like mud.

He forced himself partially to his feet in order to see the river over some low bushes. Smoke hung in the woods like fog, making the far shore a faint outline, but he could see ghostlike movement there and wondered if another attack would come. Then he saw a man dash from woods, grab a wounded soldier, and drag him back to safety. He blinked then focused on the ground in front of him. Clear to the water, he saw a dozen bodies. Two moved, moaned, were even trying to crawl back toward rebel lines while the rest lay still, their arms and legs in grotesque positions, red splotches marking the grass, rocks, water, and ground around them. Their uniforms were a mixture of blue and gray, but both sides had such uniforms from their state militias. Neither army had fixed on just one color, making it difficult to determine who was your own comrade and who you should shoot if he rose up from the battleground.

Shoving the shock of it all aside as best as he could, Rand pushed through the bushes to help the nearest wounded soldier from his battalion. As he tried to lift the man, Hooker was at his side and grabbed an arm. They pulled and carried the man back behind the line. Others got up and followed his example, wary and afraid, furtively watching the distant shore, waiting to hear the gunfire that might end their lives as quickly as it had ended others. Moments later they had retrieved all that were within a distance that would warrant risk of life and limb, but farther out, along the bank and in the river, Rand could hear the pitiful moans of wounded or dying men who no one dared to approach.

Rand focused on listening to the artillery and rifle fire down the line to the east. A battle still ensued; he realized he must get his men ready for more. While pulling cartridges from his ammo bag, he looked along the line for any sign of Malone or Daines.

"Captain Hooker," he said.

"Yes, sir," Hooker replied.

"Are Mr. Malone and Mr. Daines still with us?"

"Yes, sir. They've gone to the end of our line to see who's still standin'," Hooker reported.

The first cannonball struck the bank of the run; the second covered his men in dirt, rock, and shredded timber. He threw himself to the ground and covered his head as ball after ball punched around them. The painful cries of wounded soldiers penetrated the air as the rebels blasted again and again to drive them back from the river's edge. Rand had no new orders; all they could do was keep their heads down until Union cannons, now responding from the hill above his position, found those of the rebels and either devastated their assault or drove them from the field.

After nearly twenty minutes of shelling, the balls began landing farther up the hill as the rebel artillery tried to reach the Union cannons on the far knoll. Rand finally felt safe enough to sit up, bracing his back against a tree, his eyes watching the river, waiting for any attack that might follow. Except for the boom of cannons and the occasional zip or punch of a mini-ball, the field of battle was relatively quiet. He stood behind a large oak, hiding most of his frame from rebel fire.

Hooker joined him. "Seems they decided to test our metal," he said with a wry grin. He wiped blood from the blade of his knife and sheaved it, then he began reloading his revolver. He followed, helping Rand make sure the wounded were getting proper attention. Rand ordered several be taken to the rear immediately.

"Major!" The anxious word came from a nearby soldier, and Rand looked his direction.

"Yes, Mr. Judkins."

"Is they comin' agin or isn't they?" Judkins said with some irritation.

Rand smiled. "Keep your head down, Mr. Judkins. If they don't come today, they'll come another, and I'd like to see you there."

* * *

They waited for another hour, the cannons doing most of the fighting; no more rebels tried their line. Gradually, about dusk, the cannon fire diminished and then halted altogether.

"I think both sides have had their fill," Hooker said. "At least fer this day." He looked at the sky. The sun was lying low on the western horizon.

Rand heard movement behind them and turned to see Sherman's messenger dismounting near where Samson was still tethered. The man worked his way through the trees, searching.

"Here," Hooker called. The man made eye contact then quickly closed the distance.

"Major Hudson, you and your men are commended by General Tyler and Colonel Sherman. Your battalion will be relieved just after dark. Colonel Sherman wants your men encamped outside Centreville tonight."

"Tell Colonel Sherman we'll be there."

"The wounded are to be taken to Centreville. Those sent to the rear are on their way now. We have wagons for any others."

"Thank you, Lieutenant."

The lieutenant saluted and made his way back to his horse.

"We're being replaced at dusk," Rand told both Malone and Hooker. "Pass the order along the line, but do it quietly. No sense alerting the rebels. And get the rest of our wounded up to the edge of the trees. When the wagons arrive, I want them loaded and sent to Centreville immediately."

He paused as he holstered his revolver. "Isaac, get an estimate of our casualties and bring Captain Daines back with you. Captain,"—he faced Malone—"you are to see personally to the wounded. Go with them in the wagons. Find us in camp as soon as you are assured of their care." He paused. "And gentlemen, well done. We have added seasoning to our men's training. Hopefully it will pay off in the days ahead."

Both men only nodded and began moving along the line, giving the orders. A few men picked up the nearest wounded and began moving them up the gentle slope of the hill toward the edge of the trees. Rand counted half a dozen injured, two of them serious enough to be unconscious, one so blood soaked that Rand wondered if he could survive. The rest of the men remained in the line, the word of being replaced temporarily relieving their exhaustion, fear, and confusion. Rand knew that the attack had crushed their ideal of the supposed glory of battle, and though they had stood and fought—and would do so again—they would not spurn any relief offered.

Shaking off his own exhaustion, he picked up his Sharps and walked to where Samson and Hooker's gelding waited. He placed the Sharps in his scabbard and retrieved a jar of horse salve. He removed the shard of wood embedded in Hooker's gelding before applying the salve. The injury was not serious. Putting the salve back in his saddlebags, he removed his binoculars before returning to the line. He carefully scanned the woods and far shore of the run as Hooker and Daines joined him. At the sound of a wagon, he glanced uphill to see several pull up to the edge of trees. Malone and the others began loading the wounded.

"How bad at your end, Captain?" Rand asked Daines.

"Two wounded, one dead." He shook his head. "The rebels gah the worst o' this one. They should 'ave stayed on their side o' tha' run."

Rand nodded as Isaac handed him a canteen. He drank as Newton spoke again.

"They di' nah come at us as they di' you, but the cannon fire . . ." He took a deep breath. "They di' nah want us movin', tha's sure. We would have been cut to pieces if we ha'," he said.

Isaac spoke. "It seems that Beauregard was testin' yer end of the line, Randolph." He paused, a sober look on his face. "I figure they have five thousand men over there. Probably another five at McLean and Mitchell Fords. They'll move them here by morning. Then they'll come straight at this point."

"If they do, McDowell gets what he wants. He hits their right flank and rolls them up," Rand said.

"McDowell doesn't have enough men up to pull that off, not yet. It will be another day, maybe two," Hooker said.

Rand only nodded, a knot in his stomach. He knew how many were still on the road. He'd seen it with his own eyes. Wiping the sweat from his brow, he lifted the binoculars again, scanning the ground in front of him. Most of the bodies he had seen earlier in the run itself had disappeared, and he silently thanked God for it. He looked carefully at those remaining on this side of the river. As near as he could tell, none were federal soldiers. With the smoke lifted, he searched deeper in the far side of the woods. He could see men moving about and finally focused on several standing near some trees looking his direction. He fine-tuned his focus and settled on one officer looking directly at him with a spyglass. As the man lowered the glass, Rand's breath caught in his throat. He squinted, making sure of what he thought he was seeing, then he lowered the binoculars.

"Andrew!" he said under his breath. His mouth felt dry and his knees weak. Andrew Clay! Surely it could not be! He put the binoculars back to his eyes and looked again. The man stood alone now; the others had turned to walk away. He continued staring at Rand. They eyed each other for a long moment before Andrew dropped the glass, folding its sections into one another, moving his head left to right in disbelief. Then he turned and walked away. Rand dropped his binoculars. It was definitely Andrew.

"Sir?" Daines had noticed Rand's stillness.

Rand wet his lips, shaking it off, knowing he must say something.

"Nothing, Captain." He turned to Hooker. "Tell the men to be vigilant until we move out. It shouldn't be long." With that he turned back toward the wagon of wounded soldiers, his mind still a muddle.

He and Andrew Clay had become friends at the Academy, but Andrew was from Virginia, a slave holder, his father one of the most prominent plantation owners in the state.

And he was probably the only man Elizabeth Hudson had ever loved.

*   *   *

Andrew Clay could not concentrate, the movement of men and animals around him a blur. It had been Rand all right, and it had been Rand's command that had repelled their effort to breach the federal line. Andrew had not been in the attack but had watched it from the rear with General Longstreet. He was cavalry now, and his company, along with eight others, had been held in reserve to make the final breach of federal lines if it started to give. It hadn't. The federal line was strong, and from the look of its length, they might be amassing here as their point of attack. But then again they might not. They didn't come across they river when they could have, and he knew Rand—he would have taken the opportunity.

He shook his head. Randolph Hudson. He couldn't believe it. Longstreet's ordered attack had hit Rand's unit directly, and they had repelled the attempt. Rand's first battle command, and it had been a success. But then, Rand was top in their class in tactical training. If any one held, it would be Rand's unit.

"Captain Clay, are you with us?"

Andrew looked up into the hard eyes of Longstreet and quickly pushed aside his thoughts. "Yes, sir. Sorry, sir."

The annoyance on Longstreet's face was obvious, and Andrew felt his face turn red.

"Your opinion, Captain. I would like to hear it."

Andrew paused only a moment. He had only two options. He decided on the latter. "My guess is General McDowell is massing his forces to hit us here. We should prepare for it. If we don't, nothing will stop them before they get to Richmond."

One of the others spoke. "Begging your pardon, sir, but our intelligence tells us that McDowell's men are strung out from here to Washington, and he will not have sufficient force to break through for at least another day and probably two. If we make a push now, right here, we could chase McDowell back to Washington with his tail between his legs." Several of the men chuckled, and Longstreet gave a rare smile then sobered, thinking. Thank the good Lord, McDowell's army was moving at a snail's pace! Hopefully it would buy them enough time for Johnston's army to elude Patterson and get here! If it didn't, they would lose.

"Gentlemen, tend to your dead and wounded and hold this position. I will report to General Beauregard. Mr. Clay, you and your cavalry are to move into the line and fill in any gaps. Make a show of it. I want the federals to think we're stronger than we are at this point." He paused.

"Thank you for your opinions, gentlemen. I will bring both views before General Beauregard."

He turned, took the reins of the horse being held for him, mounted, and rode off. Andrew lifted himself into the saddle and started back toward his men. As he rode, his mind turned back to Rand again. He had never let himself dwell on the possibility that they would actually face one another in battle, but now here it was. He didn't know what Rand would do if it came to a fight, but Andrew knew that he could not shoot Rand Hudson or have anything to do with his death. No, he couldn't do it. Not just because of his friendship with Rand but because of Lizzy. She was probably already questioning their relationship because he was fighting for Southern rights, and if he killed Rand . . . well, she would never forgive him. He took a deep breath. Hopefully the brief sighting of Rand would be all he would see of his friend until this damnable war was over. And it would be over soon. He could not, would not think otherwise. If they could beat McDowell—and beat him badly here—it would surely end. Hopefully Beauregard would hit the federals hard tomorrow, before McDowell had all his men. If they could drive the federal troops back to Washington, it must end. It must!

He only prayed both he and Randolph would survive it.

Chapter Five

FLORENCE, NEBRASKA, WAS NAMED AFTER Florence Kilbourn, niece of a land speculator who had sought in vain to have the small village named Nebraska's capital and the terminal city for the Chicago, Rock Island and Pacific Railroad. Previous to that, the town had been known only as Winter Quarters to most, including Jacob Gates, who had buried his wife and child here in the year the Saints had been driven from Nauvoo, Illinois. It still pained Jacob to visit Florence, but there was no choice. Florence was where the Saints gathered before moving west.

Florence wasn't much to look at. After the failure of speculators to make Florence the state's capital and after most Mormons had moved west, the town became nothing more than a handful of houses and deserted buildings. Jacob found several of these suitable to house the influx of Saints that began as a trickle in May and turned into a flood in June and July.

Much more lively was Bluff City, just a ferryboat ride across the muddy waters of the Missouri. In 1849, the gold rush had started a wave of western immigration that funneled more than fifteen thousand people through Bluff City, setting off a boom in business. Jacob knew that Hudson shipping had profited from the boom because of the heavy increase in steamer traffic that brought more than a thousand people up the Missouri each day, depositing them in Bluff City, where they would be outfitted with wagons. Then they would cross the river to Florence, where they would launch across the plains toward the Colorado, Oregon, and California gold fields. Two ferries worked the distance between Bluff City and Florence. One of them belonged to Hudson shipping.

Jacob shielded his eyes against the noonday sun. The ferry now nearing the dock was packed with people, wagons, and animals. Though the movement to the western goldfields continued, it had slowed to a trickle. The war demanded most young men's attention now, and this ferry was carrying more Mormons than men headed for the gold fields. The wagons aboard this steamer would be carrying wagon parts, supplies, and canvas for assembling more wagons.

"William," Jacob said to one of the men standing next to him. "You get those wagons to the assembly area. James, Heinric, Olaf, see that the people understand where to go for shelter and instructions. I will meet Miss Hudson and take her to the hotel."

His eyes scanned the crowded decks to see if he could find Lizzy, but he was disappointed. Lizzy was tall, blonde, and would stand out in any crowd, but he was looking for the wrong attire. Expecting her to dress as the woman she was, he looked past her until she waved frantically at him. He smiled. Yes, he should have known. Elizabeth Hudson was not a typical woman.

The ship's ramp was quickly slid onto shore, and teamsters whipped the rumps of oxen, mules, and workhorses to get the wagons onto solid ground. William Blake shouted at the drivers of the first three wagons—all drawn by solid working horses and driven by Mormon teamsters—ordering them to take the wagons directly to the assembly warehouse. The last two—pulled by oxen—inched forward until the impatient passengers, excited to have finally reached their destination, began streaming down the ramp. Startled by the cackle of exuberant tongues and jostling bodies, the last team of oxen bolted sideways, knocking several unfortunate passengers into the water and scattering the others. Jacob could not help the smile. If there was one thing he'd learned from moving Saints across the plains, it was that most Europeans had no concept of oxen, mules, and wagons. Most had to be instructed on camp life and cooking. He took a deep breath. Obviously this group would be no exception.

But immigrants from Europe weren't the only ones preparing to go west. Remnants of the Saints who had lingered at Florence and other branches in the East had been reminded by missionaries of the Prophet Joseph's prophecy on war and saw the present as a good time to leave as God poured out his wrath upon the nation. Hearing that the Church was sending wagons from Salt Lake to hasten their effort and help even the poorest move west, they had come to join the flood of Saints fleeing to Zion.

Jacob saw Elizabeth coming off the ramp, a fine horse trailing behind her. She gave him a wide smile then dropped the horse's reins long enough to give him a hug. He noted several wagons coming from the ship's hold behind teams of strong Belgian workhorses, black teamsters at the reins.

"What's all this?" he asked, surprised.

"When the army started taking everything they could lay their hands on, I thought I had better stockpile a few things you might find hard to come by. Good wool blankets, cooking utensils, tents, wagon parts, and a dozen of the sheet-iron stoves. Flour, salt pork, beans, and a few other food stuffs as well." She grinned and hugged him a second time. "It's so good to see you, Jacob." Then her brow wrinkled. "But you look exhausted. How can I help?" She put her arm through his, and they started walking into the town, the horse keeping pace, and the wagons following.

"We do need the supplies, Elizabeth, thank you, but we will pay you for them. And, yes it's very busy right now. With those that have come with you, the three companies from Europe have all arrived now, and we have several hundred from Eastern missions that are also getting ready to leave." He pointed at the street ahead of them. "As you can see, there are several thousand."

"We can talk about payment later," Lizzy said. Her eyes were on the chaos around them. "My goodness, how are you going to provide wagons for all of them?"

"I ordered the wagons from a company out of Chicago. The last parts arrived on those wagons that got off the steamer before you did. We have a shop there." He pointed to the far end of the street where wagons stood in front of a small building, men adding wheels, boxes, and canvas tops. There were dozens in production, and the loud clang of several blacksmiths' hammers against hard steel lifted above the din of hundreds loading their own wagons for the journey ahead. She could see that beneath the seeming chaos of people and activity, there was an organized pattern to everything. And there was an excitement to it all that cut through the dust and commotion like a sharp knife.

He pointed at a large, cattle-filled corral beyond the shops and wagons. "The first of the oxen have arrived from Salt Lake, and the drovers are selling them to the immigrants for a good price—far better than we could have gotten from the thieves at Bluff City—and they're showing the immigrants how to handle them."

Lizzy had handled oxen before. Not often but often enough to know they were unwieldy, difficult even to get in their traces, but they were strong and could travel longer days than mules or horses.

"President Young's Down and Back Plan," she said. Jacob had told her of the prophet's plan to send wagons east along with extra oxen. The wagons carried products made in Salt Lake for sale in the East, then those wagons would fill up with supplies for Salt Lake. These same supplies brought exorbitant prices from the "gentile" store owners who had followed the Saints to the valley. This would force prices down and allow members to make profits instead of just gentile merchantmen. They also brought men who were expert on the trail and could lead the vast numbers of immigrants across the plains. And, of course the Saints who sent the oxen were getting a fair price, while the immigrants were not forced to pay Council Bluff prices.

And then there were the poor. Lizzy knew that some were arriving at Florence with nothing more than a few coins in their pockets—hardly enough to pay for a wagon that would cost sixty-five to eighty dollars and a team that would cost double or triple that. She wondered how they could possibly fare in such a journey.

"You'll run out of money before you get all these people in wagons," she said.

Jacob grinned. "Come. Let me introduce you to someone." Lizzy grabbed the reins of her horse and gave instructions for the wagon masters to follow. She and Jacob walked along the street, skirting wagons and dodging smiling immigrants who scurried about in their preparations. Lizzy recognized several tongues as Scottish, Scandanavian, German, and British English. They finally reached a store where Lizzy tied her horse to a crowded hitching post.

"Robert," she called to the first teamster. "Hold here until I find out where to deliver our supplies."

"Yes'm, Miss Lizzy," Robert Pendrake replied. He tied the reins about the post and climbed down to direct the other two teamsters as Lizzy and Jacob went inside.

There were several clerks helping customers, but one seemed to be at the heart of the entire clamor. She followed Jacob through the mash of people until they stood next to this clerk who put thread, thimble, and a half dozen other small items in front of the customer, then jotted them down carefully in a ledger.

"There ya go, Brother Thorsen," the clerk smiled. "That completes your order. Pull your cart or wagon around back, pick up your items, and get them loaded."

"Tank you, Brudder Young," the man said in a strong accent that indicated a Nordic background. "Tank da prophit for us too. Ita be a fine ting what he's a doin fer us."

"It is indeed," Brother Young smiled. "But once you're in the valley and making a living, he's sure you'll do your best to repay the Lord. Now off with you. Your group is going out to camp today, and you need to get loaded."

With that Brother Thorsen turned and worked his way to the door; Brother Young turned to face Jacob and Lizzy. "Brother Jacob, who is this fine lady you're keepin' company with?"

"Elizabeth Hudson from St. Louis. You remember . . ."

Brother Young grinned. "The daughter of Brother Baker Hudson, a fine Saint." He looked over the top of a pair of pince-nez glasses. "And I remember you as well, Miss Hudson, but it has been a while, and you were only a child then. I see your mother in you though. Very much so." He extended his hand to shake.

Lizzy could not remember him, but she knew she should and was grateful when he finished his introduction.

"Joseph Young, nephew of the prophet. I just arrived from Salt Lake, and Brother Jacob informed me of your help in getting the Saints here to Florence. It is most appreciated." He smiled.

Lizzy remembered. Joseph Young and her father had been in the Seventies Quorum together at Nauvoo when Brother Young was head of that Quorum. He had a large family, some of whom were near Lizzy's age, mostly boys; she'd played with them in and about the quarry where stone was being cut for the temple.

Lizzy removed her flop-eared hat and gave him a warm hug, her braided blonde hair hanging midway down her back. "I remember you, Brother Young. Your son Brig used to tease me without mercy."

Joseph smiled. "He would be less inclined if he saw you now. You have grown up a good deal." He glanced out the broken window and saw the wagons. He looked at Jacob with a questioning glance.

"Sister Hudson purchased some things I think you will find quite helpful. Where would you like them?"

"In the warehouse. I hope they are blankets and—"

"Utensils. Pots, pans, fire kettles, and the like. Wagon parts, flour, beans, and salt pork, among other things," Lizzy said.

"Wonderful!" Joseph replied with a wide grin and seeming relief. "The first wagons leave in the next few days and need a few of those items, and the wagons we are outfitting now . . . well, they'll need most everything."

"Then they are yours to give," Lizzy said. She removed a bulging envelope from her pocket and handed it to Jacob. "Tithing for Rand and me for the last few months."

"No, no, we'll credit these goods to your tithing," Jacob said. "It's the way Brother Brigham would want it. And from the looks of things, it may pay your tithes for some time to come."

"Consider the goods back tithing, Brother Jacob," Lizzy said. "It's what Randolph and I wish. God has blessed us, and we are not about to pinch His pennies."

A tall, young, and clean-shaven man came in through a side door, wiping his hands on a cloth as he approached, his eyes on Joseph Young. Several of the younger women in the store noticed his sudden appearance, and some of the younger ones made whispered comments and even giggled; he didn't seem to notice.

"Brother Young, the axles, brake shoes, and hubs on a half dozen of the wagons need replacing before we return to the valley, and unless I miss my guess, there will be need for more of the same before we reach the mountains. It is a hard trip and—"

"I have most of those in my wagons," Lizzy said. "They are mostly for Schuttlers, but I brought a few for the Prairie Schooner as well. Which do you need?"

The man looked up, a bit confused at first, but his eyes did a quick scan of the woman in front of him and showed some admiration for what he saw. "Schuttlers," he said. He had only a hint of a British accent, and Lizzy figured he was an immigrant who had been among the Saints for a few years.

"This is Elizabeth Hudson," Jacob said. "Lizzy, this is Benjamin Connelly, one of our young drovers. He came with the down and back wagons."

"Miss Hudson." Connelly smiled.

"Mr. Connelly. The parts you want are in the third of the three wagons in the street out front. There are several dozen of each. With Brother Young's permission you're welcome to use them."

"Yes, yes, of course. Go on, Ben. They're already bought and paid for"—he smiled at Lizzy—"and then some. How long will it be before you'll have the wagons ready for the return?"

"Two, maybe three days." He seemed to hesitate. "I don't mean to tell you brethren your job, but the members are loading the wagons too heavily. Especially the Schuttlers. They should have no more than twenty-five hundred pounds. We must reduce the weight or some of these wagons will never make it back to Salt Lake."

Jacob and Joseph exchanged a glace as they both shook their heads in frustration. Obviously it was something they had already tried to impress upon the immigrants. "We'll tell them again," Brother Young sighed. With that Benjamin Connelly left the store and headed toward the wagons. The endless line of folks needing help prompted Lizzy to let Brother Young get back to business.

"I will aid Mr. Connelly. Brother Young, I am staying at the Florence House. I hope you and Jacob will join me for dinner this evening. I have a hundred questions and—"

"I am afraid I'll be busy here until dark," Brother Young said ruefully. "Jacob can—"

"Then we shall eat at dark. Please, won't you come?"

"Yes, of course. At dark, then." With that another customer pushed through the crowd to the counter, and Joseph turned his attention to her. Lizzy and Jacob gently pressed through to the door. Jacob was immediately approached by one of his men, and Lizzy kept moving to the wagons where Benjamin Connelly was trying his best to convince Robert Pendrake he was not a thief.

"Robert, it's quite all right. These goods belong to the Church now, and Mr. Connelly here is one of their agents."

"Yes'm," Robert said, stepping back. He was a stocky black man who'd been working for Hudson Shipping since his youth. His parents had been freed from slavery and had moved to Alton, Illinois, where Robert had been educated in the schools of Charles Hunter, a friend of Lizzy's mother. He had come to St. Louis after Hunter had asked Lizzy's mother to give him work. Since then Robert had married a woman from Hunterville (a town for freed blacks, established by Charles Hunter), and they had one daughter. Robert was good with a team and a trusted employee who had taken over for Felix Coulon when Felix had been forced to flee St. Louis. Robert had been working the Missouri

Underground Railroad but had been discovered and was being sought by Missouri slavers when he had come aboard Lizzy's steamer at Jefferson City. She decided to take him onto Florence with her until the hunt cooled down and he could safely go back to St. Louis.

Ben Connelly dropped the back gate of the wagon and stared at the crates and boxes in front of him. Literally stacked to its canvas ceiling, the wagon contained an impressive amount of goods. He was reading some of the labels when Lizzy pointed to one at the very bottom. "That's a crate of hubs, and there"—she pointed to another—"is one with a half dozen brake assemblies. Possibly we should unload the rest of this before you try to remove those."

Ben nodded, stepped back, and shut the tailgate. "Have your men follow me." He walked around the side of the wagon, and Lizzy went to her horse, unhitching him and mounting.

"Robert, follow me please. Mr. Connelly will be our guide."

Lizzy saw Ben eyeing the Sharps rifle in its scabbard and the holstered pistol that hung over the saddle horn, a slight smile on his face.

"I suppose you know how to use those," he said.

Lizzy smiled. "I don't pack them around as an accessory, Mr. Connelly."

There was a slight glint in his eye. "No, I don't suppose you do." This was an unusual woman. He started down the street as she brought the deep brown gelding alongside him.

"How long does it take to get from Salt Lake to Florence?" she asked after a moment.

"Seven, eight weeks by wagon. If the Indians don't steal your cattle and the grass is still good enough so you don't have to go far to get feed. Why do you ask?"

"I intend to make the trip someday," she said.

"Best do it now. All Hades is going to break loose in these parts. Already is, from what I hear," Ben replied.

"Yes, that's why I have to stay. My brother is with the federal troops defending Washington, and my fiancé is fighting for the South." She wondered why she'd said it. It wasn't necessary, not really, but she needed him to know, she supposed. Just in case . . .

"That puts you between a rock and hard place," he said.

They turned down a space between two old, dilapidated buildings where Lizzy could see the large opening to a third. There were men working inside and out loading wagons with goods.

"What's it like in Salt Lake?" Lizzy asked.

"Busy, chaotic, and grand." He smiled. "I'll miss it."

"Miss it? But you are returning with the out and back wagons, aren't you?"

"No ma'am, I've been called to serve a mission. I meet Elder Orson Pratt in New York as soon as I can get there. From there, I'll go to Maryland and Washington. I'm assigned to bring another party of stragglers to Zion next spring and preach the gospel along the way." He smiled. "Try to convince a few heathens to get wet and save their souls."

"And your wife? Is she going with you?"

"My wife passed away giving birth to our child. I lost them both," he said then smiled, trying to lighten the weight he had just thrown at her.

"I'm sorry, Mr. Connelly."

"Thank you. It was some time ago. How long have you been engaged?"

"Not long." She was glad when they reached the warehouse and Mr. Connelly was distracted with the business of the wagons. She felt embarrassed for bringing up such a delicate subject when they were nothing but strangers.

"Sam, Peter, we have some supplies that need to be unloaded so I can get to some wagon parts. Can you give us a hand?"

The two men nodded as they closed the tailgate of the wagon they'd just finished loading with several bags of flour. As the wagon pulled away, one of them signaled for Robert to circle the wagon and pull it up parallel to the door. As Robert followed the instructions, the two men sauntered toward Lizzy and Ben, their eyes on Lizzy.

"This is Elizabeth Hudson, Hudson Shipping out of St. Louis. The supplies were brought by her. I assume she'll need a receipt." Ben looked up at Lizzy.

"That won't be necessary. They belong to the Church now, and their use is up to Brother Gates and Brother Young."

She dismounted and secured her horse as the three men headed toward the back of Robert's wagon. The youngest piped something to Ben that got him a good slap across the back of the head. He stumbled forward with a wide grin until he saw that Lizzy was watching, then he sobered quickly, lowered his head, and turned away a bit sheepish. The whole thing made Lizzy smile even as she wondered at Benjamin Connelly. He was at least Rand's age and had sunlit hair that was long enough to reach his broad shoulders. The sleeves of his shirt were rolled up above his elbows, and his arms were muscled and tanned. At about five foot ten, he moved quick and easy, his blue eyes flashing as he kidded with the two young men.

They soon had the crates of wagon parts sitting on the ground, and Ben used a small crowbar to pry off the lids and peer inside while Robert and the others continued unloading. He found what he needed, and as the last of the wagon's goods were taken inside the warehouse, Ben put the crates holding the parts he wanted back in her wagon.

"If you don't mind, I'll have your slave take them to my workplace. It isn't far and—"

Lizzy stiffened. "That is something you will have to ask Robert, but so that you don't make the same mistake twice, he is not a slave. He is a freedman, works for a wage that would equal anything you might receive, and is a family friend as well. We have no slaves, Mr. Connelly, and do not forget that my brother is fighting against the devilish practice even as we speak." She mounted and quickly turned back the way she had come leaving Ben with his mouth wide open and face red. By the time his tongue lost its paralysis, she had already turned into Main Street and disappeared.

Ben Connelly was stunned.

* * *

Isaac Hooker and his twelve horsemen were afoot but leading their horses by their reins. Isaac had shown the men how to wrap leather around the horses' hooves and hocks in order to muffle the sound as they moved past a nearby Confederate camp. Isaac estimated several hundred soldiers in the camp. He could hear the songs, the laughter— some of which sounded liquor induced—and even the voices of men in conversation as they changed their picket line along the far right of the Confederate line.

Sherman's orders had been clear—get behind the rebels, find out their strength at Manassas, then get word back to McDowell. They were within a few miles of the junction now, and the slightest misstep could mean detection, even capture.

As they moved south through the moonlit darkness along the east side of Bull Run, voices began to dim until Isaac could hear nothing at all. He went another hundred yards before he turned west, reached the run, and dropped the reins of his horse. Signaling for his men to wait, he picked out a large oak tree, leaned his rifle against its trunk, and quickly pulled himself up into the cover of its thick branches and dense foliage. Scampering high into its branches, he slithered out as far as the thickness would still hold his weight then pushed aside the leaves until he could get a clear look.

He saw no fires along the other side of the river, saw no movement, but in the distance he could see the campfires dotting the meadow where he knew McLean, Virginia, was located. Word was that was where Beauregard had his headquarters. Squinting for greater concentration, he let his eyes search along Bull Run farther to the south then to the east, where he could see a few lights that identified Manassas Junction. Then he listened. Would there be pickets hidden along the run as they moved south? He didn't think so. Beauregard's troops were already spread out along at least ten miles of front. He couldn't afford to stretch them any thinner by sending men this far south and east. There would be patrols—cavalry, like his own—but he couldn't worry about those. There was no time. It would be dawn in three hours, and he must get to Manassas and back before then to be of any help.

He slithered back to the trunk and was on the ground so quietly that his sudden appearance startled his men.

"We cross here. Single file. Stay behind me, and keep them leathers on your horses' hooves. Move slow. The less splashin', the less chance you'll have someone shootin' at you 'fore you reach t' uther side."

Isaac heard one of them spit a chaw of tobacco and heard the plop of the scrunge as it hit some leaves. "Fishbone, get rid of that chaw for's I makes you choke on it."

"Yes, sir," Fishbone replied. "Jus' calms my nerves tha's all."

"May as well as shout out yer whereabouts as spit that chaw," Isaac said. He never had much use for chaw spitters. Messy, ugly stuff and made 'em smell like the open end of a spittoon. "We cross one at a time. I'll go first and scout about a bit while the rest o' you gits across. Once yer on the other side, turn south again but get mounted. We'll be movin' fast once we clear them trees." He stood, picked up the reins of his gelding, and led him through the bushes to the edge of the run. He listened carefully while he stared at the water, trying to figure out which track would be best, then he stepped into the shallow water and quickly worked his way toward the other side. He hit a hole near the far bank and sunk to his shoulders, but he kept moving. The gelding floated and swam behind him, and Isaac let him catch up, grabbing the saddle horn and floating into the saddle just as the gelding reached shallow water again and pushed out of it, up the shore and into the trees.

The water wasn't warm, but it wasn't cold either, and Isaac felt a bit refreshed. His boots would need to be emptied, but he didn't worry about it at the moment. Instead, he worked through the trees quietly, listening for the slightest change of sound or unfamiliar rustle in the trees or underbrush. There was nothing. Moving south, he scouted clear to the edge of the forest then waited. His nostrils flared as he stared across the open land that lay before him. He could see no shadow, no movement, but that didn't mean someone wasn't there waiting, even sleeping. Someone who might be disturbed by their passing and sound the alarm.

The rustle of trees behind him was minimal as his men approached. He glanced over his shoulder and counted, noting that Fishbone was wet from head to toe. Isaac figured he probably hadn't seen the hole. It didn't help that he was short, a thin man who probably hadn't been able to find bottom until his hat was floating.

But Fishbone had a talent. He could use his old musket to shoot the eyes out of a squirrel at two hundred yards and put a man down at five hundred. It was the reason Isaac had picked Fishbone. He needed that talent.

Isaac knew they were all sloshing in their boots, but now was not the time for comfort.

He glanced up at the sky. There were a few clouds forming; the moon disappeared from time to time. He waited until it went behind a thick cloud then nudged his horse into the open field. If there were someone watching, they would find out now.

Chapter Six

RICHARD ATWATER APPROACHED THE GUARD with a smile meant to disarm. It had no effect, so he handed the soldier his papers. A moment later Richard was being manhandled toward a small building. The door was opened, and he was shoved inside, pushed toward a chair, and ordered to sit. His hands were then shackled behind him and his feet tied to the chair legs. He felt like throwing up even as he demanded to know what was going on. He was told to be quiet or he would be gagged.

Twenty minutes later, a short, stocky man came through the door, a woman in a floor-length linen dress at his side. The man sat on the desk and tossed an envelope into Richard's lap, making him gulp.

"Mr. Atwater I *should* have you hanged, and if you attempt to lie to me about the source of that letter, I will see it done using the closest tree," Joe Polanski threatened.

Richard felt his lip quiver, his gut wrench, then his food start to come up. He bent over as best he could and deposited it on the floor.

Polanski smiled. Richard Atwater would give him what he wanted.

* * *

Isaac figured they were within an hour of sunrise as the long train rolled into Manassas Junction from the west. He watched as hundreds of troops unloaded and began to form in quick, marching lines before double-timing it up the road toward McLean. So much for Patterson holding Johnston's rebel troops in the Shenandoah Valley.

"Hey, that's ol' Tom Jackson," one of Isaac's men whispered. Isaac squinted and saw that the man was right. Thomas J. Jackson was one of Johnston's top commanders, and here he was at Manassas. He continued to watch as more troops unloaded, formed into ranks, and followed Jackson's first regiments up the road.

Isaac knew Tom Jackson. He was a good soldier, had little fear if any. The man would make a difference for the Confederates.

"Mount up," he said, getting to his feet. They walked deeper into the woods and began untying and mounting their horses. "Boys, our soldiers will be at a disadvantage if we don't get back and let 'em know what's comin'. I figure that means we take a direct route." He pointed. If one followed his finger, the natural line of the eye fell straight across where Jackson and at least two regiments were just disappearing over a small bluff on their way to McLean. Beyond that was Mitchell's Ford, where they had fought the first battle only yesterday.

"But that's right into their strength, sir, an' there . . . there'll be thousands of 'em waiting fer us," Fishbone said.

"Then they'll make fer plenty of targets," Isaac returned. "Even you might hit one or two, Mr. Fishbone."

Fishbone reddened as Isaac went on. "We'll skirt Jackson, turn behind the rebs along Mitchell's Ford, and cross higher up. I figure McDowell will be on his way to the Stone Bridge this morning, and we'll find the fightin' there." He paused. "Trouble is we'll be in the open, so keep yer heads low and your revolvers at hand." With that he kicked his horse in the flanks and worked his way out of the woods directly down into Manassas. His men looked at one another only for a second or two before they followed.

Manassas Junction had only a few buildings and stores, and now that the troops had left, it was pretty much empty. Isaac moved his horse to a gallop as he hit the main street that paralleled the train tracks, tipped his hat to the conductor standing next to the train, and kept riding. By the time they hit the end of the street, more citizens had come out to get a look, and Fishbone, last in line, noted the perplexed look on their faces. As they fled into open land, he saw the smoke of another train coming through. He figured the passengers'd be a bit cautious when they arrived at Manassas and were told the federal cavalry had just blown through town.

With a chuckle he pushed his gelding for more speed and quickly topped the hill. Hooker had pushed his mount to full run, and Fishbone urged his horse to match the pace. At this rate, and with Hooker's audacity, they'd see McDowell before sun up.

*   *   *

Rand sat in the saddle. Colonel Sherman sat on his own mount next to him. It was dawn, and they watched as Tyler's entire division demonstrated near the Stone Bridge on the Warrenton Turnpike. It was a feint, and as Rand saw it, a poor one. Two other divisions were moving toward the enemy's flank west of them and would try to roll it up if Tyler's division could keep them busy here. With a halfhearted push by Tyler's men, their ploy would be read by the enemy and make the plan harder if not impossible to execute. Rand heard Sherman swear under his breath. He saw it as well.

Rand glanced over his shoulder to where his men waited, anxious and scared, but more seasoned than the day before. He had confidence they'd do their part.

Yesterday's brief attack had awakened them to the reality of war, and their demeanor hadn't been the bravado of the past this morning. Only silence. And cold, hard determination tinged with fear. It was a better formula for survival.

Rand hadn't slept a wink, his own near death causing him to toss and turn most of the night. It didn't help that they hadn't heard anything from Hooker. Rand worried that the rebs had managed to capture Isaac and his men. He didn't think so. Hooker was too good, but the wedge of doubt was still there. Hooker was the cement for the company right now, and if he didn't get back to them . . .

"Gentlemen, look," Sherman said to Rand and the other officers.

Rand looked the direction Sherman was pointing and saw a cloud of dust coming from the west. "They're moving up reinforcements."

"And yet there's a full scale battle going on at Mitchell's Ford. Listen."

Rand cocked his ear and could hear the firing of cannons. Lots of cannons.

"Beauregard is attacking our left," Rand said. "Hopefully the boys down there can hold him, but who's kicking up the dust?"

"That's the road to Manassas Junction. That could only mean Johnston has sent reinforcements," Sherman replied, his face etched with concern. "We need to break through here, Captain, and we need to do it now." He yanked on the reins of his horse and bolted back toward where General Tyler was watching the fight.

As the sun rose above the eastern hills, Rand raised his binoculars and scanned the far side of the run. Men were moving to the west instead of into battle at Mitchell's Ford. If they attacked here now, in force . . .

He didn't finish the thought as Sherman returned and ordered him and the other company commanders still in reserve to get their men moving in support of the Second Wisconsin, who were waiting to cross a half a mile upstream. Sherman drove his heels into the flanks of his gelding and headed that direction even as Rand turned, rode back to his men, and told Malone to give the order to form four columns, double time. He led them along the ridge until he saw the Second Wisconsin just beginning to form a skirmish line a hundred feet uphill from the river. He ordered his own men to fall in line behind them and watched as they executed the move from four columns to a full skirmish line. Rand joined Sherman and several other mounted commanders behind the men, urging them forward as cannon fire landed around them, ripping up the earth and putting half a dozen men down wounded, maybe dead.

"Attack!" Sherman yelled.

Rand screamed the order to his battalion, and the other officers did the same to theirs. Sherman's full division of a thousand men started off at a full run toward the open bank of the river. Several fell to a blistering wave of rebel fire, and others hesitated causing a moment of delay along the line.

"Form your battle lines!" Rand ordered. The men heard the order repeated by Malone and Daines, and the men spread out across the hill side until each end of the line touched the ends of other companies. "Ready, fire!" The sound of rifle fire came as the thunder of a fearsome storm. His men quickly reloaded, then Rand ordered a full-out attack. They plummeted down the hill. The rebels began to break then fled across the creek toward the other side. Rand's men fired then raced once more like a stampeding herd of cattle after the fleeing enemy.

They were nearly at the edge of the run, the Second Wisconsin to the left and already in the water, when the rebels formed on the other side, turned, and fired. A dozen men fell; the others ducked, ran, dodged, fired, and loaded.

"Full attack!" Rand yelled. His men stood, removed their revolvers, and fired as they ran into the water. They fired again and again, their revolvers loaded for six shots. Some fell dead in their tracks; others went down wounded. Still others reached the far shore, and the rebels began to withdraw once again. It was an orderly withdrawal at first, but as his Missouri boys and the Second Wisconsin reached the other side in force, along with most of the division, it became a rout, and the rebs ran toward the summit of Henry House Hill.

It was then Rand saw the rebel reinforcements breach the top of the hill and take up a line along a rock fence.

"Down! Take cover!" he screamed. The order was repeated, and his men shrunk themselves behind the turnpike bluff at the bottom of the hill; a hail of mini-balls rained down on them. Rand heard the scream of a cannonball and punched his spurs into Samson's flanks in hopes of evading it. The whiz that went past him tore off a dozen small trees lining the run. He dismounted, slapped Samson on the rear, and took cover with the others as an incessant and horrible fire rained down on them from the rebel lines. He looked back to see Samson standing a few feet away, his head down, blood dripping from a wound in his neck. Rand waved at him to spur a run, to get him to to move, to go anywhere. The horse finally turned and sauntered back the way they'd come, disappeared in the woods, and was gone.

Suddenly, cannons hit the rebel lines with a blistering barrage, and the Thirteenth New York surged across the run. Rand and the leader of the Second Wisconsin saw their chance. They stood and climbed over the embankment with the shout of "Now, boys!"

The rest of the company pressed after them, and suddenly they were over a fence and into a second gulley just as the rebels aimed cannon grapeshot directly at the surge. Rand watched as a dozen of his men, the last to go over the fence, were cut into shreds and blown back down the hill, then a massive crossfire devastated the rest, driving them back to find refuge, pinning them down, and killing even more. The attack up Henry House Hill was stopped before it had even begun.

*   *   *

Andrew Clay was about to lead his men into combat in front of Blackburn's Ford when he got orders to rush to the aid of forces at Henry House Hill. Beauregard intended to attack across the ford, roll up the federal left, and drive them back to Centreville then to Washington. It seemed the general's plan had been changed by an attack on the Confederate left at the Stone Bridge. With the attack at the ford already underway, Andrew's force was the only one still available. Colonel Longstreet ordered him to double-time it to Henry House Hill. His men made the march in the hot sun to arrive at the same time Johnston's reinforcements did. General Tom Jackson was the highest ranking officer, and Andrew immediately put himself and his men under Jackson's command.

Jackson ordered his troops to the reverse side of the hill and put his cannons on the crest where they could shoot directly into the federal infantry; recoil down the hill, where cover allowed them to reload; roll back up; and fire again. From his cover, Andrew watched as the fire devastated the federal charge up the hill.

Suddenly, Jackson rode up and called to Andrew. "Captain Clay, bring your men and follow me. We have our chance."

They mounted, and Andrew yelled to his company to fall in line. Jackson led them around the crest of the hill to the right, and Andrew saw immediately that the federal right was exposed and could be rolled up or driven from the field. He ordered his men into battle formation along the side of the hill behind a stone fence. When they reached the fence, he told them to fire. The smoke of the rifles erupted all along the fence, surprising the federals and felling dozens. But they did not retreat. Instead they hunkered down beneath every little dip and recess they could find and returned fired. He watched with wide eyes as half a dozen of his own men were hit and the rest were forced to hunker down behind the fence. Suddenly, he felt his horse shudder underneath him, heard the animal scream, felt its legs buckle midstride, and knew they were going down. He tried to jump free but couldn't get his foot out of the stirrup and felt the crush of the dying animal's weight on his foot and leg. His revolver and hat flew in two different directions, and his head hit the ground so hard he thought he would black out. He thought it odd he felt no pain as he pushed against the saddle and horse, trying to free himself; he couldn't. He blinked several times, heard the sound of chaos all around him, but could not seem to focus completely. He looked up to see Jackson ordering the men over the fence and on the attack. Then he saw a dozen horses leaping up the hill behind them, the riders firing weapons. It couldn't be. How could Union soldiers have gotten behind them?

In a split second, the charging horsemen were upon them. Andrew saw Jackson jerk as a bullet hit him in the hand or arm and throw him out of his saddle. He saw the attackers firing at the backs of his still-unaware men, saw several fall. He desperately searched for his own revolver but then ducked as the lead horseman drove his animal to jump directly over him. The man fired, the bullet missing Andrew's skull by a fraction of an inch.

Andrew's men finally realized they were under attack and turned and fired at the fleeing horsemen but to no effect. The rest of the rebel line were either so involved with the action before them or so surprised by this sudden and audacious appearance that no one thought to fire until the horsemen had descended the hill and splashed across to the safety of their own lines.

Andrew heard an explosion nearby and ducked as shrapnel blew through the air overhead. The sounds of other explosions, of their own cannons firing from the crest of the hill, of endless rifles and revolvers forced Andrew to realize that he must get free. He pushed with all his strength but could not budge his leg; several of his men scrambled to his aid and tugged and pulled until they had him out from under the dead weight of his gelding. Jackson had already remounted and was surveying the field as if nothing had happened, but his blood-soaked hand attested otherwise. Andrew found his revolver and quickly went to Jackson's side.

"Sir, you're hurt. You must go back. We will hold the line here."

Jackson did not seem to hear him, his eyes on the slope of the hill. "They're retreating." It was said with a tinge of disbelief, and he continued to survey the battleground then pointed at the distant shore of Bull Run. "They're forming a line on the other side. They will try to re-form there. We must not let them."

Andrew noted a waning in both artillery and cannon fire. It was a distinct lull—like a man trying to catch his breath. They had stopped the federal charge, and both armies were feeling the horrors of what was happening.

"McDowell missed his chance," Jackson continued. "If he hadn't come at us piecemeal . . . He outnumbered you two to one until my men arrived. If he'd come hard, all at once . . ."

Several other officers rode up, and Jackson faced them. "We have stopped them; now we must attack." He turned to one of the officers. "Jeb, take your cavalry in support of the Fourth Virginia. Capture those cannons at the bottom of the hill. Once we have those, we have victory. I will have our artillery soften them up for you. Plan to hit them in one hour."

J. E. B. Stuart was a young, energetic cavalry officer who had trained his company to be fine horsemen. With Andrew's own cavalry now holding this position, Stuart's would have to take the action needed by Jackson.

"The rest of you will attack in twenty minutes' time. Tell your men to reserve their fire until within fifty yards. Then fire and give them the bayonet! And when you charge, yell like furies!" The officers saluted and rode off to fulfill their orders. Jackson looked down at Andrew again. "The man who came through and tried to kill the both of us—his name is Isaac Hooker. Don't forget him. He nearly had both our scalps today." He smiled. "Thank the Lord of Heaven that all federals aren't like him, or we'd be overrun and fleeing to Richmond." With that he rode away toward Beauregard's field headquarters as Andrew's sergeants approached.

Andrew gave them their instructions and told them to spread the word along the line. Then he retrieved his rifle from its scabbard and picked up his hat before staring down at his dead mount. The black gelding was the brother of Rand's horse. Rand was somewhere down this hill: he knew it as sure as he lived. He wondered if Samson was too. Both men prized their horses. Now one of them was gone, maybe both. But he and Rand had to survive. They must survive. Taking a deep breath, Andrew began loading his revolver. Surely a battle like this, a field littered with bodies, would force peace. Surely they would find a way, and this horror would be over.

He bent down low as he walked the short distance to the wall. The federals were still firing, still there. They would kill him as quickly as they could see him.

He stooped behind the wall next to his soldiers and noted that there were more than a few who would not return to their families. Looking through a small hole, he peered down the gentle slope toward the river. He could see bodies; hear moans; smell blood, smoke, and death. It pained his sensitivities to realize what they had done. It sickened him.

The artillery above and behind the crest of the hill opened up again. Jackson had given the order. He looked at his watch. Ten more minutes before they were to attack down the hill again. Ten more minutes for the artillery to do more damage, kill more Union soldiers. Then they would go. Then they would have their chance to end this.

"We stopped 'em, sir," said one of the soldiers. "They came at us, and we stopped 'em." His eyes were wide with excited fear.

Andrew forced a smile. "I suppose we did, Private." He glanced at one of the dead men lying next to them. "But I'm not sure Henry thinks it was worth it." His anger was evident in his tone.

"Beggin' yer pardon, sir, but Henry and me, we're from the same town, and we joined this here army together. We don't like no Northern stuffed-shirt president like ol' Abe Lincoln telling us what we kin and kin't do."

"Do you own slaves, soldier?"

"No, sir. Don't cotton to it, sir, but this ain't about slaves, is it?"

Andrew checked his watch. Still eight minutes. Each explosion made him cringe; each meant more death, more destruction. He took a deep breath, controlling his bitter hatred of what they were doing. "I forget your name, soldier." He thought it odd that he could remember the one who died and not the one who had survived, but let it go.

"Furness, sir. Miles Furness."

"Well, Miles, what is it exactly that Mr. Lincoln was telling you that you didn't like and want to kill others because of it?"

Miles thought a moment, scratching his soft, sparse whiskers. "Well, I . . ."

"He says we have to stop holdin' slaves," said another man who had picked up on the conversation.

"He does. That's a fact," said another. "I read it in the papers."

Andrew looked at him, trying to remember a name. The soldier seemed to guess his dilemma. "Colter Hickson, sir."

"And you don't want him to stop you from holdin' them, is that right Private Hickson?" Andrew asked.

"I don't," said Colter.

"Well that ain't right," Miles said adamantly. "If'n we's fighting to keep men slaves . . . well, God won't appreciate *that* much."

"It ain't *jist* about slaves, Miles," said Colter with a little frustration. "It's about being *told* we can't have 'em. It should be a man's right to decide that fer himself. Old Abe should keep his nose out of it."

Miles scratched his head, a confused look on his face. He then shrugged as if it was all a bit much for him.

"Colter's right, Miles. Man should have the right to choose, and that's what the papers will say. But what they don't say is that slavery takes that very right away from someone, and if we're fighting for the right of self-destiny, the right to choose, shouldn't we be fighting for *their* freedom as much as our own?"

It went silent for a moment before Colter spoke again. "Beggin' yer pardon, Captain, but I hear you own slaves, sir."

"My father owns slaves, but I do not, nor will I."

"Then why are you here, Captain?" Miles said with a look of genuine curiosity.

"Good question, Private. A very good question. One I am still trying to answer."

"He's a Virginian," Colter said. "That's why."

Andrew smiled. "I suppose that's as good reason as the others. Honor. Commitment to friends, family, neighbors. Pride. It doesn't really matter. Doesn't even matter if it was a good or bad choice. Here I am," he said sarcastically, looking at his watch again. "And right now it's just about staying alive. Can't think of much worse than dying on this miserable hill today. But it would be worse to run away and be called a coward. Can't think of anything worse than being called a coward or a deserter, can you?"

"No, sir," Miles said. Colter and a few others who had been listening agreed, though their faces suddenly grew ashen as they mused over the possibilities that awaited them on the other side of the wall, where a dozen of their comrades had already caught a federal bullet.

"You were all close enough to hear General Jackson's orders, so let's see if we can end this war today, shall we? And let's do it in fine fashion, shall we? No cowards today. Not here. Agreed?" He forced another smile then stood and yelled the order.

"Hit 'em, boys!" With one accord the entire line raised to their feet, jumping and climbing over the wall. The response was a horrifying fire that cut men down left and right, decimating the screaming wave of forward movement which still seemed unstoppable.

Andrew saw Colter fall, then Miles. Maybe death would give them a different perspective, but he didn't care. All he wanted now was to survive. He fired, killed, drove forward only to survive.

*   *   *

Anger welled up in Rand, and he lifted and fired his Sharps then emptied his pistol at the line of rebels that was trying to come down upon them in a rush. Men fell like branches chopped from a tree. He loaded again, the sound of battle raging all around him, the cries and calls of the wounded and dying like a sword cutting through his heart. But he could do nothing but fire. Fire and fire again until the barrel of both his rifle and revolver were so hot he could scarcely touch them.

The sun was high in the sky, the heat and humidity burning into his flesh. Suddenly, he heard more soldiers behind him and looked to see Union reinforcements running up the gulley toward him. He yelled, trying to warn them to get low but could only watch as one after the other dropped, a sudden end to their lives coming from a source Rand tried to identify. Finally, he realized that the rebels had moved into a position that offered them a withering crossfire from another fence to the right. The rebel reninforcements! They were rolling up the Union right!

He looked down the line, his men still firing, hanging on with courageous tenacity. Some were dead, others wounded but still fighting. Another hit, then another. To even lift a head was suicide. They could not stay here. They must fall back, find a better position to hold or all would be lost.

"Fall back!" he ordered with a croaking voice. "Twos and threes. Cover fire! Fall back!"

He saw Newton Daines moving along the line, his body half-exposed as he spread the word and the men began to crawl their way out of the gulley, dragging what wounded they could; he felt someone jerk on his shoulder.

"Major, your turn," Hooker said.

Rand looked up at the grimy face and tried to smile. "Captain. You're a sight for sore eyes. Thought for sure you were a dead man."

"If I'm anything, it's hard to kill." But he pointed uphill where the rebels were in a full run and moving toward them. "But they're five times our numbers and are comin'. We best skidaddle if ya want to be alive in the mornin'."

They stood and ran down the gulley behind Malone until they reached a small hollow in the riverbank surrounded by trees. He found Newton Daines and a few others there, and they all collapsed into the recess.

"Think we can hold 'em here?" one man asked.

"Nah likely," Malone said. "We're beat." He looked over his shoulder, and Rand matched his stare at the flood of soldiers splashing through the water in retreat. He watched as some went down under a scathing fire, others looking with horror over their shoulders as a company of rebel horsemen drove their animals into the water after them, stomping, driving, punishing the retreating federals and increasing both their panic and the chaos of retreat. "Now tha's 'ow ya use the cavalry," Malone said in awe. "Look at 'em. They've go' our boys scatterin' like mice afore a fire!"

Rand raised and fired his revolver, felling one rebel from his animal, then another. Malone and Hooker felled a third, fourth, and then a fifth. Before the animals could bolt, Newton darted from the recess and grabbed the reins of a couple of the riderless horses. He ordered two of their men to get aboard and sent them toward safety with a slap of his hand. Rand had used all his bullets, was trying to reload, give cover, when a dark, powerful form came out of nowhere and hit him like a battering ram. He launched backward into the water, felt his head crack against a rock; then something hit him hard in the side. He felt his mind begin to slip into a dark hole, the sounds of gunshots and voices suddenly muffled as his body floated helplessly downstream.

Then there was nothing.

* * *

Hooker saw Rand get hit, tried to get to him, but was attacked by another horseman. He saw it coming, stepped aside in time, then grabbed hold of the rider, pulling him from the saddle. He saw his own horse still tied where he'd left him and splashed through the water to get to him as Malone, Daines, and the others were surrounded and fighting for their lives. He untied his animal and mounted just as another rebel came at him swinging a saber. He felt the cut in his side but used his revolver to shoot the man. In pain, he drove his heels into his gelding's flanks and dove into the water. He must find Rand.

* * *

Polanski sat with Pinkerton and two other agents as their carriage pulled up to Rose Greenhow's house. Three other carriages filled with agents were following. Polanski followed Pinkerton, climbing out just as Rose Greenhow was returning from an apparent walk. Pinkerton grabbed her arm, and she faced him. "You're Mrs. Greenhow, aren't you?" Pinkerton said.

"Yes. Who are you, and what do you want?" Rose answered. She had a hanky in her hand, which she immediately raised. Polanski realized it was a signal and looked about in time to see another carriage rushing away. He ordered his men to follow it as Pinkerton arrested Greenhow and took her quickly inside.

"I have no power to resist you, but had I been inside my house, I'd have killed you before submitting to this illegal process!" Greenhow said angrily.

Polanski was already inside ordering his men to do a thorough search. Over the next few hours, they found enough evidence, including Rose's diary, to put her under house arrest until they could get her to prison.

After dark, Polanski took several men and arrested the others Richard Atwater had incriminated.

By the next morning, the rebel spy of Washington was out of business. She had plans of fortifications, and she and her friends had established a plan to overthrow Washington if the rebels ever got to her walls. Pinkerton now had a dozen people in custody, but there were still others.

As he entered the office, he heard about the defeat at Manassas Junction. He sat at his desk, lit a cigar, and then drank a bit of whiskey. It was tough to be a week too late.

* * *

Newton Daines sat amongst a dozen other prisoners watching the rebels enjoy their victory. It had started as a retreat, turned into a panic, and ended up a rout. Newton had been jumped by two cavalry who had put a gun to his head; Malone had been coldcocked with a rifle butt. Now they sat together, Malone with a broken nose and dried blood on his face, and Newton wondering what would come next. Newton had last seen Captain Hudson floating face up, motionless, down the run. He dreaded the thought of having to tell Ann Hudson. And where was Hooker? He hadn't seen him since the captain had been hit.

"Hey, Yank!"

Newton looked up to see a rebel staring down at him with cold eyes.

"If ya be talkin' t' me, you'll be doin' it wi' me name. It's Cap'n Daines. Cap'n Newton Daines, most recently o' St. Lou, Missouri." He forced a smile.

"Well now, ain't we huffy." He jammed his rifle into Newton's stomach. "Y'all best not furgit who just licked yer carcass! Now, y'all git of'n thet grass an' fall in line with the rest a them prisoners 'fore I shoot y'all. Git," the soldier commanded. The accent was definitely Southern, and Newton wondered if the meanness was just natural.

"Private, mind your manners."

Newton and Malone looked in the direction of the voice to find a Confederate soldier standing a few feet away. His clothes were splotched with blood, and he had a cut over his right eye that wasn't deep enough to do more than ooze a little blood. His face was covered with dust and sweat as was his hair.

"Cap'n," the soldier protested. "These men—"

"Are soldiers and to be treated with respect."

"Yes, suh."

"Get the rest of the prisoners in the shade before you have to start burying them, then get a wagon with food and water down here," the captain said.

"But, sir, we have no—"

"The federals left everything but their pants behind. Find food for these men and for our own. There's plenty."

The voice had softened, and the soldier's belligerence seemed to do the same. He called to several other men, giving them the orders. The prisoners, spent from battle and the hot sun, tumbled into the shade, where they collapsed. The captain approached Newton and Malone.

"Hello, Mr. Malone," the captain said.

Malone shaded his eyes from the sun now peeping out between heavy clouds, a curious look on his face.

"We met in St. Louis. A party held at the Hudson place." He extended a hand to shake. "Andrew Clay."

Malone's eyes lit up with recognition. "Ah, Mr. Clay." Malone shook the hand. "Mr. Daines, this 'ere's Lizzy Hudson's fiancé. The rebel she was so worried abou'."

Newton took a closer look. "Nah near as 'ansome as I though' 'e'd be," Newton said without changing expressions.

"'Tis the blud on 'is shirt tha' does it t' ya. Belongs t' our boys is me guess," Malone said with cold eyes. "You'll be movin' along, Mr. Clay. Yer blockin' me view, an' it be such a pretty scene—all them dead. Mighty fine wha' yer rebellion 'as done. Ya shou' be real proud o' yer work."

Andrew was not surprised, but it still cut deep. They'd beat the federals back, routed them, but the hill was littered with hundreds of dead. He'd lost half his company coming down that hill and had shot at least a half dozen men himself. They all had blood on their hands now. But it was over. No one in their right mind would want more of this.

"Rand . . .?" He asked.

Malone looked down, "'e was commander," he said softly. "'e was hit. I—none o' us coul' ge' t' 'im."

Andrew felt weak in the knees and sick to his stomach all at once and had to sit down, his mind dizzy. "Then he—"

"'e was floatin' downriver las' I seen o' 'im, still as death," Malone said in a near whisper.

Andrew sat silent, unable to speak, unsure of what to say even if he had the strength. Rand had to be alive; he had to be. He looked across the run to the hill they'd fought on, to the bodies that covered it, motionless, their lives over. So many! He looked around him. There were several hundred prisoners, all exhausted, as dirty as him or worse. Their eyes were filled with disbelief, sadness. They were beaten, not by men but by death and fear. They had come on a lark and found war instead. They would never be the same. No one would ever be the same!

Anger welled up inside Andrew, his eyes on the closest rebel guards who were busy gloating, their demeanor one of bravado and victory. He whispered to Malone, "The prisoners will be marched to Richmond in the morning. If I were you, I'd try to disappear before then. The horses are kept in a corral about half a mile north. Get to them, and you're home free." He forced himself to his feet. "Try not to kill anyone, Malone. I have enough blood on my hands for one day." With that he turned and walked away.

"I' seems Lizzy's beau canah decide which side 'e's on," Newton said.

"'Tis so," Malone said. His eyes were on Andrew. He shouldn't have been so hard on him. He was a fine young man or Lizzy Hudson wouldn't have had a thing to do with him. Just caught on the wrong side, that's all. Malone felt a sudden sorrow for Andrew Clay. How did one fight for a cause he didn't believe in? Rand told him once that Andrew Clay hated slavery, but he was trapped—trapped by family, by Southern pride, by loyalty. Malone shook his head. Nothing would be worse than being trapped in a fight you didn't believe in.

The thunder struck overhead, and everyone looked up to find heavy, dark clouds moving in. Moments later it started to pour. Malone and Newton crawled closer to a tree trunk and hunkered down, waiting for their chance.

They weren't finished yet.

Chapter Seven

ANN WATCHED FROM THE WINDOW as the stream of beaten, exhausted soldiers dragged themselves through Georgetown toward Washington. The news was everywhere. The Union army had been thrashed. And though it was nearly noon on the second day, there was no sight of Rand.

Ann felt sick, apprehensive, the constant drizzle of rain making things seem even darker. And the look on the soldiers' faces—a look of confusion, their eyes full of shock, their bodies haggard. Ann felt the horror clear to her heart, any dream of this being a short war was dashed. She knew that the Confederate States would be emboldened by this victory. There would be no compromise now. They would declare themselves a free and independent people, and she knew this would only lead to deeper anger in the North. They were humiliated, and pride would demand retribution. She hated the thought.

"Miss Ann, you is gonna fret yo'self right into bed if'n yo' isn't careful." Lydijah spoke as she came through the door with a cup of hot herbal tea on a tray.

Ann saw a wagon coming up the street. It was filled with soldiers that had bloodstained bandages wrapped around heads, arms, and legs. They were the most despondent looking group of men she had ever seen. Then she saw a second wagon and a third. Her hand went to her mouth as the impact of it hit her. "Oh my!" she gasped.

"What is it, dear girl?" Lydijah asked, coming to the window.

Ann knew that there was no hospital in Georgetown and that the one in Washington would surely be overrun by now. "We must do something, Lydijah. Those poor men . . ." she said. "Look at them. Wagonloads, and there"—she pointed to several stragglers, one using a tree branch as a crutch—"some don't even have transport." She turned and started for the door. "Get Mose into the kitchen. Start preparing all the food you can. They'll be hungry. And bandages, we'll need bandages."

"But Miss Ann, what—what is yo' plannin' to do? We—"

"Feed them, nurse them, whatever it takes, Lydijah. Now hurry, and tell Mose to send Maple for Doctor Finch." She had reached the door and quickly went outside into the rain. She hesitated only a moment—there were so many—then stepped to the side of two men trying to help one another along. "You are to come into my home this instant. We have food and bandages and—"

The two men looked at her with disbelief. "Food . . ." one of them rasped. His eyes were filled with a pain Ann could not fathom, and she grasped his arm and began helping him toward the door.

"Yes, dear boy, food. How is your arm?" She looked at the bandage. The blood was fresh, and she grimaced at the thought of what lay beneath.

"My arm . . ." the boy said without much emotion. "It . . ."

"Never mind, we'll do what we can. I've sent for a doctor."

The other man limped after them, dragging his leg as two others called after them.

"Where you goin', Billy?"

As the boy she was helping turned to look, she glanced over her shoulder to find two more men standing in the street, confused pleading in their eyes, their coats hanging wet on slumped shoulders. "Come along, both of you," she invited. "We'll get you food, tend to your wounds, then find transport if you need it." She helped each of them into the living room, telling them to sit as Lydijah came into the room with a bucket of steaming water. Ann helped Billy remove his coat and then took a deep breath as she began unwrapping the bandage. "Dear Father," she prayed in her mind. "Give me strength to do this." She stiffened her resolve as Lydijah helped two more men into the room and Mose appeared with a plate stacked high with bread and with a large bowl of dried fruit, passing it out to eager hands.

Billy's wound was raw, clotted with dark blood, and Ann felt her stomach churn, but she forced a smile as she pulled a cloth from Lydijah's stack of bandages, dipped it into hot water, and began cleaning the blood from the wound.

*   *   *

Mose was starting a fire outside to heat more water when he heard the sound of hooves coming up the cobblestone drive. Maple dropped his wood, ran to the horse, and grabbed the reins.

"Nevah seen dis horse befo'," the boy said.

Mose felt sick inside as he walked quickly to Samson. "It's Massa Rand's horse, Samson." He looked over the lathered animal, finding blood on the horse's flank, then the hole that caused it. The bag carrying Rand's scriptures hung from the saddle horn, and Mose gently unstrapped it, his heart aching. "Get him unsaddled, Maple," Mose instructed. "Rub him down. I'll take care o' dis wound soon as he's cleaned and fed."

As Maple led Samson, the horse's head hung nearly to the ground. He watched them disappear into the barn before he turned and started for the house. He needed to tell Lydijah.

*   *   *

Lydijah watched Ann as she passed out the last of the bread and fruit. She fought her own tears as she struggled with whether or not to tell her mistress about Samson's return. But she must. She waited for the right moment, then she pulled Ann into the kitchen, helped her sit, and knelt to face her.

"Misses Ann, I don' know how to say this 'or'ble news but to jus' say it: Samson jus' come back, all bloody 'n sweaty; Misses Ann, Massa Rand mus' be awful hurt or maybe worse."

Ann turned pale, her strength gone. Her mind scrambled for answers as Lydijah folded her arms and began to pray. It was all either of them could do.

*   *   *

Rand woke up slowly to the sound of rain splashing against leaves and falling in larger drops to the ground. He blinked, trying to keep the water out of his eyes. He tried to roll over and felt the pain in his arm and side.

"Keep still."

Rand blinked away the haze and focused on the face above him. "Isaac? Where . . . where are we?"

"Hidin' from the entire Confederate army, so mind yer voice."

Rand tried to sit up, and Isaac gave him a hand, bracing him against a tree. It was then he noticed his stomach was wrapped heavily in pieces of linen cloth that looked to be mostly of his own shirt, seeing as how it was missing. The rest of it was around his wrist and arm. He winced at the pain as he tried to move his fingers.

"Ya had a ball pass through yer side. Bled some, but near as I can tell, no real damage. Yer arm has a chunk taken out of the skin and bone, but 'mazin' as it seems, the bone isn't broken. It'll never be the same though. Seen it before. Leaves a man stiff."

"That's what I always liked about you, Isaac—you don't mince words."

"Didn't think you wanted it sugarcoated." Isaac shrugged.

"Where's your men?"

"Probably half way to Washington like the rest of the army."

"That bad, huh?"

"A rout. Never seen such cowardice . . ." He shook his head in disgust. "But ol' Tom knew what he was doin' when he sent down them horse soldiers. Scared the daylights out of an already panicked army that had lost its stomach for blood. Their cavalry had them new British shotguns. Put 'em against their chests and fired both barrels at the same time. Cuts a man in half and sounds like a cannon. Kills one and scares the rest half to death."

"Ol' Tom?"

"Thomas Jackson. Met him once. Heart o' stone when it comes to battle." He gave a wry smile. "I left him a callin' card when I come at 'em from behind. Trouble is my aim was a bit off or things might be different."

"You shot him?" Rand tried to follow.

"Hit 'im in the hand. I'd a stopped and given him a bit more, but there were several hundred lookin' to kill us so we kept on goin'."

"How did you find me?"

"Seen you hit by that horseman. Got caught up in the fray fer a bit, then come lookin' fer you. You was caught in some snags, and by the time I got you aboard the Colonel, there was nothing to do but find a good place to hide." He paused. "What happened to Samson?"

"I sent him packing after he was hit. He's probably halfway back to Washington by now . . . or dead by the roadside." The thought was not a pleasant one, and he shook it off. "Where are we exactly?"

"East of Centreville. The railroad to Alexandria is just through them trees. I figured the rebels would focus on Centreville and the turnpike at first then spread out. Haven't seen anyone yet, but I expect to 'fore long."

"Malone, Daines, the rest?"

"Last I seen 'em, they was surrounded by rebels," he said softly. Rand was soaked clear to the skin and felt chilled. He suddenly became aware of his shaking.

"We've got to get you to a doctor," Isaac said, standing. He reached down and lifted Rand to his feet. It was then Rand noticed Isaac wasn't using his right arm.

"How bad are you?"

"Saber went through my shoulder clean. I already took care of it, but it pains me some. Ain't the first time. Consarned blade cut right through the scar where I was hit before. Tough skin t' put needle and thread to." He forced a smile then helped Rand to the horse, where the two men worked together to get him in the saddle. Isaac picked up the reins and started to lead the horse through the trees. When they reached the railroad tracks, the clouds broke a bit and the rain eased as they looked each direction and entered the cut. They turned north and continued on. Rand could tell Isaac needed a doctor nearly as bad as he did.

"Fairfax Court House. There should be a doctor there," Rand said. The village was east and north of Centreville, fifteen miles from Alexandria, twenty from Washington. It seemed a lot farther.

Isaac nodded. "Probably, but if the rebs beat us to it . . ."

Isaac didn't need to finish; Rand understood. If the rebels were smart they would pursue the federal army clear to Washington. If that happened, Fairfax Court House could already be in their hands, and Washington itself would be at risk.

Would the fortifications be enough? Was there even enough of the army left to defend it? He felt cold, and he shuddered. Ann was in Washington. He had to get to Ann.

*   *   *

It seemed the rebels weren't quite sure what to do with prisoners of war. Probably not something to which they had given much thought before the Battle of Bull Run.

But until they decided, they kept the prisoners busy digging graves and burying the dead.

Newton and Malone were both covered head to foot in mud as they dug yet another dark and gruesome hole. They'd dug too many to count since morning, and as Newton took a breather and scanned the landscape, he figured there were nearly a thousand. He had no idea which were rebels and which were not—it didn't matter. They represented too many lost dreams. He started digging again.

More prisoners had come in during the night. The count was probably eleven, twelve hundred. He'd been a little shocked by the lack of movement toward Washington on the part of the Confederates but then had overheard the guards talk of a federal retrenchment and attempt to circumvent the Confederate right. The order for the rebels had been to retreat back across the run, dig in, and prepare. By this morning the rebels had learned the information was at least partially incorrect, but still they didn't move. Newton figured they'd either lost their advantage or were too exhausted to take it. And then there was the rain. It had turned the run into a quagmire, the roads into mud deep enough to swallow a mule. No one was moving, North or South, and for the moment it seemed to Newton that the battle had come to an end.

"Hey, Newt," Malone called from the hole in which he stood, shovel in hand and ankle deep in mud. Newton turned to see Malone staring at a group of horsemen riding along the crest of the hill above them.

"Tha' one on the dapple grey is Beauregard, the one on the black is Johnston, and tha' fellow in th' middle is Jeff Davis."

"Terrible time t' be withou' a rifle, ain't it," Newton said.

Malone chuckled. "If Davis is here it'll be t' gloat and make a speech. The man's a politician clear t' 'is black heart." He looked at the group trailing behind the three rebel leaders. "Tha' be the press core, along wi' more politicians an' a few more generals an' their staff officers. Nah a one o' 'em saw either end o' a rifle yesterday, but they'll be taken credit fer such a grea' victory, tha's fer sure." There was a good deal of disgust in his voice, and Newton didn't blame him. It was the likes of these that called for this disgusting bit of butchery, yet not a one of them would ever find themselves dodging bullets. It made him sick.

Malone eyed the pickets that stood about then stuck his hand up for Newton to lift him from the three feet of muddy hole. When he was up, he wiped his hands on his pants as the Confederate soldiers spread around the hill and gave their leaders a hurrah. Sudden excitement spread, and most came out of their tents or makeshift shelters to stand in the pouring rain and give the vaunted leaders as hearty a cheer as they could muster. Even the pickets moved higher up the slope, a wary eye on the prisoners still digging the graves. "Lord of heaven, the blind leadin' the blind," Malone said. "'Tis like they ain't got the sense God gave a crowbar."

"Mice followin' the pied pieper, but then aren't we all," Newton said. "Are ya still willin', Mr. Malone?" Newton asked staring into the hole. "Looks t' be you'll be restin' in cold water and mud and—"

"'Tis still me wish, so le's nah bother wi' further examination." The two men picked up the drenched, blanket-covered body and eased it down into the hole. Then Malone looked about, making sure no one was watching before removing an item from under his shirt and lying himself down next to the corpse.

Malone had spent the night pounding on the bark of a willow branch with a rock until it had loosened and slid easily along the wood. Now he removed the bark entirely and placed it in his mouth while Newton threw another blanket over the top of him and began shoveling muddy and wet dirt into the hole, careful not to push it too tight around the breathing tube Malone had fashioned from the bark.

Newton kept one eye on the pickets but quickly finished his task. He put an ear to the hole in the bark tube to make sure Malone was getting air. Satisfied, he stood and slipped over to a few of the other Missouri boys digging graves nearby.

"He's in," Newton said quietly. The others nodded then watched as Davis and his victorious generals disappeared into the house at the top of Henry Hill. With the Confederate president and his commanders no longer in sight, rebel soldiers scampered back to where they had come from.

An hour later, the gray sky had turned dark as the sun began to set somewhere far beyond the thick clouds; the dead were finally buried, and the prisoners were herded back to the temporary holding pens surrounded by rebel guards. Newton was relieved that the guards took no accounting of numbers but scampered off for cover, leaving the prisoners to fend for themselves.

The rebels had been kind enough to deliver some of the federal tents to the prisoners, and the Missouri boys had put up a large one on high ground near the east side of the temporary fence. As they hurried to get there, Newton noted that the number of prisoners was still growing and wondered if more Missouri boys had been captured. As he entered the tent, his question was answered; two additional men huddled around a campfire trying to dry out. A hole in the top of the tent let in some rain but allowed much of the smoke to exit, though still leaving them in a thick haze.

The tent sat on small slope, and water was running under the upper edge then flowing into a gulley the men had dug to drain it out and keep the rest of the place dry. The two new captives stood, gave a halfhearted salute, and then tossed Newton and the other gravediggers some ears of corn they had been roasting on the fire.

"Rebs delivered the food. Say it's ours, but it's nearly gone since they're feastin' on it."

"Sam, Cyril," Newton said. "Goo' t' see yer still among the livin'."

The two men smiled but went back to digging the last of the corn from the cob with their teeth.

"When yer done chewin' on tha' cob maybe ya can gi' us a report on wha' ya seen as they brung ya in."

Cyril finished the last of his but shoved the cob into his pocket. Cyril had been one of the first to sign up back in St. Louis. A small, thin man who always looked pale, he didn't say much, but when he did, it was usually worth listening to.

"Our Missouri boys retreated well, but the ninety-dayers fled like they's tails was on fire. Sherman tried to regroup, but only us regulars stuck around. It wasn't enough, so we retreated as best as we could back to Centreville. Sam and I," he continued, motioning to the second man, "was caught when we ran into some rebels from Longstreet's command. They come in from Blackburn's Ford and started rolling up our left. We ran out of ammo and got cut off from the others."

"Are our boys forming a line?" one of the men asked.

"North of Centreville is what we hear. But they wouldn't be if Longstreet had his way."

Cyril looked at Sam, who explained. "Longstreet had artillery, and we seen 'em set up to let our boys have it. If they had"—he shook his head—"they'd a turned us, taken Centreville too, but they didn't."

"Why not? Did some of our boys . . . ?"

"Nah, nothing as good as that. The only boys we had a' Centreville was reg'lars and a few others who stopped runnin' 'cause someone put a gun in their chest. Maybe a few thousand strong, if that. Longstreet had an advantage and he knew it, and—"

Cyril interrupted. "Then some other general come in and stopped 'em, and all of a sudden they're pullin' back." He shrugged. "God saved our boys a worse thrashin'." He shook his head then smiled. "I never seen anyone so mad as old Longstreet, and when them other rebs started pullin' back, he stayed put. If'n he'd had his way they'd a chased our boys all the way to Washington."

"They'd a probably had to as fast as those cowards run off," said one of the other men with disgust. There was a general mumble of agreement.

"Where are the rest of our men?" Newton asked.

"My guess is Centreville with Sherman. They'll try to hold there," Cyril said.

"With this rain they'll have time to regroup then come at these rebs again, won't they, Captain?" Sam asked hopefully.

"Ain't no one movin' in this rain," Newton said. "Is Longstreet still east of us, then?"

"Nah, he musta got other orders last night. He pulled back across the run himself about ten o'clock. Brung us with 'im," Cyril finished. "No reason near as I could tell. But he done it, and he wouldn't have if Beauregard hadn't ordered him to." He shrugged. "Good thing, I suppose. Ain't no man crossin' that run till this rain stops. Never seen it so high and mean."

"Maybe McDowell has more men than you think. Maybe the army has turned around again." The man who spoke was Tom Baxter.

The group went silent, each of them deep in thought. Newton knew they were mostly thinking about being set free if McDowell came back, but that would take days, and by then the rebs would have sent their prisoners south to Richmond. Waiting for McDowell would do no good.

Sam spoke up just to end the silence. "Never seen such cowardice than what I seen yesterday. Why, them boys that was in reserve, they didn't even pick up their rifles when we was thrown back. Even when General McDowell come thundering down on 'em, tryin' to get 'em to stand firm. They just kept runnin'. After that we was sunk and McDowell knew it. Ordered us to fall back to Centreville."

"While you boys was out diggin' graves, I seen wagons full of our stuff hauled away all day by the rebs. Got enough rifles from our boys to make a whole new army of their own." Cyril shook his head and spit at the flow of water passing in their little ditch. "I see any of them boys in Washington, and I'm gonna give 'em what fer."

"Green," Tom said. "That's the problem. We was all *green*, and when it come down to it . . . well, it took all I had to keep movin' forward. Can't say as if I hadn't had the major behind us pushin' us on but what I would a run too, an' just as far."

"Anybody know what happened to the major?" Sam asked. He turned to Newton. "Captain, did you—"

"He was shot," answered one of the others.

"Captain told us afore you boys come into this devil's hole," said Tom Baxter.

No one spoke, the air heavy with the news. Newton had thought about it all day. He had seen Rand shot but had been so busy trying to stay alive that there hadn't been a thing he could do. It haunted him. He shoved the thought aside. He had seen Hooker. He'd gotten away, gone after the major. Rand was alive. He had to be. "Sam, Cyril, we're leavin' 'ere t'night, so you be gettin' yer rest." He paused. "An' ya be ready t' kill anyone who tries t' stop us. We're in a war now an' these rebel lads are th' enemy, da ya understan'? It was them wha' killed all them lads we finished burin' t'day, and wha' will be buryin' you too if ya let 'em. They ain' bein' gentle abou' wha' they want, so if ya feel t' survive ya best be ready fer fightin' yer way ou'."

He noted the stiffening of backs, the nodding of heads, the renewed resolve in the eyes of each of the men. He felt it himself. He had no intention of quitting, and unless Lincoln ordered an end to the war, he would not be giving in any time soon.

"How come they beat us, Cap'n? We had 'em on the run at first, and—"

"Reinforcements. Johnston's army escaped Patterson and got here in time to stop us," Cyril said. "Patterson let 'em go, and we paid fer it."

"Wasn't jus' Patterson," Sam said. "We had our chance early yesterday, and if McDowell had thrown our entire army at 'em early . . . well, we'd be the ones feastin' on Confederate beef and plannin' t' march on ta Richmond in the mornin'. Instead, he went in half measures. Must a been a real shock t' ol' McDowell to see all them reinforcements comin at 'im. Musta been worse to realize if he had committed early, afore Johnston's army got here, he'd a already had 'em on the run." Sam paused. "McDowell's probably up in Washington now, makin' his excuses to all them scared politicians, blamin' Patterson, tryin' t' save his job, but he's finished. He shoulda won an' he didn't, and I'll be glad to be rid of him an' Patterson both."

Cyril smiled wryly. "We seen one of them politician fellers get his come upins yesterday. Come out with them other folks from Washington who figured t' watch us rout the rebs. Well, when things turned sour, the rebs caught 'im an' brought 'im into Longstreet's camp same time as they did us. One of them Confederate officers wanted t' shoot 'im on the spot, but them with cooler heads stopped it. Nuthin' but a coward, comin' out here t' watch the rest of us die while he picnics on roast beef and coleslaw!" He spit into the fire to show his disgust.

"So is it over?"

"Lincoln doan' seem the type to quit fightin' 'cause he took a shot to the jaw," Tom said. "And if he does I'll be disappoin'ed. I don't like makin' deals just 'cause we got thumped once."

"Well, we be findin' ou' soon enough," Newton said. "You boys ge' sum sleep now. It be a long night if things go as they shoul'."

The men all tried to stretch out, and Newton did the same, closing his eyes though nowhere near sleep. The ground was wet where Malone was half buried—wet and cold. He couldn't be there long and survive it. And if he didn't . . . well, they'd be on their own, and that would make it more difficult. With Malone on the outside, a guard could be waylaid, a gun taken, a run made. Without it . . .

Newton rolled onto his side. Malone was as tough a man as Newton knew. He'd make it. He listened. The rain had stopped; at least, it was nothing but a soft drizzle. Maybe they'd have sun by morning.

He tossed and turned for another hour, the sounds around him slowly dying into silence as the prisoners tried to find rest, but Newton couldn't sleep, the battle playing through his head again and again, the faces of dead and dying men haunting him. He hadn't slept much last night and had played the whole affair over and over in his mind all day. He had killed at least six, maybe eight men while also nearly being killed himself. How did one deal with the thoughts, the images, the memories?

He heard the sound of men slogging through mud. They were in the distance at first, then closer, and he realized there were not just a few. Getting to his feet he went to the tent door, opened the flap, and looked across the mass of sleeping humanity to the fires where rebel guards warmed themselves against a misting chill. He could see horsemen pull up, then an endless line of infantry soldiers just beyond the fires. They separated at the far end of the temporary enclosure near what was supposed to be the gate. It was open, and rebels moved in and walked through the camp giving orders.

"Get up ya miserable Yanks! Y'all wanted t' see Richmond, an' we're here to oblige." Newton saw other soldiers encircle the camp as the prisoners stirred and got sleepily to their feet. As he turned to tell his men to get up, Newton felt his stomach drop. Their plan had taken too long.

Chapter Eight

THOUGH HE COULD BREATHE, MALONE was far from comfortable. The cold earth had taken his body heat faster than he'd expected. To further complicate things, it was heavier than he'd expected, and he felt the press on his ribs and lungs. He knew he couldn't leave the grave until dark, but he couldn't tell if it had actually become dark enough. Now he was at his lowest point, and though he did not think enough time had passed, he pushed with all his remaining strength against the wet, cold earth and forced first one hand and then the other through the soil. Clawing at the earth over his face, he finally moved to a sitting position and pulled the blanket away so he could see. What he found was a relief.

Darkness enveloped him, and the rained had stopped. The only voices he heard were in the distance. The air was warm, but the chill that had crept into his body made him shake uncontrollably. He forced himself from the wet earth and willed his eyes to adjust. There were fires burning along the bottom of the hill near the run, and he quickly oriented himself. Pulling the small handgun from his boot, he worked his way down the slope toward the spot he and Newton had decided was the weakest link in the picket line around the prisoners. It was then he heard the sound of orders and looked into the enclosure to find the men being put in a long line between rebel infantry.

Afraid of what it meant, he scampered to get closer and saw the prisoners already on the move along the turnpike that ran along the bottom of the hill. They were taking the prisoners to Richmond.

It was too dark to pick out faces, even to make a count, but he knew that somewhere in that line were Newton and the others, and his mind struggled with how to find them then help them escape.

Then he felt the thrust of something hard in the middle of his back. "Put them hands up, mister, then get up."

Malone slowly got to his feet. They were far enough away from the road that no one seemed to notice what was happening. Malone figured he still had a chance. He turned slowly around to face his captor then acted in one quick motion to grab the rifle and jerk it left using the side of his hard fist as a bludgeon. The soldier went down, but as his finger tightened on the trigger, the rifle went off. The ball passed by Malone's ear as he ripped the rifle from the man's hands then hit him in the skull with it. He didn't move. Malone turned to find that the entire line of prisoners had come to a sudden halt, the rebels kneeling, searching the darkness, their rifles at the ready, officers on horseback giving orders to hold their position and their fire. Malone cursed under his breath and ran back the way he had come, knowing it would only take a moment until those commands turned into more torches and a search. He slipped and slid through the mud and mounds of graves and was well down the hillside when he heard the command given. He was into the woods when the first torch was lit. He burrowed into some thick underbrush, knowing the rebels would find the unconscious soldier. It wouldn't take long for the entire rebel army to be on the alert, and unless he was far away he would be caught.

He felt sick inside, and yet there was nothing else to do. It would do no good for the others if he got himself caught. He figured there was an entire company guarding the wagons, and there would be little chance of him helping his men escape. It was finished, and Newton and the others knew it as well as he did.

He slammed a fist against the wet ground then scrambled to his feet and bolted to the river. He threw himself into the run to get across quickly but found himself in the midst of a horrible torrent. He struggled to keep his head above the water as it pummeled him, dragged him under, then tossed him to the surface again. He felt something hard hit him in the side, shook off the pain, and grabbed onto the solid surface of a floating tree trunk in an effort to keep from going under again. He floated into a wider area of the river where the speed of the flow calmed some, and he released the branch and swam for all he was worth to the far side. Minutes later he was dragging himself up the bank, clawing his way through mud and water into the cover of underbrush. He lay there, cold, shaking, exhausted, trying to catch his breath. He heard voices and forced himself to look out from his hiding place. Torches were visible on the far side of the river. Probably about fifty men, some of them mounted.

Taking a deep breath, he pushed out of the brush and began to run through the darkness. He would go west, get around the rebel lines, then head north. His gut ached at having to leave the others, but there was nothing to do. Nothing at all.

* * *

Newton and the others were in line behind a half dozen men from the Thirty-Ninth New York. Behind them were prisoners who had fought with the Second Wisconsin. They were all part of Sherman's regiment, and Newton remembered they had fought as well as any sent into the fray.

He and his Missouri boys had avoided getting into line as long as they could, hoping they wouldn't take everyone, but it had been to no avail. They were nearly the last in line and had just come onto the turnpike when they heard the gunshot. Newton knew immediately what it meant and felt his heart sink. Either Malone had been shot, or he had been forced to shoot someone. Whichever it was, the complete rebel contingent of guards suddenly scrambled for cover as if an entire federal regiment had them in their sights. There were yells farther up the line, orders given, officers on horseback prancing about and giving orders to hold. Then the torches came out.

"Ain't often that one shot can keep an entire army at bay," Sam chuckled.

"They're comin', rebs!" Tom Baxter yelled. "You all keep yer heads down now!" He chuckled, and the rest of the men joined in the heckling. It caught on quickly, and the men all up and down the line chimed in until the entire contingent was a cacophony of taunts. Then one of the prisoners, seeing an opportunity, decided to take it to the next level and leapt onto the back of a rebel soldier a few feet away. Suddenly, it was a chaotic attempt at wholesale escape. The Missouri boys were about to join the fray when a fast moving line of rebel soldiers came down the hill to put a stop to the brawl. Rifles were fired; screams were heard. Sam thought he saw a chance to run and was about to take off when Newton grabbed his arm and pulled him back just as a dozen soldiers appeared out of the darkness, their rifles aimed and ready to fire.

A minute later the brawl was over, and the prisoners were told to get on the ground. They spent the next hour shivering face down in the mud, waiting, but the mumbled word was that a couple dozen rebs had been busted up, one killed, and at least five prisoners shot. Newton watched as more soldiers were brought along to keep them company. They were finally told to get to their feet just as it started to rain again. There had been no sign of Malone.

They didn't move. Instead the soldiers that had come down from the fortifications were organized into battle formation and began sweeping across the hill.

"Not taking any chances, are they?" Sam said with a wry smile.

"Captain Malone is out there. They'll find 'im, sure as a drunk finds whiskey," another of the men added.

"Unless 'e's dead, it's nah likely," Newton said.

"You mean you boys had someone out there?" asked one of the men from the Thirty-Ninth. No one answered.

It was nearly sunup before they started to move. Newton wondered if Malone had been found, but if he was, he hadn't been alive or they would have brought him in. Newton figured Malone was long gone. He'd had no choice.

As they moved forward, they passed by the spot farther up the hill where a rebel soldier was sitting on a stump having his head attended to. Sam chuckled. "Hey reb, some ghost bust yer head?"

"Twern't no ghost, Yank!" the man returned angrily.

"Well, musta been since I don't see no body kneelin' at yer lordship's feet," Sam replied. "Woooo." He tried his best to imitate a ghost. "We Yanks aren't finished with you, reb. By mornin' this whole graveyard'll come back to life. Woooo!" He made a mocking face as he acted the part of a ghost, and even Newton couldn't help laughing.

They reached a bend in the road, and Newton noticed a wagon coming across the ford from the other side of the river. The commander leading the prisoners called for a halt as they awaited the wagon's approach. Moments later, the rebel soldiers were being handed shackles and were spreading out to put them on the prisoners while the rest of the guards readied their rifles in case someone disagreed with their effort. Newton could see that they meant business.

"Well, boys, now yer gonna know what we does with nigras when they smarts off to their betters," said one of the rebels with a cold laugh.

"You try to put them things on me, and I'll bust yer head wide as all outdoors," Sam yelled, fists clenched. Another rebel stepped out of the line and aimed his rifle at Sam's chest. Newton recognized it too late. He tried to grab Sam but was too slow. Sam launched himself at the rebel soldier, death and destruction in his eyes.

"Sam! NO!" yelled Cyril. The gun went off, Sam fell into the soldier, and they both went to the ground. The rebel scrambled to get out from under Sam's lifeless body, rolling him onto his back. Sam's eyes were empty, a gaping hole in his chest.

The entire train of prisoners went suddenly silent, everyone looking their direction, wondering what happened as a dozen soldiers were ordered to surround their small group. Newton felt the strain as the prisoners tensed like caged lions, both angered and shocked, but he also saw the fear and tension in the eyes of their captors. Newton knew that the slightest move would end in a disastrous massacre.

"Steady, boys," he said evenly. "Now is nah th' time." He placed his arm Cyril's and pulled him back slowly as several officers rode up and reined in their horses. They weren't part of the contingent guarding the prisoners, but one dismounted and went to Sam's side, noting immediately that he was dead. He turned to the still-mounted rebel officers and addressed the closest.

"He's dead, General."

The general, a dark haired and bearded man, was nursing an injured hand wrapped in red-stained bandages. Several mounted officers from the prisoner detail rode up, the one in charge visibly pale as he saluted.

"General Jackson," he addressed the man with the bandaged hand.

"Captain," Jackson replied. Newton had heard about Jackson from pickets all day. It seemed the man had become a hero overnight, arriving just in time to keep the rebel line from being overrun. Stood like a "stone wall," some said. Newton had been there. It was more than Jackson's reinforcements that had turned the tide—it was McDowell's refusal to hit them early and hard enough. But then he supposed that was what made one man a hero and the other a scapegoat. He noted the wounded hand. Somebody came close to putting the general out of the war. Too bad they hadn't succeeded; maybe it would be Yanks marching rebs off to jail.

Jackson looked down at Sam's body then at the set of shackles lying next to him. "What happened here, Lieutenant?"

The lieutenant swallowed hard, causing his Adam's apple to bob in his long neck. He frantically looked at the rebel soldiers hoping one of them would answer the question.

"That there Yank jumped Bannister, sir," said one of the privates. "Bannister killed him. Simple as that."

Jackson scanned the prisoners, his eyes falling on Newton. "Captain, is that what happened?"

"Sam did nah like the idea of bein' pu' in irons. It's true enuf, bu' you'll 'ave t' shoo' th' rest o' us if ya decide t' try sooch a thing again."

The general turned and faced his lieutnant. "Who gave the order to put these men in irons?" he asked harshly. It was obvious that this was one Southern gentleman who didn't like the use of irons much.

The lieutenant's eyes went to the ground, and he cleared his throat. "We had an incident . . . I thought . . . It's a long way to Richmond and—"

"These men are *not* to be put in shackles, Lieutenant. Do you understand me?"

"Yes, General, I understand," the lieutenant said sheepishly.

Jackson turned back to Newton. "I'm sorry that you were threatened with shackles, but I will not apologize for this soldier's reaction to being attacked, and I warn you if there are any further attempts, our soldiers are justified under the articles of war to defend themselves. I hope that is understood."

"An' we thank ya fer the warnin', General, bu' do nah expect us to sit idle while ya drag us off t' prisons t' be starved t' death or turned inta more slaves fer yer factories. If the chance comes t' run an' i' means bustin' a few heads o' traitors, we'll be doin' it wi' a clear conscience." Newton forced a hard smile. "Same articles o' war apply is me guess."

The prisoners chuckled, but Jackson did not smile and the rebels around them stiffened. "There are no traitors here, Captain, only patriots defending their homes," Jackson said coldly.

Newton wiped the dripping water from his nose. "Beggin' yer pardon, General, but to be a patriot one has to be true to 'is country, and y' an' yer boys betrayed it. You can make up a new one an' say yer defendin' yer homes if ya like, but ya were traitors first, an' we aren't abou' t' let ya forget i' an' then make ou' like it be us who is the offender." He nodded at the field of graves that now dotted the side of the hill. "The blood o' them boys is on yer heads, nah ours."

Jackson turned a bright red, and Newton felt the tension clear to his toes, but Jackson didn't respond; instead, he turned to the Confederate lieutenant. "You have your instructions, but carry them out without shackles. That's an order."

"Yes, sir," the lieutenant said. A salute followed, and Jackson and his officers rode up toward Henry Hill House. The tension did not ease and may even have worsened when the lieutenant told the soldiers to get rid of the shackles. There was a good deal of anger in his voice, and not for one instant did he stop glaring at Newton.

"You'll pay for those words before I'm through with you, Yank. Now get that man buried with the rest of yer bloody murderers." With that he rode off toward the front of the wagon train, barking orders to remove the shackles as he went. Newton,

Cyril, Tom, and three others were given shovels and were soon digging a grave for Sam under the hateful eyes of a dozen armed soldiers. Newton figured he should have kept his mouth shut, but he'd never been one to mince words. He considered Jackson the worst kind of traitor. It was men like Jackson, reputable men with influence, who could have prevented this war altogether if they'd taken a stand and refused to lead traitors against their country. Newton wasn't about to let him or anyone like him get off thinking they were some sort of patriot for it.

"That reb has fire in his eyes, Captain," Cyril said softly. They were standing in the hole. The others stood around them, waiting their turn but close enough to hear the conversation. Cyril looked at the Confederate soldiers that encircled them then at the rebel lieutenant who was leaning down quietly talking to a few of his soldiers near the wagon. "And these boys don't love you much neither." He smiled slightly. "I figure 'fore we get back in that line, they'll try to get in a lick or two. Watch yerself." He looked around at Tom and the others. "And if the chance comes, we're all in fer makin' a good run, ain't we boys." The others nodded warily. "We'd rather die right here than be stuck in some stinkin' rebel prison."

Newton nodded lightly as he glanced around at the men but kept his shovel moving. "Alright then, bu' ya be waitin' my say so, an' tha's an order." Newton knew this was no time. The rebels were itching to pay them back and would relish a chance to shoot anyone who even thought about running.

They all nodded, and Newton threw another shovel of dirt on the growing pile. They finished ten minutes later, lay Sam in the hole, and covered him up.

They returned to the wagon, shovels in hand, wary guards encircling them. Newton hesitated to let go of the shovel, but it was jerked from his grip and tossed aside by one of the soldiers. As he turned to get in line, he braced himself, sensing what was about to happen as several rebs came closer. The first blow shook him clear to his toes, the pain in the back of his neck excruciating. Then the mobility went out of his limbs, and a strong arm shoved him down as a blunt instrument crashed into his ribs. He was cognizant of the guns above him, all pointed at those around him, keeping them at bay while he was dealt with. He felt each blow until blackness crept into his vision and he slowly slipped into oblivion, unsure if he would ever wake again.

Chapter Nine

LIZZY HEARD THE NEWS WHEN she came down for breakfast. The entire town was alive with what it all meant, and there were only a few who thought it was a good omen for Northern victory.

She finished reading the story in the morning paper, worried about Rand. She would send a wire to Ann as soon as she crossed over to Bluff City to catch the steamer back to St. Louis.

And then there was Andrew. Where was he? Had he also been in this fight? Had anything happened to him? If it had, his family would surely know, but how could she contact them? She had received no reply from them lately. Should she try again?

She went back to the paper, reading it again, looking for any details she had missed the first two times. The story did not mince words. It had been a resounding defeat for the Union. Of course the paper was the *Bluff City Sentinel*, and its publisher obviously favored the South. However, he did quote directly from Northern papers. From the *New Yorker*: "We are utterly and disgracefully routed, beaten, whipped." The words angered Elizabeth. Did they expect the South to lie down and roll over for them? She slapped the paper onto the table. If anything, it should stiffen resolve, not settle into such defeatism, despondency. But deep down, she too had hoped that the North would have beaten *them* badly, that the South would beg for compromise and give up their horrid rebellion. She had hoped it would be a quick war and that Rand and Andrew would come home and they could get on with their lives. That secret hope had now been dashed, and she ached inside just as everyone else did.

"Good morning."

The voice jerked her out of her thoughts, and she looked up to see Benjamin Connelly standing across the table from her.

"May I join you?" he asked with a pleasant enough smile.

"Yes, of course." She nodded at the chair in front of him, and he pulled it out and sat. She picked up the coffee pot, but he turned his cup face down and raised a hand. "No, thank you. I have given it up at the request of President Young."

She found it curious. "And why has he made such a request?"

"Hot drinks are not for the belly. He has asked that the Church be more willing to consider coffee as a part of that commandment."

"And are most Saints willing?"

He smiled. "Let us just say that *more* are willing." He paused. "Actually, I have felt quite a bit better since giving it up, and my breath . . ." He smiled. "Jacob says that it is . . . more pleasant than it used to be."

She chuckled. "Yes, well I suppose that's as good a reason as any. And what have you replaced it with?"

"Water, milk, juices. I think I shall start a juice-making plant of some kind. The trouble is fermentation." He smiled again. "From hot drinks to drinks that leave you stupid. From the frying pan into the fire. Ironic, isn't it."

"Well if there is to be no hot drinks for the belly, I suppose that includes tea, and then your juices would be used up very quickly and fermentation less a problem, wouldn't you think?"

"Yes, I suppose, but there may be another way." He grew serious now. "Louis Pasteur, a French chemist, has shown that the growth of microorganisms is responsible for spoiling beverages like milk and juice. They say he is inventing a process in which liquids such as milk are heated to kill the bacteria and molds." He sat back, excitement in his eyes. "If he's successful, the process will allow milk and juices to be stored for quite sometime without souring or fermenting. It could lead to a whole new—" Realizing he was rambling, he stopped midsentence, his face turning a bit red. "Sorry, I'm probably boring—"

"He's also doing studies on bacteria and wounds. He believes that the elimination of bacteria will prevent infections that now require amputations, cause sepsis, and eventually lead to death. I've read his studies, and because of my own experience with a breakout of typhoid a few months ago, I know he's right. I only wish things were moving quicker, especially now that war has come."

"You've read Pasteur's work?"

"Does that surprise you?"

"I don't suppose it should, but yes. Most women do not seem to have either the interest—" He stopped himself. "I best be careful. As you know, I'm good at putting my foot in my mouth."

She chuckled. "Yes, that's true."

"I hope you will forgive me my remark about your black worker. I made an assumption. Well, it was a terrible, thoughtless assumption, and I'm sorry for it."

The waiter came and asked what he would like. He ordered eggs, sausage, and grits. She had already ordered and asked that both meals be brought at the same time. "And bring Mr. Connelly some orange juice," she smiled. "Unfermented."

The waiter nodded and left the table.

"You are forgiven, Mr. Connelly. It is an easy mistake to make when one considers where my home is."

"Thank you." He looked down. "Now to another confession. I really did not intend to have breakfast; I have come to ask a favor," he said.

"And what would that be?"

"I need passage to Quincy and thought I could travel aboard your steamship. It leaves this afternoon, doesn't it? I could sleep on the bales and work . . ."

"I am sure we can find you a room, Mr. Connelly, but we do have a couple of stops to make along the way. It may delay you a day or so."

"I can afford a few days, but I insist on working for my passage. Possibly in the boiler room or—"

Her smile stopped him. "I have something else in mind, Mr. Connelly. It's a bit dangerous, but you don't mind a little of that, do you?" She lifted her eyebrows, challenging him. "After all you've crossed the plains, stood against Indians, and been at the mercy of Mother Nature. What I have in mind should be quite simple, really."

He gave her a curious look. "What *do* you have in mind?"

"Freeing slaves, Mr. Connelly." She smiled as he sat back in his chair and looked into her eyes watching for some sign she might be joking.

As near as he could tell, she wasn't.

* * *

Matthew arrived in Richmond a day after the victory at Manassas to find the city electrified by the news of the battle. As he checked in to the Richmond Hotel, he overheard a half dozen partial conversations indicating the speakers thought the war was surely over, and the federals—even the Europeans—would soon recognize their new government.

Matthew had found himself outside Winchester, Virginia, just after Johnston had deserted the place to join Beauregard at Manassas. He tried to send a wire to Washington to warn them, but Johnston had shut down the telegraph offices to prevent just such an occurrence. Unable to warn federal forces by wire, he'd bought a horse and saddle and struck out after them. He arrived at Piedmont Station in time to watch the last train pull out, loaded with rebel reinforcements. He knew he could never catch them and could only pray McDowell would discover the calamity before it was too late. That night, word came to the hotel dining room that the North had been beaten. He didn't join in the celebration. Instead he purchased a slicker, mounted, and headed south to Rappahanock, where he ate a good breakfast and waited for trains to start running again. By late afternoon, he'd sold his horse at the local livery, purchased a ticket, and rode the rest of the way to Richmond.

He'd used the services of a bath and tub—enjoying the luxury after nearly five days with nothing but rain for cleaning—then got a good night's sleep in one of the finest hotels in the country. The next morning he ate a big breakfast and prepared to leave for the office of Henry Hyde Jr., an old friend and dedicated Confederate whose father was a colonel in the Louisiana state militia and most likely an officer at the Battle of Manassas, called the Battle of Bull Run by the Union. Henry Jr. practiced law in Richmond but hadn't joined the military yet, and Matthew doubted that he ever would. Henry had a physical malady as well as a lust for money. He would look at the war as an advantage to make a good profit while using the former as an excuse to avoid getting his hands dirty. Henry Hyde Jr. did not consider himself a coward, nor did Matthew think of him as such. Henry was just greedy, one of those men who loved money more than he loved anything or anyone else. He would exploit the war, but he couldn't if he were in it.

In the process of satiating his greed, Henry had become connected. He knew who to curry and who to toss under the carriage. He had helped men like James Seddon—the new Confederate secretary of war—and even Jefferson Davis himself make money and obtain office. A letter of recommendation from Henry, one of Richmond's most prominent and wealthy attorneys, would go a long way in getting Matthew the position he wanted in the Confederate War Department.

As Matthew waited in front of the hotel for a carriage, he heard the cry of a newspaper boy and purchased a copy. The front page contained articles that assured citizens that they had won their country and that Lincoln and the federals were beat. One went so far as to say that the war was over, that the Northern cowards had learned their lesson and would crawl back home to their mothers for solace. Another article, hidden deep inside the paper was more realistic and quoted Northern officials' resolve to not only continue the fight but to win. At least some men spoke with the voice of reason instead of senseless rhetoric.

He finally hailed a carriage and told the driver to take him to an address on Rampart Street. Settling into his seat, he watched the familiar buildings pass by. He had come here to see Henry more than a few times and had always loved Richmond. It was a vibrant city of constant growth and change, but now it was different. He had come with a purpose, and most of the people who lived here were now enemies against their own country and thus against him. If they knew what he was about to do, they would hang him from the nearest strong limb. As he watched them through the carriage window going about their business, it was a sobering thought.

The carriage pulled up in front of the offices of H. Hyde and Associates. Matthew and Henry had been the closest of friends while growing up in New Orleans, but then Matthew had left for the Academy and Henry for law school, and only on rare occasions had they seen one another since: occasional visits on holidays or when Matthew was passing through. He was a bit nervous about using Henry. The man was shrewd and seemed to know the thoughts of others better than they did. Matched with a silver tongue that could talk any man out of his last penny and make him feel good about it, Henry was not a man to be trifled with, and deceiving him would not be easy.

Matthew climbed from the carriage, paid the driver, and entered Henry's office. It was time to see if he was good enough to fool even his oldest friend.

The moment the office door opened, Henry was there to greet him and quickly pull him into his rather large private office. Matthew noted the trappings of a wealthy man as Henry asked all the obvious questions and they updated one another. With their friendship verified and properly coifed, Henry finally leaned forward and smiled.

"So, my dear and probably only real friend, how can I help?"

"Introduce me to the right people," Matthew said.

"That's easy enough, but for what purpose?"

"I want an appointment in the war department," Matthew said, smiling.

Henry sat back, measuring him. "You're serious."

"Yes, I am. I was number one in my class in tactical and operational analysis. It's where I can serve best."

"But such appointments usually are given to seasoned soldiers. To seek one at your age and with no actual battlefield experience will be difficult."

"That would be true if I were seeking a position for decision makers. I'll start as an analyst—a clerk who gathers information. I'll work my way up from there."

Henry nodded but did not speak immediately, and Matthew knew why. "You wonder why I don't want a command in the field."

Henry looked up. "It is something you spoke of all the time when we were young and even at your last visit. It does seem odd that you will settle for something far less."

"I have told no one this, Henry, but I was injured at Harpers Ferry. I have only partial sight in my right eye."

Henry looked up, his eyes intent. "You were at Harpers Ferry? But I thought that was a group of regular Union soldiers?"

"Several of us from the Academy were assigned to that unit for training maneuvers. As students, we were given the worst weapons they had. Mine misfired and damaged my eye. It was very hard for me to accept at the time, but I no longer feel I can ask for a command where my injury might endanger others. But I still have the knowledge, the ability to analyze and give others the best possible information to make battlefield decisions. I don't know where it will be needed more than in the war department."

Henry's eyes showed understanding, and he nodded. "Very well, we shall do our best." He leaned forward. "And I have just the place to begin." He flashed a grin Matthew had come to know far too well. He'd seen it whenever Henry had wanted to play a prank on someone.

"I've seen that smile before, Henry. It usually means trouble."

Henry laughed. "Not at all, not at all. I think you will actually find it quite enjoyable. All the young belles of Richmond will be there, and knowing you to have superior interest in the opposite sex, I—"

Matthew felt a sudden dread. "Henry, you know I hate coming out parties," he said adamantly.

Henry's grin did not disappear. "Well, dear boy, it's the price you'll have to pay."

Chapter Ten

RAND AND ISAAC APPROACHED THE village of Fairfax Court House cautiously. The federal flag still waved in the wind above the courthouse, but there was little else to witness a federal presence.

"Seems our boys have hightailed it to Washington," Isaac said. "That means the rebs ain't far behind."

Rand nodded. The rebels had only been driven out of the village a few days earlier as McDowell moved the army south. Many Virginians sympathetic to the Southern cause went with the Confederate army, afraid the US government wouldn't treat them kindly for their treason, but Rand knew some had stayed. Now they watched and waited for a Confederate return. They would not be friendly to federals, but both of them needed a doctor, and Rand wasn't about to pass one by because of Southern prejudice. Isaac removed his rifle from its scabbard and checked the flint to make sure it was dry. Satisfied, he handed his revolver to Rand.

"Just in case," he said. They left the shelter of the trees and approached the main street of the village. He noted a curtain pulled back then quickly dropped; the man stepped outside for a moment's glance at them before rushing back in. There were no horses tied at hitching rails, no carriages waiting for their owners. Except for the sound of birds and the distant bark of a dog or two, the place was as quiet as a Quaker meeting.

"Look," Isaac said pointing at the far end of the muddy street. Rand saw a half dozen deserted wagons and even a turned over cannon caisson. "Seems our boys left here as quick as they did Bull Run."

Isaac and Rand both saw the sign they were looking for, and Isaac led his horse to the hitching rail, slapped the reins around its bulk, and helped Rand slide from the saddle. He helped him to the porch, where Isaac rattled the door with a knock. Rand looked up at the sky, grateful that the rain had stopped but disappointed to see the blue sky once more disappearing behind dark clouds.

"Nobody home," Isaac said. He knocked again then tried the knob. It turned, and the door swung open slowly. The house was cool, empty, the doctor apparently gone.

"The army may have come for him," Isaac said. "As many as were wounded they'd be needin' all the help they could find." He helped Rand to a wooden rocking chair then went back and closed the door as it started to rain again. There was kindling and dry timber in the woodbox, and Isaac used his knees to hold one of the smaller pieces while cutting some shavings with his bowie knife. Sticking them in the cold fireplace, he used a match sitting on the mantle to light a fire. A moment later it caught in the kindling, and Isaac added larger pieces.

When he had a good blaze going, Isaac removed his wet coat then turned to Rand and helped him do the same. Seeing that Rand's pants were soaked with blood, he quickly removed the bandage to get a better look; the wound was bleeding again. He looked about. An archway revealed another room that looked to be the doctor's workroom. There, he quickly began rifling through drawers and cupboards to find fresh bandages and medicines. When he returned, he was staring down the twin barrels of a shotgun.

It was held by a boy who Isaac figured was ten, maybe twelve years old. He was dripping wet and the door was open, but the boy had a firm set to his jaw that told Isaac he did not intent to be trifled with. Isaac ignored him, walked to Rand, and knelt down to do what he could to stop the bleeding.

"I'll need to cauterize it," Isaac said. He reached for his big knife to place it in the fire, and the boy stepped back, stiffening.

"Mister, if you move I'll shoot you."

"Then shoot, boy," Isaac said evenly. He stood and stuck his knife blade in the fire. He turned quickly and grabbed the shotgun before the boy could blink. "But you might want to take the safety off afore you do." He flipped the safety off and handed it back to the boy whose eyes were wide at this sudden action. He took the double-barreled British but wasn't quite sure what to do with it now. Finally, he flipped the safety on again, stood the gun against the wall, and shut the door while Isaac returned to caring for Rand.

"You live here?" Rand asked, forcing a weak smile.

"Me and my pa do." The boy eyes were focused on the growing pool of blood on the floor. "Yes, sir. That's a lot of blood, sir."

"Where's yer pa?"

"With your troops, sir. He told me he'd be a while and I should come home. I think he thought I'd seen enough blood for my entire lifetime. Didn't bother me, but I got stock to take care of and—"

Isaac looked up. "My horse needs care. I'll pay you for feed and a warm stall."

The boy nodded. "A dollar and fifty cents, no less."

Isaac smiled. "Your pa needs to teach you about stealin'." He picked up the knife and was about to use it on Rand's wound when the boy spoke up. "Best use alcohol. Stings at first but helps deaden the pain. I'll get it while you get your friend laid down on Pa's bed. That will help slow the bleeding too." He went into the office while Isaac lifted Rand from the chair and helped him stumble to a bed in another adjoining room.

"I'll not be bleedin' on the doctor's good quilts. Pull 'em off," Rand said.

Isaac did then helped Rand sit on the edge of the bed. He gritted against the pain in his own shoulder and felt queasy as the boy entered the room with a bottle of whiskey. "Mister, you're nearly as bad off as your friend. Go back in there and sit down before you fall down. I'll dress your friend's wound." He took Isaac's knife out of his hand.

Feeling dizzy, Isaac didn't argue, took the few steps to the chair where Rand had been sitting, and collapsed into it. He felt tired and knew he'd lost too much blood. He tried to fight off the weariness, but his head began to spin then fell onto his chest and he blacked out.

When he woke up, he was lying on the floor covered in blankets. His shirt had been removed and his wound bandaged. The fire was nothing but embers, and the boy was in the chair, his mouth agape from a deep sleep. He could see through the door to the bedroom where Rand was unconscious or sleeping—he hoped the latter.

It was then he noticed a good deal of noise outside and quickly forced himself to throw off the covers and get to his feet. Going to the window, he parted the curtain slightly to get a better look. The day was still overcast, but the rain had stopped and rebel soldiers marched past in parade while a few citizens smiled, clapped, and gave them hurrahs. Fairfax Court House was back in the hands of the Confederates.

Dropping the curtain, Isaac shook the boy's shoulder, waking him. "What's your name, son?"

The boy stared at him, his eyes half closed. He rubbed them and spoke at the same time. "Joseph, sir. Joseph Getty."

"Well, Joseph, I figure we're just minutes away from having visitors, and I need to get my friend and I outa here afore then." He was gathering any evidence of their presence as he spoke, putting it all out of sight in the doctor's medical room as Joseph went to the window.

"Your friend ain't up to much, mister. He's lost a lot of blood and—"

Isaac turned to see the boy drop the curtain. "Them is Confederates," Joseph said softly.

"We was seen by some of yer neighbors. My guess is all of 'em aren't Unionists."

Joseph only nodded. He was thinking, and Isaac was sure those thoughts included his neighbors.

"Old man Pitchford. If he seen you . . ." He went back to the window, scanned the street, then turned back to Isaac. "He spends most of his time ranting against Lincoln and says if he was young enough, he'd shoot the old buzzard himself. His words, not mine. You can bet if he seen you he'll be wanting to share it with them rebs."

"Do you have a wagon?" Rand said. Isaac and Joseph turned to find him standing in the doorway to the bedroom even as they heard the sound of boots on the board sidewalk out front.

"No, sir, just my horse, but you can take him if—"

Isaac grabbed the two-barreled shotgun as a rap came on the front door, and Rand went back in the bedroom.

Isaac stood against the wall behind the door and flipped the safety off the shotgun. "Take a deep breath. Invite 'em in. I got an idea," Isaac whispered.

Joseph nodded, rubbed his hands on his pants, took that deep breath, turned the knob, and opened the door to face two rebels. One touched the brim of his plumed hat and spoke.

"Good mornin', young fella. I'm Lieutenant Detweiller. We have need of a doctor and—"

"My pa ain't here," Joseph said evenly. Wisely he opened the door a bit so the two men could see into the room. As they cast an eye over his shoulder, Detweiller spoke. "And when will he return?"

"He was kidnapped by some federal soldiers. Last I seen, they rode off toward Centreville," Joseph lied with just the right amount of bitterness.

"I see," Detweiller said with a frown. "Well, the federals are retreatin' to Washington. I'm sure your father will return soon. In the meantime we have a man who was shot by a sniper on our way here. Possibly y'all have some chloroform or calomel."

Joseph stepped back, an invitation for them to enter. When they were past the swing of the door, Isaac pushed it shut and put the barrel into Detweiller's back. Shocked by this sudden attack, the lieutenant was about to protest when Isaac used the butt of the gun on his jaw, and he fell to the floor. The other man clamped his jaw shut as Isaac pushed the barrel under his chin. It was then Isaac felt the pain in his side and nearly dropped the shotgun. The rebel thought he had a chance but suddenly changed his mind as he felt a hard object in the middle of his back. He slowly turned to find Rand with a revolver.

"Joseph," Rand said. "I think we need some rope."

*   *   *

Isaac finished tying Joseph loosely next to the two unconscious federals, who had been stripped of their uniforms. "If no one comes, you can get outa them ropes when Detweiller comes conscious, but not afore we have a chance to get outa the village," Isaac instructed.

"Yes, sir," he said.

"Thanks for your help, Joseph, and if you and your father decide to leave here, you're welcome at my house in Georgetown," Rand said.

"Thank you, sir," Joseph said. "But I know you'll be comin' back and we won't have to put up with rebs too long, right, sir?"

Rand forced a smile. "Yes, we'll be back."

"Sorry to have to do this, but you gotta be gagged to make this look good."

"That's fine, Mr. Hooker," Joseph said. "You best get goin'."

Hooker gently pushed the cloth into Joseph's opened mouth and then stood and followed Rand out the back door to the stable. Isaac had already saddled both horses, boosted Rand into the saddle of Joseph's horse, then handed him the reins. "You sure about this?" Isaac asked.

"No other way, is there?"

Isaac shook his head. He'd looked for a way to sneak out, but there were rebels everywhere. "Short a surrender, I guess not," he quipped. Mounting his gelding, he straightened his rebel uniform and tried to pull the sleeves down. Detweiller was the taller of the two men, but even he didn't match Isaac's size. Rand took a deep breath and nudged the flanks of Joseph's horse. They walked them out of the barn and down the lane to the main street then turned right. He resisted the urge to run but instead pulled his hat a little lower over his eyes.

Wagons filled with supplies were parked near the courthouse, and men had built fires and were setting up tents on the grass. The mercantile store had a line of men standing outside trying to get in to make purchases, and soldiers walked about the muddy streets in small groups carrying rifles and visiting with friendly villagers. As Rand and Isaac passed, some would give them a look then get on with their business, but most ignored them as just two more rebs moving into the newest front line of the army.

As the pair passed the courthouse, several officers came through the door, and Rand quickly looked away. Isaac noticed this sudden move and glanced at the officers. General Beauregard stood next to General Jackson and two other officers. Beauregard seemed to be giving them some sort of instruction. One of them, a captain, wasn't paying attention. Instead, he was looking directly at Hooker.

Hooker did not look away. Instead he tipped his hat, gave a quick salute, and just kept going. They were nearly past when the captain came down the steps slowly and called after them.

"Lieutenant, hold up please," the officer said.

Hooker pulled back on his horse's reins and brought his gelding to a stop. Rand was next to him but stopped in a position that he couldn't be seen clearly by the captain who came and stood next to Isaac's gelding, patting him lightly on the neck. "Is this your horse?"

"Yes, sir," Isaac said. "Why do you ask, sir?"

"I saw one just like him in battle. Nearly ran over me and—" His eyes widened as he realized it had been Hooker. "You!"

Isaac moved his half hidden revolver so the barrel pointed directly between Andrew's eyes. "Captain, you so much as twitch and I'll blow yer head off," Isaac said. Andrew kept still then looked at Isaac's companion and nearly fainted.

"Rand!" Andrew hissed. "You're a fool for trying to come through here!"

"We were already here when you boys arrived. That didn't leave us much choice. Now, I'm going to dismount, and you and I are going to walk to the edge of town while Isaac keeps his gun on you. I'll ask him not to kill you for Lizzy's sake, but neither of us is about to be taken prisoner." He dismounted, leaned for just a second against his horse to get his strength, then started walking, Andrew at his side.

"I can't just let you walk away, Rand," Andrew said.

Rand looked at men as they passed by, watched their faces, looked for any sign that things weren't right. "I have six bullets in my revolver, Andrew. I'll use them, and at this range I won't miss. And Isaac, he's a dead shot and has six of his own. You'll have to decide if twelve lives are worth keeping your mouth shut."

Andrew kept walking. He was trapped. There really wasn't anything he could do, but did he want to anyway? He took a deep breath. "How's Lizzy?"

"Waiting for word from you. I'll let her know you're still alive."

"I sent letters, but I suppose they don't get through anymore."

"We could take you with us, Andrew. You would be out of it."

There was a long silence. "Honor still matters to me, Rand. Foolish maybe, but it's the way I was raised."

"How are your parents and sisters?" Rand asked.

"Half the farm is a military camp, but life goes on."

They were nearly to the end of the street, and the number of rebels was dwindling. Rand noticed cannon emplacements being built on small hills on both sides of the street. "You boys act like you intend to stay," he said.

"McDowell missed his chance at Manassas, but so did Beauregard and he knows it. This isn't a defensible position. He'll have to move back. Right now he's just trying to make a point."

"That you can hit Washington if you want," Rand said.

"He figures putting a scare into Northern politicians will make them think twice about coming south again."

"You know he's wrong," Rand said.

Andrew took another deep breath. "I'm glad you're alive, Rand. Tell Lizzy—"

"I will," Rand said. He turned to his horse and tried to mount but didn't have the strength.

"You're hurt," Andrew said, coming quickly to his side.

"Nothing seeing Ann won't fix," Rand said with a forced smile. Andrew grabbed his leg and boosted him up as Isaac put his revolver back in his holster.

Rand looked down at his friend. "Stay alive, Andrew."

Andrew nodded then hit Rand's horse on the rump, and it cantered away. Isaac tipped his hat and then followed. Andrew watched as they disappeared up the road toward Washington then turned back to the village wondering if they would ever see one another again.

*   *   *

Ann Hudson was exhausted. The soldiers she had bandaged and fed had finally either left to find their units or had been taken to the hospital for more extended care. Lydijah scrubbed at the bloodstained floor and carpet in the sitting room as Ann tried to pick up the last of the clothes the wounded had discarded as they were bandaged. Mose had started a fire behind the summer kitchen and in front of the barn to heat more hot water. She went out the back door and dumped the last of the rags next to it so that Mose could either burn or boil them according to their condition. As she leaned against the hitching post nearby, she heard the sound of horses hooves echo off the narrow cobbled drive. Her breath caught as she turned to see Rand and Isaac coming toward her. She ran toward them as Lydijah, who had seen them from the window, burst from the house. They both arrived at Rand's side at the same time. Ann could not help the tears as she examined her obviously exhausted husband.

"My lady," Rand said with a weary smile. "Would you have a soft bed for a weary traveler? I can pay."

Ann burst into joyous tears mingled with fear as she saw the blood on his pants and shirt. Mose had reached them as had Maple, and they quickly helped Rand down and all but carried him into the house. Ann stood back and wiped the tears from her eyes, smiling up at Isaac.

"Thank you," she said, choking back the tears. It was then she noticed that Isaac had fresh blood staining his shirt. Ann was about to give him a hand when Isaac waved her toward the house. "Take care of him, Ann. I'll be fine."

Ann hesitated then darted for the house as Isaac wearily put a foot in the stirrup and then slid down the side of his gelding. He reached the steps and sat down, grimacing. He had never been so tired, but they had made it. He'd kept his promise.

Mose came out of the house and took an arm, but Isaac only smiled. "Just need a minute more, Mose."

Mose nodded then sat down beside him. "You is bleedin', Massa. I needs to see t' yo' wound."

Isaac nodded and let Mose help him remove his shirt. They had discarded their rebel coats and hats before crossing the chain bridge. The guards had tried to get them to see a doctor, but Rand wanted no delay in getting home.

"Dis is no good; red 'round de edges, and infection sho' to come," Mose said.

Isaac didn't move. He had passed out again.

Mose held him up and called for Maple. Both the boy and Lydijah appeared a moment later. Between the three of them, they carried Isaac into the house. Knowing they couldn't get him upstairs, Lydijah suggested they put him in their room at the back of the house. Isaac opened his eyes as they lay him on the bed. He'd never felt worse, and he wondered if this was the time he'd finally meet his Maker. He didn't have the strength to talk as they took off his boots; Mose pulled off Isaac's pants and covered him up. It was all a haze to him, disjointed, a sort of in and out of consciousness where he missed some things and heard others and time had no meaning. When he finally woke up and felt to stay awake, he remembered only one thing that really mattered. Rand had been there, had laid his hands on Isaac's head, had said a prayer and commanded him to get well. It had been a peaceful feeling, and after that he had slept the sleep of angels.

He blinked several times and looked up to find Ann standing over him.

"Good morning," Ann said with a smile.

Isaac tried to lift himself up, but she put a hand on his head and gently pushed back. "Catch your breath first, Isaac," she said.

He tried to talk, croaked, cleared his throat, then tried again. "How long I been here?"

"Four days," Ann said, her hand on his forehead. "Fever's gone, and your wound is no longer infected. Seems a piece of the blade broke off in your shoulder. After giving you a blessing, Rand had the doctor look for it. It was stuck in the bone. If it hadn't been found, it probably would have killed you."

"How is Rand?"

"I'm fine," Rand said from the doorway. His arm was in a sling and he looked pale and tired, but he was standing of his own volition.

Isaac figured it was time he tried to do the same, and with Ann's help he slowed raised up and put his feet on the floor. He felt dizzy for a moment, shook it off, and ran his hand through his hair, pushing it back out of his eyes.

Ann handed him a cup of water and told him to drink. "You saved Rand's life. We're both very grateful."

Isaac gave a weak smile. "Seems he saved mine if I recollect rightly."

"If you mean the blessing, I was just expressing the Lord's will, Isaac. Seems you have a few things to do yet."

Hooker nodded. "I ain't anxious to greet the devil, so I'm obliged." He paused. "I ain't a religious man and you both know it, but I felt that prayer clear to my toes. Thank you for sayin' it."

"My honor," Rand said. He stepped forward and handed Isaac a book. Isaac recognized it as one Rand had given him but he'd never opened. "I notified Sherman of our return. He's been here and even stopped in to say hello to you, but you ignored him."

"Never had much use fer colonels," Isaac said.

"He says we can return when we're ready. Until then you might want some reading material."

Isaac smiled. "You don't give up easy."

"No, it's not in my nature."

Isaac took a deep breath. "It ain't that I don't appreciate the gesture, Rand; it's just . . . well, I cain't read. Well, I can, but not enough . . . well, these words are like written in Spanish or something." He extended the hand to return the book. "You just as well keep it; I cain't read it."

"Then we'll read it with you," Ann said. "Will you let us?"

Isaac was out of words and only nodded. Then he sipped a little water. "Yer tryin' to save a lost soul, Ann, but yer welcome t' try."

Ann smiled, reached for the book, and opened it to the first page. Then she began to read.

There was more hurting to be fixed.

Chapter Eleven

MALONE HAD WALKED FOR TWO days when he decided enough was enough and stole a horse, saddle, and bridle and rode the rest of the way. He ran into Confederate lines south of Harpers Ferry, decided he was too tired to play it safe, and rode like a demon directly through them in pitch black darkness. He heard rifles fire but felt no result and rode on, arriving at Union lines five minutes later. After a good night's sleep, he went onto Washington and reported to Sherman before learning the whereabouts of Hooker and Rand. With Sherman's permission, he rode onto Georgetown and knocked on Rand's door, where Lydijah greeted him with a shrill haleleujah and Rand join him in Isaac's room to hear the story.

"We should go after them," Hooker said. "Surprise the dickens out of the rebs if we rode in and created a little havoc. Shoot ol' Jeff Davis while we're at it."

Rand smiled. "And get ourselves shot in the process." He paused. All of them knew there was nothing to be done, and it pained them more than a little. "Malone, rest a couple of days, then round up the brigade. Get them organized, back to training. We'll join you as soon as we can." He stood and went to the door. "Glad you're safe."

As he shut the door behind him, Malone looked at Isaac. "We ought t' be doin somethin.'"

"Nothin' we can do, Brenden, 'cept maybe conquer Richmond." He paused. "Newton will escape, and so will the others if they can. For now we just make sure it don't happen again. You tell the boys we'll be seein' 'em in a few days. Do what Rand says; get 'em ready. We ain't done with them rebs, and they ain't done with us. Best thing we can do now is give a little payback for Newton and the others."

Malone only nodded as Isaac picked up his Book of Mormon. "Lord of heaven, 'tis a miracle. I thought you couldn't read."

"Can't, least not very well, but I can't wait on Ann to come and do it so's I muddles along."

"Wha's in them pages tha' ya would suffer so much fer it?"

Hooker smiled. "You'll have to find out for youself, but I'll tell ya this: it's given me a good deal of comfort and understandin' that I never knew existed."

"Abou' wha'?"

"The good Lord, Malone, and my place in the scheme of His creations."

"Then 'tis surely a miracle. Hooker's gettin' religion, is he?"

"I wouldn't be goin' that far, not yet. Now be quiet, and I might read you a few words. Then maybe, just maybe, you'll see what I mean."

Malone chuckled as he stood. "I'm a Catholic through and through, and you'll nah be changin' it with a few words from Rand's religious book. I respect the man and his choices, and I got no fight with 'is religion as some seem t' 'ave, bu' the Church of Peter and its grace is sufficient fer Brenden Peter Malone."

"Then you'll be headin' to purgatory fer sure, Malone, which by the way is a matter of fiction and should be discarded as quickly as whiskers that are both unkept and unnecessary. And your sprinkling don't count fer much neither."

"Now, Mr. Hooker, 'tis not Christian to be attackin' another man's faith, so you'll be watchin' yer step or I'll put a sword through yer other arm."

"I ain't attackin' it, just tellin' ya truth, and it won't do a bit a good to be hidin' behind a facade of persnickety self-righteousness just so ya won't have to change. I was a Methodist, born one too, but I ain't no more. They just didn't get it right, Malone, and the good Lord had to restore what they lost, simple as that, and if you'd just break down yer prideful walls of tradition and open yer eyes, you'd see it as clear as I do."

Malone was about to open his jaw for a mean retort but decided against it. "'Tis a man's right to choose his own path, Hooker, so get on with it if ya must, but leave me alone or I'll break yer head." With that he left the room and closed the door with a bit of a slam. Hooker only smiled. It was a step in the right direction.

*   *   *

The steamer didn't have many passengers. It never did on the return trip from Bluff City. These days most traffic along the Missouri was moving west, and even it was beginning to slow. Only the Mormons seemed in a rush to go west anymore. The young and hearty were joining the war effort, seeking glory and excitement. After Bull Run, Lizzy figured some were sorely disappointed but also embarrassed and inflamed. They wanted to redeem their honor, and others were joining for the honor of the North.

Lizzy watched from the rail that ran around the walkway of the upper deck as the crew prepared for docking at Jefferson City. It was nearly two in the morning, and the only people moving along the dock were those who would retrieve the ropes of the steamer and tie her off.

They had feigned the need to make repairs earlier in the day and had pulled to shore, letting time pass so that they would arrive at Missouri's capital at this very hour. The passengers were sleeping and so was the city. And Lizzy had a run to make.

"Are you ready, Mr. Connelly?" she asked, putting on her hat and tightening the leather thong under her chin.

Ben nodded, following her down the stairs to the wagon and team of four horses. As two of her crew lifted themselves into the back of the wagon, she and Benjamin climbed into the seat and waited for the bridge to drop.

"You know they'll hang us if we get caught," she said.

"So you've said," Benjamin answered.

"You've been warned, that's all." Lizzy took the reins in her hands and released the brake as the two men in the wagon bed lifted the lid on a storage box and removed Sharps breechloading rifles. "There is a shotgun and another rifle under the seat," Lizzy told Ben. "Ammo for both in the box to your side there. Pick whichever you like."

He glanced at her then leaned over and fished out the first one his hand found. It was the British shotgun. Opening the lid of the ammo box, he pulled out a handful of shells, putting most in his coat pocket then breaking the breach and shoving two in the double barrels of the gun before snapping it closed. Lizzy was gratified that he knew what he was doing but said nothing. Hopefully they would have no need of firepower.

The bridge hit the dock, and the ropes were quickly tied off. "Heyaw!" Lizzy shouted, as she slapped the reins on the horses' backsides.

They immediately lurched forward and were on the dock then into the
street. Lizzy kept them at a fast trot as they moved through the town.
She noted that a few federal soldiers were picketed at each intersection,
but the streets where otherwise deserted. The city was under the control
of the federal government now. The old government had been dissolved
and the governors seat declared empty once Governor Claybourne Fox
had decided to side with the secessionists. Many of the former members
of the legislature who had sided with him were no longer living in
Jefferson City but had returned to their homes in parts of Missouri
controlled by secessionists and under attack from the Union army.

They reached the outskirts of the city, and Lizzy slapped the horses
with the reins moving them to greater speed.

"Where to, Miss Hudson?"

Lizzy smiled. "Little Dixie, Mr. Connelly."

He only nodded and grabbed the side of his seat as the wagon
careened about in the rutted road. It had rained hard yesterday, but the
warm summer sun had quickly dried the muddy gullies into ruts that in
only a few days would flatten out once more.

On the trip from Florence, Lizzy had been busy in her room doing
paperwork Dickson had sent along but which she'd put off. Benjamin
had tried to get her to let him work around the steamer for his passage,
but she reminded him that he would earn his keep soon. Most of the
trip, he'd sat on deck reading a familiar book, and at dinner they had
discussed its teachings until bedtime. It was a wonderfully fruitful
evening for Lizzy as Benjamin shared what President Young and the
Twelve were teaching about the Book of Mormon passages she wanted
so desperately to understand. She hadn't slept much last night as she
went over the things she learned again and again in her mind, especially
with regard to mercy and the Atonement. They had not talked of plural
marriage. She found she did not care about it, not now at least. For
Lizzy, the truth of the gospel was in doctrines and principles that never
would change. She had questions about everything from the nature of
God to exaltation and the difference between power and authority in
the priesthood. It made no sense to waste time on things that would not
matter if she fully understood eternal truths.

They traveled the seven miles quickly, and Lizzy slowed the horses
and pulled into a side road, bringing the team to a walk as they entered
the deep woods along the Osage River. As she brought the team to a halt,

the two men in the back jumped out and quickly used halter ropes to tie the lead horses to trees as Lizzy and Benjamin got down.

"We walk from here," she said. "Mr. Connelly, this is Purdy Summers and Bryce Hanlon. Purdy doesn't stand for any jokes about his name, and *that* should explain Bryce's broken nose." She smiled. The two men grinned at the introduction, and Ben extended a hand to shake.

"Name's Ben," he said. "Glad to meet you."

"Glad to have you along," Purdy said. "Miss Lizzy loses one or two on these trips, so with you here that means we have a better chance of survivin'."

Bryce grinned. "Lost a dozen just like you in one night. Dangerous place, Missouri."

"Lying always did come too natural to you boys." She smiled as she finished lighting a lantern. "Let's get moving." She led the way through bushes too dense for a trail. They quietly hurried along the bank of the river until they reached a large house with several barns. Lizzy blew out the lantern and set it aside then started across the open land toward the house. Ben and the others followed until they reached the outside door to a root cellar. She knocked lightly, and the door swung open. They quickly descended into a large room where Ben found a dozen black faces, their eyes wide with expectation. Ben noticed an immediate tension, and Lizzy turned to an older white gentleman who stood next to a black woman, his hand firmly on her shoulder. She was obviously very frightened and had been crying.

"We have a problem, Miss Hudson," the older gentleman said, trying to stay calm.

"Mr. Henderson," Lizzy said softly. "What's happened?"

Henderson looked down at the black woman. "It would be best if she told you."

Lizzy went to the woman, stooped down, then looked up into her eyes. "What's your name?" Lizzy asked.

"Tess, Missy," she said in a quiet, shaky voice.

"What do you need to tell me, Tess?"

Tess broke down, and her words came spilling out. "Dey made me do it, Missy! Dey made me! Dey say if I doan do as dey say they kill mah husband. Kill him dead, Missy. I had to do it. Had to!"

Ben looked around the room and found the others just as frightened as Tess.

"Tess, what did you do?" Lizzy asked firmly.

"I led 'em here, Missy. Deys outside right now, waitin' for you to run! Just waitin' to shoot y'all. I knows it!" She put her head in her hands and sobbed; another black woman stepped out and tried to give comfort.

Lizzy patted Tess on the leg, stood, and paced a bit before turning to Henderson.

"Harness up your wagon and bring it around to the door. I have an idea."

Ben looked at her quizzically but listened. When she finished he knew it could work.

*   *   *

William Quantrill had been a schoolteacher, had even been an abolitionist once. But neither had provided the lifestyle he wanted, so he turned gambler and went west for a few years, ending up in Salt Lake City. Then he'd come back to Missouri and ended up switching sides, more for money than out of philosophy. Slaves were running, and hunting them down and bringing them back had become lucrative. He had been doing it in Arkansas and even in some places in Kansas until Missouri landowners had sent for him. Now he worked for them.

Quantrill hadn't always been a gunman. He'd actually learned how to use guns and the long bowie knife that hung from his belt while raising the devil in the new saloons and back alleys of Salt Lake City. He hadn't used them on anyone there. Porter Rockwell was better than him, so he kept a low profile. But when he lived in Kansas, he'd killed his first man while running with the Jayhawkers. Others had followed, and it had become a habit. He found he didn't mind killing for money.

He used the black woman, forced her to lead them here. Threatened her by telling her they'd kill her husband if she didn't obey. Even though killing a buck would cost money, he meant what he'd said, and he'd have done it. He found this the best way to find slave runners. Less work, like a bird following a trail of bread to the whole loaf.

A man came out of the darkness and slipped to Quantrill's side. "We're ready, Bill," he said. "Ain't no way they can get away."

John Little had been running with Quantrill for a full year along with William Haller, George Todd, and a half dozen others. They were also fighting with Sterling Price's Confederate Missourians, but they didn't hang around camp. Just wasn't profitable.

They heard the noise before they actually saw the wagon. It came out of the darkness of the barn in a rush and pulled up behind the root cellar. The door flew open, and in the light of a lantern, he saw a half dozen people come out and get into the back. Another larger man hopped up to the driver's seat, took the reins, and whipped the horses. The wagon was on the move before Quantrill could react.

Quantrill cursed. "No other way, huh, John?" He added a second curse aimed particularly at John's parentage as he turned and ran through the woods to get to his horse. They had to catch that wagon.

* * *

Ben slapped the reins against the horses again after they made a turn in the road that took them directly east. They were quickly at a full run and reached the road to the river just as the first rays of daylight flashed through the trees. He pulled back on the reins, slowing just enough to make the turn as the wagon slid around behind them. He looked over his shoulder, saw no one behind them, then glanced down at his passengers as they tried to reseat themselves after the turn.

"How far?" he asked.

"A mile."

Ben slapped the reins again and picked up speed. Their timing should be just about right.

* * *

Lizzy watched from the window at the front of the house as a half dozen riders flew past in pursuit of the wagon. She smiled then quickly returned to the basement where she, Purdy, and Bryce helped the runaways out of the cellar and across the yard to the forest. Five minutes later they were loading their own wagon. Lizzy hopped up and took the reins. She whipped the horses, and they lurched into their traces. Moments later they were on the road and headed for one more stop. They had to get to Tess's husband.

* * *

Quantrill saw the wagon in front of the church by the river. They galloped down the slope and quickly dismounted, pulling their weapons and climbing the steps. He flung the door open to find a preacher at the pulpit with several dozen black members listening to his sermon. There was an older white man sitting up front, and he immediately stood.

"What is the meaning of this?" he asked. "This is a house of God! Surely—"

Quantrill cocked his revolver, and the white man bit his tongue.

"Hello, William."

Quantrill saw another white man stand up from the front pew where he'd been sitting. "Well, well, Ben Connelly. You're a bit far from home, aren't you?"

"On a mission. The pastor asked that I speak to his congregation, and I was about to oblige him when you boys came in. What seems to be the problem?"

"That wagon was carrying a dozen runaways. Where are they?"

"I beg your pardon," the older fellow spoke again. "I brought my servants here for services in that wagon. I do every Sunday."

Quantrill felt his stomach churn. "And you are?" he asked.

"Thomas Henderson. My home—"

"And I suppose you have papers for all these people," Quantrill said.

Henderson frowned. "Of course not. They are not *all* my servants. I do have papers for mine, but these other folks will have their own."

Papers suddenly appeared in every hand and were gently waved at Quantrill. "Yas, suh," said one. "We all has papahs. Sho nuf. Our massas they let us come, but they makes sho' we has dees passes. Why, do youse know dey's slave catchers around what takes us po' black folks from our massas and sells us to someone else. Yas, suh, we carries 'em." A woman came out of the pew toward Quantrill waving her papers. "You kin see 'im, massa. We's all slaves heah, 'cept'n for Massa Henderson's folks, deys free, dey is."

Quantrill gently waved his revolver at the woman. She came to a quick stop, her eyes wide, then she backed up a bit. "Doan you want t' see 'em, massa?" she asked.

"John, you and the boys check 'em all. Then I want this place searched."

John gave the order, and the men spread out. Quantrill was about to tell John to help when he remembered the man couldn't read. "Search the place, John. Now."

It didn't take long. The church was a one-room building with no other exits and a floor made of solid oak. There were no hiding places, but they checked every nook and cranny just to be sure. Ben hid his smile then cleared his throat as Bill looked at him.

"They all have papers, boss," said one of the men.

Quantrill played with the hammer of his gun. He had been duped, and Benjamin Connelly was a part of it. This was no more than a decoy, and he'd played right into it. "I should kill you, Ben."

"Don't make me regret saving your life, William."

Bill gave a wan smile then holstered his weapon before turning to leave.

"You bought them some time, Ben, but not enough. They have to pick up the woman's husband. If they don't, I'll keep my promise. I'll kill him."

Ben felt the hair on his neck stand up. He knew Bill Quantrill well enough to know when he meant what he said. As the last of his men disappeared out the door, Ben went to the window and watched them gallop up the road. He gave a nod then went to the woman who had approached Quantrill with her papers.

"Mrs. Curtis, a fine job." She was Henderson's housekeeper, and the rest of his servants gathered around to congratulate her fine acting when Ben saw some motion outside the window. He went to it in time to see two of Quantrill's men a hundred yards away at the top of the hill. Each had dismounted and was wrapping a branch with cloth. Ben shouted for everyone to get out of the building as one of the men lit his makeshift torch and mounted his horse.

Ben ran out the front door, jumped off the porch, and ran for the wagon as the first horseman came down the road and made the turn toward the church. Knowing it was too late to get to his shotgun, he crouched, waited until the rider was nearly on him, then stepped to one side, grabbing the horse's reins and jerking them hard toward the ground. The horse went down, launching the rider into a tree. As the horse flailed about, Ben pulled the rifle from its scabbard in time to turn and aim it at the other rider, who had turned off the road and back toward the church. The man pulled back on the reins so hard his horse nearly sat down on its haunches. Ben grabbed the butt of the gun, took a few steps, and knocked the rider out of the saddle. The pastor and others quickly extinguished the torches as Ben swung up into the saddle of the second horse. "Henderson, tie them up then have them thrown in jail. I have to catch up to Miss Hudson. Watch out for Quantrill, Henderson. As you can tell, he is a vengeful man." He spurred his horse into a gallop. He had to catch up.

Chapter Twelve

MILLIE WAS WAITING FOR DIX. The sun was rising, and they would need to be at work soon. They were ahead of schedule until the rain; now they were behind. Two slaves had run away since her arrival, and only one had been retrieved by her overseer, Silas French, who had done little to find the second—his way of objecting to Millie's "dangerous sympathy" regarding her slaves. She had immediately sent him packing.

French's presence had been a surprise to her. Apparently, her uncle had fired the overseer her father had worked with and had replaced him with Mr. French. Because of it, she'd found the workers angry, recalcitrant, and dragging their feet, the crop suffering and the buildings in some disrepair. After French left, she went immediately to her workers to tell them of her plans. Of course, without an overseer, all but Old Dix could have walked away. He was the patriarch of her workers and their families, a man who had been a friend to Millie since her childhood.

She told them that she would give them each a paper declaring them freed men and women if they would sign on as her workers for two years. During those two years, they would share equally in any profit. They could use the money as they wished, and she would allow them to fix up their cabins and make other improvements using timber from her property. They seemed pleased with her proposal. She reminded them that she would expect them to work hard. If they didn't, they would be asked to leave Beauchapel and would be replaced by someone willing to improve the plantation and make it profitable. There would be no loafing about as they sometimes did in an effort to show their anger at being slaves. They would be free and responsible to do their best.

They did not respond as quickly as she had hoped, nor did they all stay. Two of the younger men took the papers she offered and left the next morning with their wives and children. They were going north. If the Confederates had won at Manassas, there was no assurance that the federals would come again. The men figured real freedom would only be found in New York or Pennsylvania. Millie couldn't blame them, but she made one last plea, reminding them that every freedom would be offered on the plantation *and* she would protect them. They would have no protection if they left. After some discussion, they thanked her but still left at sunrise.

The others had another request, which she quickly granted. They wanted to have larger garden plots that would allow them to sell some products at the markets in Petersburg or even Richmond. She thought it a good idea but told them they would have to buy their own seed and tools after the first year. They agreed. Since these changes were made, the crop had dramatically improved, and things looked much more hopeful for the success of her plans.

Millie watched as Dix, a bit slumped from age and hard work, shambled across the creek bridge, giving her a warm smile and a good morning. She returned both and then began discussing the day.

"I want you to get the men started in the fields. I must go to my office and get ready for Mr. Huggins. He's coming this morning. We must get the rest of the tobacco cut and hung before the end of the week."

They talked of other chores and concerns as they walked back toward the house. Families were coming out of their homes and gathering for their morning ritual of prayers and a song before going to the field. Millie loved this part of the day but could not join them. She must go over the papers one more time before her attorney arrived from Petersburg. She left Dix at the gathering, knowing he would get them in the fields and working hard. They were a happier group now than she had ever seen them. There was hope in their eyes, but that hope was based in her promises. After going through her accounts, she had many questions and concerns that needed to be addressed, not the least of which would be the suing of her uncle, who had finally arrived back in Richmond. He said little of why he had been delayed so long, but Millie had a good idea that was verified when the papers announced the arrest of Rose Greenhow in Washington. Mr. Polanski had obviously detained him.

Going inside she was handed a cup of coffee and a plate of hot bread as she passed through the kitchen. The coffee was too hot to drink, but a bite of bread, butter, and honey hit the spot as she turned into her father's study at the left of the wide entry.

She put the remaining bread and her cup on the desk and began looking for her last figures. Though the banker had refused to discuss anything with her, her withdrawal of what remained had stopped the flow of her money into her uncle's pockets, but it didn't stop the waterfall of letters from creditors threatening suits for non-payment. Some had not been paid for more than a year. Her uncle claimed there was an agent in Richmond paying the bills, but she found no such agent. While they were in Europe, everything had gone into arrears except payment of wages for French, who also used the money from last year's crop to pay for food and a few other necessities. Thus, no income, only bank drafts in New York against their Europe trip and his personal debt—all while feigning that *he* had paid for everything. Even if she deducted the amount for her share of the trip, he had stolen nearly twenty-five thousand dollars from her accounts, leaving her just enough to pay the accounts in arrears. But there was still money owed to Daniel Geery. It was that money her attorney was coming to discuss.

Finding her notes, she reviewed them along with any papers she thought she might need, drank her coffee, and ate the rest of her bread. She heard the carriage approaching and hurried to the mirror to check her appearance. The woman who stared back at her was darker than she had been even a week ago, her naturally brown skin coming from descendants who must be Italian or Spanish, raising questions about her bright green eyes. Her dark hair normally hung in curls to her shoulders but was done up in a bun this morning—a more mature look for her young age of twenty-one. She stared at the round face and could see that she had even lost a little of that chubbiness as she worked out in the hot sun. She was thin, about average in height, with heavier calves than she liked, and a posterior that was, well, also shrinking, and she was grateful for it. The thought occurred to her that Matthew Alexander would probably not even recognize her if he saw her today, but he would surely be pleased with the difference.

She pinched her cheeks and patted her hair while calling out for coffee and bread for Mr. Huggins. She closed the study door to prevent herself from looking too anxious then waited. The house worker welcomed him and proceeded to lead him to the sitting room. He requested the porch instead. It was already turning warm. She heard the screen door close as they went out and heard Huggins thank Tiera for the coffee and bread. The screen door creaked again, and Tiera spoke at the study door.

"Miss Millie."

"Yes," she answered.

"It is Massa Huggins. He's a waitin' on the front porch, ma'am."

"He is *Mr.* Huggins. You have no masters, Tiera. Remember?"

"Oh, yes'm. I forgot," the voice said with a pleasant chuckle that made Millie smile while taking one last look in the mirror. Beads of sweat pinpointed her forehead and cheeks. She cringed and grabbed a hanky, dabbing her face as she opened the study door. Taking a deep breath, she went out onto the porch. Huggins stood and bowed slightly then stepped forward, took her hand, and kissed it lightly.

"Miss Atwater, you are looking lovely this morning."

Huggins was an older gentleman—a landowner and an attorney with a reputation for honesty but also tenacity. He had a tender place in his heart for the underdog and had defended the rights of many a small farmer against larger ones. He had also defended freed blacks who had been caught and resold. More than one Southerner had paid stiff fines or spent time in jail because of Mr. Huggins, and in those circles he was not a popular man. Daniel Geery ran in such circles. It was one reason she had hired him.

"Mr. Huggins, you are very kind. How are things in Petersburg?"

"Fine, fine. There's more talk of a compromise this morning, but it is all fluff and no substance. More troops gather in Washington, and in the west they continue to fight. Some say our Confederate troops are preparing to drive into Kentucky. Anyone who thinks this war is over is a fool."

"Please, sit," she said. "And what of the Union blockade of our coastline?"

"A few of our ships are being caught, their shipments confiscated. Most are getting through though, but the North will send more if the war goes on much longer. They'll strangle us if they have to."

"Yes, that's what I fear." Her stomach was churning at the thought, but she kept her feelings hidden. If her shipment was confiscated, it meant the loss of everything.

She sat in a chair facing him, thankful for a breeze that came across the porch, cooling her face.

"I am afraid that the report you asked for is very mixed," Huggins said.

Millie felt her mouth go dry and busied herself pouring a cup of coffee. "Let's start with the good news, shall we?" She forced a smile.

"You do have recourse against your uncle for what he took from your accounts. I sent him a letter demanding payment and threatening suit if I did not receive it." He sat back in the chair, his brow furrowing. "As you know it's a considerable amount of money."

"Yes, around twenty-five thousand dollars."

Huggins brow wrinkled. Millie could see that the bad news was about to follow.

"I investigated his holdings. Until a few months ago, he was very heavily in debt, nearly twice what he owes you. Then, suddenly, it was all paid off."

"Then he has the money to repay me?"

"If that were true, I could collect my retainer and conclude our business. Unfortunately, it's not. He's spent most of those funds, but worse still . . ." He paused, leaning forward. "It is as you thought, Millie; he used your plantation as collateral to obtain the money and spend as if he were well-heeled. I believe he even gambled some of it away, but I can't be sure."

Millie felt her heart stop and the blood drain from her face. "How could he do such a thing?" she said in a near whisper.

"He made some very bad decisions even before the death of your parents. This scheme seems to be what he came up with to pay them." He took a deep breath. "There is a lien against your property that your uncle signed. Daniel Geery and Geery Tobacco Company hold that lien."

"How much debt is it?" Millie asked, bracing herself for the answer.

"Forty-eight thousand dollars," Huggins answered softly.

Millie felt faint and had to force the next question. "And when is the debt due?"

"The seventh of January, next year," he answered.

It was August. Less than six months. She leaned forward, her forearms on her knees, thinking of her uncle's incessant advice to sell the plantation after her parents' deaths. "No wonder he wanted me to sell Beauchapel," she said softly. "He could clear the debt and still have power of attorney then hand me the surplus, claiming that the land didn't bring a good price." She sat back, "Then again, I may never have seen a dime."

After a few moments of silence, Millie stood, put her cup on the table, and went to the porch railing, her fingers rubbing her forehead in an attempt to make the pain of a sudden headache dissapate. After several moments she found the strength to speak. "Daniel Geery has wanted this property for years. It seems he's found a way to get it."

"It may not just be about the property, Millie."

She turned and faced him. "What do you mean?"

"It is no secret to anyone but you that Geery has laid claim to you. Anyone who has shown some interest in having a son court you has received a visit from Mr. Geery." He smiled. "He approached your father once, but your father sent him away. He swore then that he would have you. I heard him say it that same night. He boasted of his ability to force you into his bed."

"But why haven't you . . . why hasn't anyone said anything about such insolence?! Surely . . ."

"I should have . . . Someone should have. Forgive me, forgive them, but the point is he may think he has enough leverage now and—"

"I will never marry him! He is a fool if he thinks otherwise!"

Huggins countenance saddened. "Then you may have to sell Beauchapel. It's a fine piece of property and will bring far more than what is owed to Geery."

The thought of having to sell Beauchapel nearly brought her to tears, and she nodded in mute response.

"If you can force your uncle to sell what assets he has and pay you what he owes you, the debt is cut in half. If the crop does well, it would earn the rest, but if it doesn't . . . and, well, there's the blockade. If it worsens you may not be able to sell it all, not with Geery controlling the market. In your case he'll surely try to keep you from selling. Whether he wants to force a marriage or just to steal Beauchapel, he will try to keep your profits to a minimum." He thought a moment. "Do you have any other property you might sell? Anything at all?"

She felt sick as she shook her head. "No, nothing."

There was a long pause. "Then you must find another investor. Someone you trust, who will give you more time. However, he may demand more interest in Beauchapel. No one will loan you money without a price."

"Or if they're told my crop won't sell. Geery could spread such rumors, use his influence to turn others away."

"Start in Richmond. Geery has too many friends in Petersburg. There are men in Richmond who do not care a stitch for Daniel Geery, but I warn you, they will look at it strictly on the profit possible to them. If they do not like your proposition—"

"I'll leave immediately." She went to him and planted a kiss on his cheek. "Thank you, Mr. Huggins. You have given me hope."

He blushed. Standing, he descended the steps and mounted his waiting horse. She threw him a second kiss, and he waved then walked his horse down the drive. Millie went to her father's desk and thumbed quickly through his papers until she found the list she was looking for. Men her father did business with, had borrowed from, had helped. Most of them were in Richmond. Yes, this was an option.

"Tiera," she called as she went to the foot of the stairs in the entry. Tiera appeared at the kitchen door. "Tell Dix I need a carriage to take me to the train station and that I'll be gone for a few days. Tell him to come to the study as soon as he can. I'll pack and then visit with him."

Tiera nodded, and Millie launched herself up the steps. She must hurry. The afternoon train to Richmond would leave in less than three hours.

Chapter Thirteen

QUANTRILL ARRIVED TO FIND HIS men locked up in the slave quarters, tied and gagged. He quickly pulled the gag aside for one of them and asked for answers.

"Some woman come up here in a empty wagon. Said she was here to pick up cotton. Handsome woman but wearing men's clothes." He looked down at his feet as Quantrill cut his bonds. "We all went out to get a good look, and afore we knew it she had the drop on us. Two other men joined her, and we was put in here. They took five slaves that were housed here—includin' the husband of that woman you sid you'd kill if she didn't help us—and headed out about ten minutes ago."

Quantrill stood, brushed the man off, then slapped him across the face, hard. "Another mistake like that one, George, and I'll bury you. Understand?"

Quantrill was back at his horse and mounted when George came out of the cabin. "I suppose they took your guns," he said.

"Chased off the horses too," George replied.

Quantrill turned and headed for the road, his men behind him. He stopped at the end of the lane and checked the ground for fresh wheel tracks. He found the set he wanted and drove his spurs into his mount. They were headed for Jefferson City.

* * *

From the shadow of the trees, Ben had watched Quantrill and his remaining men turn down the lane. When he saw Quantrill leave the slave's house Ben spurred his horse on toward Jefferson City. Quantrill would come after the wagon, and he needed to give them warning.

He caught Lizzy about a mile outside the city. The wagon was crammed full of more slaves, and he figured she'd picked up nearly a half dozen at the last stop. He yelled his warning, and she whipped the animals harder, glad she'd brought a double team. They raced into the outskirts and through the city streets, Ben right behind them. The sun was up, and the first citizens were out and had to dodge the fast moving wagon as it careened through the mishmash of muddy or wet cobbled streets toward the docks. Ben looked over his shoulder as the wagon reached the dock, and Lizzy reined in the animals. She pushed them at a walk aboard the steamer and into the main hold. The doors were quickly closed behind them and the slaves taken down to where they'd be hidden.

Ben dismounted and tied his horse to a hitching post near the door of Hudson Shipping. As he crossed the street and walked onto the steamer, he heard the thunder of hooves and looked back to see Quantrill and his men barreling up the road. The whistle blew its warning, and the loading ramp and walking plank were quickly pulled in. As the steamer's paddles caught water, Quantrill rode onto the dock and watched the boat slip away as Lizzy came out of the hold and joined Ben by the rail.

"Nice to see you again, William," Ben called from the steamer.

Quantrill reached for his revolver then thought better of it when he saw Purdy and Bryce atop two bales of cotton, aiming their rifles in his direction. "Miss Hudson, if I find you in Missouri, I'll see you hanged. You too, Ben." He turned and rode back up the street, his men in tow.

"Tell the captain it would be wise if he made no stops within fifty miles of here," Ben said. "William Quantrill is a man of his word."

"So he's the gunman the plantation owners hired."

"Elizabeth, I know Quantrill. Stay out of Little Dixie until he's either gone or dead."

Lizzy was surprised. "How do you know the likes of him?"

"I went to Utah with the army when the federal judges spread their lies. Before I joined the Church, I met Bill in my nightly rounds of every saloon in the Salt Lake Valley. He was a gambler then. Not much good with a gun. He and a half dozen other drifters used to spend their mornings shooting up tree limbs and empty whiskey bottles. Porter Rockwell chased most of 'em out of the territory, but Quantrill was smart enough to keep a low profile. He didn't drink much, cause a ruckus in the saloons, or shoot people like some of his friends did. Eventually, though, he decided to move on. Not enough loose money in Salt Lake when the soldiers all started leaving to join one army or the other."

"And you became friends?" Lizzy said.

"I drank, and on slow evenings at the tables he kept me company. After a couple months, I realized where I was headed and stopped. Never went into a bar or cried into a bottle again. He came looking for me." Ben smiled. "Thought maybe I had jumped off a cliff or something."

"What were you doing?"

"Getting religion. I wandered into the bowery one day and heard Brother Young and half a dozen others teach the gospel. Haven't had a drink since. A month later I was out of the army and a baptized Mormon working as a wagon maker for President Young."

"But Quantrill came looking for you?" she prodded.

"Once. He was cheated by another gambler. Busted the man up pretty bad. The fellow hired a couple of gunman to put Bill in his grave. I was in the saloon at the time looking for a wayward member of our ward. I saw it coming and busted one of the gunmen's jaws before he could get his gun out of his belt. William was faster than the other one." He paused. "He thought about killing me today, thought on it real hard, but he didn't. Instead he just sent two of his men back to burn down the church. He doesn't like being beat, Elizabeth, and he'll keep after you until he hangs you. Stay out of Little Dixie."

The steamer caught in the main current and lurched forward, causing Lizzy to stumble against him. He put an arm around her to steady her but removed it quickly. Lizzy found herself wishing he hadn't, and it caused her to blush. She stepped to the side of the vessel and put a hand on a rail to steady herself as she watched Jefferson City slip away in the sunlight of day. She regained her composure.

He came up next to her and leaned on the rail with both forearms. "How many did you end up bringing aboard?"

"Seventeen. When we freed Tess's husband, we brought along four others," she said. "It'll be eighteen sometime today. A new baby." She smiled before turning around and leaning back against the rail, her long hair blowing in the wind. "You handled that shotgun like it was second nature."

"When the army went to Utah and found out the Mormons weren't a threat, we were put in charge of the trails going west. Indians attacked wagon trains regularly, and we spent a lot of time chasing them. We got into a few skirmishes. You practice when there's a chance your life will be on the line."

A steward approached, several papers in hand. He gave them to Lizzy. "These came to the office at Jefferson City. I thought you would want to see them right away."

She thanked him and quickly thumbed through the wires. She scanned one, relief showing on her face.

"Rand is back in Washington, but it's chaos there." She scanned further. "Hooker and Malone are with him." Then her countenance fell slightly. "Newton and eight other Missouri boys were taken prisoner."

In her conversations with Ben, she'd told him about Newton and Hooker and even Malone. She had a fondness for all of them and was saddened by the news.

"They're already talking prisoner exchange," she went on. "Ann says Malone is confident Newton is alive and will either escape and find his way home or be exchanged when the time comes." She thumbed through the other wires, but when she didn't see any word about Andrew, she couldn't hide her disappointment, and it bothered her that she cared if Ben noticed.

Straightening, Lizzy did her best to smile through a tired countenance. "We'll be in Alton this evening. You best get some sleep if you plan to take the train to Chicago."

"Breakfast first, then some reading. I'd be honored if you'd join me," he said.

She wanted to, very much, but she knew it would be dangerous. She was beginning to like Ben Connelly more than she should. It was time to make excuses.

"I have to check on our new arrivals. Possibly I can join you later." She faced him, extending a hand. He handed her the shotgun.

"Yours, I believe, and handshakes are much too final. Without warning, he leaned over, kissed her softly on the lips, looked into her eyes, and smiled. He turned and went toward the steps that led to their rooms, leaving Lizzy Hudson speechless for one of the first times in her life.

Chapter Fourteen

MATTHEW DID NOT LIKE PARTIES, especially those involving the coming out of young Southern belles and to which all her friends were invited. It seemed inevitable that once a young girl had such a party, she thought that she was somehow a woman and began looking to capture an older beau with "prospects." But this was the oldest niece of Henry Hyde Jr., and Henry had insisted that if Matthew wanted an appointment in the war department, it would be important for him to attend the party.

Henry's sister was married to Thomas Seddon, son of James Seddon, good friend to Jefferson Davis. Matthew knew James Seddon. There was not a more rabid proponent of secession than James. He had come to Washington as part of the Virginia peace delegation and did everything he could to undermine the effort. It was rumored that Davis was looking for a place for Seddon in his cabinet. Making an impression on the Seddons would go far in getting Matthew the appointment he sought.

As he entered the Seddon family mansion, Matthew gave his coat to a servant as he scanned the crowd. There were few familiar faces, not surprising since he wasn't from Richmond. However, he knew the city, state, and Confederate government would be well represented, and at the very least he might glean a few tidbits to pass along to Pinkerton.

His visit with Henry had gone better than expected. In a relatively short period of time, Henry had become an integral part of society in Richmond, and so far at least, he had not given a second thought to Matthew's loyalty. Though it caused Matthew some grief to use his friend in this way, the guilt didn't last long. Treason was the same whether accomplished by friend or foe, and Henry had chosen a side for which Matthew felt no sympathy. Nor did he have any illusions that if Henry discovered Matthew's intent, he would have him shot and possibly even do it himself. He played a dangerous game, but if Southern treason were to be met with a strong hand, he would do his part.

He saw Henry, nodded, then waited for his friend to finish his conversation with several men. He regretted the wait as two young belles came forward to greet him, their fans held in front of their giddy faces.

"You are Matthew Alexander, aren't you?" the first asked. "I am Henry's sister, Tersa." She bowed slightly, her eyelashes flashing.

"Ah yes, Tersa. I remember you. Such a sweet young girl. Henry used to bounce you on his knee when home from college for the summer," he said as affably as he could. "And who is your friend?"

"Marjorie, Marjorie Kempton," the second girl said. She raised a hand, ostensibly to have Matthew kiss it, but Matthew shook it lightly and bowed, silently questioning if there were any muscle in her arm as it waved about with his slightest motion. "Nice to meet you, Miss Kempton. I wish I could stay and chat, but Henry is waiting for me. Enjoy the evening." Giggles punctuated his slide past them, and he quickly joined his friend.

"Lovely, aren't they," Henry said, facetiously. He pulled Matthew toward the open door of another room, leaning lightly on his cane. "Father went to war, and Tersa came to live with me. At times I wonder who has the better end of it."

"Children that age are always lovely and innocent, aren't they, Henry?" Matthew said.

Henry laughed. "Yes, well, be careful. Tersa has had a crush on you for years, and she may try to corner you again." They were near the open door. "For now, Thomas and his father are gathering the most prominent among this crowd to talk a little politics. I think we should join them."

Matthew knew the conversation would be laced with the recent victory at Bull Run and the assurance of Confederate superiority. He cringed at the thought of having to bear it silently; he pacified himself with the knowledge it could also be fruitful. "Maybe Tersa's company wouldn't be so bad after all. You know how I hate to discuss such things," Matthew said.

"Bear with me. I think you will find this most interesting, and if you really do want a letter of recommendation, the signature of James Seddon will go far in procuring it." They passed through the study door, and Henry closed it behind them.

Matthew knew his presence would be noted and was not disappointed. Several groups eyed him with whispered curiosity as Henry quietly identified the most important guests for Matthew.

"That's Governor John Letcher over there." Henry nodded. "And the man next to him is Mr. Mayo, city mayor. Most of the city council is here as well, as are the editors of our newspapers. That's James Seddon standing near the fireplace. He will be the central figure of this little gathering and the one you might find a way to impress, but Leroy Walker, the present secretary of war, will do you the most immediate good. He is the tall thin one with a beard but no moustache next to Mr. Seddon." He pointed at another man. "That dear boy is Robert M. T. Hunter, Confederate secretary of state."

Matthew smiled as he looked at Hunter, but he was more interested in the older gentleman with a white beard to his right, a man encircled by several others and answering their enquiries. He had met Robert E. Lee, but he doubted if the general would remember it.

"Even President Davis himself may join us later, we shall see, but as you can see, this is fertile ground for what you seek, my friend. Fertile ground indeed," Henry said with some pride.

Matthew nodded but was thinking how much good having all these men imprisoned might accomplish. But that would be a subject to dwell on later. James Seddon was clearing his throat and discarding his cigar.

"Gentlemen, as all of you know, we have won a great victory at Manassas."

He needed no pause to invite a response; it came automatically, an eruption that rattled the windows and made Matthew grit his teeth while joining in. He noted that General Lee was not among those applauding, but Lee had a reputation for being reserved when it came to counting chickens before they hatched.

"Well, do not think it means anything," Seddon went on. "The Rail Splitter is not about to give us peace that easily."

Several derogatory statements about Lincoln and the Northerners jumped from lips around the room, and Seddon let them be heard before going on.

"We must not allow ourselves to become complacent. Our freedom will be hard won. We are outnumbered ten to one, and we have only a fraction of the industrial might of the North." He paused, the room growing sober. "But we do have Southern will and the right on our side, gentlemen, and if we keep these brightly lit, we will have our freedom. It is the will of God!"

The room reacted to this last impassioned sentence with enough applause that Seddon had to wait upon them before he continued.

Matthew noted that he seemed to enjoy the wait. Finally, as it died, he wrinkled his brow and cleared his throat. "We must prepare Richmond for war, gentlemen. We should increase our steel and lead production by 100 percent in the next few months, and we must have factories for the manufacture of tents, uniforms, swords, and especially cannons and the newest sort of rifles that surpass those of the North in their effectiveness, or in the end, they will outlast us and beat us."

The room remained silent. "Gentlemen, I met with Mr. Joseph Anderson of Tredegar Iron Works only this morning. They have begun production of iron sufficient to arm our first ironclad warship and are also developing the Brooke rifle, a giant rail-mounted siege cannon that will play an instrumental role in our military ability to lay siege to Washington and other Northern cities *when the time comes.*"

The room was afloat with murmuring approval, and Matthew could not believe his luck. In a single moment he had gleaned important information about Confederate weaponry that he had not expected. Possibly the most fertile ground for information wasn't the war department after all but the parlors of Richmond. He glanced at Lee. The man's face was red with anger, and he chewed hard on an unlit cigar. There was at least one other person in the room who saw the error of making such information public. Secretary of War Walker was even less happy with Seddon's obvious indiscretion than Lee was.

"We must also raise fortifications," Seddon went on, "just as Lincoln has at Washington."

The room went silent again. "For this part of our discussion, Secretary of War Walker will take the lead." He bowed his head slightly to the younger Walker, who stepped forward, grabbing his lapels in his hands.

"Gentlemen, as you know, General Lee has already begun to build earthworks and forts around the city." He looked at Lee, and others glanced his way with murmuring approval. Lee forced himself to look pleasant.

"Unfortunately, with our recent victory, this process was slowed considerably. We must impress upon our citizens the need to increase our dedication to the protection of the city. As Mr. Seddon has advised you, the Rail Splitter has called for more soldiers, more armament, and has begun production that would rival any that provided for all the wars in Europe. He is not doing so for defensive purposes, I assure you." He paused, giving time for more derogatory remarks about Northern leaders and their unwillingness to learn their lesson.

"We must have artillery batteries strategically placed to stop federal capture, more forts to house our growing army, and much more in the way of supplies." He paused. "You men hold in your hands the ability—through your newspapers and your influential positions—to impress upon the people of Richmond a greater urgency for this effort." He looked directly at Lee. "The general is requesting that we send our slaves to work on these fortifications at least three days a week and that we add our financial strength to buying the materials necessary for the fortifications."

Lee was highly respected by most of these men, but Matthew sensed grumblers in the crowd. Perhaps they simply did not believe there was a need for such fortifications, and if that was the case, they were fools.

Henry said it had been Lee who had developed the strategy for Manassas, adding glitter to an already sterling reputation. Matthew was just glad he was behind a desk. Though General Robert E. Lee would be a tremendous asset to the Confederacy no matter where he served, his greatest strength would be in the field. Davis was doing the North a tremendous favor by keeping him in Richmond.

"I read to you from one of our morning newspapers," Walker continued. *"The mayor of Danville has sent down twenty-four able-bodied free negroes. Not one free negro from the city of Richmond or county of Henrico has been on the works. Why is this? Two gentlemen, eminent physicians from the county of Lunenburg, have brought, the one fifteen and the other six men (the best we have) and have given their services to attend to such as needed medical aid on the works. May I not, from these facts appeal to those men immediately interested in the speedy completion of these defenses, to render us all aid in their power, and that speedily?"*

He lowered the paper to his side, pausing, the room quiet. "We appeal to you, the leaders of this city and state to move this work forward with a more determined speed." He paused again. "Now to another matter. As you know, even though Manassas was a victory, we have hundreds of wounded. Prisoners have been brought here as well. We need hospitals; we need better prisons."

"Hospitals we can handle, but let them Northern boys rot," said someone in the back of the room.

Walker's face hardened. "We are not inhumane, and do not forget that the North captured several hundred of our own patriots. If we expect them to be treated humanely, we must do the same until we can find common ground for their release." Another pause and the room fell silent again, but Matthew was a bit chilled by the obvious feel in the room. Prisoners represented the enemy who had killed some of their own and who were still a threat. They would not be high on the list of priorities of Richmond's citizens.

"Gentlemen, we need your support both in getting others to work and in funding what must be done. Can President Davis and the entire Confederacy count on you?"

"It will cost tens of thousands—" said one man.

"Aren't you being a bit hasty?" asked another guest with some distaste. "Surely a compromise . . . !"

"I agree," said another. "We should wait until Lincoln responds to our efforts to achieve peace. Even though he is asking for more men and speeding up industry, could it be simply for purposes of defense or even negotiation? Building fortifications we may not need and alarming the people prematurely will put a great strain on all our citizens."

Matthew decided now was the time to speak. "Gentlemen, may I speak?" The room was filling with cigar smoke fast, and he nearly choked as he took a deep breath. Seeing his discomfort, Henry signaled to one of the servants to open the windows.

Walker looked at him quizzically. "I am afraid I do not know you, Mr. . . ."

"Alexander. Matthew Alexander of New Orleans. I have recently come from West Point."

"Please, Mr. Alexander," Walker said over the hum of curious voices. His face showed relief at some kind of support.

"I have been at the Academy for nearly four years, and I can tell you this: the North means business. They have no intention of allowing us to secede and will use every force at their disposal to stop it. I came by way of Washington only a few days before Manassas. As you know, we still have friends there, and if they have not already done so, they will second what I tell you now." He paused trying to measure the crowd, how much they would need to make them believers. He knew much more, but he wasn't about to reveal what he had heard discussed in the halls of the White House. Just enough to increase his air of loyalty—enough to make an impression. "They are particularly obsessed with the defeat of Richmond, and even before our great victory at Manassas, there was talk of an immediate campaign through the Shenandoah."

There were some looks of approval but also a good deal of grumbling and the murmur of discussion that seemed more than a little unsupportive.

Walker gave a nod of thanks and then spoke again. "Mr. Alexander's understanding of our situation is correct, gentlemen, and I will begin the support with a pledge of five thousand dollars and hope that all of you will at least match that amount." He waited, but the reaction was mixed.

"I am not a wealthy man, Mr. Walker," Matthew said. "But my father did have some property in New York State, and I demanded it be sold when I left that country. I expect the money to be in my possession within a month's time and will match your five thousand dollars."

Walker was even more impressed, and several others immediately chimed in with matching donations, including one from Henry. Both Walker and Seddon seemed relieved and grateful.

Matthew did not have any land and certainly didn't have the money, but getting money into the South from Northern banks was already a serious problem, and confiscation by the federal government would make an acceptable excuse if needed.

Others made other pledges, and further discussion ensued concerning labor for the fortifications. Within half an hour Seddon and Walker seemed to have a good beginning. Finally, Seddon raised his hands for quiet. "Gentlemen, our wives are probably ready to string us up by our thumbs. But I do have one other matter." He was standing again, his chest blown out like a rooster. This was obviously a man who liked to be the center of attention. He cleared his throat, glancing at both Walker and Lee before going on. After a slight hesitation, he seemed to cast any reluctance to the wind and proceeded. "We are sending emissaries to Europe soon. With our victory at Manassas, we are sure they will find success."

The placed suddenly buzzed, and Lee fumed. Walker seemed a bit shocked but quickly hid his concerns.

"When will they leave?" asked one of the group.

"Soon," Seddon said with a wry smile. "After all, even these walls may have ears. Thank you, gentlemen."

The laughter was general as the doors were opened, and the mood changed to one of full celebration as servants brought glasses of wine. One man offered a toast to victory at Manassas. Having drifted toward the door, Matthew stepped through it quickly enough that it didn't look unseemly not to raise his glass. More followed into the large living and dining area where the small orchestra greeted them with a rendition of "Dixie."

Matthew felt a hand on his arm and turned to face Robert E. Lee as Henry Hyde joined him.

"General, how good to see you," Matthew said with feeling.

"Lieutenant Alexander, how is that eye of yours?" Lee asked, looking into the eye with concern.

"Mostly lost to me, sir, but I don't mind. We did put down Mr. Brown, didn't we?"

Lee gave a wan smile. "Yes, I suppose we did."

"General," Henry said. "Because of his injury, Matthew is seeking an appointment as analyst in the war department. It is a minor position and beneath his talents, but he wishes it just the same. Possibly you could give him a recommendation."

Lee did not have a chance to answer as Walker inserted himself into the conversation. "General," Walker fumed. "What are we do with him?" he said, referring to Seddon.

"Hang him, I suppose," Lee said, only partially smiling. "But that would embarrass his wife, so possibly Jeff should sit down with him tomorrow."

Matthew knew "Jeff" was Jefferson Davis, and James Seddon would get an earful if Davis learned of his prideful revelations.

Lee turned back to Matthew then looked at Walker. "Leroy, this is Matthew Alexander. He was at Harpers Ferry with me and was injured sufficient enough to keep him from combat, but he graduated top of his class in tactical analysis and would be quite suited to your department. Possibly you could find a place for him."

Walker looked him over while Lee addressed Matthew. "It's good to see you, Lieutenant. I am sorry that it hasn't worked out for you. You were one of the best assigned from the Academy to our unit. God bless you. And Henry, thank you for your donation. I knew we could count on you." He looked to Walker. "I will give Mr. Alexander a full recommendation, and, Leroy, Jeff will be here shortly, but I must leave. Please visit with him about James. Something really must be done."

Walker smiled and nodded as Lee turned and walked away. Matthew could not believe his luck.

Mr. . . . uh, Alexander, is it?"

"Yes, Mr. Secretary," Matthew replied.

"Normally Robert's recommendation carries a good deal of weight, but I have already determined for most positions to take only seasoned men who have served in the field. You are welcome to apply for a small opportunity in our internal analysis department. It isn't much, but if it works out, possibly something else will open for you." He quickly backtracked. "I am not saying it's yours. We do have other applicants, and it will take some time to process their applications, but if you're willing to give it a try . . ."

"I would be honored, sir." Matthew bowed slightly. "I will bring in my letters of recommendation in the next few days."

"Then you have others?" he asked.

"He has mine," Henry chimed in. "He has a talent for seeing things most others can't, Mr. Secretary."

"Yes, well, we'll look at your letters." Walker forced a smile. "Robert's is definitely a start. Now, please excuse me. My wife is giving me a look that would crush walnuts." Walker forced a smile then walked away.

"A start, harumph!" Henry said. "A recommendation from Lee would make most men's careers."

"Walker's a politician, Henry. He'll need a letter from someone of like profession."

"Seddon might write a letter for you. I could try to arrange something with him."

"Yes, Seddon would work."

A woman approached and immediately seemed to make Henry anxious. "Good evening, Mr. Hyde. Who is this fine gentleman you have with you?" She extended her hand for Henry to kiss, but he merely touched it and then let it go. She did not seem to notice, her eyes on Matthew.

"Matthew Alexander, may I introduce you to Miss Elizabeth Van Lew," Henry said flatly. "Her friends call her Beth. Elizabeth, how are you?"

Matthew noted the disagreeable tone and also noticed a number of whispers and snippy looks thrown in the direction of Miss Van Lew. He also remembered Pinkerton's instructions. Elizabeth Van Lew was friendly to the Union.

A middle age woman with birdlike features and quick, bright eyes of green that were set off by dangling ringlets of dark brown hair, Miss Van Lew seemed unaware or uncaring of the negative attention. "Miss Van Lew," he said, taking her hand and kissing it lightly.

"Mr. Alexander, you are new to Richmond." The tone was soft, warm, and confident.

"Yes. I just arrived a few days ago."

Henry seemed nervous at Matthew's courtesy and grabbed an elbow as if to turn him away. "You will have to excuse us, Miss Van Lew," he said. "Matthew is—"

"Handsome, single, and probably a very good catch," Elizabeth said, falling in next to Matthew as Henry tried to pull him away. She took the other arm in an obvious attempt to further needle Henry. "Shall we have some refreshment, Mr. Alexander? Henry, you are certainly welcome to join us unless you feel you would be neglecting your wife and sister, and they do look neglected. Why, I believe they both are quite upset. Look at them, standing there, glaring at you."

Henry looked and so did Matthew. They *were* glaring, but Matthew could see it was at Miss Van Lew not Henry.

"Go on, take care of them. Don't be so uncaring. Go!" She waved him away, and Henry finally stopped and threw Matthew a look of warning. Matthew only shrugged, a slight smile on his face.

They reached the punch bowl and were given two glasses, then he led her to a quiet corner, his heart in his throat. Could he trust her? He must; there simply wasn't anyone else. "Miss Van Lew, I believe we have a mutual goal."

She looked at him quizzically. "And what would that be, Mr. Alxander?"

"The demise of the Confederacy. Are you willing?"

She looked at him, measuring, trying to discern if he was serious. "Quite."

"Then we must meet." He kept his face passive, acting as if it was a normal conversation.

"My, my, you are a bold one, aren't you? How do I know I can trust such a proposal? I do have enemies in this fair city."

"Surely it is I who have the most to lose, Mrs. Van Lew, but I trust Allan Pinkerton's estimation of your desire to support the Constitution."

She smiled. "Come to my house later tonight. Walk the last two blocks, and make sure you are not followed." She gave the address then extended her hand for another kiss, and he took it. "Later, Mr. Alexander." With that she was gone, disappearing through the doors of the veranda as Henry rejoined him.

"Beware of that woman, Matthew," Henry said with some distaste.

"She seems innocent enough," Matthew lied.

"She's an abolitionist with a sword for a tongue. She used to be highly respected, but since secession . . . well, she has no qualms about stating her position. She'll turn traitor someday. You'll see it," Henry said stiffly.

"Traitors don't usually make their views so public," Matthew said.

"Yes, well, she's at least a thorn in the side of Richmond society, and as you can see, we wish to pull it out. Do not be seen with her again unless you have no real interest in getting your appointment," he warned.

Matthew only nodded as they went to the edge of the dance floor to watch Henry's niece dance with her father. After it was over, others went onto the dancing area for a waltz, and Henry leaned toward Matthew to speak above the noise of the orchestra.

"Well, well, look who has come to grace Richmond society with her presence," Henry said.

Matthew looked in the direction Henry was staring. The woman at whom he was looking was stunningly beautiful, and Matthew had to remind himself that Ninette Benjamin was also the most self-centered, jealous, and money-oriented woman he had ever met.

"I thought she was living in Paris with her mother?"

"She is, but she's come home to celebrate her father's appointment as our new attorney general," Henry explained.

"Judah Benjamin is in the government?"

"Despite his being Jewish *and* having challenged President Davis to a duel when they were both legislators in Washington," Henry said with a smile.

Matthew chuckled. "Yes, but remember they worked out a mutually beneficial end to the duel and became friends, and don't forget Benjamin is considered one of the finest political minds and orators of our time. His service in the United States legislature was highly successful."

"Yes, well Davis seems to think so at least." He paused. "Have you seen Ninette since leaving New Orleans?"

Matthew shook his head, but his eyes were on the woman next to Ninette. His vision prevented him from seeing her clearly, and he asked Henry for verification. "And who is the woman next to her?"

"Millicent Atwater. Her father owned a plantation outside Petersburg, but both her parents are gone now and she has decided to run it herself," The last was said with some disbelief, as if a woman certainly would fail at such an endeavor. Matthew had grown up in a house of strong women and knew better.

Matthew had not forgotten his meeting with Millicent back in Washington. In fact, he'd thought of her quite often.

"She's only in town for a few days. On business. Something to do with bad handling of her estate by her uncle. The gossips say Daniel

Geery manipulated the entire affair. That's only gossip but supported by one single thing. She's looking for a loan." He smiled. "I'm sure she would love to talk to you if you have fifty thousand dollars."

"That much?" Matthew said in awe. "She should sue her uncle if he absconded with those kind of funds."

"We're looking at that too," Henry said with a grin.

"We? So your information is more than just rumor," Matthew said.

"I'm not her only attorney. A Mr. Huggins of Petersburg and I are working together." Henry grew serious. "She is a fine woman, and I really do wish her the best, but how anyone in her position can come up with that kind of money is beyond me. The men of the South are being very cautious with their funds at present for obvious reasons. Rumor has it she's finding her path a very difficult climb."

Matthew had been only halfway listening. It had dawned on him that Judah Benjamin could get him the letter Walker needed, and Ninette might just be the way . . . "Excuse me, Hank. I feel the urge to dance."

"You know I hate that name, and Ninette won't dance with you. As I recall, she dropped you years ago."

"Miss Atwater might," Matthew said, working his way through the crowd and leaving Henry with a look of curiosity on his face.

Matthew approached the two women, stood halfway between them, and smiled. "Miss Benjamin, Miss Atwater, how are you this evening?" he said, bowing slightly.

Ninette looked down her nose at him and gave a forced smile. "Well, well, Matthew Alexander. Have you deserted, or are you just a coward come to hide?"

Matthew wanted to ring her neck but decided, good as it might feel, it wouldn't forward his aims and in fact might prevent them.

"I see you have put tongue to whetstone, Ninette. Sharp as ever." He turned to Miss Atwater. "Would you honor me with a dance."

Millie was shocked to actually see him standing in front of her and was momentarily speechless.

"She's with me, Matthew, and does not dance."

Millie glared at Ninette. She had no fondness toward her and wasn't about to let the woman put her in her pocket with some kind of idiotic statement. "Miss Benjamin, I have a tongue, and even better, I know how to use it," she snapped then looked at Matthew. "Yes, Mr. Alexander, I would love to dance with you."

Her answer seemed to shock Ninette, and Millie found pleasure in it. She took Matthew's hand, and they entered the dance floor.

"I would apologize for her, but I don't know her well enough to even consider trying to cover her horrid remarks," Millie said.

Matthew glanced at Ninette. His dancing with Millie was having the desired effect. "Ninette and I used to court. Once she dumps you she feels the need to walk up and down your back just to make sure you know your place."

Millie laughed. "Yes, she seems the type."

"And how have you come to know Ninette?"

"I met with her father today on business. He asked me to accompany her. It seems she has no friends in Richmond." She smiled. "It would surprise me if she had any friends at all. I have spent only an hour in her presence and cannot for the life of me see what anyone would see in the woman."

Matthew laughed. "Ouch."

"Oh, I'm sorry, Mr. Alexander, I did not mean . . . She's quite beautiful, and I'm sure—"

"It is quite all right, Miss Atwater, you are quite right about Ninette; her beauty runs only skin deep, and I thank God everyday that I came to my senses." He looked down at her. "I am glad you made it safely home. I hope all is well at your plantation?"

"It's not. My uncle has made a mess of my affairs." She looked up, forcing a smile. "But, it's nothing that cannot be fixed. And your journey, was it a safe one?"

"Safe enough." He apologized for stepping on her toe. "I am afraid dancing is not a part of the curriculum at the Academy, though we do rather well at a march."

"Quite a different cadence is my guess." Millie faked a grimace.

He chuckled. "Possibly." He attempted to turn her about and stepped on her toe again. She did not flinch, and he left the apology in his throat.

Matthew liked Millicent Atwater. She was not the raving beauty Ninette was, but there was something in her eyes and face that made him want to talk, to share with her. It was a beauty he could not really define, but it shined in her countenance and was most enticing and far more magical than most women. The dance came to its conclusion, and he bowed slightly. "Would you like to get some fresh air?" he asked.

"You read minds, then?" Millie said.

"A mere hobby, but I find it helpful at times."

"And what is Miss Benjamin thinking?"

He glanced over at Ninette only briefly. "That she would like to kill someone. It could be me, but I think not as the daggers coming from her eyes are bouncing off your back."

"Ah, I wondered what those sharp pains were," Millie said. "I assume her sudden hatred of me is your fault."

"Yes, I suppose so. I am sure she thought my approach was so that I could grovel at her feet. When I didn't, well, she looks for the reason, and in this case has rightly determined it is you. Now she feels the need to punish you."

"Well, at least the ride home won't be filled with her incessant chatter about herself. That certainly got old in a rush. How long did you court?"

"Six months. Makes you think I'm a mental case, doesn't it."

"You do read minds!"

He laughed then cleared his throat. "I fear to say that like most men, her beauty caused me temporary but quite complete insanity."

"But now, in my presence, you do not feel in danger of such?" Millie teased.

"Quite the contrary. I fear it even more," he said, looking at her. She had her arm through his, and he placed a hand on hers. She felt the warmth and flushed a little. The repartee she had considered fled. Instead, her eyes went to a passerby in an attempt to calm her feelings. Millie found Matthew Alexander a contradiction. He did not have the bombastic character of most avid secessionists, nor did he seem in any rush to justify the Southern position to her in attempt to have a convert, and yet here he was, seeking a commission at the very heart of Confederate belligerence. It made no sense to her.

They went through the doors to a large patio area where several couples visited. They spent the next hour deciding to call one another Matthew and Millie, talking about the Academy, and discussing her dreams for Beauchapel. In the midst of their enjoyment, there was a stir inside the house, and the name of Jefferson Davis drifted out to them.

"It seems the president has arrived," Matthew said. "Would you like to . . ."

"I'm quite comfortable here," she answered quickly. "But if you're interested, I shan't consider you a fool for it."

"The garden is more inviting. Would you like to take a walk?" He stood, and she joined him. They went down the steps as others rushed toward the house. They found a quiet, moonlit path and walked slowly away from the sound of Davis's speech.

"Tell me more about your parents," he said.

"They were fine, gentle people. Father was a gifted businessman and Mother a talented artist. I have many of her paintings hanging at the house. They were wonderful people. I miss them very much." He lay his hand on hers and squeezed it gently. "I'm sorry, Millie. I know how hard it is to lose a parent, but to lose both must be horrible."

Millie nodded but didn't speak for a moment, getting control of her emotions. "Tell me about your family."

"My father is gone as well. My mother lives at the home of my sister and brother-in-law in St. Louis. I have not seen them for quite sometime, and now I suppose it will be a bit longer."

"Because of the war. Yes, I suppose. Do they have the same convictions as you?"

Matthew wanted to say yes but knew he could not. As much as he wanted Millicent Atwater to know that he agreed with her, he must not. It would be dangerous. "No, I am afraid she and her husband have quite different feelings, as does my mother. They hoped I would stay loyal to the federal government, and Rand Hudson, my brother-in-law, is a major in the federal army."

"And do you have other family?" she asked.

"A brother. He serves in the Seventh Louisiana, but we have not had contact for months." He had no wish to discuss Adam, whom he considered a traitor. "And you? Do you have other brothers and sisters?"

"Mother had difficulty bearing children. Two were stillborn before I came. She could have no others." She sighed. "I supposed it's why I am so spoiled and must have my way," she said with a grin.

"*Spoiled* is not a word I would use to describe you, Millie," Matthew said.

They had reached the end of the path, where a white bench greeted them. They sat close to one another, and she continued clutching his arm.

"What words would you use then?" she asked.

"*Independent, determined.* A woman of strong will and conviction."

"Attributes most men would not want in their women," she replied.

"You remind me of Ann, my sister. She's probably the finest woman I know," Matthew said.

"Then I'm flattered."

Matthew looked into her eyes and could not help himself. He leaned close and kissed her gently on the lips. Her response was to put a hand on the back of his neck and pull him gently to her lips again. This time the kiss was longer, more heartfelt, but interrupted by someone clearing his throat. They quickly separated, and Matthew got to his feet to face Henry.

"Marvelous timing, *Hank*," he said.

"Yes, well, I would apologize, but I've been sent by her majesty, Queen Ninette."

"Ah, that explains everything," Matthew said with some irritation.

Henry looked at Millie, who had also stood and was patting at her hair, a pleasant flush to her face. "I do apologize, Miss Atwater, but it seems Miss Benjamin is ready to leave and says that you are to accompany her."

"She isn't capable of leaving alone?" Millie asked sharply.

Henry smiled at Millie. "It seems she came in your carriage."

Millie laughed lightly. "Oh, yes, I had forgotten. Please tell her I'll be there shortly."

Henry turned and left, throwing a curious glance at Matthew. When he was out of sight, Millie turned into Matthew, took his arms, and placed them around her before laying her head against his shoulder.

"Someone I met before leaving Washington said I should thank for your help with the destruction of Rose Greenhow's letter," she said.

"Really? And who might have said such a thing?"

"His name is Polanski." She looked up at him. "You were quite right. They had been following Rose and saw us at breakfast that morning. They searched my possessions before letting me board the steamer." She smiled. "I think they also searched Uncle Richard's; he was delayed for nearly a week."

Matthew was enjoying their closeness but allowed himself a smile. Joe had received his message.

"Thank you for a wonderful evening, Matthew." She looked up at him, and they kissed again. Then he held her close for a long moment before she took his arm, and they walked back toward the house. "I'll be honest with you. After riding here with Ninette, I had hoped for a quick conclusion to the evening; now I find myself unhappy at it having to end at all."

"Then we must see one another again," Matthew said.

"I am afraid I must return home early in the morning. Possibly when I come to town again, but that may not be for sometime, I'm afraid. You're always welcome at Beauchapel. I hope you will come. It's a wonderful, peaceful place."

"I will. I promise." As they reached the bottom of the stairs leading to the raised veranda, he kissed her hand gently when he saw Beth Van Lew coming down the wide steps. She saw them and smiled, giving Matthew a moment's apprehension until he realized she was smiling at Millie.

"Millie, dear girl, how are you?"

"Elizabeth!" Millie said with a wide smile and extended hands. They hugged as Matthew watched, a bit perplexed. "I thought I saw you earlier. It's good to see you. How is your mother?" Millie asked.

"Fine, fine. My goodness it has been a year or better. How was Europe?"

"Interesting, but I am glad to be back." She turned to Matthew. "This is Matthew Alexander from New Orleans. He is seeking a place in the government."

Beth kept her face passive. "I have met Mr. Alexander. He is Henry's friend, and we were introduced earlier." She smiled then concentrated on Millie.

"And where are you staying? You know my house has plenty of rooms, and to spend money on a hotel is silly."

"I'm sorry, Beth, but I didn't want to intrude."

"Nonsense. If you come again you will stay with us, is that understood?" She looked at Matthew. "Tell her, Mr. Alexander. It is a waste of good money for her to stay in a hotel, isn't it!"

"Yes, it would be," Matthew said with a smile.

"Then it's settled. I'm sorry I don't have more time to talk, dear girl. Stop by and see me before you leave. It is wonderful to see you. Good-bye to you both." With that she went along to the path where carriages awaited their owners.

"An interesting woman," Matthew said with a slight smile.

"Very. She loves to come to these parties just to raise eyebrows. She's an abolitionist, and you know how everyone in Richmond feels about abolitionists." She smiled. "But she's really quite harmless and as fine a woman as I have known."

"Millicent, there you are."

They looked up to see Ninette at the top of the steps.

"Was that that horrible Van Lew person? How embarrassing for you! Come along, now," Ninette said. "I really must get home." With that she turned and walked away, treating Millie as if she were some kind of servant and without even acknowledging Matthew's existence.

"Mr. Alexander, I think I shall challenge Miss Benjamin to a duel," Millie said with some frustration.

"A duel?" Matthew said with a wry smile.

"Yes. At least that way one of us would be put out of misery before I have to climb into that carriage." She gave a tired smile and turned into him, kissing him lightly on the cheek. "Good night, Matthew. I do want to see you again. Come to Beauchapel soon. Please." She lifted her dress to take the steps two at a time and was soon running across the veranda toward the house, then she disappeared inside.

He had never met a woman quite like Millie Atwater, and he wondered just exactly where Beauchapel might be.

* * *

Matthew didn't go home immediately. Instead, he had the carriage driver take him to the street in which Elizabeth Van Lew lived.

The carriage pulled up to the curb, and Matthew paid the driver then asked him to return in an hour's time. If he did, Matthew would give him a handsome retainer. Once the carriage disappeared along the dark street, Matthew walked several blocks to the address Beth had given him.

The house was a two-story white mansion. Half a dozen round columns fronted a wide porch and held a thick roof at the top of the second story. Three gas-powered chandeliers hung from the high ceiling of the porch. It was a bold, powerful, stately home that spoke of a good deal of wealth while carrying the personality of its owner. There were rows of well-lit windows on both levels, and a maid was just pulling the curtains in the rooms on the second floor when Matthew walked past the house. He turned down a side street and finally slipped into the shadows, climbed over a six-foot stone fence, and crept through the trees and a small flower garden before stepping up the dark back stairs and knocking on the door. He was quickly let in by a house servant.

Beth Van Lew greeted him in the entry then took him in the sitting room, where he was greeted by a half a dozen men.

"Gentlemen, this man has come from Washington. Shall we shoot him or shake his hand?"

One man reached inside his jacket then smiled and stepped forward extending his hand. "Welcome," he said, "What can we do to help?"

Matthew started breathing again.

Chapter Fifteen

RAND DIDN'T STAY IN BED long. Ann found him in the sitting room the morning after his return, pacing, wondering what had gone wrong, worried about his men, how many he'd lost, where they were, and if they were being cared for. After only a week at home, and against her wishes, he'd asked Mose to bring up a carriage at eight in the morning, and soon he and Isaac were headed in the direction of Fort Corcoran to see to their worries.

When they'd arrived, Sherman sent them directly back to their carriage and told them not to come back until they were fit for duty. But they didn't exactly obey the order. Instead, they wandered about the fort and the growing tent encampment around it looking for their men. By noon, they were both exhausted, but they'd found more than one hundred fifty of the Missouri boys. Rand had called a meeting at the parade ground at three that day then sent all of them searching the city for any remaining stragglers. He slept in the carriage until the appointed hour and then spoke to nearly two hundred of his men. He told them he appreciated their service but reminded them that they'd been thoroughly trounced and he didn't intend to have it happen again. If they didn't wish to be worked hard, they could transfer to other units with his blessing, but he wanted no slackers for what lay ahead.

Ann sat in the shadows of the carriage. She watched as soldiers from other units stopped to listen, and she had watched their reactions. Rand had a gift for forthright honesty. He didn't hide behind his officer's stripes but spoke with a conviction that settled into the minds and hearts of others. And he never spoke anything but the truth. At that moment she realized how much he had to offer, how his leadership could make a difference. Though her fears wanted him to resign and take her back to Missouri, she knew that doing so would break him.

They had ridden home quietly, Rand and Isaac too weak and she too fearful to speak. Since then she had prayed fervently for the ability to be strong for him and for the war effort. Otherwise she would just mope about until she became paralyzed. A few days later, when he'd gone back to his men and his duty permanently, she had gone off to the hospitals bearing books and socks and a listening ear. When most of the injured were well enough to go back to their units or return home, she had offered her services to Dorothea Dix, who asked her to help at one of the medical supply depots. She was busy now, and it made a big difference, both to her and to Rand. War was a horrible thing, and one did not survive it by sitting about, worrying. Keep busy. She must just keep busy.

* * *

Matthew sat on the divan in the Benjamin mansion waiting for Ninette to join him. The letter had come the morning after the party at the Seddon mansion. It literally oozed kindness and a desire to see him again while opening the door for him to call as soon as he could. He had decided to come unannounced. Ninette hated it when people came unannounced. But it was not Ninette that Matthew wanted to see. It was her father.

With Henry's help, Matthew had learned Judah Benjamin's schedule, a schedule Matthew knew the Confederate attorney general would adhere to fanatically unless he had changed his nature since living in New Orleans. The man was obsessive when it came to time, and Matthew intended to use that obsession to get a meeting with him. Leroy Walker would be hard pressed to ignore this recommendation.

Judah Benjamin was Jewish and had moved to New Orleans from North Carolina to practice law. When he was twenty-two, he married Natalie Bauché de St. Martin, the sixteen-year-old Catholic daughter of a prominent and wealthy New Orleans French Creole family—no small thing for a man of Jewish heritage. But Benjamin was not one who wore his Jewish background on his sleeve, then or now, and they were married in a Roman Catholic ceremony at the St. Louis Cathedral. Shortly thereafter, he purchased a sugar cane plantation in Belle Chasse, Louisiana, and became a slaveholder. His plantation and legal practice were both very successful.

Natalie Benjamin had trouble giving birth, but nine years after their marriage, she was finally able to give her husband their only child, Ninette. When the couple became estranged in 1847, Natalie took Ninette and moved to Paris, France. Benjamin traveled there each summer to see them, and once Ninette was old enough to travel alone, she spent some winters in Louisiana. It was during one of those winters that Matthew met and courted the beautiful Ninette.

Judah Benjamin launched his political career in 1845 when he was elected to the US Senate by the state legislature. He became famous as an orator and was the first Jewish American to be nominated to the Supreme Court, a nomination which he declined. A strong adherent of slavery, Benjamin was once called "a Hebrew with Egyptian principles." He was one of the first to resign from his congressional position when the Southern states began declaring their secession.

Matthew spied Ninette's short, stocky father, with a round, almost pudgy shaven face, as he came into the entryway where a house slave met him to take his hat and cane. He asked several questions without noticing Matthew's presence but was brought up short when the servant leaned over a bit and whispered something. Benjamin looked at Matthew curiously then forced a smile as he strode from the entry into the sitting room to greet his unexpected guest.

"Matthew Alexander," Benjamin said. "What a surprise." He extended his chubby hand for shaking. Matthew was already on his feet and took the hand.

"Mr. Benjamin, it's nice to see you again. I apologize for coming unannounced, but Ninette insisted she wanted to . . ." He intentionally let his voice trail off.

"Ninette asked you to come?" Benjamin said, his face showing a little confusion. "Well, she is a precocious woman, and one with a mind of her own. So much like her mother. How is your family?"

"Well, but unfortunately, my mother is living in St. Louis. But then it's where she ought to be, I suppose. Her only daughter, my sister Ann, married a man from that city." Matthew knew Benjamin well enough to be up front about Ann's whereabouts. Any man who showed an interest in Ninette was carefully scrutinized by her obsessive father, and if Matthew asked for a recommendation, he was doubly sure Benjamin would learn all he could.

"Ah, how wonderful for her. An abolitionist?" Benjamin said with a forced smile.

"Unfortunately, yes. I believe you used to do business with him. Randolph Hudson." It was no secret that Hudson Shipping had more steamers along the Mississippi than any other company. Nor was it a secret that most Southern plantation owners used Hudson's steamers to move their cotton, sugar, and other products to Northern markets.

Benjamin lost the smile. "Yes, *used to* is the correct phrase, that is certain. His politics—"

"Are certainly different than ours," Matthew said, feigning strong dislike. "I haven't spoken to my sister since her disastrous decision," Matthew said. He hadn't spoken to Ann personally since her marriage, but he was quite pleased with her decision.

"You have left the Academy and come to Richmond. I assume you have a position here?" Benjamin said.

"Henry Hyde Jr. and General Lee are supporting me for a recommendation for a commission in the war department. My studies in tactics at the Academy and my experience with Lee at Harpers Ferry—"

"You were with Lee at Harpers Ferry? The man will win the war for us, and Mr. Hyde is a good judge of men. Both will help you a good deal." His tone seemed to soften, and he pointed at the divan and Matthew sat. Judah placed himself in a chair a few feet away.

"My daughter hasn't said much about the two of you lately. Of course, she spends most of her time in Paris with her mother, but, well, I really must ask, is this some sort of reconciliation?"

"One can only hope so. We saw one another the other night at the Seddon party. I received a note a few days later and was overjoyed by it. I have always thought highly of Ninette," he lied.

Mr. Benjamin cleared his throat. "And your finances?"

Now came an even bigger lie. "They have changed a good deal. My father's estate was finally able to sell a very large piece of land we held in New York State. My brother and I will inherit most of the two hundred and fifty thousand dollars, but with the change in governments, it will take some time. As you know all transactions have to be done through England these days, and I have yet to instruct our bank in New York just where to send it." He smiled. Adam's regiment was somewhere in South Carolina, and unless fate were really against him, Matthew didn't think his brother would learn of this little ploy and make his deception known. And some funds *were* on the way. One of the messages he sent to Pinkerton through Miss Van Lew's courier system was for a large enough sum of money to continue his ruse.

Benjamin's countenance lit up as if he had seen a vision. "How wonderful for you, and how do you intend to invest it?"

"In land, of course. I would hope that you would give me some guidance. I know of no other man that I respect more when it comes to such things. Your plantation cost you a small fortune, yet you paid it off in only ten years, and it is well known that your other investments have added a good deal to your wealth."

The flattery seemed to puff up Judah's barrel-like chest as if someone had blown hot air into him. "I would be more than happy to do so," he answered. It was common knowledge that he very much wanted to get Ninette married to someone on this continent and had done his very best to make a half dozen matches that never seemed to quite pan out—mostly due to Ninette. The man was headed for another disappointment.

"Thank you. I hope to have the funds in a few months. However, if I don't get that commission, I'll attach myself to the Seventh Regiment and be indisposed for sometime."

"Then we must get you that commission. Would a letter from someone as unimportant as myself be of help?" Benjamin feigned humility.

"You are too modest, Mr. Benjamin. I feel that a letter from you would assure it." Matthew didn't know that it would. Henry had learned that Benjamin and Walker were often at odds concerning the war and that Walker was even considering resigning. But President Davis trusted Judah Benjamin more than he trusted most others, and if Walker resigned, Benjamin or someone close to him would be Walker's replacement. Benjamin's letter might not have an immediate effect, but it would have the effect Matthew desired.

"Then you shall have it," Benjamin said.

"I am most grateful," Matthew said.

"Now, about Ninette," Benjamin said, glancing toward the entry then moving his chair closer. "She has never stopped loving you, Matthew. I hope you understand that. Her, uh . . . need to move on was simply a matter of, uh . . . future."

"I understand, and I would not have come today if I couldn't give her exactly what she deserves," Matthew assured him.

"Good, good. She is a beautiful woman, and there are so many offers for her hand, but with this new development in your finances, well, I know she'll be relieved and quite happy to renew your, uh . . . relationship."

Matthew faked concern with a raise of the brow. "Until the money arrives, it may be best to keep it to ourselves. Though it now sits in a safe place, the war has caused some delay of exchange. As you are aware everything is in turmoil and—"

"Yes, yes, I understand. I have funds invested in mills up north, and it is proving to be of great concern."

"My honor will not allow me to make any promises to Ninette—or to you—until the money arrives safely from New York. For now, I ask only that you allow me to see Ninette as occasion permits. After all, in the end it really is her decision, and if her interests lie elsewhere . . ." He shrugged. "There is little to do but to mourn my loss."

"I am sure she will be elated, and you have my permission and my blessing." He leaned forward as if to speak in confidence. "A little advice, my boy. Your money may be safer in New York, at least for now. I would advise care in its transfer until things settle a bit. And Ninette is going back to Paris for a few months. By then we will have a clear picture of events and can move forward with confidence."

Matthew had to hide both his shock and his pleasure at these revelations. Here was one of the leaders of the new Confederacy suggesting that his money would be better off in a Union bank than in a Confederate one! And not to have to deal with Ninette in the near future was something else he was elated with. His luck was holding.

"I'm disappointed that Ninette is leaving, but you're quite right, and I thank you, sir, for counsel about the funds. May I converse with you as a way of keeping well informed in such, uh . . . timing?"

"You may," Benjamin said.

Judah Benjamin stood, seemingly pleased at the prospect of the future. They shook hands, and he left the room, a new energy in his step. Matthew only smiled. It could not have gone better.

He heard Ninette dressing down a servant as she came down the stairs, and Matthew prepared himself for the next act while noting that it was actually a good deal of fun making fools of the arrogant rich.

As she entered, her dark countenance immediately brightened. Ninette's greatest gift was her ability as a social chameleon to change her entire demeanor to suit any opportunity in the time it took most people to blink.

"Matthew, how nice to see you," she said, her voice oozing friendship. She held out her hand, and Matthew crossed the sitting room to take it and kiss it lightly. As he lifted his head, he looked over Ninette's shoulder. The door to the study creaked open a few inches. Apparently Mr. Benjamin's interest had been piqued.

"Ninette, you look lovely as ever." She was a beautiful and very passionate woman, and she used those attributes as skillfully as a swordsman who had perfected every part of his skill. She could tease one into submission and then rip his heart out as easy as a lion playing with its prey.

She put her arm through his and pulled him close, her warmth and softness pressing against him. She took him to the divan even as she spoke.

"Billie, please close the doors. Mr. Alexander and I wish to be alone."

Billie was Ninette's personal female slave and immediately materialized out of nowhere. Matthew could only wonder at the treatment poor Billie received from Miss Ninette Benjamin, but it showed in Billie's eyes—nervous, frightened, fearful. Matthew felt anger as Billie quickly closed the doors and Ninette sat on the divan and patted a spot next to her, indicating Matthew should join her. Matthew remained standing. He saw the cold look of disapproval, but it was quickly replaced with her famous pout.

"You do not wish to sit with me?"

He did not. Now that he had what he'd come for, he wanted to give her a good tongue-lashing and be done with her, but he couldn't, not yet. It took all of his self-restraint to resist. "I am afraid that such close proximity would only be a danger to my honor." He took a step and sat in the chair to her left, the one Judah Benjamin had vacated only moments earlier.

"You are such a beast, Matthew Alexander," she pouted.

The door opened, and another servant brought in a tray with a teapot, cups, and sweetbreads. He put them on the table in front of the divan then quickly left the room, closing the doors. Ninette poured tea and put sugar and cream in each cup. Matthew took his when offered and sipped.

"How are things in Paris?" he asked.

"Beautiful, wonderful, *merveilleux*, as they would say in France. I miss it dearly and must return soon or die of a broken heart."

"My, such a love affair is to be envied," Matthew said.

She sipped her tea, her eyes looking at him over the rim of the cup. She lowered it to the saucer in her other hand before speaking. "So what are *your* plans, Matthew?"

The question actually bordered on sincere, but Matthew knew Ninette was only beginning to build her web. He'd been trapped in it before, knew exactly what to expect, but Ninette's physical gifts too often made one ignore such machinations. Men simply could not help themselves when it came to Ninette. Women on the other hand, despised her. Most because they simply didn't have a chance when Ninette was in the room. Others, like Millie, despised her because they saw how shallow Ninette really was.

"To do all I can to support the Confederacy," Matthew said, taking another sip.

"Henry says you are seeking a commission in the government's new war department. Surely that will take some very high recommendations. If—"

"Actually, I have what I need and will present my credentials soon," Matthew said. He sat his cup in its saucer and then put both on the table. "I'm sorry that I don't have much time today. I have an appointment with General Lee. His letter should be ready to pick up by now."

"General Robert E. Lee? You know him that well?"

"I served with him at Harpers Ferry," Matthew told her.

"Which begs the question, why are you not applying for a military command? Isn't that the quickest way to honor and fame?" she asked coquettishly.

He explained the accident to his eye. "The doctor has said my service in the field is over, but I still wish to aid our cause. General Lee feels I can in the war department."

"If anyone knows where your talents could aid our new government the most, it would be General Lee," she said.

"You know him as well?"

"We've met." She leaned forward as if to share a secret. "My father says he will leave Richmond soon. Things are growing troublesome in the western part of Virginia, and Lee will be sent to keep those rebellious fools in the Confederacy."

A tasty morsel, Matthew thought. "Well, if anyone can do it, General Lee can." He pulled out his watch then stood. "I mustn't be late."

"Of course not." Ninette was quickly on her feet in front of him, her dark eyes looking into his and even showing a little moisture.

"I must see you again, Matthew. I *need* to see you again." She put her hand on his shirt collar and touched his throat with one finger. The smell of her hair brought a rush of memories, the passion, the touch of lips and soft skin. Sensing his sudden desire, she put her arms around his neck and kissed him passionately. He tried to resist but couldn't and finally pulled her to him and responded with an old and disquieted passion of his own. Then she pushed away, straightened her hair, and headed for the door. As she opened it, she glanced over her shoulder, gave a wry smile of conquest, and spoke. "We shan't see one another again, Matthew. Good-bye." Her power confirmed, she was gone.

Matthew could only smile. She was the most irresistible woman he had ever known, but there were none who could be as cold and calculating as Ninette Benjamin. In her mind, she had made him pay for his treatment of her—leading him to the trough, letting him sip a little, only to jerk away, leaving him thirsty.

He walked to the entry, where another slave waited, Matthew's hat in hand. He also handed Matthew a letter of recommendation signed by Judah Benjamin.

"Mr. Benjamin said to see that you received it. He was called away. He hopes to see you often in the presence of his daughter once she returns from Paris." He bowed slightly, and Matthew thanked him. In his departure, he glanced to the top of the stairs to see Ninette standing there, arms folded—the defiant pose of the conqueror. He put on his bowler hat and tipped it lightly to her, waved the letter lightly before putting it in his pocket with a smile, then exited the door.

As he climbed in the carriage, he was relieved. She had set him aside once more, and Judah Benjamin couldn't fault him for it. It was she who had said good-bye.

Climbing into the carriage loaned to him by Henry Hyde, he sat back in his seat, looking at the sealed letter. He had what he'd come for.

* * *

Millie was relaxing after a long day's work. Sitting on the front porch in her mother's well-used rocking chair, she was enjoying the soft fall breeze that spoke of a change to winter. Suddenly, the sound of singing then the clatter and thump of what she knew to be another large group of men forced her out of her reverie to look down the road. Her workers came from behind the house as well, watching from the railed fence that separated her land from the road.

It was the third group in the last few days. The road would take them northeast down the peninsula, where fortifications were being thrown up on plantations that bordered the Chickahominy River. Even the farm of Horatio Clay was being used, and he was one of the most prominent plantation owners in Virginia. Though she did not know them well, she knew this would be a blow to the Clays economically. One couldn't till ground occupied by battlements and campgrounds.

She pushed the thought aside. The Chickahominy was still a good distance from Beauchapel. She concentrated on the seemingly endless rows of soldiers passing along the road. As always, they were a motley mass of men dressed in all kinds of clothing, carrying weapons and loaded down with packs stuffed with personal items to make their lives more comfortable in their gallant search for glory. The first group, much smaller than this one, had come to the house looking for water and a rest. She had ordered her workers to provide buckets from the well and doled out what fresh bread she had while prying them with questions. She discovered that most were from Mississippi or Louisiana and were surrounding Richmond so as to "keep the Yanks out of the Southern states."

"Won't take long," one of them added. "Yanks is chicken to come down and fight us country boys. See how they run at Manassas. Cluck, cluck," he mocked, "Chickens, pure and simple."

The group had laughed, and another had chimed in. "They know we'd skin 'em like raccoons and eat 'em fer lunch."

Millie wondered if most of them wouldn't die long before the Chickahominy under the weight of such comforts and their own misplaced pride.

Now she watched as the third group passed by. The number indicated more and more men wanted in; the chance for good pay, recognition, even glory too hard to resist. They could tell their grandchildren they'd fought to free the South and won. Or maybe they'd have to tell them they'd lost. But she was sure that either way, the story would be told with bravado and relish.

A few saw her and waved as greeting a neighbor on a morning stroll. When the last of them disappeared over a distant hill and the dust began to settle, her workers went back to the chores, and she went back to her rocker. Her uncle should be arriving soon.

She had tried to get a loan from a dozen different men, all to no avail. But there were others, and both Mr. Huggins, her local attorney, and Henry Hyde Jr., in Richmond, were still looking into them. Both had recommended that she sue her uncle. That would be part of the discussion today. He wouldn't take the news well.

Daniel Geery was coming with him, as was Geery's attorney. The time had come to get everything in the open. Geery was still talking to others as if he was courting her, and it rankled her a good deal. She had turned down his requests to call, and she hoped to end it completely today; yet she must be cautious. She must do everything she could to save Beauchapel.

The carriage appeared in the distance and was soon making its way up the lane to the house. Millie stood, bracing herself for what was to come.

The coachman came down from his perch and opened the door. Her uncle was the first to step out, then Geery, and finally Geery's lawyer. She gave her uncle a forced but pleasant smile and a hug, ignored Geery, and greeted the lawyer. Geery seemed quite sure of himself and unconcerned by the snub. His smile was pleasant but did not deceive her. This was a man with a black heart, and she would be watchful.

"Gentlemen," she said planting a smile on her lips. "Please, come inside. Uncle, I know it was a long trip from Richmond, and you must be tired and thirsty." She took them in the sitting room, where several brands of liquor waited—along with Mr. Huggins. She introduced them all while a servant prepared their requested drinks. Millie noted that Geery took no liquor, but she waited for her uncle and Geery's attorney to satiate their thirst before speaking. It was time to get to business.

"Mr. Geery, it seems you have some papers you feel give you a right to this plantation. May I see them please?"

Geery smiled—if you could call anything formed by his lips a smile—and nodded to her uncle Richard's attorney, who opened a valise and removed some papers. Millie noted with some satisfaction that her uncle could not bring his eyes to meet hers. He had been a greedy fool, and now it had come back to haunt them both.

Millie took the papers as the lawyer began to explain them, but Millie raised a hand to bring him up short. "I am quite capable of reading, Mr. Blunck. If you gentlemen will be patient, Mr. Huggins and I will review these papers in my study. We will only be a moment." She gave no smile and left the room, crossing the entry, entering her study, and closing the door behind her attorney after he entered.

She turned the papers over to him and let him read them carefully. Fifteen minutes later Huggins looked up, a troubled, near hopeless look on his face. "It is as I feared Millicent. His hold is very solid. I see nothing that would allow us to challenge it in a court of law."

"And the date of payment is as you were told?"

"Yes. January seventh of the coming year."

Millie felt sick but was prepared. "Then we still have time." She left the study and went back to the sitting room. She must be pleasant, at least outwardly, to Daniel Geery. But inwardly she could not help but despise him.

"It seems I have a debt to clear with you, Mr. Geery. You will have your payment by the date given in these documents."

Geery stood slowly, savoring the moment. "Miss Atwater, I do not wish to hurt you. I have sufficient lands and money that I do not *need* that which belongs to you. Surely, you can see that the long-term solution for everyone lies in a union between our two families. In that case you will never need to worry about losing Beauchapel again."

Millie felt like throwing up but kept her face unchanged.

"I am flattered, but that is quite out of the question. I have no interest in you, Mr. Geery." She turned to her uncle. "Mr. Hyde of Richmond has been instructed to begin a suit against you, Uncle Richard. If you do not wish the humiliation of such a public suit, I suggest that you sell your property and see that the debt is paid no later than Thanksgiving Day."

Her uncle seemed to stop breathing, his face falling a bit. "But, surely you see—"

"I see that you have acted against my best interests for your own personal gain. You have gone so far as to break the law, claiming false debts were incurred at this plantation. That debt was yours, not mine, and if you wish to make amends, you will arrange for a repayment of at least 50 percent of Mr. Geery's money before the date given on this document." She forced a smile. "You can go to jail, and do not think for a moment that I will not put you there."

"But I . . . I do not know where—" Her uncle started to opine.

"Why, Uncle, you will sell your Richmond home."

"But I will be on the street, humiliated and—"

"A soldier needs no home, Uncle."

"You expect me to join the army? But I have no—"

"Then live on the street. It's your choice. But joining the army will help you save face while paying your portion of this debt. I do not care about the former, but I demand the latter."

"Now see here, I will not be blackmailed—"

"I am not blackmailing you, Uncle. You stole from me, and you will repay it. Mr. Hyde has already placed a lien on your home, and if you do not sell it, he will do it for you. You have until Thanksgiving, no longer."

"She is quite right," Geery said. "Your property should be sold."

My, how quickly the devil deserts his own, Millie thought. But she kept it to herself. "There, you see, Mr. Geery and I do agree on something," Millie said with a hard smile.

"But I cannot . . . I . . . I . . ."

"I am resolved, Uncle," Millie said firmly. "Either you agree, or I will sue you and take your shirt and pants as well as your house. Do you understand?"

Her uncle collapsed into the chair, the despondent look on his face giving Millie a good deal of satisfaction. Now to Geery.

"Our business is finished, Mr. Geery. You will not come onto this property again without my express invitation. You knew what you were doing when you loaned Uncle Richard that money, and I will countenance no such chicanery. You will have your payment by the seventh of January, but I will have no more to do with you. Now if you will excuse—"

"Mr. Blunck," Geery said with an evil smile. "Possibly you should inform Miss Atwater of the addendum."

Millie felt her stomach wrench. "What are you talking about? What addendum," she said without changing expression.

Blunck handed her a paper. "An addendum. Signed by your uncle. Mr. Geery's debt includes rights to administer this property until the debt is paid. He must be consulted on every decision made concerning the property and has the controlling voice of what can and cannot be sold, including slaves." He cleared his throat. "We understand that you have freed yours without his permission. That makes your decision null and void by contract."

She felt her stomach turn over and even had to fight dizziness.

She turned and glared at her uncle. "I made it clear to my uncle that he had no right to sign anything concerning Beauchapel."

"I am afraid he does, or did, until you actually began running the property. It's in your father's will, and those papers were signed in Washington before you returned home."

Millie now understood what Geery was really doing in Washington and why her uncle rushed her off to Europe before she could start running Beauchapel. She also remembered being read the will by her uncle. He had obviously left out one of its most important paragraphs.

"However, we agree that he did not have the right to use the money Mr. Geery loaned him to pay his own debts. Mr. Geery had the understanding that the money would be used to improve the property and Beauchapel."

Her uncle came quickly and angrily to his feet. "That's a lie!" he shouted at Geery. "You knew exactly what I was doing with that money! You . . . you said—"

"Sit down, Uncle!" Millie said firmly. She felt to panic but forced herself to remain calm, to think.

The attorney spoke. "I assure you, Miss Atwater, Mr. Geery had no knowledge of—"

"Mr. Geery has a tongue, Mr. Blunck. Let *him* deny it!" Her uncle responded vehemently.

"I do deny it," Geery said evenly and without emotion. He never took his eye off of Millie as he spoke, and she could see he was measuring her, calculating.

"Your attorney can verify that the paperwork is in order if you like."

Millie felt sick. Though she knew this man to be shrewd and cunning, she had still underestimated him. She handed a pale Huggins the latest document, and Huggins scanned it carefully. "It seems legal, but I would have to do some research . . ."

Geery was still looking at Millie. "He can waste your time and money, or we can resolve this now."

Millies head was spinning, and she could not think clearly. She prayed silently for guidance and then took a deep breath. "We will need a few days to verify your papers."

She saw a flash of doubt in Geery's eyes, but it was gone quickly. "You will find them in complete order."

Mr. Blunck spoke again. "Until then nothing is to be sold without Mr. Geery's permission. The constable has been apprised of the addendum and will enforce it. Your slaves should be told they are no longer free and every effort made to keep them on the plantation. If they are lost, the cost will be added to your present debt."

"Then I will sell immediately to another and the debt paid. I will countenance no interference in my affairs here, none."

Gerry gave a haughty smile. "I think you will find that the latest addendum also states that the first right of refusal is mine. If you decide to sell, I will buy the property, giving you only the difference between the debt amount and the appraised value." He gave as pleasant a smile as such a man could. As if by mechanical means, his smile softened. "However, there is another option. A union between our families." He paused. "Give me time, Miss Atwater. I will show you that I can be a generous man. I have only the best interests of you and your property at heart. Though I know you despise what may look like chicanery to you, it's only business and quite separate from my feelings for you. I truly hope you will not sell, but give me the chance to win your heart and satisfy everyone's needs. I must say there is no other in the entire state of Virginia that can provide more completely for you than I. You will never want for anything and will be accepted among the most prominent families of this state and the Confederacy. You will have only the finest things money can buy and so will any children that come by our union. That is my solemn word to you."

Millie was sure steam must be coming out of her ears. "You fool! Do you honestly believe that I would marry the very man who is consciously trying to destroy me? Get out, Mr. Geery. Get out now, and do not darken my door again!"

Geery's face darkened, and both her uncle and Blunck paled. "You will regret this, Millicent!" Geery hissed.

"I will regret it more if I have to stand in your presence even one more instant. Go!"

Geery's expression tightened, his eyes filling with fire, and he stepped toward her with a doubled-up fist when Blunck grabbed his arm and pulled him away toward the door.

"And Mr. Geery, if I hear one more rumor that you and I are somehow courting, I will sue you for defamation of character!"

Geery cursed her as Blunck pulled him from the house and to their carriage, his ranting chilling the air. If the devil himself had been leashed from hell, it could have been no worse. Finally, the carriage driver whipped the horses, and they bolted for the gate. Millie stood there, angry, her hands in fists as if to defy him to return.

Finally, Huggins spoke softly. "You have made the worst possible enemy, Millicent."

Millie blinked several times then turned back into the house, where her uncle was standing, pale, his mouth agape.

"Uncle, you will wait in the study," she hissed as she darted by. She went immediately up to her bedroom and closed the door behind her. She paced back and forth, angry and upset beyond words.

A knock came at the door, and she asked who it was.

"Tiera, Missy. May I come in?"

"Of course, Tiera."

The black servant entered and quickly began helping Millie undo her formal attire. "Missy, I hear it all. Yo' uncle has done yo' dirt, tha's fo' sure, and if'n yo' want I take dat gun a yo' pappy's and shoot him right now!"

The edges of Mille's lips twitched in an attempt at a smile. "I shall reserve that honor to myself, Tiera. Is Mr. Huggins still with us?"

"Yes'm. He say he wait." She helped Millie step out of her dress. "I heard what dat lawya say about us bein' free. You doan worry none 'bout dat. We intends t' stay and work fo' dat freedom sure as de good Lor' come again and save us all! We know you find a way, Missy. We know it, and we wait fo' it." She hung up the dress as Millie removed her pantaloons and pulled on pants and a shirt. After dressing, Millie hugged her and left the room, going back down to the study where her uncle and Mr. Huggins waited. From the tension still hanging in the air, Millie knew they had not spoken to one another.

Now under control, Millie spoke in an even voice. "Uncle, I meant what I said. Sell you land or Mr. Huggins and my attorney in Richmond will sue you. I want that money by Thanksgiving."

"Millie, you can't do this to me. I had no intention—Geery is lying. He knew exactly—"

"Yes, I know he knew what he was doing, but the fact that you let him do it is unforgivable. Now get out of my house, and do not return— ever. Do you understand me?" She pointed at the door to be sure he knew the way.

He turned on his heel, fuming, then turned back. "I have no way back to the train station."

"Walk, Uncle! It'll be the first honest thing you've done since my parents passed. Go!"

He left, and the screen door banged behind him. She went to the window and watched him trudge angrily down the lane. She disliked herself for her meanness but knew it must be so. There must be consequences or he would just go on being the fool. She turned back to Huggins.

"I'm surprised you didn't know of the addendum," she said evenly.

"If it *was* filed, it was filed in Washington. I had no idea."

"And if it wasn't filed, but kept secret until now, is it still a legal document?"

Huggins managed a smile. "You amaze me, Millicent. No, if it wasn't filed, it would not be a legal document. But with the war . . . I . . . I'm not sure how to find out. I can send a letter to a fellow I have done business with before, but there's no guarantee that the letter will ever arrive or that he'll do anything with it if it does."

Millie paced, thinking. "I know a gentleman who has just come from New York and who is trying to sell some land in that state. Possibly he has contacts there that can give me some assistance."

Huggins nodded. "I'll mail my letter tomorrow, but the more channels we use the better chance we have of finding out what we need to know." He took a deep breath. "But what if it has been filed?"

"I don't know," she said softly.

There was a long silence before Huggins spoke again. "Geery is the most vengeful of men. Have you sold your crop?"

She shook her head as the sudden realization of what she had done hit her.

"I fear that he will make certain you get no market. If he makes his feelings known . . . well, if Daniel Geery is good at anything it's at intimidation. Now he'll stop at nothing to destroy you."

She closed her eyes and nodded.

"I must get back to town. I will inform you if I hear anything about the filing of that addendum. I hope your friend can send a letter soon as well." He picked up his hat and Millie faced him, forcing a stop to her self-hate long enough to give him the warm hug and peck on the cheek he deserved.

"You are a good friend, Mr. Huggins." She put a hand through his elbow and accompanied him through the kitchen and out to the barn, where his horse waited. She had seen that moment of doubt in Geery's eyes when he announced the addendum in perfect order. It may be nothing, but it could be everything.

"Fantow," she said to one of the workers. "Saddle a extra horse to send with Mr. Huggins. My uncle should have sore feet by now and could probably use a mount. Mr. Huggins, tell him to leave the horse at the livery and I'll pick it up tomorrow when I go to town to catch the train to Richmond."

"Your heart is showing, Millicent," Huggins said with a smile. "And why to Richmond?"

She was already heading back to the house and spoke over her shoulder. "To get that letter sent, Mr. Huggins." She waved good-bye and went back into the house. She had no idea of exactly how to find Matthew Alexander, but she must.

And she wanted to very, very badly.

Chapter Sixteen

LIZZY STOPPED HER WORK BRIEFLY to watch the sun come up over the eastern hills and light the bank of mist hanging low over the fields behind the barns. She loved this time of morning. The waking of the birds and smell of the damp soil all engendered memories and a sort of peaceful loneliness that made her both melancholy and happy. The first smells of fall were in the air even though temperatures were still humid and hot during the day, and she relished the time when the leaves would begin to array themselves across the landscape in reds, golds, and purples, making the land look bright and royal.

"Missy, do yo' want me to prepare the carriage this mornin'?"

Lizzy turned to face Elliott with a smile. "Good morning, Elliot. No, no carriage. I will saddle Cruz for the ride to town." Cruz stood in his stall, his head turning as she walked through the door. He began to whinny lightly and stamp one foot, his way of saying he was glad to see her. She fed him some oats from a bucket, then opened the stall and put on his halter before leading him out to curry and saddle him.

"Have you heard from Miss Ann?" Elliott asked.

The question was a normal part of their morning. Elliott's parents, Mose and Lydijah, were usually mentioned in every wire, and he was really asking about them. It had been more than a month since her return from Florence, and battles occurred every day somewhere. Washington, though more settled, was still preparing to send an army south, though Rand didn't think it would be soon. He had been impressed with General McClellan at first but was now beginning to talk about the man's seeming reticence to move. Each day made immediate success less and less possible.

"They're all doing fine. Rand has recovered and returned to duty, and Ann is busy managing one of the medical supply depots."

"Has Mr. Newt showed up yet, Missy?"

Lizzy's brow wrinkled with worry. "No, Elliott, he hasn't. They think he's in prison in Richmond."

Elliott only nodded.

After Lizzy's return from Florence, it had taken nearly a week for her to force herself to go back to work. She had done nothing but worry about those she loved in Washington and about Andrew and his family. She was simply depressed about so many things she just couldn't bring herself to face paperwork. Not that it didn't catch up to her. The clerks brought it every day, gave her an update, and got their orders.

But once she finally returned, she felt quite happy again. The company continued to thrive, though in different places than it used to. Most of their steamers were plying the Ohio now and carrying an increased number of soldiers and military goods headed into war zones. She and Rand had talked of investing in the railroad, and she had made their first big deposit in the line moving toward California. It would be some time before it paid dividends, but it was the future, and they weren't about to be left behind.

And then there was Mr. Benjamin Connelly. After the sudden kiss, Lizzy hadn't seen Benjamin again, at least not face to face. Fearful of her feelings, she had stayed in her room, coming out only long enough to see the steamer off-load the runaways into skiffs for the short row to shore a mile above Alton, Illinois. Benjamin had been with them. Though they would dock at Alton, where he could have caught a train to Chicago then to Philadelphia and New York, he had apparently decided to travel with the runaways to their next stop and make his way from there. It was the last time she had seen him but not the last time he had been on her mind, and that both frightened and confused her. She loved Andrew and she knew it, and having anyone else on her mind seemed like a sort of infidelity; it definitely bothered her.

She heard the horses coming up the lane but continued to saddle Cruz. Moments later Elliott entered the barn, his face somber, a uniformed Union soldier at his side. "This is Captain Hillyer. General Grant sent him up from Cairo," Elliott said.

The soldier ungloved his hand and extended it. Lizzy shook it firmly. "Captain, what can we do for you?"

"General Grant sends his regards and has asked me to deliver this to you." He handed her a sealed letter. Lizzy opened and read it while

Elliott finished putting the bridle on Cruz. She turned back to Captain Hillyer. "Our steamers are at the general's disposal. We have several at Cairo, and I will bring two larger ones as soon as I can get them up to steam. Of course, you'll accompany them, won't you, Captain?"

Hillyer nodded as Lizzy took the reins of Cruz, and they walked toward the house. "Breakfast is nearly ready," Lizzy said. "I insist that you have some before we leave."

"We? But surely you're not coming. The general would not approve."

"The price for using my steamers, Captain. Now, come along and have some breakfast while I gather my papers and a few other things. Give me fifteen minutes." She tied Cruz to the hitching post at the back of the house and hurried inside, Hillyer and Elliott trailing her. She passed through the kitchen taking a cup of coffee from Ann's mother and asking her to see that the two men were fed. Since Lizzy had been so busy, Amanda Alexander had taken over all things domestic in the Hudson home since Ann left. She immediately told the servants what to prepare. Adelia, a slave Amanda had brought out of New Orleans and freed, had filled in for Lydijah; she quickly began preparing food. Lizzy rushed through the dining room and into the entry before taking the stairs two at a time to get to her bedroom on the second floor. Quickly pulling a carpetbag from under her bed, she threw extra underwear, pants, and shirts into it along with personal items. She grabbed a second large valise and put two dresses inside along with slips and other needed items. If Grant was moving south as rumored, there would be runaways to gather and care for then transport north to safety. She might be gone for some time. She looked about her. She would need more but would send for it all later.

She had not been back to Little Dixie since their run in with Quantrill. Since he couldn't reach her personally, he'd gone after her steamers, destroying one of them. She'd been forced to move them all downstream until a few days ago, leaving her without a safe method of transferring runaways downriver from above Jefferson City. But Purdy and Bryce were still making dashes into Little Dixie by land when needed and were quick and smart enough that Quantrill hadn't caught up to them. When she knew he was gone she'd go back, but for now, though it rankled her, she couldn't afford more lost steamers.

But now Grant was opening another opportunity, whether he knew it or not. He might not like it, but she intended to accompany his troops and set up a line of the Underground Railroad out of the Deep South.

She grabbed her Book of Mormon from the reading table and placed it on top of the other items in her carpetbag before slinging her saddlebags over her shoulder. The weight bore witness to what she already knew—there was shot and powder encased in each pocket.

Strapping on her holster, she put her revolver in place before removing her Sharps rifle from above the fireplace. Adelia entered the room and offered her help; Lizzy asked her to bring the valise and follow her. When she reached the bottom of the stairs, she grabbed her hat and put it on, sliding the latch on the leather cords until they were hitched under her chin. She entered the dining room and smiled at the two men who were busy eating.

"Gentlemen, if you please." She walked past them and into the kitchen. They scarfed down what they could, grabbed some biscuits, and followed.

"Amanda, I'll be gone for a few days," Lizzy said.

"Imagine that," Amanda said with a smile. She had come to love Elizabeth Hudson nearly as much as her own daughter and hid the concern on her face. Lizzy was a determined woman, and Amanda had learned quickly to simply smile and get out of the way. She handed Lizzy a small bag of food. "Your breakfast, dear girl," she said.

Lizzy gave her a kiss on the cheek. "Thank you." She threw her a warm smile as she continued out the back door. Hanging the carpetbag over her saddlehorn, she shoved the Sharps in its scabbard, tied on the saddlebags, and then mounted.

"I must protest once again, Miss Hudson," Hillyer said as he mounted his horse.

"Adelia, give the captain my valise." With that she urged Cruz to a trot then turned back to Eliott. "I'll take Cruz with me." She waved, faced forward, and was quickly galloping toward the gate and the city beyond. Hillyer trotted behind, trying to balance the large valise and keep up. They should be in Cairo by evening.

* * *

Millie waited in the lobby, her heart pounding. She had sent a telegram asking Henry Hyde where Matthew was staying and had arrived early in hopes of catching him before he left the hotel. The clerk had sent her message up to his room and had returned with word that Matthew would join her momentarily. She sat on a divan near a center post watching the bustle in the crowded room. The St. Claire Hotel had become the center of business in Richmond. Anyone coming to discuss contracts with the new government stayed here. So did politicians and beaurecrats who weren't yet established in their own homes. It was chaos.

"Good morning, Millie."

Millie looked up at Matthew then stood, her hand extended. He kissed it lightly. "Are you hungry?"

"Starved." She smiled, looking through the crowd toward the dining room where a long line had formed. "But I do not believe we will eat very soon if we wait here."

"I have a carriage this morning and know another place—small but the food is excellent," Matthew said. He offered his arm, and they dodged their way around nonattentive people to the door and outside. The street was packed with carriages, but Matthew led her down the steps and into the street, where a driver helped her inside. The carriage pulled away from the curb, and they settled in next to one another.

He wrapped his arm around her, she turned in to him, and they kissed. "I've missed you," he said.

"And I, you." She kissed him gently a second time, but it was interrupted by a bump that nearly tossed her hat off. They laughed lightly then settled, her arm through his.

"How are things at Beauchapel?"

"My plan to sharecrop was well accepted by my workers. They are freedmen now, but most have stayed and are working very long hours preparing the land for next season. Having a stake in the profits is a strong incentive."

Matthew smiled. "Snubbing your nose at the South's most prominent institution, are you?"

She laughed lightly. "I suppose that is one view of it. Have you received your commission?"

"Soon. I have obtained a recommendation from the new attorney general of the Confederacy."

Millie knew who he meant and had a sudden tinge of jealousy crawl up her spine. "My, my, no small task. And how is Mr. Benjamin's daughter?"

"Fickle as ever. She said to give you her regards next time I saw you."

"A surprise. The night I took her home she was quite clear about us never having any further social contact. I told her I was quite agreeable to that since I found her to be both a bore and bad company."

Matthew laughed. "She must have taken that well."

"I thought her hair might catch fire. I feared for the entire city."

"Well, you need fear no longer. She has gone off to Paris again."

"Then that city should tremble," she said relieved. She knew Ninette, and no woman's man would be safe if the girl set her bonnet for him.

"And did her father—"

"Give me a loan? No, but he did send a letter. It was a polite no but a no just the same."

"I'm sorry to hear it. I hope Ninette wasn't responsible."

"No, I knew that day that Mr. Benjamin never intended to give me the loan. I should never have let him use me the way he did."

"I'm glad you did," Matthew said. "We wouldn't have met again if you hadn't."

"Yes, that is a silver lining, isn't it?" She smiled.

They arrived at Mrs. Gilbert's coffee house and were soon seated at a small table beside a window. They both removed their hats and placed them on unused chairs at their table before ordering their meal. Millie thought it best to get right to the point. She glanced about her. Though the place was busy, the table nearest them was empty, and she felt comfortable speaking.

"I have come to ask you a favor that I'm not even sure you can deliver," she said.

"I'll do my best."

She explained openly about her uncle's deceit and his debt on her property. "My attorney in Petersburg tells me that if the addendum wasn't recorded properly, it's invalid. I heard you have property in New York State and hoped you might have contacts that could verify the recording for me."

Matthew felt a bit of a panic but hid it under a thoughtful exterior as he realized he could help but not exactly in the way she thought he could. "Getting word to them will be the difficulty, but yes, I believe I know someone who could help. In fact, he lives right in Washington." He leaned forward. "If you can write down the details of the transaction, I will try to get word to him." He could use the courier system Mrs. Van Lew and her group had set up to get information to Joe Polanski in

Washington. Polanski could hire an attorney and get Matthew what he needed, though the return route would have to go through Europe. All legal documents went that route.

She reached across the table and took his hand. "Thank you, Matthew. If I lost Beauchapel . . ." She felt herself tearing up and cleared her throat. "I'm sorry," she said, shaking her head slightly. "I don't know what is the matter with me lately."

"Tell me about Mr. Geery," Matthew said.

"Rich, greedy, arrogant, and mean. Beyond that there isn't much to tell."

Matthew chuckled. "How old?"

"His early thirties I would guess."

"He should be in the army."

"He would only get people killed trying to hide behind them."

Matthew laughed louder this time. "Well, we'd better avoid that, hadn't we."

"If you don't get your commission what will you do?"

"Pout." He grinned but knew he must change the subject. "What are you doing the rest of the day?"

"I hadn't thought about it. Why?"

"I have only one appointment this morning. After that we could go for a ride in the country. Have a picnic."

"I'd like that."

The waiter brought their food and placed it in front of them. Matthew directed the conversation toward Beauchapel and then spent the rest of their meal listening to Millie's plans for the future. She leaned forward and quieted her voice as she told him about her intention to provide a school for her workers.

"I thought that was against the law," he said with a slight smile.

She looked at him coyly. "You won't tell, will you?"

"That depends," he said as he dabbed at his lips with a cloth napkin.

She stopped chewing, a curious look on her face. "Depends on what?"

He leaned forward. "On whether or not you'll let me provide books."

"Books are always welcome." She used her own napkin as she sat back. "But you couldn't ship them. It would raise eyebrows. They would require personal delivery."

"Consider it done."

"And how soon could you arrange it?"

"Oh, considering the need to purchase them discreetly, I would think the weekend after next. Of course, I realize my presence may inconvenience your relationship with Mr. Geery, but—"

She threw her napkin, hitting him in the chin. "Ohh, how dare you even . . ."

He retrieved the napkin that had fallen into his lap and handed it back to her with a smile. "I am sure it's a tiring and difficult trip to Beauchapel. Is there an inn nearby?"

"I'll arrange something, Mr. Alexander." She had picked up her coffee cup and sipped, her eyes on his, her heart pounding.

"Then we have an appointment," Matthew said.

"We have," she said.

"Good. But I do have one other question."

She waited, taking another sip of her coffee.

"Should I bring a weapon? Mr. Geery may take offense that I am in your presence and possibly challenge me to a duel."

This time the napkin hit him square in the middle of the face. As he peeled it away, he noted that customers at nearby tables were staring at him. He smiled and put the napkin on the table nearer to him than Millie.

"You are very quick, Miss Atwater. And very accurate," he said.

"You are a tease, Mr. Alexander, and deserve anything required to make you stop."

The waiter brought the check, and Matthew removed the coins for payment. "Where can I drop you while I am in my appointment?" Matthew asked, glancing at his pocket watch. He stood and pulled back her chair, allowing her to stand.

"A friend's house," she said. "I stayed there last night and can put together a picnic lunch for us."

They left the restaurant, and Matthew signaled the carriage driver forward. As it pulled up, he asked Millie for the address and nearly stopped breathing when he heard it.

He looked up at the driver and gave it to him before climbing inside. Moments later they were pulling up to the front door of Beth Van Lew. Apparently Beth's invitation to Millie had been accepted.

Chapter Seventeen

Matthew was a bit distracted as he rode with Millie through the country going north out of Richmond. He felt a bit guilty about mixing "business" with pleasure, but he had no choice if he wanted to spend the day with Millie and carry out his reconnaissance of the defenses of northern Richmond in daylight. He also had a message to deliver to the first stop on the Van Lew courier route.

His appointment had been with a clerk serving in the Confederate Department of Naval Operations. A man who privately wished for a Union victory, he was willing to share information that showed just how big a blow the successful Union takeover of Hatteras Inlet could be. According to reports, the possibility had caused a shudder across the entire Confederacy, and Davis was pouring money into the building of new iron-clads in response. Matthew had their place of construction and their possible sailing dates. He also had information about a new ship, a submersible, being built at Tredegar Iron Works. Somehow he had to get in to see it.

As they moved along Meadow Bridge Road, Matthew noted a new raised cannon emplacement being thrown up just south of Deer Run, giving the rebels a direct line of fire at the bridges that crossed the run, certain devastation to any attack by Union troops from that quarter. He also noticed that the emplacements east and west of the Virginia railroad line were completed and that at least fifty cannons had been put in place. Soldier encampments surrounded each emplacement, and earth and wood works ran between each fort so that men could be moved discreetly from position to position—Robert E. Lee's handiwork; each day the Union delayed he was making Richmond stronger.

"My goodness!" Millie said. "I have never seen such . . . such weaponry! And all these soldiers. How could anyone possibly succeed in attacking the city?"

Matthew smiled. "That, my dear, is the whole point. But there are weaknesses." Unfortunately, if McClellan continued his delay even those would be gone soon.

"Weaknesses? I don't see any. Those cannons up there"—she pointed to one of the raised emplacements—"would destroy anyone who tries to cross Meadow Bridge or Taylor Bridge. And that one over there—"

"Covers the same set of bridges with a crossfire. And Fort Johnston—you see it in the distance over there to the east—protects the city from attack by way of Woodbury Bridge, the Mechanicsville Pike, or the two possible fords between them. General Lee knows exactly what he's doing."

"But the Union army hasn't moved from Washington since Manassas, and everyone feels that they won't, that they're beat. Why . . . ?"

"Because 'everyone' is wrong, and Lee and Jefferson Davis know it. The Union needs only capture this city and capture or scare off Confederate leaders in order to win. If Richmond falls, the Confederacy falls."

"Then why does the Union delay? The longer they wait, the more men will die trying to do that very thing! Is their army led by a fool?"

"Time will tell, Millie, but whether they are or not, even a fool can come to Richmond and give it a try. Lee and Davis are attempting to be ready."

Crossing over Meadow Bridge, they quickly left the city behind. For the most part they rode in silence, comfortably sitting close and watching the scenery change from war battlements to the open fields of the countryside, where fall was beginning to show in the changing color of trees and bushes. They passed a long line of troops marching north, and Matthew noted their flag and unit banners while wondering about the soldiers' destination. He didn't have to wait long for his curiosity to be satiated as they passed by a fairly new encampment at Mechanicsville.

"I haven't seen Beth's farm for several years. It's a lovely place. I'm glad she suggested it," Millie said.

When Matthew had returned to pick up Millie, Beth had continued their little charade about his real purposes in being in Richmond while also suggesting they have their picnic at her small farm north of town. Knowing Matthew had a message to deliver there, her recommendation had met both needs at once. Her quick thinking and shrewd ability to improvise had saved the day.

"I'm sure it's a lovely place," Matthew said. The carriage turned onto a side road lined with trees and rock fences following a small creek eastward.

"Have you heard anything from your family?" Millie asked.

He nodded. "A letter from my brother at Manassas. He's being transferred with Johnston's army to Tennessee." Matthew hadn't expected his brother to be a source of information, but he had become such. His details about Johnston's orders and numbers and where he would be headquartered would all be helpful to the Union. "I haven't heard from my mother and sister."

"Nor have they heard from you is my guess," Millie said then paused deciding whether to speak her mind. "If you can get word to the North that might help me, surely you can get word to your mother—and your sister—that you are all right, Matthew. They love you and deserve this consideration."

"Yes, you're right." He smiled at her while squeezing her hand as it lay on his arm. "I'll try." He had given it a good deal of thought but had not found a private enough channel to consider it safe. He couldn't send it by Miss Van Lew's route because if it were captured, it would surely reveal his identity, but he could send it by way of Europe. He would try.

They arrived at the small farmhouse and a single barn surrounded by several acres of apple, cherry, and plum trees. A half dozen workers were in the fields removing old vines of harvested vegetable plants, pruning old grape vines, or working in small buildings, drying or canning food for winter. As the carriage halted in front of the house, a small, rustic-looking woman with tanned leather skin lined with wrinkles stepped from the expansive flower gardens nearby. She had a pipe clinched between toothless gums, and she squinted against the light to focus on Matthew as he descended from the carriage.

"Mister, what can I do fer ye," she said in a rasping voice.

"Hello, Mrs. Tuck," Millie said from the carriage window.

The old lady squinted, the pipe pushed off to one side of her mouth. "Well, well, if it ain't Miss Millie Atwater," she said with a cackle and little dance. "Come on outa that thar carriage, Missy!"

Millie got down, and the smaller woman embraced her so completely that Millie was lifted off the ground and turned in a full circle, the other woman cackling with joy the whole time. Finally, putting the scarlet-faced Millie back on the ground, she stood back and gave her the once over. "My, you has become a fine lookin' woman. Fine lookin'." Her countenance finally clouded over. "I ain't seen you since yer pap and mama was buried. Horrible thing." She turned to Matthew. "And who's this fella ya brung to see me?" She gave *him* the once over. "Average face, broad shoulders though. Good firm legs. Make a good stud if he was a horse."

Millie laughed, and Matthew couldn't help himself either. "Why, thank you, Miss . . ."

"This is Amberline Tuck," Millie said.

"It's Tuck. If you call me Amberline, I'll shoot and bury ya in my garden."

"Well then *Tuck*, my name is Matthew Alexander, and I'm glad to meet you."

Tuck grabbed Millie, then Matthew by the arm. "Come on inside fer a bit, then we'll be sendin' ya down to the prettiest spot on the run where you two can spoon all ya like. First ya has to tell me about Beauchapel, Missy. Beautiful as ever is my guess."

They went inside, the two women chatting while Matthew looked over the place. He didn't know Beth Van Lew's courier by name or sight but had been given instructions as to where to leave his messages. He would need to slip away to make the delivery.

Following the two women inside, he found himself in a one-room home about twenty feet deep and thirty feet long. On one end was a bed and cabinet with a basin sink for washing; on the other was the fireplace, table, and some cupboards for cooking utensils, food, and other sundry items. It had a wood floor and was neat and clean. Above the fireplace hung an old flintlock rifle and two single-shot flintlock pistols. A powder horn and shot bag hung from a nail fastened to the thick oak mantle, and a five-by-seven framed painting of a couple was prominently displayed in its center. There was no fire and from the looks of it, there hadn't been one for some time. A bowl of cherries sat in the middle of the table along with a number of books, papers, and what looked like a hand-drawn map of the area. Tuck quickly removed these and set them on the bed while inviting her visitors to sit on the straight-backed wooden chairs at the table.

"Summer and fall we don't cook much in the house, but we does have fresh juice from them fruit trees. Ain't fermented yet but good just the same. What's t' yer likin', apple or cherry?"

They both said apple at the same time, and Tuck opened an icebox, pulled out a jar, retrieved glasses, and filled each before sitting down and lifting her own glass of thick juice. "T' yer health," she said as she removed her pipe. They all drank, and Matthew appreciated the cool liquid. The day was getting warmer. The two women were talking like old friends, eager to catch up on each other's lives.

Seeing an opportunity, Matthew spoke. "Excuse me, Tuck, where is your privy?"

"Down behind the barn. You'll see the trail." She said it without missing a word of what she was saying to Millie. Matthew went outside, walked down the short path to the gate of the picket fence, and then crossed the open space to the barn. He saw no workers around and entered, double-checking that no one was near. It was large enough to hold a hayloft and house stalls for a dozen animals from his right clear to the rear of the building with storage rooms to his left. He counted the doors as he passed them, and at the third he glanced about again before entering. Inside, he found a small workbench with tools and a self-standing grinder. He bent low to look under the workbench and located the handcrafted toolbox. Opening the box, he removed several items, examined the bottom, saw the small string, and pulled on it, removing a false floor. Taking the already-prepared missives from his pocket, he lay them inside before replacing the false bottom and putting the tools back inside. He put the toolbox back where he'd found it before turning to leave the room and running smack into Tuck.

"Lost yer way?" she questioned with a hard look.

"I've never seen a barn quite like this one," Matthew said. "Couldn't help my curiosity. How much hay can you put up there?" He looked up at the loft.

Tuck didn't answer at first, her eyes digging into his, looking for the lie.

"Enough to feed twelve animals for the winter" was the reply. She banged her pipe against one of the posts holding up the hayloft above them. Tobacco dust drifted to the floor before she pulled a small pouch from her pocket, removed more dried tobacco, and stuffed it in the pipe bowl.

"And where do you store your fruits and vegetables?"

"Cellar underneath. Door's in the first room back there," Tuck said, lighting her pipe. "Mr. Alexander, Millicent Atwater is as fine a young woman as there is. She don't need no Northern spy makin' her promises he can't keep 'cause he gets hisself hung." She sucked on the pipe and blew smoke out the sides of her mostly toothless mouth.

It was Matthew's turn to measure the sun-worn woman confronting him. "Where is Millie?"

"In the women's privy down towards the river."

"Well then, *Amberline* Tuck, your challenge to me is both misplaced and offensive, and if you weren't a woman, I would shove that pipe down your throat and make you choke on it." With that he walked toward the door, leaving her behind, a slight smile on her face. He went directly to the carriage and retrieved their picnic basket and a blanket just as Millie joined him. Offering his arm, they walked past an orchard until they reached a standing of tall, thick trees. Locating a shaded grassy spot, they spread the blanket. Millie sat and Matthew handed her the picnic basket. She retrieved a cloth and set upon it a meal of cold fried chicken, rolls, and a cabbage salad. Matthew removed his jacket, rolled up his sleeves, and sat down.

"Tuck was right; it is a beautiful spot," he said looking down the wide run at the gurgling water glistening in the afternoon sun.

"I used to come here as a child. Beth, her mother, and my parents would work in the gardens or pick fruit while I played with the workers' children. We would swim in that water hole over there." She pointed.

Matthew had to turn to see the spot and noticed a rope that hung out over the water, its loose end wrapped around a limb. He smiled, grabbed a boot and pulled it off, then the other, then his socks before standing.

"What on earth—"

He was already heading along the shore as he removed his shirt. When he reached the rope, he was in only his pants, suspenders, and underwear. He grabbed the end, stepped back far enough to stretch it to its length, then ran and lofted himself over the water. The rope carried him to the far side of the deep pool, and he lifted his feet, let go, and did a somersault into its deepest point. The water encircled and refreshed him, and he rose to the surface with a big smile on his face. He opened his eyes to see Millie standing on shore laughing at this sudden exuberance, and he swam to a spot just below her feet, where a well-worn path allowed him to exit the pool. He smoothed back his hair and wiped the water from his face, his pants dripping profusely as he sat down on the shore then plopped onto his back, staring at the slightly golden leaves of the tree above him.

Millie sat down next to him. "My, that was sudden. Are you always so impetuous?"

"Always," he grinned. "You should try it. The water is wonderful."

Millie chuckled. "It's easy enough for a man to doff his shirt and soak his pants, but it's quite another thing for a woman to do, especially in a man's presence."

"I'll close my eyes," he answered.

"You expect a good deal of trust for us having known one another for such a short time." She smiled as she got to her feet. "I'm sure the ants have gotten to our food. Grab your shirt and come eat before they carry it off."

He got up, lifted her into his arms, and started for the river. "Not until you're wet."

She kicked against his strong hold, laughing but her eyes wide. "Don't you dare! I'll never—"

He launched them both from the shore into the shallow part of the pool and stood her on her own two feet before turning back and pushing hard for shore. Millie's eyes were wide, both with the sudden coolness and Matthew's action, but she started after him. "You! I will get you for this!" She struggled against the water that held her linen dress. She tried to catch him, but he was out, had his shirt in hand, and was running for the blanket before she could even get to shore. Glad she had worn only light, slip-on shoes, she removed them quickly and ran after him as fast as her dripping dress would allow. She caught him just as he finished putting on his shirt, and she threw herself against him, knocking him off balance. They sprawled across the blanket, food flying in all directions. She landed on his back and immediately straddled him and grabbed at his hair, but he was too strong and turned her over, threw her to one side, and quickly had her arms pinned. They were both laughing and struggling when Millie stopped, her eyes on his, her heart suddenly knowing how deeply she felt about him. His grip on her arms slackened, and she eased them from his hands, put them around his neck, and pulled his lips to hers. The kiss was filled with tender passion, and after it she held him close.

"I love you, Matthew," she said in his ear.

"And I love you." He released her and pulled away, sitting as she did the same. They sat side by side. She lay her head against his shoulder, and he put an arm around her. They said nothing more for what seemed like long minutes, then she spoke. "Lunch is spoiled," she said evenly, looking about at the scattered food.

He laughed lightly as he kissed the top of her head then picked up a chicken wing from the blanket. "Well, we have this at least." He offered it to her. "Ladies first."

She took it, flung it over her shoulder, then turned to him, and they kissed again.

Neither of them saw the dark shadows moving through the woods. Matthew only became aware of their presence when one of them stepped into the sunlight and snapped a twig with a careless foot. Matthew got to his feet quickly then helped Millie to hers, wishing he hadn't left his revolver in the carriage as four rebel soldiers approached. He didn't like the look of these men. Millie tensed and grasped his hand and arm tightly.

"Gentlemen," Matthew said, tucking his dry shirt into still-wet pants. "What can we do for you?" Each carried a rifle, and two were armed with knives and a revolver.

The first smiled. "What you was doin' was entertainin' enough. You kin go on if ya like."

The others snickered a bit, lust in their eyes. One of them saw a piece of chicken near his feet and picked it up. Ignoring the ants, he took a bite, chewing slowly.

"What's your name . . ." Matthew looked for some insignia but found nothing on the sleeve of the man. "Private?"

"Don't matter," he said, losing the smile. He waved the gun toward the path leading back to the farm. "Git movin'. Captain wants everyone up at the house."

Matthew picked up his shoes and socks while Millie grabbed his jacket and quickly gathered the dishes and the basket. Matthew grabbed the blanket and threw it over his arm, and they started back up the hill, arriving at the cabin a few minutes later to see what looked like an entire company of soldiers moving about the premises as if searching for something. Matthew forced himself to breathe normally, keeping his face passive as they found Tuck talking to the captain. As they were seen, the conversation stopped, and the captain stepped toward them. "You are Mr. Alexander?" he said stiffly.

"Yes, and this is Millicent Atwater. We came out from Richmond for a picnic, but how do you know . . ."

"Mrs. Tuck informed us of who you are. How do you know the owners of this place?"

"I came to Richmond on business and am staying at the Van Lews' home," Millie said.

"How long have you known them?"

"At least ten years. My parents, who were killed a few years ago in a steamer accident, knew the Van Lews. We used to come here when I was child. Mrs. Tuck can verify—"

"Yes, she has already done so," the captain said.

"What is this about, Captain?" Matthew asked.

"We have it on good authority that this place is used as a pick-up point for letters of information being sent north."

"That's ridiculous," Millie said immediately.

Matthew glanced at Amberline Tuck but got no reading; her face remained passive. Had she revealed his being in the barn? He looked over her shoulder at the large building. There were at least twenty men searching the place. If they found the toolbox, the false bottom . . .

"Is it?" the captain smiled. "Well, I hope you're right. But we've been sent to search the place thoroughly just in case." He forced a smile. At least Matthew thought it to be a smile. The thick, bushy beard covered most of his lips, and his eyes were sunken so deep that Matthew couldn't read what might be in them.

A man was hurrying from the barn directly toward them. Matthew's heart sank as he saw the toolbox in the man's right hand. The tools had been removed. He strode up to the captain, handed him the box, then whispered something Matthew couldn't hear but which caused the captain to look at the box. He dismissed the soldier then put the toolbox on the ground, stooped, and put his hand inside. Matthew thought he would faint as the captain jerked up with his hand, removing the string, the false floor dangling from it.

As the captain reached down again as if to fetch something, Matthew considered all his options only to discover he had but one. He kept a straight face and refused to let his instinct to flee take over. He had nowhere to go.

The captain's hand came up empty, and he stared up at Mrs. Tuck, a curious look on his face. "It seems odd to have such a hidden compartment in a toolbox, Mrs. Tuck. Possibly you could give us an explanation."

Matthew felt the blood rush back into his face as he realized the papers he'd put there had disappeared. He forced himself to quit holding his breath as Tuck spoke.

"'Taint nothin' hidden about it, Captain. House plans. That is where they were kept in order t' prevent 'em from weather and loss. Harumph! City boy, ain't ya."

The captain stood and patted his hands together to remove dust, his face red.

"If you don't mind, Captain, it's getting late, and we really must get back to town. My train leaves tonight, and I cannot miss it," Millie said. She waited but got no response, the captain in his thoughts.

"Nothing out here, sir," someone shouted from the orchard.

"Nothing here either, sir," said another soldier from the cabin door.

"We're done in here, Captain. What da ya want us t' do next?" said a soldier at the entrance to the barn.

The captain rubbed his hands together again as if there was still dust on them. "Miss Atwater, I would advise you to avoid the Van Lew home in the future. They are under suspicion, and their reputation—"

"Thank you," Millie said curtly. "But my friends are my business, not yours. Now, may we leave?"

The captain reddened some at this chastening and nodded before turning to his sergeant. "Call the men together. We'll camp at the spot along the run a mile back." He turned to Tuck. "This area will be the outside perimeter of the Richmond defenses, and soldiers will throw up earthworks along the entire run. We expect that you'll support our efforts and that some of your crops will be sold to our quartermasters for the use of the army. We'll be here often, Mrs. Tuck, and we expect your full cooperation even though Mrs. Van Lew is not fully supportive of the new government. Is that understood?"

"Captain, yer speakin' to the wrong person if ya think I be against ya. I ain't, and I'll be sellin' ya whatever ya need. Ma son is in yer army, and I ain't about to let no Yankees come in here and spy fer 'em. Hope ya understand that."

"Thank you," the captain said. He looked directly at Matthew. "You and Miss Atwater may leave."

The sergeant had already given the order to group, and two long lines of soldiers had formed along the road. The captain mounted a dapple gray gelding and quickly spurred the animal to the front of the line, and the march was ordered. Dust flew up immediately as the soldiers stomped backed toward Richmond.

"I didn't know you had a son serving in the army, Tuck," Millie said finally.

"Don't, but the captain wanted to hear it." She shrugged. "The man's a fool. I'll have these crops peeled off and put away safe and sound afore them boys come lookin' fer 'em. Ain't about to feed 'em, no sir." She bent over to pick up the toolbox, glancing at Matthew. "Makes ya wonder who them soldiers been talkin' to, don't it, comin' here like they done."

Matthew only nodded. They would have to be more careful.

Millie looked at the two of them with some curiosity until Matthew suggested that they should leave in order to get her back to her train in time. He bent down and picked up Tuck, giving her a hug and whispering a thank you in her ear, bringing a broad smile to her face. She and Millie hugged before Matthew helped Millie into the carriage and climbed in after her. As they drove away, Millie gave Tuck one last wave before settling down next to Matthew.

"Now, darling," she said. "What was in that box?"

For possibly the first time in his life, Matthew was not ready with a sure answer.

Chapter Eighteen

ANN HAD BEEN AT THE medical depot only a week when the woman in charge became sick with typhoid and recommended Ann as her replacement. There were several other women who worked with Ann—all of them army "widows" just as she was. They were of varied backgrounds, but all of them had one thing in common: they were tireless in their service, working long hours each day to receive, shelve, and prepare to disburse endless amounts of bandages, medicines, blankets, medical instruments, and even wooden legs and arms in order to be ready for what Mr. Lincoln said was yet to come.

"Ann, do you have the forms for these crates?" Jane Terpo asked.

Ann was at the desk, so she located the papers and took them to Jane, who was watching as Mose used a crowbar to open the first of two large sealed crates. Mose had asked to help. With only a few animals to care for, he had little to do, especially with Maple around. But she knew it was more than that. Mose felt obligated to do what he could, and if they weren't going to let his people into the fight, at least he could help behind the lines. As the job got bigger, he had approached a black man in Georgetown who he had met the day of his arrival—a man by the name of Thospe—and found others to lend a hand. There were five now, all under Mose's direction, each working a few hours a day so as to still be able to support their families. So far it was working out well.

As she returned to her chair, shoving aside a strand of wayward hair that covered her right eye, she felt the twinge of nausea and pain in her stomach; she gently pushed against it for some relief. It was not long or especially hard and quickly went away. But it had happened several times in the last few days, and it was becoming bothersome and more painful.

As she was about to return to her work, she noted a tall figure in a stovepipe hat coming through the door to the warehouse. She heard a gasp behind her and glanced over her shoulder to see Jane doing her best to pat her hair into place as the other workers slowly stood, unsure of just what to do.

Though she herself had stopped breathing normally at this unexpected visit, Ann quickly rose and moved forward to greet him.

"Mr. Lincoln! This is a surprise," she said. Unsure of whether to curtsy or just offer her hand, she finally did the later. Unfortunately, her pencil was still in it. Mr. Lincoln calmly removed it from between her fingers before kissing her hand lightly then offering her the pencil back.

"Miss . . ."

"Hudson. Ann Hudson." She turned. "And this is Mrs. Jane Terpo." She introduced each of the other workers, who came forward, shook his hand, and then stepped back, ending with Elijah Benton and finally Mose.

"This is Mose Brown, formerly of Virginia, presently employed by us along with Mr. Benton and several others to help with the heavy work that confronts us." Mose, unsure of just what to do, stood still, quietly gripping the crowbar in his hand. Ann went to his side, took his arm, and brought him forward. Mr. Lincoln offered a hand to shake, and Mose used his pant leg to wipe the sweat off his own before reciprocating. Lincoln then stepped to Elijah and shook his hand as well.

"Mr. Brown, Mr. Benton, are you freedmen or runaways?" Lincoln said with a smile.

Elijah looked at Ann, and Mose smiled.

"Mose has been with my husband's family for a very long time but is a freedman. Mr. Benton is what your government seems to be calling contraband, Mr. President," Ann said. As more and more slaves fled north, there was a cry from the rebel government for their return. At first some slaves were put in wagons and sent south to their owners, but General Butler, the commander at Fort Monroe, Virginia, refused, calling them "contraband of war." Since then thousands more had fled and were being put to work in the war effort in warehouses, forts, and camps. They waited on Mr. Lincoln and his government to decide just how to make them freedmen.

"Mr. Benton," Lincoln said with his usual somber smile, "welcome to freedom."

"Than' yo', suh," Elijah said, his eyes on the ground.

"Suh?" Mose said sheepishly.

Lincoln looked at him. "Yes, Mr. Brown."

"Us black folk would like t' do mo', suh. We'd like t' fight jus' like all dem white folks. Is dat possible, suh?"

Ann held her breath. She had not expected it, yet it was a fair question that even she wanted an answer to. She looked at the president, who seemed to be contemplating.

"Mr. Brown, your desire is most honorable, but I must ask your patience." He paused. "I was on board a steamer one time, coming up the Ohio. It was in spring. and there had been a terrible storm. Debris floating downriver as thick as fleas on a dog. In the distance we saw a large tree floating along headed right for us. Of course, it could badly damage the steamer, even severely enough to send it to the bottom. The captain blew his whistle and ordered the wheelsman to turn the ship." He paused, smiling lightly. "As you know, it's not easy to turn such a large ship in such a short distance, but gradually it moved, just a bit, then a bit more. I watched as the tree bumped into the vessel's side—a glancing blow—and then went on its way." He smiled again. "'Tis hard to turn a ship on a dime, and 'tis even harder to turn a government to its proper course, but the whistle has been blown, the warning sounded, and the ship has begun to change course. A little more time, Mr. Brown. Just give this old captain a little more time."

Mose nodded, seemingly satisfied, and Ann smiled. She hadn't fully noticed the two people with Mr. Lincoln but turned her attention to them now.

"Mr. Bellows, Mr. Chase." Ann did curtsy this time. Henry Bellows was the president of the US Sanitary Commission, created only in June. They were to investigate and advise the military on medical matters, but Bellows was working hard to expand their powers to create a more unitified response to the challenges they all knew were coming. Bellows had already recommended and pushed for at least ten more hospitals in Washington, and he was the power behind stockpiling medical supplies, thus the power behind Ann's warehouse.

Salmon Chase was the secretary of the treasury, a former opponent of Lincoln for president and probably one of the most powerful men in Washington. His daughter, Kate Chase, was vying with Mary Todd Lincoln for the most prominent socialite in Washington and was working with Bellows and others, holding "sanitary fairs" to raise money for additional supplies. Though Ann was wary of Kate Chase and her father in many ways, she applauded the effort to prepare for the medical firestorm everyone knew would surely come.

"Mrs. Hudson," Bellows replied, bowing slightly. Chase also bowed, smiled, and then asked after her husband.

"The captain is back with his men," she said smiling.

"Then he has healed?" Lincoln asked.

Ann was a bit surprised that he knew of Rand's wound. "Yes, but how—"

"General McDowell provided a list of the wounded and killed. I remember the captain's name from a visit we had some time ago before the election. He came to Springfield to quiz me about my politics, and then he returned to St. Louis to support my nomination." He smiled. "One does not forget those who fight for them."

Ann had not remembered Lincoln being so tall. Her shorter stature forced him to look down on her, and yet she had the distinct impression that he considered her quite equal to him. "What—what brings you gentlemen here?"

"You do, Mrs. Hudson," Lincoln said. "You wrote Mr. Bellows a note about some of the supplies you have been receiving. It alarmed Mr. Bellows and Mr. Chase, and they brought it directly to me. We were out visiting the troops and thought it good to get your personal view."

Ann felt the blood climb into her face. She had written a letter, but she never thought it would cause an inconvenience to any of these men.

"Could you show us the supplies you mentioned?" Linclon prodded.

"Of course," Ann said. She turned, gave Jane a quick glance, and then walked to the first row of long shelves that extended a hundred feet to the other end of the building. There were fifty such rows filled with various items, but this row had been set aside to hold those items that were not what they were said to be.

She reached the first items and removed the cork from the throat of a bottle. She stepped to Mr. Lincoln and put the bottle near his nose, causing him to move his head back a bit. "I apologize," Ann said, her face reddening again. "But what do you smell?"

Lincoln sniffed at the bottle. "Possibly . . . something sweet?"

"Please, Mr. Bellows, read the label." She handed him the bottle and returned to the shelf to retrieve a blanket.

"Chloroform," Bellows said. "Why, surely you smelled something, Mr. President. I . . ." He put the bottle to his nose.

"Water, gentlemen, mixed with a little bit of rose petal." She handed Chase the blanket and asked him to unfold it. As he did, he revealed a ragged hole in its middle. "These are supposed to be new, but as you see they're not. Some are worse than this, some less so, but there are far too many that are as thin as paper and hardly able to keep our boys from freezing even in fall weather."

She returned to the shelf and pointed to another row of bottles. "The labels say this is quinine. It's nothing of the sort, though I have no idea what it is. Here we have bandages that are so thin they will do no one a bit of good, and here we have cutting instruments that show rust and use and are as dull as the edge of your finger." She pointed down the shelf. "As you can see we have a good many items that are not what they should be." She walked angrily back to her desk. "Yet they have been received by our government and paid for at costs that make one wonder if you gentlemen have discovered the mother lode in the Rocky Mountains."

Lincoln was frowning. "What companies shipped these items?" he asked.

She read the names from the shipping bills, and Lincoln glanced at Chase. "Do these strike a familiar chord, Mr. Chase?"

Chase nodded. "They do."

"We have received reports from several different sources of a similar deception, Mrs. Hudson. We are aware of who is behind this skulduggery and assure you that we will see it end."

Ann could see he meant what he said and nodded to thank him.

"Now, Mrs. Hudson, I understand that you tended to some of our soldiers in your own home as they returned from the debacle at Manassas. Since then, Mrs. Dix tells me you visit the hospital often to give comfort and offer your services. I personally thank you for your efforts, but I also have a question."

"Yes, Mr. President?"

"What did we lack that could have eased their suffering?"

Ann was humbled by the question. With all Mr. Lincoln had on his plate, it was this that obviously concerned him most deeply. But she had given it some thought and had even talked to many of the soldiers about what they needed. In almost all instances, it was the same.

"They need proper transport from the battlefield to medical services. Even wagons are horribly uncomfortable. Why, some of the soldiers told me that they were taken from the field in wagons and they cried to be left behind because it caused them such horrible pain. Surely something better, even altered carriages with a . . . a . . . more giving . . ." She turned to Mose as she struggled for the word. Mose smiled.

"Suspension system, Miss Ann. That's what it called."

"Yes, a more giving suspension system. And then there's always the need for prevention in spreading disease. Patients who contact smallpox, mumps, and malaria should not be kept in the same rooms or even in the same hospital with those who do not have them. And when I watch surgeries and see doctors using the same instruments on patient after patient with no regard to diseases that might be transmitted, I cringe at the possibilities."

"There has been no evidence of disease being transmitted in such a way," Chase said almost patronizingly.

"They're doing studies in England on that very thing, Mr. Chase. One of your doctors showed me an article he'd been sent by a friend in London. There seems to be a growing concern that there might be a very real and deadly connection."

"We're advising the doctors to sterilize when they can, but after a battle, in a field hospital . . ." Bellows shook his head slowly. "They are simply overwhelmed by numbers."

"And what would be the cost of such sterilization?" Chase asked. "Why, the price of alcohol these days is exorbitant with everything being produced going to . . . ah, well, alcohol that is used in other ways."

"Yes, well it's time the government reduced the one in favor of the other. Heaven only knows how many fools are made every day by drinking away the stuff that should be used to save lives," Ann said forcefully.

Lincoln chuckled. "Asking our politicians to give up something that helps them forget their bad decisions may be a considerable mountain to climb, Mrs. Hudson."

Ann smiled. "You have not struck either my husband or me as a man afraid of a little climb, Mr. President."

He bowed his head in deference. "Thank you for your counsel. It will not be forgotten, I assure you. Gentlemen." He started to leave the building then turned back. "My wife is having a ball at the White House next Friday. I invite you to attend, Mrs. Hudson."

Ann was flattered. "I'm honored that you would ask, but I do not usually go to such things without Randolph."

He nodded, that sober smile creasing his lips. "I am sorry to hear that." With that he was gone.

Jane had been standing to one side watching it all, her smile bent upward in satisfaction. "I think that if you don't go, he may send his personal guard to retrieve you."

Ann chuckled. "He was being kind, that's all." She returned to her desk. "We've been idle long enough. Back to work." She waved her hand impatiently as she renewed her focus on her paperwork. The moment she sat down, however, a man in a dark suit came through the door, walked briskly to her desk, and handed her a paper.

"From Mr. Lincoln. He asks you to see that it's delivered." He turned on his heel and quickly disappeared.

"His bodyguard, I would suppose," Jane said, moving closer as her curiosity got the best of her.

Ann opened the paper. It was simply a piece torn in such a way that the presidential seal was intact.

General Sherman,

On the 24th of October, Mr. Randolph Hudson should be dismissed from his duties and appear with his wife at the White House by 5:00 p.m. He will return to his duties on the 28th at 8:00 a.m."

It was signed *Abraham Lincoln.*

* * *

Rand and Isaac stood together listening to General Sherman's instructions for the day. Most of the other officers in the room seemed bored, but Rand wasn't. Each one gave him opportunity for further preparation.

Rand's battalion had been one of the least bruised by the Battle of Bull Run. Of his nearly three hundred men, only ten were dead with fifteen wounded, eight captured. Rand knew why. Before Bull Run, officers and soldiers alike had given little credence to preparation while Rand had worked his men hard each day, not only drilling them relentlessly, but taking them on long marches, where they'd come to understand the physical demands soldiering would take. He had also provided the best weapons he could find and taught his men how to use them efficiently.

More than a few had died because of poor weaponry. Most of the men in other units had brought along whatever weapons they had. Many had double-barreled shotguns or old flintlocks and muzzle-loaders that had served them well for hunting but had proven woefully insufficient at Bull Run. Others, those who had no weapon such as city slickers, foreigners, or those who'd joined to get out of poverty's deadly grasp, were issued similar weapons. Some of these were the huge .69 or .70 caliber smoothbore muskets that one officer declared about as efficient as pitchforks, and another said of them, "I think it would be a masterful stroke of policy to allow the secessionists to steal them, for they kick further than they shoot. Five shots, and they'll be in Richmond." Rand knew that such weapons were so short in their range and so inaccurate that even after two hundred shots their users would have been lucky to hit a target three or four times. Rand had watched practices before Manassas where the barrels of the "pumpkin slingers" or "European stovepipes"—names stemming from their origin—blew up at the first firing. They were more dangerous to the person shooting than they were to any enemy not firmly attached to the end of the barrel. Since Manassas, the word was the army was doing their best to replace such weapons with the .577 Springfield that most of Rand's men used. Though still a muzzle-loader, it was much more accurate. Those who had them accounted for ten times more punishment to the enemy than all the others put together. Fortunately, the rebels were just as poorly armed.

But weaponry was not the most egregious cause of the loss at Bull Run; it was lack of discipline and poor leadership. He looked around the room. Of the officers who had led men at Bull Run, only half remained. Since the battle, McClellan had set up a board of review, and the board had washed out as many officers as it had kept. Though Rand knew that most of those who were given other duties were good men, they'd been political appointees who knew nothing about war, and though some had fought bravely, they hadn't done the training necessary to win the battle. McClellan intended to see that change, and Rand was gratified at the effort.

The parade grounds were now filled with men much more intense in their effort to learn the art of war than he had seen before Bull Run. The men had stared death and dishonor in the face and wished to see neither again. Their efforts were far improved, but there was still much to do, a fact that was compounded by the addition of new recruits.

Since Bull Run, Lincoln had called for an additional five hundred thousand men. Though many were being sent to the western theater, most were showing up here just as full of themselves and unprepared as many had been before Bull Run. McClellan had made certain that the novices were intermingled with the veterans so they would learn quickly, but it was still a mighty task to get them ready for future battles. Rand had received seventy-five new recruits and was working hard to integrate and prepare them.

Sherman finished as one of the officers asked a question. "Will we be moving south soon, sir?"

Sherman shook his head. "General McClellan has no intention of going into battle as unprepared as we were at Bull Run. When he sees we are ready, we'll move."

Isaac leaned over to Rand and whispered, "Just as well start buildin' cabins, then. We'll be here well into 1870."

Rand smiled. It was September of 1861.

"We'll begin forced marches tomorrow."

One of Sherman's staff quickly handed out the schedule to company commanders. Rand glanced at his.

"We'll begin with five-mile marches with haversack and weapons. You're to make three miles per hour. If you do not, you'll march again tomorrow and the next day and the next until you do. Two and a half miles out, two and a half miles back. You should be gone no more than two hours, including rest stops. Major Hudson, your brigade will set the pace and begin at 5:00 a.m." He then went on to review with the other companies the times they would follow. "When you return, you will be immediately submitted to a mock battle. There will be extensive cannon fire for the effect of noise alone. Targets will be set up at the enemy position built in the shape of men. Your hits on these targets will be counted. The intent is to get the men ready for the sounds of battle so they're not so easily frightened and will hold their positions. We will do these mock battles regularly until we are ready to move south. Any questions?"

"Will anyone be firing back at us?" one solider asked with humor. Others in the room snickered at the lighthearted question.

"It wouldn't surprise me," Sherman said. He forced a smile. "But not with the intent to kill, Captain. As long as you keep your head down, you should be fine. Dismissed."

A mumble through the room revealed their wonder as to whether Sherman was serious. They were about to fall in line to leave when Sherman called.

"Major Hudson, Captain Hooker, stay a moment," Sherman said.

Rand and Isaac stepped out of line and waited until Sherman's orderly left and closed the door behind him, leaving Rand and Isaac alone with Sherman.

"I'll get right to the point. I'm leaving for the western theater—Kentucky—and will be gone in a few days."

Rand felt his stomach lurch. He felt comfortable with Sherman and didn't like the thought of change. "And your position, sir?"

"I'm to become one of those fools I spent a good deal of time criticizing, a general. I'll command a brigade under Robert Anderson. It seems that the rebels are trying to coerce Kentucky into the fold." He leaned forward, his arms on the desk. "You both fought well at Bull Run. If you wish to ask for a transfer, I would gladly accept you under my command. Good day, gentlemen." He stood and extended his hand. Isaac shook it, and then Rand did. "Tell your lovely wife good-bye for me, Randolph. I enjoyed very much her hospitality while visiting you and Mr. Hooker at home."

"I will. God go with you, General. I would be honored to serve with you again."

They turned to leave.

"Major, McClellan is a foot dragger," Sherman warned. "He will not move south before spring no matter how prepared the army may be. Even then, I doubt his resolve is much greater than McDowell's was. He'll hesitate rather than force his will on Richmond. The war will be won in the west, then in the east."

He stuck his cigar in his mouth and focused on some papers on his desk. He expected no response.

Rand and Isaac left the house, mounted, and rode to their section of the camp. They rode in silence, passing through the straight rows of tents, most of which were Sibley's version of an Indian teepee. Sibley was the most cursed man who now served in the Confederacy, not because he served the rebels but because he had been the fool who'd invented the Sibley tent. Though spacious, the central pole was held in place by an iron tripod that was constantly getting tangled with men's feet. The army packed men in them like sardines, their feet to the center. If one caught a cold, the rest were sure to as well, and already full tents of men had been hauled to hospitals with chicken pox or mumps. They were like furnaces in summer and iceboxes in winter. The army was looking for a replacement and was supposed to receive something smaller by winter.

Officers were housed in wall tents. A large, box-shaped structure with upright sides and sloping roofs, the tent was roomy enough a man could move about the center without stooping. Unfortunately, it was too heavy and too expensive to provide for everyone. Rand supposed it was an incentive to become an officer—the only incentive.

Rand and Isaac hitched their horses to the rail outside their battalion command tent, saluted Farley Judkins—who had become the new master sergeant of the battalion—and then went inside. Malone was sitting on his cot, a book in his hand.

Since his getaway, Malone had looked every day for Newton Daines and the others in hopes that somehow they had escaped. So far he'd waited in vain.

Malone closed the book as Rand began reporting what Sherman had told them.

"'T w'll be interestin' t' see wha' the new regiment commander thinks abou' our present arrangement," Malone said. "'Tis not often tha' ya 'ave a battalion set up jus' fer one group. The new colonel migh' nah like it."

A soldier came to the tent opening and gave a halfhearted salute. "Mail," he announced. He handed a stack of letters to Isaac and was gone as quickly as he'd come.

Isaac went through the lot of them, removing theirs before calling to Judkins to get them to the men, who were just finishing up their lunch.

"'Tis a fine day," Malone said as he eyed the letter handed to him. Rand knew it was from Malone's wife and his son, Dillon. They wrote nearly every day. Malone's wife was not a well woman but didn't complain and told him if he came home before the South was properly put in its place, she would shoot him herself. She was living with Dillon and his family and was doing fine.

"Dillon says the business is goo' as ever an' nah t' worry. The Kerry Patch is quiet since O'Brien an' 'is toughs went south to join up with David Atchison's rebel regiment." He smiled. "Be nice t' see 'em on the field o' battle. Settle a few scores once and fer all."

"How's your darlin' wife?" Isaac asked.

"Same as ever—charmin' and never a word o' complaint. Dillon and 'is goo' wife be lookin' after 'er."

Rand noted that Isaac again received no letter; there had only been one or two since they had come to Washington. Isaac joked about how she must have run out of money and married someone else, but Rand knew her lack of writing was worrisome. His business was well cared for by a trusted partner, but his wife was a bit younger and had voiced her disapproval about his leaving from the start. Not much worried Isaac Hooker, but Rand could tell this did.

Rand's mail came to Ann at the house. He hadn't seen her for nearly a month, but she had Mose deliver the letters to him. The last letter from Lizzy had been filled with business matters. Except for the loss of a single steamer, things were in good shape at Hudson Shipping, and his response on that count wasn't long.

He had told her about his encounter with Andrew, at least in part. He didn't recount that he'd nearly had to shoot her fiancé.

Isaac stretched out on his cot and continued reading. Rand noted that he was probably halfway through. Since their return, Isaac had started to study. He read the New Testament first; now he was in the Book of Mormon. After he'd first finished 1 Nephi, he'd had some questions. Even Malone had been listening to the answers.

The camp was set up to work like clockwork, and the timetable for the day had been given to Judkins that morning. At exactly one o'clock by Judkins's watch, the sound of his voice cut through the air as he ordered men to the parade field for the afternoon training. Isaac and Malone went out the door, dropping their plates in a bucket of hot water as they passed. Rand's dishes joined theirs, and he returned to his desk. There were still several letters to write to the families of those who had died at Manassas. Before beginning, he removed his Book of Mormon from his knapsack and began to read. He was near the end of the book for the third time in less than a year. Not only had it become a habit but a need.

But he didn't go to where he had finished reading this morning. Instead, he went to the page with the folded upper right-hand corner. He found the spot that described Captain Moroni and began to read:

And Moroni was a strong and a mighty man; he was a man of perfect understanding; yea, a man that did not delight in bloodshed; a man whose soul did joy in the liberty and the freedom of his country, and his brethren from bondage and slavery; Yea, a man whose heart did swell with thanksgiving to his God, for the many privileges and blessings which he bestowed upon his people; a man who did labor exceedingly for the welfare and safety of his people. Yea, and he was a man who was firm in his faith of Christ, and he had sworn with an oath to defend his people, his rights, and his country, and his religion, even to the loss of his blood.

He leaned back in his straight-backed wooden chair to think as he turned the corner of the page over again and gently shut the book. How did one become such a man?

Farley hadn't noticed Rand's contemplation and was halfway through the entrance when he did. "Sorry, sir. I—"

"Not to worry, Sergeant. What do you need?"

"I have a friend up at McClellan's headquarters. He says our government received a list of prisoners down in Richmond. Newt—Sergeant Daines is on the list, sir. He's in Ligon Prison."

Rand let the front legs of the chair fall to the ground. "It's good to know he's alive, Sergeant. Please tell the rest of the men, will you?"

"Yes, sir," Judkins smiled. "They'll exchange for him, won't they?"

"Let's hope so," Rand said. "Politicians are slower than tar on a cold day, but the papers seem to be putting on the pressure to get it done. Maybe the heat will soften them up a bit."

Farley stepped closer and handed Rand an envelope. "And this come from Sherman's headquarters just now. The courier says it's urgent."

Rand nodded as he used his thumb to break the wax seal and pull out a letter as well as a small piece of paper with rough edges.

The short note was from Sherman. *It seems the president has requested your presence this weekend. When you return, I will be gone. I hope to see you in the army of the west. God go with you, Randolph.* It was signed *Cump.*

Rand unfolded the second paper, read the order from Lincoln, and smiled. It seemed the president had met Ann.

Chapter Nineteen

MARY TODD LINCOLN WAS WORKING very hard to overcome her unfortunate reputation as a backwood's wife by holding elaborate parties and teas for all the ladies of Washington while also spending inordinate and even disgraceful amounts of money on clothing and redecorating the White House. Ann did not move about in any of the city's many social circles, but she did hear the rumors as they ran their course through servants who gossiped in the markets and shops as well as through Jane Terpo, who seemed to have an endless amount of unverifiable gossip at tongue's end. To have spent twenty thousand dollars on redecoration when soldiers went without warm blankets and socks was a disgrace in some circles and reason for outright condemnation in others. Ann did not trust in rumor and had decided to withhold judgment until at least meeting Mrs. Lincoln. She was not about to denounce the First Lady behind her back while eating her food and enjoying her parties, as so many were apt to do.

The carriage jostled Ann a bit, and she held tightly to Rand's arm to keep her balance, the pain in her midsection harder than usual. She ignored it as best as she could, grateful to have Rand at her side. He had arrived home just in time to change before they had to leave. She had kissed and hugged him, even helped him bathe, and longed to be alone with him. She hoped the party would not be long, even suggesting to Rand that they skip it altogether. He had reminded her that he was under orders from the president to see that she attended.

"You might want to know that Cump Sherman is being transferred," Rand said.

"Oh, dear, I am sorry for it. He was most concerned about you and Isaac."

"He said to tell you good-bye and that he was very grateful for your hospitality."

"I never did meet his wife. Is she going with him?" Ann asked.

"I am not sure," Rand replied.

"Please try to find out. If she remains behind, she will need company from time to time. I'd be glad to visit."

"I'm sure she would like that." He paused, grabbing the strap as the carriage hit several hardened ruts in the street. Though the city was expanding its population, it was not doing much about improving its infrastructure, and most streets were either unpaved mud bogs when it rained or hard, rutty wheel busters when it didn't.

He looked at her. "In the rush I didn't have time to ask you how this order came about, and don't say it had nothing to do with you. Mose already informed me that you had a visit from the president last week."

Ann told him as she clung to his arm. "I don't have the slightest idea why he would want me there, but he must have some purpose."

Rand chuckled. "You light up any room, my love, and in these dismal days such a light is badly needed."

"There are plenty of women more radiant than I, dear Rand. Why, I hear this Miss Agnes Leclercq cuts quite a figure. The papers say she rides about the city on a white steed in a gilt-buttoned, gold-braided habit with captain's straps, her black groom mounted on a black steed of just as high a quality prancing behind her. They say she's a dashing and beautiful figure with blonde hair and bright blue eyes. Every man's head turns when she passes."

"Yes, I have seen her and a dozen others like her—or very similar, though none so brash as to wear a captain's shoulder straps. She pales next to you, my love, I assure you."

"You've met her?"

"I've seen her. She comes often to the camps to pay the men a visit. Kate Chase comes quite often as well. And then there are the women of the theater and . . ."

"And . . ."

"And endless others all looking to be flattered and drooled over. Do not compare yourself to such women, dearest. You are far above them in both beauty and character."

He turned into her and gave her a gentle kiss. "Now, less of the wenches of society and more of what you do with your time when I am suffering in the heat of camp."

"Let's see . . . nothing unusual, really. We've made a dozen quilts for our soldiers, canned fruit, stored vegetables, painted the house, and . . ." She tapped her chin with a finger as if thinking. "Oh yes. You are to be a father."

He was only partially listening, his eyes on the street, which seemed somewhat deserted. Then it hit him. "What?" He looked at her with wide eyes.

"Yes, it's true." She grinned. "I was sick for nearly a month, and it's all your fault."

He turned in his seat, took her in his arms, then leaned back and looked into her eyes. "You're sure?"

"Quite sure. It's been three months now, and I fear I'm beginning to need larger dresses. But these are facts you would know, my dear, if you ever came home long enough to accompany me to our bedroom."

"I will do my best to verify your beliefs this very night." He kissed her again then held her tight as the carriage pulled into the drive of the White House. "But should you be out and about like this? The carriage . . . it jostles about so . . ."

She laughed lightly as he held her tight again. "I am quite all right, darling." She thought of telling him about her pains but let it go. She was sure they were nothing but indigestion or overexertion to her muscles. "I go to the warehouse every day and feel quite strong. I'll have to slow down a little as the time for the child's birth draws closer, but for now, I'm quite all right."

He wrapped his arms around her and gave her a long and passionate kiss, letting her go only when they arrived near the door of the White House and the carriage slowed then stopped. "I love you, Ann."

"And I you, darling. I don't suppose we can just go home, can we?"

"It is a temptation, isn't it."

"A few minutes, maybe an hour, then we shall leave."

The driver had jumped from his seat and opened the door, and Rand got out then helped Ann do the same. As she stepped to the cobblestone, she felt her stomach wrench hard enough that she was tempted to bend over, but she forced it aside with a grimace, gripped Rand's arm more firmly, and made herself smile. After a moment, it lessened, but it didn't go away, a dull throb. She feared it this time but could not bring herself to tell Rand. She would be fine in a few moments, she was sure of it. After all, the pains had always left shortly after they'd come. This time was a bit different but nothing to be alarmed about.

As they neared the door, they could both see there was a line and that each couple carried an invitation. Rand pulled the order from his pocket to present at the door. Neither of them recognized many faces, and even those they did gave no indication that the recognition was mutual. Rand whispered to Ann, "Even an hour may be more than I can bear."

As they reached the butler, they could hear the sound of music coming from inside. The entry was well lit by gas-fired lamps and chandeliers, giving it a bright and cheery feeling. They were each handed a dance card, then ushered to a reception line to greet President and Mrs. Lincoln. Rand did see General McClellan near the door at the far end of the entry, and he also spotted Secretary Seward.

He listened to Mrs. Lincoln greet each guest in front of them; he recognized some names and had no idea about others.

"Randolph, Ann." Rand turned about to see Frank and Apolline Blair approaching, wide grins on their faces. They hugged one another quickly.

"Aunt Apolline, I thought you were still in St. Louis," Ann said with a blush of happiness.

"We only arrived last night. Frank had to come to see the president about matters in Missouri and to carry out his duties as senator," Apolline said in a quiet voice.

Frank leaned toward Rand. "Randolph you must tell me about Bull Run and—"

They reached the Lincolns, and Ann extended a hand to the First Lady, who squeezed it as she tried desperately to remember a name. "I'm so sorry," she finally said.

"I invited them," the president said. "This is Ann and Randolph Hudson of St. Louis. Mr. Hudson and I met before the election. He is one of the few who supported my presidency in the state of Missouri. His family owns Hudson Shipping, the largest of its kind on the Mississippi, and I met Mrs. Hudson several days ago at one of our medical supply depots. I have learned that Mr. Hudson was at Manassas. He only recently returned to duty after a severe wound that nearly took his life."

Both Rand and Ann blushed as Mrs. Lincoln spoke. "Oh my, welcome, both of you. Make yourself quite comfortable in our home, and Mrs. Hudson, we must visit more about your service to our soldiers. Several prominent women of this fair city are trying to get Congress to do more, and your voice will surely be helpful." She looked at Frank. "Especially as it applies to Mr. Blair, representative of Missouri in our

Congress and a bit recalcitrant in his support of funds for more hospitals. Where have you been, Franklin? We need your support for this change."

"Your husband's fault, Mary," Frank said a bit sheepishly. "He asked that I continue my efforts to enlist another full regiment of Missourians before I came to Washington." He shrugged as if there was really nothing he could do about it.

"And were you successful?" the president asked.

"Completely. They're under command of Ulysses Grant at Cairo." He cleared his throat slightly and stepped closer to Lincoln. "I do need to speak with you about another matter, Mr. President, and very soon."

Lincoln visibly sighed. "About Mr. Fremont, I assume?"

"Yes, Mr. President. As you know he had *me* arrested and—"

"Come tomorrow." He smiled as he took Apolline's hand. "All of you enjoy yourselves tonight." They passed on and were soon in the East Ballroom, where a waltz played and dancers filled the center of the room. Others visited and mingled on the perimeter, and Frank and Apolline were immediately pulled away to greet several others, leaving Rand and Ann to fend for themselves.

"Who is that talking to Frank?" Ann asked.

"Secretary Cameron of the war department," Rand responded. "General Fremont is acting the fool in Missouri. He arrested Frank for voicing his concerns about Fremont's decisions publicly. The president had to demand a release. Fremont seems both incompetent and belligerent. My guess is Frank wants to put a stop to it." John C. Fremont, former explorer of the Northwest and former governor of California had sought and been granted the command of the Department of the West when General Harney, thought to be sympathetic to secessionism, was forced to resign.

"Ah yes, I remember Lizzy writing us about his troubles," Ann said. "Fremont passed out contracts to corrupt contractors and even declared himself the great liberator by declaring all Missouri slaves free. Lizzy was quite pleased about that part but was angry with Fremont's seeming desire to feast upon the fatted lamb in St. Louis while his troops died in fights with the rabble Confederates in Little Dixie. A mixed bag at best."

"The president is not pleased with any of it, including Fremont's premature announcement. He has no authority over such matters, especially in light of the attitude of the border states, whom he is still trying to hold in the Union."

"He gives the border states too much, Rand. Freeing the slaves—"

"Will come in time, dearest, but by Lincoln's hand, not by Fremont's."

The song ended, and the Lincolns entered the ballroom; the crowd separated to allow them to the center of the room where the president thanked them all for coming then launched into one of his humorous stories, creating smiles and laughs around the room. "Please, enjoy yourselves," the president said. "But tomorrow, when the silk dresses and the fancy duds are put in closets and trunks, do not forget we need you to be diligent in putting down this rebellion."

The room suddenly went quiet.

"Mr. President," said someone in the back on the far side of the hall. Lincoln turned that direction and gave his somber smile. "Tell us, how is the war going? Is General McClellan ready yet, sir?" The tone was one of frustration.

Mr. Lincoln looked at the floor and seemed to be thinking. "A few weeks ago, just before we had to declare martial law because of riots, a brawl broke out near the old national theater at about eleven o'clock at night." He turned to the left, his hands holding his lapels. "An officer, in passing the place, observed what was going on, and seeing the great numbers of persons involved he felt it his duty to command the peace. And this he did. Now, this is not an ordinary man but one with a voice of thunder and fists likes granite. Unfortunately, one bully roughly pushed the officer and told him to go away or he would whip him. The officer proceeded to arrest the troublemaker and put a hand on his shoulder to control him. Of course, the bully, half drunk with his hate of Northern views took a hard and mean swing at our officer."

He turned a bit and faced the front. "The officer parried the blow and used his iron fist to strike the fellow under the chin and knock him senseless. It was believed the officer had killed the man, broken his neck."

There was an audible gasp in the room from the ladies while the men seemed assured the man deserved it. It was very quiet and the president went on.

"Of course, the officer took the man to the nearest hospital where the surgeon declared there was no hope. The man died though they did their best to save him."

He paused again, standing straight and tall, his eyes filled with a mixture of sobriety and mirth. "The officer was inconsolable, and because we are friends, he came to me and told me what had happened.

I listened and then asked a few question before I remarked that I was sorry that he'd had to kill the man, but these are times of war, and a great many men deserve killing. This man seemed to be one of them, and I told the officer to feel no guilt about the matter and that I would stand by him."

He turned to the man who had asked the question, all eyes riveted on Lincoln. "And then I told him this. You go home and get some sleep; but let me give you this piece of advice—hereafter, when you have occasion to strike a man, don't hit him with your fist; strike him with a club, a crowbar, or with something that won't kill him."

There was genuine laughter, but Rand could see confusion on the faces of many. The president deemed it wise to make his meaning clear. "We are not to the point where I wish to kill our Southern brothers and sisters, only teach them a lesson so that we do not have to hit them any harder. Peace is my goal, at as little cost as possible, but if after a good thumping with a stick they continue to fight the peace . . ." He paused. "Well, the story tells the truth of our determination." He looked at the orchestra leader. "Maestro, a good reel after a bad story, if you please."

The song was immediately forthcoming, and the mood lightened. Rand watched Lincoln as he walked through the crowd toward the door, greeting but never fully stopping. It was obvious he wished only to be free of the distraction, and his wife fell back, visiting some of the women and introducing them to others.

A moment later, Lincoln disappeared out the door, a half dozen men following. Rand knew each had something to solicit from the president and felt sorry for the man. Such things would be a nuisance in the daytime, a burden in the evening.

Mrs. Lincoln was suddenly in front of them and taking Ann by the arm. "Excuse us, Mr. Hudson, but your wife and I really do need to visit. I'm sure you won't mind."

Ann gave him a sorrowful, helpless glance as she was whisked away. He felt a bit naked standing alone and was grateful when he felt someone gently grab his elbow. He turned to face Elmer Ellsworth, one of Lincoln's personal secretaries and the man who had attended the Blair meeting in which they'd made plans about the arsenal months earlier. It had been the first time he met Ellsworth but had been impressed.

"Mr. Ellsworth," Rand said with a wide smile. "How good to see you again."

"And you." Ellsworth gently directed him toward the door. "I wish this were a social meeting, but unfortunately it's not." He glanced about quickly then leaned closer to Rand. "Mr. Lincoln would like to see you in his study. Do you have a minute?" It was obviously a rhetorical question, and Rand let himself be ushered from the room, his stomach in knots. They passed by men in deep conversation who took little note of Rand and Ellsworth. They entered a door into the long hallway and passed several doors before Ellsworth opened the last, ushered Rand through it, and closed it behind them. Lincoln was standing near the window, his hands clasped behind him as he listened to a man sitting in a chair, back to the door. Lincoln did not acknowledge Rand's presence immediately, intent on the other man's words.

"Fremont is right to do what he has done," the man in the chair said. "If you force him to recant, you set back our goals by months!" The voice was angry, adamant, forceful.

"It's a matter of timing," Lincoln said as calmly as he could. "Six months, a year. I need more time." Lincoln turned and looked directly down at the man whose dark hair was all Rand could see. "I need you to concentrate on repealing the Crittenden-Johnson Resolution by the end of the year. Once that's out of the way and Kentucky and Maryland are secure, I will begin to move our feelings into public view but not now. There is too much at stake."

The man stood, and Rand immediately recognized him. Thaddeus Stevens was one of the North's most active universal emancipation proponents in the House of Representatives. He was also the chairman of the House's Ways and Means Committee that controlled the country's purse strings.

Stevens was stiff, resolute when he stood, but after a few seconds in front of the taller and even more determined Lincoln, his shoulders sagged, and he shook his head.

"Very well, Abraham, but I warn you if you don't—"

Lincoln interrupted him. "Thaddeus, let me introduce you to one of our officers, Randolph Hudson of Missouri."

Stevens turned and faced Rand, then stepped directly to him as if to intimidate the newcomer. Rand extended his hand to keep him at a fair distance. "Mr. Stevens."

Stevens shook his hand while measuring Rand. "Missouri, is it? Slave owner?"

"No, sir."

"Mr. Hudson and I had a conversation a while back while I was still trying to secure the nomination. He is an abolitionist, Thaddeus, and one who thinks this war *should* be about slavery," Lincoln said.

Stevens was still in the midst of shaking Rand's hand and gripped it harder and shook it more energetically at the pronouncement. "Then possibly you can pound some sense into Abraham's thick skull. Do you agree with General Fremont's order to free slaves that escape their owners?" He opened one eye further, lifting his eyebrow, and giving Rand a hard look.

"In substance, but the president is right. This is not the time."

"Harumph," Stevens said. "Already indoctrinated, are you?"

"No, sir, but you cannot win the war if Kentucky and Maryland turn against you. For the present, General Butler has the right idea—call them contraband, put them to work for the Union. With the Confederacy moving into Kentucky against the promise to honor its neutrality, most of the men there will be in the Union fold in a matter of two, maybe three months. Maryland will take a bit longer, but if McClellan is even partially successful against Richmond, by the end of the year you'll be in a good spot to begin introducing a more complete and lasting emancipation."

Stevens glared then turned to Lincoln. "All right then. I'll buy you some time." He stepped toe-to-toe with the president and looked up at him. "But I need you to control Mary, Abraham. She is spending far too much on this . . . this . . . *palace*. People are going to start thinking you want to be king if she keeps it up!"

"I have already been very frank with her, Thaddeus. Pay the present bills, and there will be no more."

"Harumph." He started for the door. "I'll find my way out. By the back door if you don't mind. Hate these balls. Fools stepping on everybody's toes! Just as well come to Congress if that's your game." The door closed with a bang.

"Interesting man," Rand said.

Lincoln gave his usual smile. "He would appreciate that analysis and then debate you for an hour to show your error." He pointed to a seat. "Sit, please. Would you like anything to drink?"

"No thanks, I don't drink."

"Because you joined the Mormons," Lincoln said without expression.

Rand felt his throat tighten. "Yes."

"Frank Blair shared your religion with me." He paused to pick up a cup and sip from it. Knowing Lincoln was a teetotaler, Rand figured it was coffee. "I knew of your people when they were at Nauvoo. Voted to give them a city charter when I was in the legislature."

"But you were silent when they were being driven from the state." Rand tried to keep his voice free of the anger he'd felt as a boy, but it was difficult. The mob had been responsible for his father's death.

Lincoln's cheek twitched a little at the attack. "I was in Washington, and what we heard from Governor Ford resembled the color of the waters of the Mississippi in spring; I just didn't realize it at the time. I am sorry to say that I was very busy here and did nothing to discover the truth until I learned of the great loss of life when you were driven out of Nauvoo in the dead of winter. My lack of action has haunted me ever since." He leaned forward. "Even by then, there was little I could have done. The mob had taken control of Nauvoo, and your people had left for the West." He sat back again. "When you came to Springfield a year ago, you said nothing of being a Mormon then."

Rand frowned. "My father died because of the mob, and my mother grew bitter. She took us to St. Louis instead of going west. She refused to let us even speak of the Church, though my sister and I disobeyed for a time and attended a branch for those immigrating to Salt Lake through St. Louis. Then I just drifted away. When I spoke with you it was no longer a part of my life."

"But you have renewed your faith in Mormonism."

"My mother's death forced me to think about things, to remember what I knew to be true."

Lincoln's eyes were dark, piercing, and he used them now to measure Rand. "One cannot fault another man for his religious beliefs even if they don't agree with his own. If he did, he would probably find his own religion soon under attack and have little ability to defend himself." He went to his desk, removed a paper from its center drawer, and handed it to Rand. "I received that recently. As you know the telegraph has reached the West Coast and runs through Salt Lake City."

Rand read the telegraph, *"Utah has not seceded, but is firm for the Constitution and laws of our once happy country."* It was signed *Brigham Young.*

"There has been some concern about Mormon loyalties. I would guess that Mr. Young's telegram is intended to put those concerns to rest, and yet reports we receive . . . Well, I'm still unsure and wish to find some peace about the matter."

Rand leaned forward. "I was just entering the Academy when Judge Drummond assailed the Mormons in every newspaper on the East Coast. Everyone believed his report and that of other non-Mormon officials given office in the new territory of Utah. That led to your predecessor sending an entire army to put down a rebellion that never existed. When it comes to the Saints and their leader, don't trust your government-appointed officials; trust the prophet, or like Mr. Buchanan you'll run your ship into the shoals of blunder."

Lincoln smiled as he picked up another telegram and handed it to Rand. "Two days after I received the wire from Mr. Young, I got another from one of our generals. He wants to recruit one to ten thousand Mormons."

"For what purpose?" Rand asked.

"To guard telegraph lines, trails, and US territory against Confederate takeover. We have word that renegades and some Indian tribes have agreed to serve the South and will try to harass our communications and forts between here and California. We've already seen some of it. The question is will Mr. Young be agreeable, or should we send a contingent of soldiers?"

"I don't pretend to know what he would or wouldn't do, but the telegram he sent should be considered an olive leaf. I can convey your feelings to President Young," Rand offered. "I can also let him know of a forthcoming request concerning help protecting federal property and roads. With your permission . . ."

Lincoln stood and extended a long, thin hand, a wry smile on his face. "You're a private citizen as well as a soldier. What messages you convey to your spiritual leader are your own business." Rand took it as a signal their conversation was finished with satisfactory results. Rand stood as well, received the president's firm grip, and they shook. But Lincoln didn't let go. "There are those in the army that would misunderstand your allegiance to your faith, Mr. Hudson. Would you consider it offensive if I asked you to be careful who you share it with? I would hate to lose your leadership."

Rand pressed the hand a bit harder then released it. "I understand your concern Mr. President. I don't wear my religion on my sleeve, but I will not hide it either. I did that once and found it didn't work. What you really believe wins out in the end, for good or ill. God sees to it."

"Then I wish you Godspeed. Enjoy the rest of the evening, and I hope Mary hasn't worn out your good wife's ear with her endless plans that never seem to take root. Mary could use someone with determination and—"

"You invited the right woman," Rand said with a smile. He turned to the door, and as he did, he noticed several books on a reading table next to a comfortable chair. He recognized the one on top and paused to touch it. Rand smiled as Ellsworth opened the door and ushered him out of the room.

"Your religion's Book of Mormon," Ellsworth said. "The Library of Congress had a copy, and the president is an avid reader." Ellsworth offered a hand. "Thank you for being frank with him and for your help with Mr. Young. The president must be careful these days." Ellsworth went back into Lincoln's office. Rand turned down the hall toward the entry when he saw Ann sitting on a divan near an outside window. She was in conversation with Mary Lincoln, and when she saw him her eyes quickly focused on his. They were pleading for relief, and Rand walked briskly toward her.

"Ladies, I fear that I have bad news," he said with an apologetic smile.

"Oh my, nothing too terrible I hope. The rebels haven't attacked our city have they?" Mary Lincoln said.

Rand regretted his approach. Mrs. Lincoln was rumored to have lost a good deal of sleep over a rebel takeover of Washington and was constantly needling her husband to do more to protect the city. His words had obviously stirred those concerns once more. "No, no, nothing as horrible as all that, but I regret that Ann and I must be on our way. I know you probably have much more to discuss, but—"

"He's right," Ann said, getting slowly to her feet. "He hasn't been home for so long and must return to his duties far too soon. I hope you don't mind."

"No, no, of course not, but you really must come to tea next Wednesday. Our committee meets at that time, and they must hear your ideas. Mr. Bellows will be there and Miss Dorothea Dix. You know them both of course, and you know they mean business, but they are both so busy. And my duties here . . ." She rolled her eyes as she took Ann by the arm and led her toward the door. "Endless. Simply endless. We need someone with energy, ideas. And you have both."

Ann glanced at Rand with a tired look of hopelessness on her face. It was then he noticed she was a bit pale, her eyes worried.

"You will come, won't you? I won't have it otherwise, and I do want you to feel free to call on me anytime. I have a good deal of influence in this city now and can open doors for you that others simply cannot. We must do something about hospitals, dear Ann; you know we must, so you must come and help us get started. Promise you will." She smiled at Ann as they reached the door.

Rand could see now that it was not just Mrs. Lincoln that was bothering Ann but that she was not feeling well. He kicked himself for not noticing it sooner.

He pulled Mrs. Lincoln aside quickly. "I'm sure Ann will try Mrs. Lincoln, but she is . . . well, expecting our first child and—"

"Oh my, why didn't you say so, dear girl? Here I am rambling on so and—yes, I see you are a bit pale. Take her home, Mr. Hudson. Immediately. And let me know how she feels. If she can come, by all means . . ."

They went quickly through the entry to the main door, where Rand looked for the carriage, waved the driver forward, and then returned to a still-talking Mrs. Lincoln and a quite distraught Ann. He gently grabbed her arm as he bade the president's wife good-bye and then helped Ann into the carriage. Telling the driver to take them home, he climbed inside and sat down beside Ann, who immediately collapsed into his arms.

"What is it, Ann?" he asked with sincere concern.

"I think I'm bleeding, darling. Get me home quickly."

Rand leaned out the window and told the driver to use the whip. The carriage lurched forward as he fell back inside and wrapped his arms around her, his eyes closing as he begged God for help.

*　　*　　*

Rand arrived at home to find a stranger waiting in his parlor. As he hurried up the stairs with Ann in his arms, he called out to Lydijah. Lydijah, sensing the fear and desperation, ran from the kitchen, saw the blood on the floor, and forced her large frame up the steps two at a time. Entering the bedroom, she found Rand helping Ann remove her dress and underskirt, saw the blood on her garments, and immediately helped Rand lower Ann into the bed.

"Did you send de driver fo' de doctah?" she asked firmly.

"Yes," Rand answered. "What's happening, Lydijah? What—"

"She's threatenin' t' lose de child." Lydijah ripped off Ann's pantaloons as she told Rand to go into the hall. "Dat man in de parlor, he a missionary from de Church. She need a blessing, Mr. Rand, and he can help."

Rand ran from the room and down the stairs. He entered the parlor to find a man of about his same height and weight but lighter in complexion and hair color. "Sir, you're a missionary?" he asked.

The man nodded. "Benjamin Connelly. Is your wife ill?"

"She is threatening to lose our child. Can you assist me in giving her a blessing?"

"Of course. Do you have oil?"

Rand went to a cabinet and pulled out a small corked glass bottle. "Follow me," he said. They went quickly upstairs, knocked, and stepped in at Lydijah's approval. Ann was covered with blankets, and Lydijah was washing out a bloody rag, concern in her wrinkled brow. Ann was obviously in a good deal of pain. Rand went to Ann's bed and sat on the edge as she gave a questioning look at the man behind him.

"This is Benjamin Connelly. He is a missionary and will help me give you a blessing." Rand stood and handed Connelly the vial.

"Mr. Connelly, I am sorry that I'm—" Ann started to say.

"Please, save your strength, Mrs. Hudson." He pulled the cork, put a drop of oil on the crown of Ann's head, then laid his hands and quickly anointed. Rand went around to the other side, his heart in prayer that he would say the right words. He stretched out his trembling hands and laid them on her head. When he felt the warmth of Benjamin Connelly's fall on his, suddenly he was very calm, his mind clear. He sealed the anointing and gave her a blessing, promising her comfort and peace while also telling her that she would yet have many children and raise them up unto the Lord. He told her firmly that she should not blame herself for this untimely event and to rely on the Lord and trust in His will. He then closed the blessing, looking down into Ann's tear-filled eyes, then he stooped and kissed her forehead gently.

"Thank you, darling," Ann said. "I'll be all right, won't I?"

He nodded, knowing that she would.

"Now, you two fine gent'men go out in de hall. When de doctor come, yo' send him right in. Shoo! Go on now! I has care t' be givin'."

Rand closed the door behind them and let himself fall into a padded chair next to a table in the wide hall. Connelly took the one on the other side of the table.

"That was a fine blessing, Mr. Hudson. The Spirit was in it," he said genuinely.

Rand only nodded. He knew what was missing. He had wanted to bless the child, but he could not say the words. He'd tried, but they simply would not come. He heard Connelly say something but missed it and had to ask him to repeat himself.

"Your sister, Elizabeth, sends her love," Benjamin said, offering what comfort he could.

Rand sat a little straighter. "You've seen Lizzy?"

"I met her in Florence. She gave me a ride back to Illinois on one of your steamers. From there I caught the train to Chicago to come here." He grinned. "We did have one side trip in Missouri." He grinned. "Your sister is quite a woman."

Rand lifted his eyebrows. "She had you help retrieve some runaways?"

Benjamin chuckled. "Yes, with William Quantrill on our tail. We had quite an adventure."

Rand shook his head, smiling. Would Lizzy ever learn? "What brings you to Washington?"

"I'm assigned to gather any remaining Saints in this city and in several others who want to go to Salt Lake and make arrangements for them in the spring. Elizabeth said I might find lodging here, for a short time at least, but—"

"No buts, Mr. Connelly. The room on the end down there will be yours. You may stay as long as you like."

"Thank you." They both sat back and each returned to their own thoughts. They were jolted out of them only by the appearance of the doctor. Rand stood, told him what had happened, and watched him disappear into Ann's room. He stood there quite helpless, afraid and unsure of just what to do.

"Mr. Hudson?"

Rand turned around to face Benjamin Connelly. "Rand, please." He forced a smile.

"Rand, experience has taught me that prayer is a man's best solace when these moments arise. Possibly you and I could go to the parlor and . . ."

"Yes, I think that would help. Thank you."

They went downstairs and into the parlor. Rand closed the door so that there was only a two-inch opening. He sat down on the divan, and Benjamin took a chair.

Two hours later, Ann lost the baby. Rand and Benjamin both shed tears as the doctor told them. Then Rand climbed the stairs, knowing his wife needed him. And knowing what God would have him say.

Chapter Twenty

LIZZY HAD EATEN, NAPPED, AND changed clothes by the time the steamer reached Cairo. She was joined by a still disgruntled Captain Hillyer as she left the ship and walked up the hill to the old house being used as Grant's headquarters. They passed lines of soldiers fully equipped and marching to the docks to be loaded aboard several steamships, most of which belonged to Hudson Shipping. Not a single soldier missed giving her a good look as they trudged to their destination, and several jokingly asked if she'd come to marry them. She gave each soldier a warm smile and light wave but neither commented on nor rebuffed their remarks as they did not strike her as being other than complimentary.

When they reached the door of the old house, several officers moved aside, tipped their hats, made a slight bow, and then whispered to one another about who she might be or what she could possibly be doing at the general's headquarters. One of the adjutants opened the door for her, and she stepped inside to find Grant standing in a half circle of men around a table, studying a map. He either did not see her come in or was too engrossed in his business to care. Hillyer pointed to a chair and offered her a cup of coffee, which she declined, removing her gloves and hat instead.

Lizzy had changed her attire for a reason. Though she could probably ride and shoot as well as any man in the room, she knew that many of them would not take kindly to such a woman. She also knew Ulysses Grant. They had met several times when Grant lived in St. Louis and ran his father-in-law's farm. His recognition of her position as a lady—and the present managing owner of Hudson Shipping—would give her a chance to make her point without her being a direct threat to his desire to protect all things feminine from the "crass sport of men."

She was in the entry, Grant and his fellows in the sitting room but in full view. She couldn't hear every word but did hear enough to know that Grant was moving the lion's share of his force down the Ohio to the mouth of the Tennessee River to capture and hold Paducah, Kentucky. As near as she could tell, the Confederates were already on the move to Paducah with the intent to fortify it and prevent Union incursions into the heartland of rebel territory.

Hudson steamers had plied the Tennessee clear to its headwaters at Knoxville. The river ran from the southwest to Chattanooga before crossing into north Alabama, where it eventually formed a part of the northern border of Mississippi. Here it turned north again, crossing the breadth of Tennessee and dumping into the Ohio at Paducah.

The Cumberland River, which also entered the Ohio near Paducah, was no less important. It ran through Kentucky to Nashville and into northern Tennessee. If the Union controlled these two rivers, they could launch expeditions deep into the heart of the Confederacy.

But to Lizzy it was more than that. As the Union moved south, slaves would flee for freedom but be surrounded by armies either unfriendly or uninterested in their plight. She wanted to help them.

Grant finished giving orders, and one of his adjutants rolled up the maps that lay on the table while making him aware of Lizzy's presence. Grant chewed on his cigar as if annoyed. Then Hillyer approached him, and he began to chew on it harder. Lizzy figured Hillyer had just updated him on her stubbornness. He sat at his desk, and Hillyer motioned for her to join them while the adjutant grabbed another chair and placed it across from Grant. Lizzy did not sit until Grant stood and pointed at the chair.

"Elizabeth Hudson. It's been a few years. You're more beautiful than ever."

"You're kind, Ulysses. How is your family?"

"Fine, fine. And your mother and brother?"

"Mother passed just last year. Randolph was with McDowell at Bull Run. He was wounded, but his wife says he's healed and has returned to his command."

"McDowell was a fool. He waited too long then didn't commit his forces." He shoved the dark scowl aside. "I'm glad Randolph survived. When I lived in St. Louis, he and I talked tactics one night at a party neither of us was enjoying very much. He knew his stuff." He tossed the entire cigar at the spittoon but missed. From the number of half-chewed, half-smoked bits and pieces, it wasn't the first time. "But, I must leave tonight. Elizabeth, we appreciate your response to our request, but you shouldn't be here."

Lizzy smiled. "You're right, General, and I do not intend to stay very long." She pulled some papers from the valise she had brought with her. "All I need is your signature on these documents, and I will be on my way."

He was surprised at her response, leaned forward, and took the documents then looked them over quickly. His face hardened. "But this is downright thievery. We can contract for steamers at half that price up the Ohio."

"But you're not up the Ohio, are you, General," Lizzy said with a smile.

He tossed the papers on the edge of the table nearest her. "I cannot pay this price, Elizabeth. I would look the fool. Don't try to take advantage of any perceived friendship we—"

"You'll look worse if the rebels reinforce Paducah and prevent Union use of the Tennessee when you could have stopped it," she said. In order to hold his tongue, he pulled another cigar from his pocket and rammed it into his mouth. Lizzy took the papers, put them in her valise, and pulled out another set. "Possibly this contract is more to your liking." She handed it to him.

He grabbed the papers, looking them over then sitting straight. "But except for the cost, there's no change on this document," he noted, confused. "What—"

"The last paragraph," Lizzy said.

Grant quickly read it, then his nostrils flared again. "You know I cannot—"

"You can, and if you're the shrewd soldier I think you are, you will."

"But this as much as grants you the right to remove slaves from Confederate territory under the protection of the federal government. You know Lincoln has already denounced Fremont's attempt at declaring rebels' slaves free and will probably force Fremont to rescind his order. This goes contrary to Lincoln's wishes."

"The president has also agreed with Butler's use of the word *contra-band* with regard to slaves who come across federal lines. Note, General, that in the contract we use that word, and you are merely giving me the right to remove said contraband from enemy territory. It falls well within already established guidelines from the government."

"Then you intend only to receive slaves that cross our lines and we declare contraband," Grant said suspiciously.

Lizzy had to be careful. Though she intended to set up a railroad that would strike deep into the heart of Tennessee and Alabama, she couldn't reveal those plans to Grant. Such efforts were *not* covered in the federal government's recent statements, and Grant could not agree to any such network. "The contract is clear, General. My ships take your men to Paducah if you agree to turn all contrabands over to me for removal north. It solves a lot of problems for you. Though you can put some of the slaves to work building fortifications, you cannot feed, house, and care for their women and children. I can get them to safety and see they're taken care of. You cannot lose, Ulysses, and we both know it."

Grant read the document more carefully then looked at Lizzy, measuring her. Finally, he shook his head. "Why do I get the feeling I am being taken by a pretty face?"

"Why, thank you, General." She smiled. "You're right in that all is not as it seems. I hope that as you move south you'll allow my ships to move with you and that other contracts will be forthcoming. In the meantime, I get the satisfaction of helping slaves flee their masters, and you get ships to help you win the war. If that makes you feel like you're being taken, then you're not the shrewd man I've assumed you are." She glanced at the small watch attached to her bodice. "Your men are waiting to load on my steamers. What will it be?"

He sat back, chewing on the new cigar then asked the adjutant to give him pen and inkwell. He stood, signed the documents, and handed the pen to Lizzy, who also signed. She picked them up and put them in her valise before turning to leave. "See you onboard, Ulysses."

Grant removed his cigar from his mouth. "What? You can't—"

"Yes, I can. Paragraph two." She quoted it: "*The agent assigned by Hudson Shipping will travel with the steamers to assure proper use and to arrange for repairs, supplies, etc., etc.* Don't be long, General. Your room is number five on the upper deck of the *New Uncle Sam*. Dinner will be served in the dining hall at eight." She grinned as she walked through the entry and outside. Hillyer didn't catch up until she was halfway down the hill.

"Is he still cussing?" she asked.

"Yes, ma'am," Hillyer said with a grin. "I never seen anyone beat the general at his own game."

"His own game? What would that be?"

"Feint, then hit 'em with all you got, ma'am." His smile was filled with respect.

Lizzy laughed, putting her arm through Hillyer's. "Well, I suppose that's what I did all right, but there's another part of the strategy the good general hasn't seen yet that always makes a man feel good about being beaten by the fairer sex."

He was enjoying her touch, his face turning a bit red at all the attention the soldiers were giving the two of them as they walked past the line.

"What's that, Miss Hudson?"

"You'll see, Captain. You'll see."

They arrived back at the ship, and Hillyer gave the order to start boarding the men. As soon as each vessel was loaded, they were to go to the middle of the channel and wait for the others. Lizzy boarded, went up to her room, and closed the door behind her before doffing her hat, removing her dress, and replacing it with the other more comfortable linen one. Picking up her apron, she made her way to the galley. She had a meal to cook.

Chapter Twenty-One

RUNAWAYS STARTED ARRIVING IN PADUCAH a few days after Union troops occupied the town and started fortifying it. True to his promise, Grant declared them contraband and began hiring some of the men to build a fort while Lizzy set up a camp for their wives and children at a farm just outside the town. Grant provided food, blankets, and even several tents, but as more runaways began showing up, Lizzy could see it wouldn't be enough and sent for more supplies from St. Louis. She also sent for Elliott. The number of runaways was growing daily, and she needed help. When Elliott arrived with the supplies, she put him to work preparing a winter camp and making arrangements for transporting those who wanted to go farther north. Lizzy was aware of a number of safe havens in Ohio but the largest was in Ripley, situated on the banks of the river. Hundreds of locals there aided runaways that crossed the river. Their leader, Jon Rankin, lived in a house atop a hill sporting a thirty-foot pole that had a candle lit every night—a sort of beacon for runaways in Kentucky unsure of where to go. Lizzy sent word to Rankin that she'd set up a camp in Paducah and had sent the first group of runaways to him.

At first, the people of Paducah were unfriendly to their occupiers. Though Grant had written an order guaranteeing that soldiers would not molest or steal from them and promised punishment for any who did, the population as a whole supported the South. The most discontented fled, leaving a mollified but cooperative population behind. It was from one of the families set on moving south that Lizzy had bought the farm.

She pulled back the curtains of her second-floor room as the sun breached the eastern sky and flowed across leaves, now beginning to fall from the trees. There was a definite crispness in the air, and the fireplace had been stoked most of the night. She had been traveling back and forth between St. Louis and Paducah, but she was planning to go back home tomorrow. It would be Thanksgiving in two weeks.

The number of runaways had slowed to a trickle of what it had been when the town was first occupied. Slavers had quickly learned of this new road to freedom and had done their best to watch for slaves heading this direction. Lizzy and Elliott had considered making forays into Tennessee to bring out runaways, but the Confederates had moved more than twenty thousand soldiers into the region, making it near impossible. Things would open up as the Union army moved south against Fort Donelson and Fort Henry then into Tennessee. But General Fremont, Grant's boss and head of all the armies of the West was dragging his feet. She would have to be patient.

She sat at her writing table and quickly wrote a letter to Rand and Ann, something she hadn't found time for in at least two weeks. Her first sentence asked after Ann's health. Lizzy had received word of the loss of the baby weeks ago and had written a long letter then. It had been hard to be so far away, but they had corresponded since, and Ann seemed much better. With the Army of the Potomac all but entrenched for the winter, Rand was staying his nights at home, and that gave Ann both the love and comfort she needed as the two of them read and prayed together. Ann shared what she had learned and felt, and Lizzy was grateful that comfort had followed. Ann's last letter was filled with the hope that she would be pregnant again before spring.

Ann had also mentioned Benjamin Connelly. He had stayed in Washington for nearly a month but was on the road most of the time, seeking out members in Maryland and New York. There were a few members in Washington, and they met together in various homes, including the one temporarily occupied by Thomas Stenhouse, who was in Washington on business but also in direct contact with President Young. They hadn't seen Ben for some time. He was traveling, visiting other small branches, and preparing for the migration in the spring.

Ann told her that feelings against the Church were high in Washington due to Senator Morrill's lies about the Saints and his determination to pass a law banning plural marriage. Brother Stenhouse had sent word to President Young of what was happening and had included Rand's conversation with Lincoln. President Young had immediately agreed to the enlistment of Saints to guard the telegraph lines, and Lincoln had authorized payment and enlistment. Since then Stenhouse had returned to Salt Lake.

Lizzy had been relieved after receiving Rand's letter telling her that Andrew was alive and well, but she still hadn't received anything directly from Andrew or his family.

She supposed that she shouldn't be surprised. Communications between North and South had been almost completely severed, and she had found no method of getting her letters through either. She could only assume that nothing was getting through unless it was hand delivered. She supposed that there were people willing to take such risks for a fee, but she hadn't found them and, apparently, neither had the Clays.

But she mustn't give up hope. She still loved Andrew, she was sure of that, and she supposed that was why she felt so guilty when the thought of Ben Connelly crossed her mind. She hadn't forgotten his stolen kiss, and that worried her, but more frightening were the thoughts that Ben was a Mormon and Andrew was not. Those feelings had finally led her to write a letter to Andrew telling him of her faith, her love of it, and her plans to never let it go. She had sent it and then instantly hoped that of all the letters she had sent, it wouldn't be the one to reach him. And those feelings had given her a good deal of guilt too.

It was all so confusing, and she'd finally gone to her knees, begging for guidance. Finally, only last week, she had come to the conclusion that she need not feel guilty on any count. Until the war was settled, nothing else could be.

She looked at the last letter from Ann, reviewing its content in order to change the direction of her thoughts. There was still no word of Newton, and the proposal of a prisoner exchange had become mired in politics. It angered Ann, and she said so in her letter. This war was the product of political intransigence, and in her opinion, that would be the cause of more deaths than any other factor. It was foolish to play politics with the lives of those who were starving or freezing to death in jails and prison camps on both sides.

The last page of Ann's letter detailed the political battle over McClellan's foot dragging and Rand's growing discontent with the general's apparent messiah complex. His political supporters considered him the savior of the Union and had finally gotten General Winfield Scott to retire and put McClellan in his place. Only then had they discovered that the dominant trait of their "Little Napoleon" was that he had little courage. For Ann, the worst part was that he'd taken a stand against the war ever being about slavery. "I am fighting to preserve the

integrity of the Union," he had said. "To gain that end we cannot afford
to mix up the negro question." It had infuriated Ann and discouraged
Rand, who was left to wonder about McClellan's ambition to preserving
the Union more than to his own political future. The army was *almost*
ready to move *almost* all of the time, but they didn't move, and Rand had
confided in Ann that he wondered if they ever would under McClellan.

Lizzy put the letter in her valise, finished writing her response,
addressed the envelope, and sealed the letter inside. She would send it
with the next mail going east.

She sat down at the mirror and began brushing out her hair. Last
evening she'd held a dinner between the fort's commanding officers and
General Grant and his staff who had come from Cairo. She had learned
long ago that most men hardly noticed a woman when they were being
served, and she had listened carefully to the entire discussion while
she made sure their plates were filled with a fine meal and their glasses
topped with good wine. She was pleased with the information she
heard as they discussed details and preparations for a campaign against
Tennessee that would move forward in late winter. As they disbursed to
their various accommodations, Grant had hung back, a slight smile on
his face. Telling her that he was impressed with her ability to spy on him,
he wondered if she would be so kind as not to share her information with
the enemy.

After a bit of a laugh, she had promised. Then he'd surprised her
with a request that she accompany him on a ride the following day. He
didn't reveal his purpose, so it caused her to toss and turn during the
night. She was glad the time had nearly come for her to learn of it.

After brushing her hair, she dressed in riding clothes and put on a
sweater and leather riding jacket before going downstairs to the kitchen
for breakfast. One of the runaway slaves whose husband was working
for the army was doing the cooking and had breakfast ready when Lizzy
got to the kitchen. Having decided to give up coffee, she sipped at a
cup of herbal tea while she waited. She didn't wait long. Grant came
through the kitchen door, greeted the help, removed his hat, and said
good morning to Lizzy, who invited him to sit in the chair opposite her.
The cook put a plate before each of them, and they ate while chatting
about her success escorting runaways out of the state, the lack of any
movement in Washington, what was happening in Missouri, and the
recent taking of Hatteras Inlet on the Carolina coast and what that would

do to Confederate shipping. Grant seemed generally upbeat but had some harsh words for McClellan as an absentminded mystery who had forgotten what generals are to be about. He also critized Lincoln's slow action toward Fremont, whom Grant considered a disorganized popinjay. Grant, who usually said very little, seemed in fine form this morning.

Breakfast finished, the two awaited their horses at the back porch. Then they rode into the street, where a dozen mounted men joined them. For a moment, Lizzy thought she was being escorted out of town, but they turned south and traveled toward the river until they reached a knoll overlooking the inlet that held the mouths of both the Cumberland and Tennessee Rivers. With their escort ordered to hold their position, Grant led Lizzy to the edge of the knoll and pointed at the land between the two rivers.

"Down there fifty miles you have Fort Donelson on the Cumberland and Forts Henry and Heiman on the Tennessee. Until we take those battlements, we cannot secure Kentucky nor can we move into Tennessee, a necessary event if we're to split the Confederacy in half."

"Then you must take them," Lizzy said, not sure why he was telling her this.

"Farther south and east, Johnston has fortified Bowling Green, Kentucky, but we cannot discover his strength there, nor do we know how many men he has at Donelson. Because General Fremont does not want us to move at the present, I think it wise to retrieve more information by . . . clandestine means."

Lizzy was getting the gist of this meeting. "And you need someone to provide you with that information."

Grant had removed a cigar and stuck it in his mouth. Lizzy seldom saw him actually light one, so she was surprised when he lit this one.

"Do you know the name John Fairfield?" he asked.

Lizzy nodded. "A former Virginian, son of a slaveholder. He hates the institution and has helped dozens if not hundreds of slaves to escape. He disappeared last year and some say he was killed in Cumberland County, Tennessee, while trying to aid some runaways."

He nodded. "We think he's in Bowling Green." He paused. "Fairfield operates different than most. You, on the one hand, set up a rendezvous, race in, pick them up, then race out. Not Fairfield. He goes in as a businessman under an assumed name. Sets himself up, ingratiates himself to the locals, puts out the word to the black community through men he claims are his slaves, and pretty soon the locals are missing half a hundred blacks. He's a planner, takes his time. The man shot in Tennessee last year came in fast for a pickup but got caught and was shot. It wasn't Fairfield."

He reached into his pocket, pulled out a yellowed piece of paper, and handed it to her. "We received that from one of your runaways yesterday."

Lizzy unfolded the paper to find an announcement for an undertaker in Bowling Green. There was a brief note written across it. *"Take this boy and the dozen with him to Rankin with my compliments. J.F."*

"The boy says the undertaker arranged their escape with a fake funeral of some kind and that it wasn't the first. He was taken to a safe house and brought out with the rest of his group. The boy's description of the undertaker meets that of John Fairfield." He paused. "The boy says his mother is still in Bowling Green. A tall, thin woman who is this mortician's housekeeper. He's worried she won't get out if Fairfield is caught."

"And you need someone to make contact with Fairfield."

"The name on that flier is John Barber. We thought Mr. Barber would enjoy a visit from his sister." Grant smiled. "If you want a way into this war, Elizabeth, I'm giving you the chance."

Lizzy stared across the landscape, thinking, her heart pounding. She'd never been into the heart of Kentucky, knew no one there. She certainly couldn't advertise herself as Elizabeth Hudson of St. Louis. Hudson Shipping's politics were well-known in both Union and Confederate circles, and when Rand had thrown his support to the Union, the rebels had tried to force him to give them his steamers. He'd not only repelled their offers but had made them look like fools. Then a thought occurred to her. "Barber's sister wouldn't have access to the places you want information about, Ulysses, but I have an idea who might."

Grant looked at her. "And who would that be?"

"Susan Davis."

"The singer? But she's made it known she supports the Confederacy. Besides, she's in California and—" The lights seemed to come on. "Ah, you will pretend to be Miss Davis." He smiled. "Shrewd, but if even one person—"

"Let me worry about that, General, but this must stay between us. Not a soul is to know. There are too many Southern sympathizers still living in Paducah and St. Louis who would love to have me in a Confederate prison, and if they learned I was playing the part of Miss Davis, they'd have it done."

"What, no additional contracts binding the government to Hudson Shipping?" Grant asked with a wry smile. "As shrewd a businesswoman as you are—"

"I already have all I can handle," she returned the smile. "Are we agreed?"

He nodded, his face sobering. "Of course. It'll be dangerous enough without some loudmouth making it worse."

"Good. Then I must make arrangements." She turned her horse to go back the way they had come. He was soon at her side. "This General Johnston who you say is commanding the army at Bowling Green. Is he the same one who reinforced Beauregard at Manassas?"

"Yes, the same."

"Well then, making a fool of him will be doubly sweet, won't it?" she said.

Grant laughed, something he didn't do often, then grew sober again. "General Fremont is sending me to mount a series of demonstrations against the rebels at Columbus. Supposedly, he is pursuing General Price and his men in southeast Missouri, and he doesn't want the rebels at Columbus to come to Price's rescue. I won't be readily available if you should run into trouble."

Lizzy only nodded. There was no sense worrying about it now. Instead, she decided to redirect the subject.

"Fremont sounds desperate," she said.

"He is. Lincoln's been asking for action for months. Fremont has delivered little to nothing, and Missouri is still up for grabs but shouldn't be. If he doesn't hand Price's scalp to Lincoln soon, Fremont knows he'll be replaced, regardless of his powerful friends." He paused. "Between you and me, Fremont will be removed. It's the reason we've been held back from going south. They want a new commander in place before they take any real action. Foolish but the reality. I want all the information I can get by the time that change takes place."

"I'll do my best, Ulysses," she said.

They rode the short distance back to the farm in silence, but when they reached it, Grant tipped his hat and wished her Godspeed before riding toward the fort. Lizzy dismounted and went inside. She would need a few things from St. Louis before she went south. She found Elliott in the makeshift office they had created in a bedroom next to the kitchen. He looked up at her from behind the desk then sat back.

He had seen that look before.

* * *

The sun lay low in the sky, and the day was turning cold. There had been a light smattering of snow in the morning, but the noonday sun had melted it and warmed the afternoon sufficiently that Ann decided to walk through a small park just down the street. Couples and families sat about on benches or strolled along at a quiet pace. As she reached the far corner, she noticed a number of people gathered around a preacher standing on the fountain wall. She recognized him immediately and quietly finagled her way through the listeners to where she could see him more clearly. Ben Connelly was looking directly at one man and seemed to be answering his question.

"The doctrine of Christ is the key," Ben said. "Faith in the Lord must come first, then repentance of sin, baptism, and reception of the Holy Ghost by the laying on of hands. But authority is necessary just as it was in the days of Christ. Recollect, my friend, that Christ himself laid hands on Peter and his fellow servants before He sent them out baptizing and preaching. If Christ thought authority necessary, why should we believe otherwise? And who has authority? Has your minister had hands laid on him? By whom? And who gave him the authority to do so?"

"We'll show ya the laying on of hands," mocked one man at the back of the crowd with a laugh. Other hecklers followed with similar derisions, but Ann noted that Ben ignored them and went on teaching the man and a few others who seemed genuinely interested. "Christ's authority was lost to this earth with the apostasy Paul preached of many times. When did it return? Through whom? I will tell you, good brother. On a bright spring day in 1829, Peter, James, and John—the Lord's Apostles and leaders of the kingdom after His death—came to this world through the veil and restored their authority to Joseph Smith, and I bear witness that we have it again upon the earth."

The hecklers booed and whistled. There were loud denunciations and even laughter until a particularly angry heckler, about the same size as Ben, shoved through the crowd and spat tobacco juice on Ben's boots. The crowd went silent as Ben stopped in midsentence, looked at his spattered boots then at the man, and smiled.

"It takes talent to hit something that size from that distance. My congratulations." He turned back to the man to whom he had been speaking and went on as snickers and outright laughter bounced around the crowd. Even Ann chuckled at the response but saw that the man who had done the spitting was not amused.

"Listen you miserable Mormon buzzard, you either shut yer mouth or I'll shut it fer ya." He shoved himself between Ben and the man to whom Ben was speaking. Ben showed no emotion but spoke plainly.

"What is your name, sir?" Ben asked.

The question and the calmness with which it was asked seemed to fluster the attacker and tie his tongue.

"His name's Hodges, Bill Hodges," called someone in the crowd.

Hodges glared at the person who spoke, but Ben smiled.

"Mr. Hodges, when I was a lad, I was small for my size, and there was this boy who used to pick on my kind. He was a bully, pure and simple. I used to get beat up by this bully quite regularly until one day my mother saw me huddling in a corner of the woodshed instead of going to school. She asked why, and I told her. She then proceeded to tell me how to handle such boys. Next time he come at me, she told me to—" With a sudden motion, Ben punched Hodges in the solar plexus, taking his breath away and causing him to bend over in pain. Ben put a hand on Hodges's head. "Then she said I was to finish him with—" Ben hit him on the back of the neck, and Hodges went flat on his stomach, unconscious. "That was all it took. The bully never bothered me again." He smiled at the crowd. "Now, brothers and sisters, it is not kind to attack a brother who is simply doing his best to preach the good word, but if there are others of you who think being a bully is better than intelligently talking about our differences, Mr. Hodges there will soon have company."

"Ain't you supposed to turn the other cheek?" someone asked.

"Ah yes, that is best at times, but you'll remember that even our Lord made a whip and drove out the money changers. 'Tis a world of conflict we live in. Sometimes it takes a soft touch to heal, and sometimes it takes it bit more of the hard approach."

The crowd went quiet, and Ben went back to preaching while two fellows came forward and dragged Hodges away. A few others followed. Ann figured they'd go to a pub, work up their ire, and come back. Hopefully Ben understood that as well.

She listened for a few more minutes until Ben addressed the entire group. "Now you have had a short lesson. I and a few others will be giving another at the community hall on Freewater Street tonight at 7:00 p.m. If you're interested in truth from the scriptures and the great plan of the Lord for your happiness, come and join with us." The crowd began to dissipate, and Ann noted their comments were mostly positive. She decided to stay put, waiting for Ben to finish talking to the interested contact, who received a copy of the Book of Mormon and left, thumbing through its pages. It was then Ben noticed her and smiled.

"Well, well, Sister Hudson. What a nice surprise."

Ann smiled back. "Mr. Connelly, you know that bully will come looking for you."

Ben gave her a sheepish look. "Then we should be on our way. May I escort you somewhere, or—"

"I was just out for a walk. Possibly you could accompany me home. Dinner will be ready, and after such exertion you're probably hungry."

"I have partaken of your lovely meals, Sister Hudson, and would be simply delighted to do so again." He picked up a bag near the fountain, offered his arm, and they started toward the street.

"How are you feeling?" he asked with genuine concern.

"Rand gave me a fine blessing. The Lord gives strength and comfort, and I thank Him for it." She smiled and leaned toward him to whisper. "I think I may be pregnant again."

"Ah, what wonderful news. You are a saint, Sister Hudson. Not unlike my wife, bless her soul."

Ann knew that Ben had been married but his wife had been lost trying to bear their child. "What was she like, Brother Connelly? I don't wish to intrude. I—"

"It isn't an intrusion at all," Ben said with a smile. "She was a survivor. Came across from England on her own, crossed the plains with the Martin Handcart Company, then spent her first winter in a small, one-room sod house with a family of strangers who took her in. They weren't strangers long, and she cared for their children when the wife died that winter. In spring, she went to work helping prepare the land for planting, along with the rest of the Saints, while also building her own house along Mill Creek. I met her that summer. We bumped into each other at a Church meeting." He smiled. "After I helped her get to her feet, she was kind enough to give me a good scolding for not looking where I was going before she pranced off toward the mercantile. Needless to say, I followed her, and we learned to get along a bit better."

He paused. "She had trouble bearing our child but made it far enough to bring our daughter into the world for about an hour. I greeted her and gave her a name before she and her mother passed and left me wondering if God had played some kind of joke on me." He smiled sadly. "It took a good deal of prayer to find my peace, but I did. You remind me of her a bit." He grinned. "I've seen you scold your husband, and it sounded familiar."

Ann laughed. "Why, thank you, Brother Connelly. I'm flattered."

"As you should be. She was the best when it came to scolding with love and making me want to be better. I believe you do the same for Brother Hudson."

Ann blushed. "Thank you, Ben. I really am honored to be compared with such a woman." She paused. "When did you return from New York?"

"Just an hour ago. There are still a few Saints there, and they're getting ready to go west in the spring, but I had to come back to check on your little branch as well."

"Then you will stay at the house," she said.

"Thank you for your kindness, Sister Hudson. Have you heard from Elizabeth?"

"Not for a while, but it doesn't surprise me. She's set up another station for runaways, this one at Paducah, Kentucky. It's an amazing thing. She no longer has to go and bring them out. They come to her."

"And less chance of running into Quantrill again," Ben said. "Of that I'm glad. And has she heard from her beau, Mr. Clay?"

"No, not a word, but we know he's alive—at least he was when Rand escaped after Manassas." Ann didn't say more. She was aware that Benjamin liked Lizzy. She could sense it in his voice, see it in his eye, but Lizzy loved Andrew and that was simply the way of it. She was not about to meddle in such affairs. "Oh dear, don't look now, but your bully from the park is standing across the street, and I believe he has less than good intentions."

"Yes, I saw him," Ben said.

"What will you do?"

He smiled. "There are only three of them, but I would ask that you stay here if they come across the street. I'll handle it. No sense getting both our heads busted."

"Does this happen often?" she asked. "I mean, do you get attacked because of your preaching?"

"Mostly heckling, but I usually ignore them or give them the quiet they want and return later to try again. Today, my temper got the best of me."

"The natural man," Ann commented.

He smiled. "Yes, I suppose."

She thought a moment then quoted: "The natural man is an enemy to God, and has been from the fall of Adam, and will be, forever and ever, unless he yields to the enticings of the Holy Spirit, and putteth off the natural man and becometh a saint through the atonement of Christ the Lord . . ."

"And becometh as a child, submissive, meek, humble, patient, full of love, willing to submit to all things which the Lord seeth fit to inflict upon him, even as a child doth submit to his father," Ben finished with a pained smile. "As well as I know it, you would think I would live it a bit better. It would certainly save me a good deal of pain."

Ann watched as one of Hodges's friends pointed out a policeman meandering down the street; they obviously decided now was not the time or place and turned back the way they had come.

"Saved by the good man in blue," Ann said.

"'Tis the Lord looking out for the sinner," he said.

"I hope to hear you preach again, but promise me you'll not be forgetting Mosiah," Ann said.

Both of them laughed lightly as they reached the house. It was time for supper.

Chapter Twenty-Two

LIZZY WATCHED THROUGH THE WINDOW as the carriage neared an apparent rebel camp north of Fort Donelson. Her heart started to pound as she realized this would be the first test of their ability to move about.

She felt the butt of the revolver under her cape then took a deep, steadying breath. Quickly removing the gun, she hit the release to the hidden compartment under the opposite seat, where several other weapons lay. She deposited it and closed the lid, sealing the compartment, as the carriage came to a halt and a soldier approached her driver, Elliott.

"Let's see your pass, nigra," came the command; he blew into his hands as he waited, his cape hanging to his knees against the cold November chill.

Lizzy stuck her head out the window and smiled from beneath a warm winter bonnet. "Hello, soldier. How are you this fine evening?"

Elliott jumped down warily, stepping through partly frozen mud to the carriage door and opening it, allowing Lizzy to exit. Even if the soldier had been her brother, he would have had difficulty recognizing her. She wore a brunette wig, small round sunglasses, and thick pasty makeup.

Lizzy extended her hand from beneath her woolen cape, revealing her long yellow silk dress with white trim. "Susan Davis," she said sweetly. "And you are?"

The soldier was instantly tongue tied, forgot to take the hand at first, then nearly crushed it when he did. "Uh, Sims, uh . . . Miss . . . Miss Davis."

Several other shivering soldiers gathered round as Elliott pulled a stack of fliers from the carriage and began handing them out while giving his announcement.

"Miss Susan Davis, form'ly o' San Francisco, Los Angelees, an' de great music halls o' Europe. She's come t' support de fine soldiers of de new Confed'racy in deys valiant efforts to defend deys rights." More soldiers came from out of nearby tents and from around warm fires where the midday meal was cooking. He spread the fliers as all eyes looked over the woman they thought to be Susan Davis. "She be singin' at de theater in Dover dis very night. Just one quarter fer soldiers and fifty cents fer dem folks what ain't." Elliott was playing the illiterate slave to the hilt, and Lizzy had to restrain a smile.

The soldier who had asked for a pass, looked at the flier, the likeness, the statement about her talent and seemed awestruck. "My brother is in them goldfields. Says he heard ya play and sing, Miss Davis. He's says it was mighty fine." He grinned.

Susan Davis was a real entertainer but one of similar height, build, and facial features as Lizzy. The wig, makeup, and small dark glasses finished the illusion. A Southern girl from Mississippi, Davis had gone west as a young girl with her parents and had lived there ever since. Knowing Davis would probably have lost some of her Southern accent, Lizzy kept hers mild but evident.

"Why, thank you, suh," she said. She stepped close enough to pat his cheek with a gloved hand, leaving him red and flustered, then turned to the other men, causing a sudden rush in her direction. Sims tried to block their way and with a loud, commanding voice ordered them to stand at attention. Most came to a sudden halt, but two managed to crash into one another and became a tangle of arms and legs sprawling on the stiff mud. The others laughed as the two men scrambled to their feet and came to attention only inches away from Lizzy. "Now, boys," she said, patting each of the two on the cheek. "Your attention is sweet, but you really must be careful. I might fall in love with one of you."

The mumbling and snickering resounded, and Lizzy knew she had them convinced. "I'll be performing tonight. I will be sorely disappointed if you don't come," she pouted. Then she turned to Sims. "I suppose I should have a pass, but you see I came through that horrible Northern country and this is the first sight of friendly and valiant men I have seen. Why, I even met that awful General Grant." She rolled her eyes. "A short squatty thing." She waved a hand in distaste. "And horrible manners. Why, he tried to keep me from coming here, and I had to flee in the middle of the night."

The mumbling turned to angry grumbles and name-calling. "Surely you or one of your officers can write me a pass, can't you?" She touched Sims's face again, looking at him over the lenses of the dark glasses and adding a flutter of eyelashes to her plea.

"Yes, ma'am, Colonel Harter, ma'am. He can do it, but he's on down the road a pace." He turned to the crowd of men, looking them over as if trying to find familiar faces. "Handby, Meagle, get your mounts and escort Miss Davis to the colonel's headquarters." The two men dashed off with a grin while the others mumbled at their bad luck but continued to admire her. Lizzy took the sergeant's arm and guided him in the direction of her carriage door, where Elliott stood waiting. "Sergeant," she whispered, "you are a fine gentleman, and I shall not forget it. If y'all can come to one of mah shows, find mah servant here and he'll see that you have a fine seat at no charge."

"Yes, ma'am. Thank you, ma'am," he said sheepishly.

Lizzy picked up more of the fliers. "I know this is asking a lot, but could you spread these around among the rest of the men. This is such a large camp and—"

"We'll need 'em all, ma'am. Why, we has a whole regiment set up in these here woods, and a there's another back with the colonel."

Lizzy smiled, "Oh mah, that must be a lot. How big is a regiment?"

"A thousand men, ma'am—on average, that is."

"Then we have little worry from that horrible General Grant."

"Yes ma'am," Sims said proudly. "Why we've got fifteen regiments in these parts and another fifteen to twenty between here and Bowling Green. That fool comes down here we'll drive him all the way back to Canada, won't we boys." His voice was loud and boastful, and the men answered with resounding shouts. Handby and Meagle rode up and proudly placed their mounts in front of Lizzy's team.

"Mah, mah, how brave y'all are. Why, I will tell the whole South of what fine soldiers I see, and I'll tell your general about your courage as well." She threw a kiss at them, took Elliott's hand, and climbed up into the carriage. The door closed, but she framed herself in the window, waving and throwing more kisses as the team responded to Elliott's encouragement, straining against their traces to drag the carriage away. The soldiers waved hands and hats, yelling hurrahs after it.

Lizzy sat back in the seat and breathed deeply, examining her shaking hands, then she laughed to release the tension, took another deep breath, and finally covered her shivering legs and feet with a blanket before removing a small writing tablet from the hidden compartment. She noted the information Sims gave her but then put in the column that she doubted such numbers and would seek better information. She removed a map from the compartment and noted where the soldiers were encamped and that it was fortified with some trenches, but she saw no cannon emplacements. She then put everything back in the compartment and sealed it again before sticking her hands in her muff to warm them.

Though scared at every moment, she had actually enjoyed playing the part. If she could keep her fears under control, this trip could be profitable, very profitable indeed.

*   *   *

Lizzy had been forced to wait for Colonel Harter, who was on some sort of inspection of his troops, but she used her time wisely, flirting with several of his staff and getting additional information. She found it particularly notable that General Loyd Tilghman had been assigned command of the entire area and had already inspected both Fort Henry and Fort Donelson and found them wanting. Additional troops and approximately five hundred slaves had arrived to begin work on the high ground across the Tennessee River at Fort Heiman, named for the man who was supervising the construction of the fortifications. She also discovered that new artillery was being shipped downriver from Nashville to both forts. Apparently, Tilghman's biggest worry was the fact that Fort Henry lay near the water and could be easily targeted from across the river, but Lizzy knew there was another worry. Winter brought a good deal of rain and snow, and in the early spring, Fort Henry would be awash in flood waters and of little value. The new fort was surely meant to alleviate that problem.

She was also getting a better idea of numbers. They were much smaller than even Sims knew them to be. The Confederate line was thinly stretched from the Cumberland Gap clear to the Mississippi, but it was growing. If the Union delayed too long, they would find their attempt to take middle Tennessee very costly.

Harter returned and awakened her from her thoughts with a knock on the door of her carriage. After quickly primping herself, she pulled back the curtains and invited him to join her. He sat across from her, and Elliott provided coffee and bread spread with jelly while they visited. Lizzy buttered him up one side and down the other. A half hour later, she had supposedly autographed a sheet of Miss Davis's music for the colonel, and he had signed a pass for her and Elliott. She was also informed that the rebel army's headquarters were not at the fort at all but at the Dover Hotel, which was close to the theater at which she would perform. She thought it all quite convenient, but she wondered if any rooms would be available if the officers were headquartered there. She gave Harter a peck on the cheek as they parted then noticed that only Meagle was still escorting the carriage.

"Where did Private Handby get off to?" she asked Harter.

"I sent him ahead. The officers will want to know you're on your way."

"And who would that be?"

"Lieutenant Colonel Randal McGavock, Miss Davis. He and Colonel Heiman are both at Fort Donelson at present."

"McGavock. Irish, isn't it?" she said searching for more information.

"Yes, ma'am. He comes from a prominent, wealthy Tennessee family, attended Harvard, then returned to enter politics in Nashville. He was elected mayor in 1858, no small accomplishment for a man of thirty-two years." Harter smiled, obviously fond of McGavock. "A fighter, ma'am, and a gentleman who will see to your every need."

"Married, I suppose," she said.

Harter looked at his feet. "Yes, ma'am, but he took a look at nearly every girl in Tennessee before he tied the knot." He cleared his throat. "His one weakness."

"And Colonel Hieman?"

"German fellow. Older, very strict, and prim. He's a veteran of the Mexican-American War. Survived the attack at Monterey and came home a hero. Set up an architectural practice in Nashville and oversees the construction while McGavock trains the troops." He shook his head lightly. "He's been in this country some twenty-five years, and he still can't speak plain English, especially when he's in a hurry."

Lizzy nodded her thanks, and Elliott slapped the reins to get the horses moving. They passed a number of small rebel encampments, where men came out and waved, some even chanting her name as they passed. She thought it amazing that word of her arrival had preceded them so rapidly since it seemed difficult for most officers to get word of their actions across a battlefield in a timely manner. She kept busy adding notes to her book and map as they continued the five miles to Dover, Elliott whistling whenever something important seemed to crop up. He whistled as they neared Dover.

She looked out the window to see earthworks and walls being put up on a high hill that overlooked the river. There were too many men to count moving about the fortifications in the cold chill, and a tent city of considerable size surrounded the actual fort but not enough for more than a regiment or two. As the road sloped down toward Dover, she lost sight of the fort altogether but noted several other sites where some sort of fortifications were taking place.

Arriving in Dover just before dark, Elliott pulled the carriage in front of the Dover Hotel and climbed down to open her door only to find another man already at the task, offering his hand to Lizzy. As she exited, applause greeted her. A number of officers formed two lines through which she would need to pass to go up the steps to the hotel's main entrance. She smiled warmly, acted overcome by such wonderful attention, and offered her hand to several men until she reached the top, where a handsome man who could not be more than in his midthirties bowed slightly, hushing the crowd. The man had a full head of red hair that matched a well-trimmed and cared-for beard. His bright eyes revealed an intense personality.

"Miss Davis," he said. "I am Randal McGavock, colonel of the Confederate army defending Fort Donelson. Y'all's reputation precedes you, and we're pleased that ya have come to share your talents with us."

"Colonel, you are too kind." She removed her hand from his and turned to face the men standing on the stairs. She thought there must have been several hundred. "Gentlemen, thank ya for your fine service. I wish I could give y'all a hug for it." There were chuckles and mumbles of agreement and other less gentlemanly things, but she ignored them and continued. "But, alas I am both tired and in need of preparing for the night's entertainment. Good-bye for now. I hope to see all y'all at my show." She turned back to McGavock. "I hope there is a room in this blessed establishment, Colonel. If I have to sleep in that cold carriage one more night, I—"

"We've made every arrangement, Miss Davis." McGavock smiled, offering his arm. Lizzy took it, and they went through the front door and up the stairs, men crowding into the small lobby behind them. She turned and invited them all to her performance then let McGavock escort her upstairs. Elliott followed behind with a couple of her bags. Going to the end of the hall, he unlocked the door then presented her with the key. "Miss Davis," he said, with a broad smile. As she took the key, he clutched her hand then leaned over and kissed it. "You are even more lovely than reports led us to understand. I hope you will allow me . . ."

His eyes warned of his intentions, and Lizzy spoke quickly. "Colonel, once again, you are too kind. I really am quite tired and do need to rest before my performance. If you would excuse me . . ."

"Yes, yes, of course," he said with a smile. "But I've planned dinner in the hotel dining room after the performance for you and our officers. I hope you don't mind."

"I look forward to it," Lizzy said.

He bowed slightly. "Good, then I will see you at the performance."

Lizzy went in the room, where Elliott was already finding places for her bags. She closed the door.

"They'll bring up the big trunk soon," Elliott said in his normal voice.

She nodded, listening at the door. She opened it and looked into the hall to make sure no one was standing about before closing and locking it. "What did you see?" she asked quietly. He'd had a much better view from atop the carriage.

"A large fort on the hill to the nor'west with cannons both inside an' outside."

She handed him paper and pencil, and he began to draw what he'd seen while verbally describing it. "There's a creek what runs along the hillside here." He pointed to his drawing. "Lottsa cannons in the fort looking down on the river. Ships come in, they be at once hurtin' fo' it. Union ain't gonna get close coming that way. Trouble is I can't see the fortifications on the western side from the road. We hasta get a closer look over there."

"How many soldiers do you estimate?" she asked.

"A couple of thousand, but there could be other camps nearby, and there are more at Henry and Hieman. Even then they is weak, Miss Lizzy." He took a deep breath. "But they is gettin' stronger day t' day. They have slaves workin' on the trenches and fortifications. I'll visit their camp while you is signin', see what else I can find out."

He left, and Lizzy looked in the mirror, wondering who the woman was that stared back at her. There were rings under her eyes and wrinkles she had never seen before. But she couldn't worry about such things. She had a show to get ready for.

Chapter Twenty-Three

NEWTON HAD SEEN LITTLE OPPORTUNITY for escape between Bull Run and Richmond. The first beating had left him in a state of off-and-on-again consciousness that lasted until after their arrival. With broken ribs, a face so swollen he couldn't see, relentless rain, and guards as thick as daisies in spring, it would have been futile anyway.

Some of the boys had tried; all of them were buried along the road to Richmond.

He was now locked up in the basement of Ligon Prison in a cell with a dirt floor and with the stench of mildew from moisture seeping through the outside wall after heavy rains. He was alone, in solitary confinement, and had been since their arrival—a further indication that the lieutenant who had said Newton would regret his belligerence intended to be true to his word.

Newton remembered his first beating—and his second—and even though it had been several months, he still smarted from the pain from broken ribs unaided by decent food or adequate sunlight and exercise. For him, food was scarce, brought once a day by Cyril or Tom and shoved through a small window.

Cyril said it was the end of November. The small window high in the outside wall allowed little evidence except for the constant chill and the amount of sunlight—or lack of it—coming through the small, high, barred window in the eastern wall.

He used his bare foot to swipe at a passing rat, another sign they were entering winter. The creatures had moved indoors en masse, awakening him nightly as they scampered about his person looking for food or a place to find warmth. He'd killed several, tossing them through the small window, but if his rations didn't improve, he figured he'd have to start eating them soon.

They'd been kept in another place for the first few weeks. The jailers had called it Lumpkin's Jail. The cells had been smaller, the food better, and he had been housed with other prisoners out of lack of room to isolate him. But it had also been where he'd managed to speak his mind in answering some rebel fools' questions and had got his second beating. After that he'd stopped speaking to rebs altogether.

On daily trips to bring Newton food, Cyril had explained that Ligon Prison was a former tobacco factory. The cells for privates had been made from storage rooms on the two upper levels, and those for officers were on the first floor. There was a building outside where meals were prepared by a black slave who did his best with scant rations. Officers were fed decently, but Cyril and Tom were getting no more than Newton. Cyril said it was so crowded in the regular soldiers' quarters that they couldn't stretch out at night. Even in good weather, they were seldom allowed to bathe in the single outdoor faucet, and now that it was winter, the guards refused to stand in the cold so some could brave the frigid water to try and get clean.

Typhoid fever had already broken out, and a dozen men had been taken to a nearby building the rebels had made into a hospital. Cyril had helped pack Tom over there only yesterday and found it roomy with beds and blankets, neither of which were found in abundance in their own quarters. Cyril thought it might be worth getting the fever just to die between blankets instead of on the cold hard floor in the upper reaches of Ligon Prison. Newton suggested that Cyril attack a guard and get himself sent to the basement. Though he'd shake from the cold every night, at least he wouldn't die from typhoid. Cyril had only smiled, saying he'd give it some serious thought.

Newton heard the creak of footsteps on the stairs down the hall and pushed himself to his feet. Cyril greeted him at his small window with a smile and handed him his plate: hard bread and what seemed to be vegetable soup with tough meat. Cyril said the meat was at least two days old.

"They cook it and then throw it in a trough out in the yard near the kitchen. Ain't used for two or three days. Collects dust, grime, and lots of flies, at least when it's sunny out. Get a little more protein with every bite." He smiled then looked back toward the steps to see if the guard had followed him down. He usually didn't. After all, where was Cyril going to go?

In the few minutes it took for Newton to eat his food, Cyril had shared the latest news garnered from new prisoners or from overheard conversations between guards. The North had not sought peace as most Southerners were sure they would. Instead, they were preparing for war in camps of tens of thousands outside Washington. Early on, Northern newspapers were filled with confidence in George A. McClellan, the new commander of the Northern army. But now McClellan had become the butt of jokes made by rebel guards. Most rebels said "Lazy" or "Foot-draggin'" George McClellan was the Confederacy's best general. It infuriated Union prisoners at first, but as time passed it became demoralizing. Prisoners wondered why they'd ever gone to Manassas if the army was all talk and no substance. McClellan had become fool's gold to most prisoners—all shine and no worth.

The guards said there was some discussion of prisoner exchange, but Northern politicians were dragging their feet. Such exchanges took place only between foreign countries, and if the North entered into negotiations, it would be recognizing the South as a separate country instead of a rebellion. Southerners figured Manassas proved the point and weren't about to compromise. Most prisoners at Ligon waited the outcome, whiling away their days playing cards and dreaming of freedom while a few decided that waiting for politicians was like waiting to be hanged when no one had a rope—the wait causing more anguish than the actual outcome. They weren't about to sit by and let politicians decide their fate. Instead, they talked of escape.

"Any word abou' Tom?" Newton asked.

Cyril looked down at his feet. "One of the lieutenants is tryin' to go and see him. We hear he's real bad, near dyin.' Same as a few others. They keep us in here long enough, and we'll all die from it—or starvation." He drew close. "The lieutenant says t' tell ya them women what started comin' to visit, Miss Van Lew and her mother, they're tryin' to set up a way for escape."

"You mean the ones who 'ave been bringin' medicine and books?" Newton asked. He picked a tough piece of meat, cleaned off a small bone, then stuck the bone in his pocket to suck on later.

"Yeah, them." He lifted his shirt and pulled a small cloth bag from behind his belt. "She said to give you this medicine, and there's some hard rock candy in there too."

Newton kept eating, knowing the time was limited before Cyril would leave. Cyril looked over his shoulder again. "They're movin' some of us t'night. Takin' us to another jail near the waterfront, name of Libby Prison. Confiscated it from a Union sympathizer or somethin'. Too

crowded here. Apparently, they's plannin' on more war, and Miss Van
Lew says it's comin' sure as snow in winter. But not if ol' Fool's Gold has
his way." He drew closer. "She says that if a fella can escape . . ." Another
nervous glance over his shoulder before he tossed something through
the window. It landed on the dirt floor. "You should go to her house. It's
only a few blocks away. That's my plate. I smudged the address on it with
charcoal, and they won't miss it once we're gone. Think I took it with me
to Libby. Maybe you could start digging an'—"

"Hey, Yank! Time's up."

Newton saw the guard at the bottom of the stairs looking hard into
the darkness. He quickly licked everything from his plate and handed it
through the window. Cyril took it and forced a half smile. "I don't know
if I'll see ya again, Captain. Godspeed and . . ." He couldn't say more.

"I be thankin' ya then, Cyril. Yer a fine man and took goo' care o' me.
I hope the next place is a bi' more comfortable fer ya an' the boys. If they
doan take ya, I'll see ya t'morrow."

Cyril nodded but moved quickly when the guard shouted a final
warning.

Newton stooped down and picked up the plate that Cyril had
thrown into the cell. Going to his blanket he sat down, memorized the
address, then rubbed it off the plate's grimy surface. Opening the bag
sent by Miss Van Lew, he found some medicinal cream and spread it on
the sores around his mouth and eyes. It stung, but he was grateful for it.
The sores had been growing. He removed one of the hard candies and
put it in his mouth, wondering when the last time was that he'd tasted
something so good. He scratched at his growing, scraggly beard. He
supped on his good fortune but felt depressed as well. Cyril had kept
him sane, grounded, and if he was gone . . . Newton wondered if they'd
send anyone with food, let alone information.

He pushed the thought aside. Cyril had given him a chance—a small
chance, but a chance just the same. He took a deep breath, picked up
the plate, and crawled to the corner near the wall, not visible from the
window in the door. And then he began to dig.

*   *   *

The small theater was packed, and Lizzy, standing just off the stage where
a piano awaited her, moved to where she could see Colonel McGavock
and other officers sitting in the front row. She was surprised to see several

women with their civilian husbands sitting behind the officers. Colonel McGavock sat in the middle next to an older soldier. From the stern look and high head, she figured it was Colonel Heiman. His face gave no sign of enjoying the festive evening.

Hearing a hint of an argument behind her, Lizzy turned to find the stage manager trying to keep a soldier from entering the back door. Though the soldier's hair was now greased back and his scruffy beard shaved, she recognized him as Sergeant Sims, who had first greeted her and quickly asked the manager to let him in. He wore enough cologne to announce his presence clear to Fort Henry and carried a small bouquet of roses that still had dirt attached to the stem. They were probably ripped from some nearby flower garden. She greeted him with a smile, took the roses, commented on their beauty, and then asked Elliott to escort him to one of several reserved seats a few rows back. He left with a bright red beaming face that both pleased and annoyed her as it reminded her that these were good men as well as the enemy.

Going to a full-length mirror to distract her mind, she checked her appearance one last time as the manager went onto the stage to announce her. A moment later she floated onstage, her stomach in her throat, bowing, her beautiful red silk dress setting off her brunette wig and pretty features that drove every soldier to the edge of their seat with admiring glances. The applause, whistles, and catcalls went on for nearly two minutes until she raised her hand and quieted them.

"Ladies, gentlemen, thank y'all for your wonderful reception, and thank you for coming. 'Tis a hard thing that causes me to come this far to see you boys and give y'all a hurrah, but I do it for God, flag, and country." She said it with some exuberance, but they thought the country she meant was the Confederacy. Under this intended misdirection, the house was raucous with applause, whistling, and yelling. Sometime later, when they found they'd been duped, maybe they'd recognize the irony.

She raised her hands again and quieted them. "Now, y'all didn't come here to hear me give a sermon, so I'll begin with a familiar number." She sat at the piano, her red dress covering the seat completely, the audience quiet, anticipating. She had learned this song as a child and knew it well enough to play it in her sleep. Lizzy launched into "Camptown Races," adding her own rendition. Her fingers flew over the keys, filling the hall with the familiar tune, and soon the audience was clapping and stomping to the music. She finished with flair, and the place erupted with applause. Everyone came to his or her feet. She stood and bowed, flushed with the sudden rush of adrenaline. She bowed again then again then raised her hands and hushed them before returning to her piano.

She started with the slower melody, "Wake! Dinah, Wake!"—this time singing the lyrics—then went back to Foster's "Oh! Susanna" and then his "Soiree Polka." Seeing how they loved Foster, a Kentuckian, she played a half dozen other songs, singing some, just playing others. She had them dancing in the aisle, clapping, loving it all, and she didn't stop until her arms were near to fall off. Finally, she stood, accepted the endless applause with a dozen bows, then left the stage for a quick intermission, waving as she went, throwing kisses, and watching the officers for their reaction. Even Heiman applauded with some exuberance, though his face remained dour and emotionless. She went to a small dressing room, closed the door behind her, and shook her hands and arms to try and relieve the pain in them. A knock came at the door, and she quickly opened it to find the stage manager, a wide grin on his face. He told her they had made good money and gave her a small container with her share along with several notes with requests from officers. She thanked him, said she would be back for the second portion of her performance shortly, closed the door, and quickly changed into a baby blue dress with cream-colored lace and trim. She would return to the stage, sing three more ballads, and end with one meant to convey the false idea that she was a Southern patriot. Primping her hair once more, she opened the door to find a soldier standing in front of her.

She gasped. "Sir, you startled me!"

"I apologize," the soldier said red faced and rigid. "From Colonel McGavock."

She read the note. She didn't like the feeling she was getting but could not refuse if she wanted to see the fortifications more closely. "Tell him that I would be glad to visit with him but that I do not see men alone in my dressing room or in my private rooms."

The soldier nodded, turned on his heel, and started to march away.

"Private." She stopped him.

He turned around on his heel again. He was really quite good at the maneuver. "Tell the colonel that it's a precaution I take to protect both his reputation and mine. I'm sure he'll understand. If there is another who wishes to accompany him, they may join me after the show."

She closed the door, caught her breath, then opened it again. She entered the stage to grand applause and had to quiet the audience again before playing several of the requests and ending with "You Are Going to the Wars, Willie Boy!" singing the lyrics:

You are going to the wars, Willie boy, Willie boy,
You are going to the wars far away,
To protect our rights and laws, Willie boy, Willie boy,
And the banner in the sun's golden ray;
With your uniform all new,
And your shining buttons too,
You'll win the hearts of pretty girls,
But none like me so true.
Oh! won't you think of me, Willie boy, Willie boy;
Oh won't you think of me when far away?
I'll often think of ye, Willie boy, Willie boy,
And ever for your life and glory pray.

You'll be fighting for the right, Willie boy, Willie boy,
You'll be fighting for the right and your home;
And you'll strike the blow with might, Willie boy, Willie boy,
'Mid the thundering of cannon and of drum;
With an arm as true as steel,
You'll make the foe-men feel
The vengeance of a Southerner
Too proud to cringe or kneel.
Oh! should you fall in strife, Willie boy, Willie boy;
Oh should you fall in strife on the plain,
I'll pine away my life, Willie boy, Willie boy,
And never, never wear a smile again.

When she lifted her hands from the keys, the place was quiet. It suddenly broke into loud applause and a scramble to the front of the stage, where several tried to climb up, one grabbing the hem of her dress with such force that it tore. The place was bedlam, and it was all Lizzy could do to step back far enough to keep from getting grabbed again. Then the sound of a gun went off, and men ducked, jumped, and dove for cover. Colonel McGavock stood with his still-smoking revolver over his head and loudly ordered the hall to be cleared and that the last one to remove himself from the stage would be shot. Lizzy smiled as a dozen men all threw themselves into the crowd standing next to the stage, each scrambling to be off before he could be caught in McGavock's sites. All except one who stood quietly to the side, hat in hand, a sheepish grin, his eyes on Lizzy.

"Colonel McGavock, geet das idioot uff das stage!" Heiman yelled.

Lizzy raised a hand, and the room fell silent. She took several steps and stood in front of Sergeant Sims. Rising to her tiptoes, she gave him a peck on the check and then turned him toward the front of the stage and gave him a slight nudge. He half stumbled into the arms of his comrades, a look of contentment on his face. She waved to everyone, gave them a warm smile, threw them a kiss, and left the stage. A moment later an expected knock came as she sat at her dressing table.

"Come in," she said.

McGavock and Colonel Hieman entered. She glanced at them in the mirror as she powdered her nose for distraction.

"Miss Davis, what a marvelous performance!" McGavock said.

"Ya, ya, twas a fine aucht. Fine!" Heiman said without a bit of change to his dour look. Lizzy believed it was to ever be thus. The man simply had no smile.

"Why, I've never seen anything quite like it, and it outstrips your reputation. Why—"

"Thank you, Colonel," she said. "Please, both of you be seated." She watched in the mirror as they did so.

"I didn't know you played so well. Usually a pianist accompanies you, doesn't he?" McGavock asked.

"My player was a Union man. I'm afraid he would just as soon shoot y'all as play for you," she said. "I thought it best to leave him in San Francisco plunking keys for two bits a day than take the chance." She gave him a wry smile.

He chuckled, nodding agreement.

"Colonel," she said, finally turning around, facing McGavock, "Forgive me, but it was a very tiring night. Do you mind if I skip dinner? I really must be on my way tomorrow and—"

McGavock's face showed disappointment. "The officers are expecting you—"

"Nein, nein, she is right, Ker-a-nel," Heiman interrupted. "Das Frau is exhausted. Possibly breakfoast den?" He smiled.

"Yes, that would be much better," Lizzy said. She pushed herself to her feet. "Thank y'all, and good night."

"Ya, ya," Heiman said, getting to his feet. He took her offered hand and kissed it. "Danke, meina Frau. It was wunderbar! Wunderbar!" He went to the door.

He really was an adorable fellow, and she gave him a light kiss on the cheek before turning to McGavock, who also kissed her hand. "I am most disappointed, Miss Davis. I was hoping we could . . ."

"Forgive me, Mr. McGavock, but I would be very poor company this evening. I did send some specially prepared rum cake and liquor to the dining room. Give my thanks and my apologies to your officers. Tell them it's a peace offering and that I look forward to breakfast."

McGavock kissed her offered hand a second time. "Yes, of course." He followed Hieman out, and she closed and locked the door. She went back to her dressing table and continued to remove the horrid amounts of makeup until two quick knocks then a third came at the door. Lizzy opened it and let Elliott in.

While she changed into her evening gown and robe behind a screen, he removed his previous drawing from a pocket specially sewn into the lining of her red silk dress. He quickly added to it while telling her verbally what he had learned.

"According to the slaves, the trenches are very extensive west, north, and south of the fort, and new cannon emplacements are being built. When the cannons arrive, they'll double the firepower of the fort." The slaves he had talked to said the soldiers talked openly about large forces of men at Bowling Green even though there weren't many at Donelson, Henry, or Heiman. They'd also heard of shortages in rifles and said only a few soldiers had good ones—most carrying the old flintlocks. But when he was finished, she realized she still didn't have enough information.

"I must see the fortifications," she said. She told him about breakfast and that she would find a way to cajol one or both of the men into a tour.

McGavock's drooling vanity should give her a better than average chance, but Heiman would be her target, his seeming penchant to protect her like a daughter an even greater vulnerability. Yes, she would target Heiman.

Chapter Twenty-Four

LIZZY FELT THE JOLT OF the carriage, felt herself falling, then hit the floor with a thud. She pushed the cobwebs aside, pulled herself back to her seat, nudged aside the window cover, and focused on the gas lamps outside several buildings. Apparently, they were in Bowling Green.

She prepared herself as best as she could, and a few moments later the carriage pulled up in front of the hotel. Elliott got down from his perch and opened her door. There were no gentlemen about to help her down, to fawn over her, and she was grateful. It was one reason she and Elliott had decided to leave Russellville early and travel well into the night.

The breakfast in Dover had been profitable. She had hinted that she would love to see their work for the protection of the Confederacy, and they had obliged with a tour of the defenses around Fort Donelson. As she walked between Colonel Heiman and Colonel McGavock, the two tried hard to outdo one another in what information they could reveal, but Heiman had been especially helpful. Though Colonel Harter had been right about his accent making it difficult to understand his speech, she had gleaned enough information about Fort Henry and Fort Heiman to know that both were still far from finished and that Fort Henry would be particularly susceptible if the Union attacked at the time of high water. He had even been kind enough to show her his well-prepared drawings of how he intended to fortify Heiman to help protect Fort Henry.

Not to be outdone, McGavock had filled in a number of blanks while the other officers that accompanied offered comments as well. No one seemed at all concerned about the amount of information being doled out like candy at Christmas, nor did anyone ever ask for her pass. She found it quite unbelievable until she remembered the success of the now imprisoned Rose Greenhow in Washington. Vain men were easy targets.

When she left both colonels, she gave each a quick kiss as thanks then returned to her hotel and carefully added everything to both the map and her notes before making a grand departure from Dover.

Russellville had been less eventful. The show went well except for the crude behavior of a few drunken soldiers and civilians who seemed to think they deserved her special attention, but there were no fortresses around the town and certainly no generals to reveal army secrets, so she had quickly departed for Bowling Green.

Stepping to the street, Lizzy felt her shoe sink in mud. It had rained and been chilly all day, and only heavy blankets had kept her and Elliott from abandoning their journey for the warmth of a fireside at some indistinct inn along their route. Holding up her dress, she walked to the steps then up them into the hotel lobby. Several men were standing about visiting—two in soldiers' uniforms, four in civilian suits, but all freshly coifed. The uniform of the youngest man revealed that he was a general. His hair was combed back from his forehead, and he sported a long moustache that hung an inch past the corners of his mouth. He was handsome, of average height, and had intelligent eyes. As he extended his hand, she gave hers, and he introduced himself as General Simon Buckner. He introduced the others as the mayor of Bowling Green, a staff officer, and three others who had just been elected to offices in the Confederate government of Kentucky. The last name she recognized as the new governor, George W. Johnson. The convention had been held only a month or so ago at Russellville, and the stage manager there had bent her ear about it for nearly twenty minutes.

"Governor, how wonderful to have you here. You are a brave man to accept the office with the enemy so close at hand."

Johnson revealed a pistol in his belt as he spoke. "I'll not be worrying too much upon it, Miss Davis. There are worse ways to die than at the hand of Yankees if two or three of 'em join the parade to heaven."

Lizzy forced a smile. "Well then, we can only hope you get the chance sooner than later," she said.

Seeing that Johnson was a bit confused by the answer, Buckner moved forward, introducing of the last of his guests. "And this is General Tilghman." He turned to a man at his side. "He would have been with you at Donelson except that we just returned from meetings with General Johnston in Nashville."

Tilghman kissed her gloved hand. "I hope Colonel McGavock took good care of you."

"He was more than helpful, General. Why, he should be made a captain immediately."

Each man covered his mouth with a fist to hide his amusement. Lizzy was more than aware such a move would be a demotion, but she wanted them to think her just another ignorant woman who knew nothing about things of the military.

"Well, that would certainly surprise the colonel," Buckner said.

The others laughed lightly at the response, and Lizzy put her hand to her mouth. "Oh my. There. I must have done it again. These military offices . . ." She rolled her eyes. "There are *so* many! How on earth do y'all ever keep them straight?"

Buckner smiled. "It's not easy, Miss Davis. Have you eaten?"

"No, and I'm quite famished, but I'm sure it's much too late for the hotel dining room . . ."

The men glanced at one another as if sharing a secret. Buckner offered his arm. "It's Thanksgiving, Miss Davis, and we have a table set for the occasion and would enjoy accompanying you. As I said, we just returned and have not eaten."

"Oh mah, I had completely forgotten. How wonderful of y'all!"

He extended his arm. She took it, and they walked through an adjoining archway into the dining hall that seemed to be filled to capacity except for one table. The place became very quiet, and all eyes turned to her. Then the men stood and applauded.

She tried to hide how tired she felt with a smile and waves and kisses to Susan Davis's adoring audience, then she allowed herself to be seated as Buckner pulled back her chair. Waiters appeared on cue, and food was brought to the table, placed in front of each person that surrounded it, then given to others in the room.

The conversation was light, and she was asked questions about the West that she simply had to make up answers for while thanking the Lord that she had always been an avid reader and knew enough to cover the fact that she'd never actually been there. She had also studied Miss Susan Davis's news clippings, and some embellishment made Miss Davis more interesting than she might have been otherwise.

As they visited, she turned the conversation to the war, politics, and particularly to Bowling Green, but this time her hosts said little that was helpful, though Johnson and the other Confederate leaders had much to say about their intentions for Kentucky as soon as they could get hold of Frankfort, the state capital.

"And when will that be?" she asked innocently.

"As soon as General Johnston deploys his men in that direction. He promised only today that troops would be forthcoming." He leaned toward her. "It's those consarned abolitionists that've caused this trouble. If I had one here now, I would ring his neck! We would have our country if not for them and their stubbornness on the issue of our slaves. Why Lincoln listens to them is a mystery. He is a Kentuckian by birth. He knows how we feel about nigras and such. But those abolitionists bend his ear and turn him against us! If I could get my hands on just one of them—"

"Yes, well, you may have your chance soon, Governor," Lizzy said.

He waved dismissively. "If you're speaking of Grant, the man is nothing but a worthless drunk. A fool. With leaders like him we have nothing to fear from the North."

Lizzy saw that this upset General Buckner and decided to find out why. "Do you agree, General?"

Buckner looked at Johnson then at Tilghman. "I was at the Academy with General Grant, and anyone who underestimates him will find themselves either buried in their own self-conceit or out of house and home."

Johnson turned red, and General Tilghman decided to settle troubled waters.

"Miss Davis, would you do us the honor of playing a tune or two? After all, we are here to celebrate your arrival, and all of these fine people are eager to hear you perform."

"I'd be honored," she said. She had already seen the piano sitting a few feet away, and as Tilghman got to his feet and quieted the crowd, she stood and removed herself to the piano bench.

The applause was polite, more in keeping with a hall filled with temperate members of high society.

Tired and unwilling to try anything very difficult, she played Foster's "My Old Kentucky Home," singing the lyrics. When she finished, the applause was much more appreciative, and there were even a few whistles. She stood and bowed, and when it grew quiet, she thanked them all for this fine reception but said she was quite tired and hoped to see them all at the performance tomorrow night. They applauded again, and she curtsied in response as Buckner approached and offered her his arm.

They were entering the lobby of the hotel when she saw a group of wet and muddy soldiers near the doors at the far end. Lizzy nearly fainted when she recognized one of them. She immediately turned into Buckner to avoid being seen and noted Buckner was interested in the same men.

"Excuse me, Miss Davis. I sent some men on patrol, and they've just returned."

"It is quite all right, General. Go ahead," she said, hiding her panic. "I'm tired and wish only to go to my room. I'll see you tomorrow, and thank you for dinner." She offered her hand even as she heard the soldiers coming their direction. Thankfully, the stairs were in front of her, and she walked past Buckner and began to climb them.

"Oh, Miss Davis?" The voice was that of the clerk, and Lizzy froze, turned slightly, and gave him a smile as he came up the steps. She had a fan in her dress pocket and quickly flashed it open and across her face to at least stay partially hidden.

"Yes?"

"Your key, Miss Davis." He handed it to her, and she took it and quickly thanked him. After a quick glance at the soldiers, she continued her journey. She nearly fainted when she realized all eyes were on her and that the eyes of Andrew Clay were among them. As she reached the top, she heard him ask Buckner who she was, heard Buckner's reply, and couldn't help but glance once more at the group. Buckner had turned Andrew toward the door, but he was looking directly at her, the confused, curious look of recognition etched there. She quickly finished climbing the steps, disappearing from view and bracing herself against the wall for fear she might faint. Struggling on to her room, she quickly unlocked it and found Elliott asleep in a chair. She fell into a second chair with such aplomb that it startled him from his sleep. He sat up straight using his hand to try and wipe the sleep from his face.

"Did you find Stanley Barber's residence?" she asked weakly.

"Yes'm. He lives above the mortuary." He described where it was. "I went in t' ask 'im about funerals and such, and he fits the description of ol' Fairfield sure enough." John Fairfield was supposed to be dead, killed while trying to help slaves escape. Apparently, he wasn't.

Lizzy stood, removing her brunette wig and shaking out her blonde hair before pulling it back and putting a comb in it. She then rubbed her forehead with her fingers, trying to rid herself of a splitting headache as well as a good deal of fear.

"Andrew Clay is here."

Elliott sat bolt upright. "Did he see you, Missy?"

"Yes, and I fear he recognized me," she said.

"Then we must run, Elizabeth," Elliott said coming to his feet.

"Not yet. If Andrew knows it's me and he betrays me, we're already too late. If not, we still have time and must use it wisely." She stood in front of the fireplace, warming herself while thinking. "Just in case we must leave quickly, I want you to prepare the horses. Hide them in the alley behind the hotel, then go to your room and be watchful. If soldiers come, you're to disappear, Elliott. Take the notebooks and maps and run. You have all the papers you need to verify you're a freedman and should be able to get to the North."

"No, Miss Elizabeth. I will not—"

"Elliott, you will!" she said firmly. "The information we have is too important. It *must* be taken to General Grant. Besides, if it's found on me, they'll have hard evidence against me. You will do it, or I'll never speak to you again."

Elliott couldn't help the smile. It was the same threat she always used. When she was going to church and needed him to keep her secret, she'd used it. When she'd told him he was fool for letting a good woman get away from him, she had told him to either marry or she'd never speak to him again. It was just her way of making sure he understood she was serious and she expected him to do it. Trouble was he loved her like a sister, and it always worked. But this time was different. Her life was at risk.

"It'll take more than childhood threats, Elizabeth, but I'll get the horses. When I come back, you and I will leave here even if I have to carry you and throw you over the saddle. Change your clothes and get ready." He turned and left the room. She heard the key turn in the lock and quickly crossed the room and tried the knob.

"Elliott! You come back here this minute!"

There was no answer and she yelled again. Still nothing.

"Oooh!" she said, stomping to her trunk and quickly removing her riding clothes, boots, revolver, holster, and a warm coat along with her flop-eared hat. She changed clothes, fastened on her holster, then pulled the red silk dress from the trunk. She removed her papers, the folded map, and notebook from their hidden pocket, shoved them inside her tucked-in shirt, then put on the heavy coat. Blowing out the lamp, she went to the window, slid it up, and stepped carefully onto the roof covering the front steps of the hotel. She kept low and moved along it around the corner. In another thirty feet, it ended above a side entrance. She got on her belly and looked over the edge. The area was empty. She let herself over the edge and then dropped to the ground. Keeping her head tucked low, she entered the busy street filled with soldiers looking for a good time. Crossing it while dodging riders, carriages, and pedestrians, she jumped up on the boardwalk and walked quickly down two blocks before turning right and walking another block to the mortuary. She was grateful there was still a light on in the rooms above the business. Climbing the staircase on the side of the building, she knocked lightly at the door. A black woman answered, a look of bewilderment on her face. "Yes?"

"Is Mr. Barber here?"

"No ma'am. He's down at Charlie's saloon."

Lizzy hesitated, her eyes on those of the woman. She seemed well educated and had a stately presence about her that aroused Lizzy's curiosity.

"Possibly you can help," Lizzy said.

"I have no knowledge of mortuary work, Miss . . ."

"Hudson. Elizabeth Hudson." She removed her hat. "I'm actually here to see John Fairfield."

The woman paled and seemed to stop breathing. Her hand went to her heart, but she still struggled to keep her composure. "I . . . I don't know any John Fairfield." She started to close the door, but Lizzy pushed against it. "Two months ago a young man was put in a coffin and smuggled out of Bowling Green. He was joined by others and escaped to Paducah, Kentucky. He said he left his mother behind. A tall, thin woman, well educated, and a freed slave. He's worried she won't join him."

The woman gasped, her shoulders sagging. Lizzy stepped in and caught her then used a foot to close the door while helping the woman to a chair. She retrieved some water from a pitcher and handed it to her.

She drank some then gave a slight smile. "He made it?" she whispered.

"Yes, he did. I need to see John. I need all the information he can give me about Confederate troops in Bowling Green, and I need it now. I have to leave before sunup."

The black woman shook her head. "John is a kind and good man. He's helped more black folk than any white man I know, but when he starts gamblin' there isn't a thing that will get in his way. Not you, not me, not nobody."

"Does he have the information I need?"

She nodded. "Yes'm. He keeps a book, but I don't know where it's at. Somewhere downstairs is my guess. I keep up this place, and I'd know if there was a hiding place in it." She looked around at the room.

"What time does he come home?"

"He don't gamble often, but when he does it's all night, lessen he gets sick or runs out of money, which ain't often. He's good and usually brings home more than he took. I guess that's why it takes so long."

"And if he thought someone was dead and waiting for his services?"

"Ha! John would say the dead ain't in no hurry." She shrugged. "They'd wait just like everyone else." She paused.

"Where is he now?"

Charlie's saloon. Down mainstreet. Last gambling house on the right." She paused. "You seems in a hurry. Are you in trouble?"

"Not if I can get out of here soon. Thank you . . ." Lizzy realized she did not know her name.

"Name's Dortha. You take good care of my boy, Miss Hudson."

"He's already in Ohio, Dortha. By the end of the week, he'll be in Canada."

"Thank you." Dortha gave Lizzy a hug, then Lizzy opened the door and went into the night, headed for Charlie's saloon. She only hoped Andrew Clay still didn't drink.

*   *   *

The day Judah Benjamin was made secretary of war, Matthew Alexander received a message to go to his office. By afternoon, Matthew was charged with keeping track of fortifications and navy preparations along the coasts of Virginia and North Carolina. Working from a small cubicle in the war department, he gathered information and funneled it up the chain to decision makers with the promise that if he did well, Benjamin would move him up the chain.

But Matthew found an even greater source of information in befriending other analysts who, feeling quite safe in the confines of the war department, talked freely of their own assignments. Soon he had a very clear picture of the strengths and weaknesses of the Confederate army and began sending information to the North via Beth Van Lew's well-oiled courier pipeline. By Thanksgiving he had relayed a good deal of information concerning weak points inside Hatteras Inslet and at other places along the Atlantic. In response, he'd received a coded note asking for more information about defenses along the James River. He'd garnered what he could but needed more, deciding to use his position to travel south and take a personal look before sending back word.

The train pulled into the station at Petersburg, Virginia, and Matthew got off and walked across the platform, a suitcase in each hand. Entering the station, he passed through it quickly and exited on the boardwalk facing the street. He saw Millie waving from a carriage then giving the driver instructions to move forward. Matthew glanced up at the bright sun, grateful it wasn't snowing as he set the bags down long enough to remove his wool winter coat. He tossed the bags up to the driver, who secured them as Matthew stepped into the carriage and a steward put a small trunk up on top. He tipped the man through the window then sat down next to Millie. She put her arms around his neck, and they kissed before she snuggled in against the cool day. "And what's in the trunk?" she asked.

"Your books, dear girl. For the children."

She sat straight. "You remembered. How wonderful of you." She gave him another kiss and then snuggled back in next to him as the carriage pulled away and they settled in for the half-hour ride to Beauchapel. "The children will be so grateful Matthew. How was the trip down?" she asked as she unfolded the blanket that lay across her knees and shared it with him.

"Until now, miserable," Matthew responded with a smile then another kiss.

The carriage jostled them about as they left the station and traveled through the town and into the country. It was a familiar journey for them both. Matthew had come to Petersburg three different times over the last month so that they could spend time together.

"I finally sold the last of our crop," Millie said with a smile.

Matthew sensed that it was not necessarily good information. Daniel Geery had done everything he could to deter any prospective buyers, and she'd finally been forced to travel into North Carolina to find a wholesaler Geery could not influence. Though prices for about everything else had gone up, tobacco had stayed about the same. It was not a hot commodity abroad because of a bumper crop in the Caribbean islands, and so far

Millie had only been able to pay her workers and her overhead, leaving very little to pay off the debt owed to Geery. Her uncle had sent her the money he owed but only after the placement of a lien on his property and a constant harangue from Henry Hyde's law firm. Henry had even gone after and successfully milked money out of the banker who had aided her uncle, but it didn't add much. She was still thirty thousand short.

He squeezed her hand but said nothing. He had a surprise for her, but now was not the time.

"How are things in the war department?"

"Chaotic. If the Confederacy wins, it'll be a miracle because the vainglory of men will prevent it otherwise."

She chuckled. "Well, from what the newspapers say, the Union has similar problems. This McClellan, did you know him?"

"I knew his reputation at the Academy. Smart but headstrong, proud. The consummate politician. Secretary Benjamin called him the best friend of the Confederacy the other day. If McClellan knew how much he was appreciated here, it would at least embarrass him."

"How are the Van Lews?" she asked.

Matthew saw them only by clandestine means, but he did see them. "They send their love."

"And are they still visiting the prison?"

"Yes. Beth gleans a little information here and there from prisoners caught in almost daily skirmishes south of Washington, but she's more concerned with setting up an escape route for them."

"Good for her."

On the way home from their picnic to the Van Lew farm, Millie had challenged him. He saw no reason to continue to deceive her, and she was actually relieved. Since then she was very aware of and even a little frightened by his work.

"Your wire said you'll only be able to stay tonight before going to Norfolk," she said.

He nodded. "I'll tour the fortifications along the James then take a ship back to Richmond. I'll also get a look at the new ironclad the rebels are building."

She smiled. "It seems your use of Miss Benjamin is working out quite well for the Union."

"Fortunately, Ninette has decided to marry a Frenchman. Of course, Judah is quite discouraged but was very consoling when he revealed her decision to me. He knew how I had my heart set on advancing my relationship with Ninette."

"And I suppose you played the martyr to the hilt," Millie said with a smile.

"Of course, my dear. I told him I would survive, given time. But it is difficult, you know," he teased. "She was such a lovely, kind, and gracious person, and—"

"Oh darling, are you all right? I mean, I could write to her and try to intervene for you."

"Well, she's returning to Richmond with her fiancé this spring. I suppose I could try to rekindle our relationship then."

"If you do, I shall have you admitted to the hospital for the mentally ill, dear boy." Millie was shaking her head.

"And rightly so. Besides I hope to be married by then."

"I see, and who did you have in mind?"

"Actually, there is one young lady. A prominent landowner, green eyed and beautiful, who, unfortunately, carries a good deal of debt. But I understand she's about to get some relief."

Millie sat straight, her eyes filled with confused curiosity.

He lifted his valise and pulled papers from it. "I received those yesterday, darling. They came from a friend in New York and were sent via England to get them back here. It took a little time, but I think you'll find them worth the wait."

Her eyes widened, and she quickly scanned them. "But . . . this says the addendum was never registered. It would therefore be invalid."

"That's correct. And if it was not filed in the state where it was signed, it has no force of law even in the Confederacy."

"Then Daniel Geery has no right to make any determination about the sale of Beauchapel or its property." Her wide eyes continued to read.

Matthew continued, "And he has no right of first refusal. If we cannot pay the debt, you can sell to whomever you want."

She looked up. "We?"

"Yes, darling, we. I intend to help you find a way."

She threw her arms around him and held him close. "Oh, Matthew, what would I do without you?" She kissed him then looked into his eyes. "Would you mind if we went back to Petersburg? I must visit with Mr. Huggins immediately."

"I've already shown these papers to Henry. There is no question about the legality of your position."

"No, no, I just want Mr. Huggins to know so that he can notify Geery. The man is spying on me, and I wish to put an end to it."

"He still holds the debt, Millie. Until we find a way to pay, it may be best to leave him in ignorance."

She hesitated only a moment. "I have a way, Matthew. I have a buyer for Beauchapel. Once he sees these papers, he'll be quite willing to give me the price I require."

"You intend to sell? But—"

She put a finger to his lips. "There's no other way, Matthew. We have less than a month to come up with thirty thousand dollars. I don't have the money and neither do you."

"Give me until New Year's Day. If I cannot get a loan, you can go to your buyer."

She pulled her legs up onto the seat so she was in a kneeling position, her eyes searching his. She had come to love him so much that it was no longer about saving Beauchapel but saving him. She intended to get him back to the North, to stop this dangerous business and flee before he was caught and hanged or shot or thrown in some horrid jail to waste away until he welcomed death. She had nightmares about it. And yet she was torn by his request. If he could save Beauchapel, if this awful war ended soon and he was never found out . . .

"All right, Matthew," she said softly, "January first. After that, I sell and move to New York."

"Good. Then there's no reason to see Mr. Huggins, correct?" Then it dawned on him. "New York? But we cannot marry if you're in New York."

"Yes, we can."

He didn't answer immediately. He knew what she was thinking. They had discussed it before, and it was always there, hovering over them like a dark cloud. "You know I can't leave," he said softly, looking out the window.

She leaned against him, her arms around his neck. She kissed him just below the ear but could not hold back a tear. "Oh, Matthew, can't you see? You can go to Washington and do just as much good! And we—"

"Millie, look where I am. The war department of the Confederacy! No one has better access to Confederate secrets than I do. I cannot just leave."

She tightened her grip. "But if I lost you . . ."

"You won't, Millie." He held her close. "I promise." After a moment they separated, and he gave her a wry smile while using his hanky to dry the tears that marked her cheeks. "Just a moment ago I proposed to you. What is your answer?"

She looked at him doubtfully, her mind going back over their conversation. "*That* was a proposal?"

"Well, yes, but I . . ." He pulled a small box from his pocket. "Will this help?" He flipped back the lid to reveal a ring. "Will you marry me, Millicent Atwater?"

She closed the lid on the box, the ring still inside. He looked at her in confusion. "Of course, the ring is beautiful, but I will expect it to be presented properly, Matthew Alexander," she teased. "After that, if you ask in just the right way, if you beg a little . . . Well, maybe I shall marry you, but I do have a very good offer you know, and yours will have to be considered in that light. After all Mr. Geery would leave me wanting for nothing and . . ."

The carriage turned so quickly that Millie started to fall from her kneeling position. Matthew caught her but did not raise her up. "Say you will, or I shall let you go."

"If you do, even that ring won't save you," she said with a threatening tone and grin.

He pulled her up and then lifted her into his lap before kissing her lips. "All right, Miss Atwater you shall have your formal proposal, but it'll be on my timetable not yours, is that clear?"

"Yes, dear," she said, kissing his nose and cheeks softly.

"Good." She kissed him on the lips, once, then twice, then on the eyes, forcing him to close them.

"Here, darling," he said softly, pointing to another spot.

She smiled, kissed the spot he pointed to, then kissed his lips again. "Is there anywhere else, dear?" He pointed to a spot near his ear. She kissed it gently.

"Millie."

She looked into his eyes. "Yes, dear."

"*Please*, marry me?"

"Of course, darling. All you had to do was ask." She kissed him again as the carriage came to a stop. It was more than a minute before the door opened and a smiling Matthew got down from the carriage then helped Millie get down. She put her arm through his, and they started up the steps to the front door, the diamond on her finger glistening in the midday sun.

*   *   *

When Lizzy walked into Charlie's, she had to push and shove her way through drinking, rowdy soldiers and citizens to try and find the gambling tables. When she finally got a visual of Fairfield, she found him sitting with three others. They were so enthralled in their game that they seemed oblivious to the constant mayhem all around them. A half dozen others stood about or watched the game from other tables, and Lizzy sidled up next to a post and leaned against it as she tried to figure out exactly how to get the mortician away from his table.

Lizzy was no stranger to gambling. When her family had first moved to St. Louis, Lizzy made friends with a girl whose father was a riverboat gambler and ran the games on several of Hudson's most elegant riverboats. Her friend's father had taught his daughter the finer points of the games, and the girl had passed them on to Lizzy behind the closed doors of their bedrooms, including how to deal from the bottom of the deck. And the one pitching cards at this table was adept at it. A plan formed in her head. There was an empty chair, and she had fifty dollars in her pocket. If she closed this game out . . .

She moved to the chair and sat down as the last hand ended and the dealer scooped up a small pot. All eyes fell on her.

"This ain't no place for a lady," the one next to her said.

"Do I look like a lady?" she asked angrily, then flipped the fellow's hat off with a quick finger. He scrambled for it while she placed her money on the table. "I'll bet one of them ten dollar pieces that I can take the first pot. If I can't, I'll go put on a dress and dance with this here fella till the cows come home." She looked at the man, who was just putting his hat back in place. "'Course, somebody'd probably have t' teach me how to dance, but I'll force myself just the same. What do you say, boys?"

"Let her play," someone said from behind the table. Others chimed in. Fairfield finally shrugged, and the cheater picked up the cards and began to shuffle. He was good, probably a professional gambler who was hustling these boys a little at time. He'd lose some, win some, but when the evening was over, he'd go home with most of the cash while they wandered back to their families mostly broke but feeling good about it. "All right, one hand, little lady, but if you lose, yer done and home to yer pa."

"Pa! Huh! Ain't got no pa. Now, deal."

The cheater finished his show, and Lizzy prayed with her eyes open, watching the deck. He was dealing from the bottom all right, but she was getting the cards he was peeling off. She knew they'd all be bad ones.

She picked up her cards, verified that she had nothing, smiled, then threw in a ten dollar coin. "You boys are about to have your come-uppins."

The man next to her folded, and then the dealer, a mild smirk on his face, matched her ten and added another ten. Fairfield matched both with a call, and the last man tossed his cards in.

"How many cards you want, lady?" the dealer asked.

"These suit me fine," she said with a smile. She matched the bet.

The dealer did the same. Fairfield tossed his cards on the table with the others. It was just her and a crooked dealer. "I'll take three," he said.

When he started to deal them, she pulled her gun and pointed it at him. "Leave all three sit right there. Move yer hands away like a good boy." She grinned. "Boys, this fella's dealin' from the bottom."

The men standing around the table went suddenly quiet. The dealer had stopped midaction and looked at her without emotion, his hands still on the three cards. He was about to move them so she cocked the pistol. He didn't move another finger.

"Move 'em away," she said. The cards he'd dealt himself lay flat on the table, and he pulled his hands away, sitting back, pulling the cigar from his lips. "I suppose you know how to use that thing," he said, glancing at the revolver, trying to act calm.

"From this distance I don't need to know much except how to point and pull." "How do you plan to prove your accusation?"

"Turn your first five cards over."

He hesitated then shrugged and turned them over.

"Nothing there that would buy you a piece of hard-tack candy," she said.

He shrugged. "So what? My guess is you don't have anything either. Just a bad hand, that's all."

"Except those last three, the ones you dealt off the bottom are a different story. Winners, all of 'em, ain't they?"

She wiggled the revolver.

Beads of sweat appeared on the dealer's forehead. "Even if it's true that don't prove nothin'."

Fairfield reached across the table and turned the cards over. "Three queens."

"My, you are a lucky fellow, aren't ya?" she said.

The men around the table were grumbling now, and the cheater stood quickly. "I ain't stickin' around to listen to this, I—"

"Miles," Fairfield said to a man standing nearby. "This is your place. Clean it up, will you?"

Miles nodded to two rather large men, and they grabbed the dealer, stood him on his head, and shook him good. When they were finished, the floor was littered with coins and a few high-ranking cards. The crowd parted like the Red Sea as they carried the dealer to the door and tossed him on his ear into the street. Lizzy figured he'd beat her out of town, and she had to be leaving pretty soon.

"You have a good eye," Fairfield said. "Did you see it before or after you joined the game?"

"Before. I don't like cheats." She put her gun back in the holster. "Mr. Barber, yer the local mortician, ain't you?"

"Yes, I am."

"Well, I need a burying, and seein's how I just saved you a good deal of money, I'd appreciate you takin' care of it now."

Fairfield looked at the pot then at the other men. It was a hard choice, but finally he slid his chair back and stood. "All right, miss. Let's take care of your problem." He picked up his winnings and a share of the money the gambler had left on the floor, and they started for the door.

They exited the front entrance, walked down the steps, and dodged their way across the street.

"Where is the body?" Fairfield asked.

"Well, there isn't any, John, but I needed to talk to you, and according to Dortha, what you just saw was the only way to get you out of there without dragging you by the ear," Lizzy said.

He stopped, and she turned to look at him as they stood under a gas lamp hanging on the wall of the mercantile store.

"Don't worry, Mr. Fairfield. Your secret is safe with me." She took him by the arm and pulled him along.

"Who are you?" he asked.

"Elizabeth Hudson of St. Louis, or Susan Davis of California. Take your pick."

He visibly relaxed. "I've heard of both. One is a singer and supposed to be performing at our local theater tomorrow night, the other is a firm abolitionist who has helped more slaves escape Missouri than I've helped escape Kentucky—well, almost." He grinned. "What are you doing here, Miss Hudson?"

"General Grant sent me."

"Then he's planning to come south."

"Yes, but he needs numbers. When he found out you might be here, he thought I could shorten my stay with a visit to you." She paused. "It seems I must leave even quicker than I thought, so I had to get to you tonight." She told him about Andrew.

"Your fans will be disappointed. From everything I've heard, Miss Davis has been better than her reputation." He paused. "I know Captain Clay. He seems a fine man but one bound by the highest form of Southern pride and honor. In your case that could be a dangerous thing."

"And why I must leave as soon as I can. Do you have any information that might help General Grant?"

"I have a ledger. Very detailed, but things change almost daily, and if he doesn't act within the next month or two, much of it will be outdated."

They reached the shop, and he used his key to let them inside. Lighting a lamp, he pulled the curtains closed, went to his fireplace, and pushed up hard on the mantle. It folded up as if on a hinge. He reached into a narrow slot and pulled out a ledger. "I have made drawings and maps and done my best to give a true accounting of numbers." He opened it and showed her his work. She was amazed at the detail.

"This will give Grant a tremendous advantage."

A knock came at the door, and both of them froze, then he shoved the ledger back in its hiding place and knocked the mantle back into place. He pointed to a room and waited until she had disappeared before going to the front of the store and opening the main entry door. He was confronted by half a dozen soldiers, armed and obviously agitated.

"Yes, what is it?"

"Our dead, sir," the first man said. "We were on patrol up by Morgantown and run into some Yanks. We drove 'em off, but we lost some men."

"Very well, Sergeant. Bring them in through the usual door, and we'll take care of them."

The sergeant gave instructions to his men, and they moved around to the side of the building. Fairfield closed the front door, worked his way around the workbench and materials, and opened the side door. Four bodies obviously beset by rigor mortis were brought in and laid on the floor.

"When did this happen?" Fairfield asked.

"Two days ago, sir, but Captain Clay wanted 'em brought here. Says it's better if their folks know where they're buried." The sergeant pointed to the one on the far end. "Except for Hanks, sir. His folks are picking him up, taking him home. Lives in Russellville. Coming tomorrow, sir."

"That's fine. Tell the captain they'll be ready for burial tomorrow afternoon."

"Yes, sir." They left, closing the door behind them. Fairfield locked it then went to the front and locked that door as well. Lizzy came out of hiding, glanced at the covered bodies, and scrunched up her nose at the strong smell of decay.

Fairfield spoke. "Most officers would just bury them where they fell, but Captain Clay takes care of his." He opened the mantle and retrieved the ledger.

"Tell Grant there's a lot of change going on. More men every day, lots more. Hopefully he can move before too long."

She smiled. "Good-bye, John. I'm glad you weren't killed in Tennessee."

"I'd like to stay dead, Miss Hudson. No one is looking for me anymore, and that makes my job a bit easier." He blew out the lamp as Lizzy shoved the small ledger under her shirt with her own books and notes. He unlocked the door, and Lizzy gave him a quick kiss on the cheek as a final thank-you before slipping out and heading back to the hotel. It was time to leave Bowling Green.

Chapter Twenty-Five

MILLIE AND MATTHEW SAT AT the round kitchen table across from one another. They had just finished a meal of fried ham, red-eye gravy and biscuits, and cold milk when a knock came at the door. A servant answered, and there was a bit of noise before she came into the room with wide, frightened eyes.

"It's Massa Geery," she said in a loud whisper. "An' he got dat lawyah wid him too, along wid some other man I nevah seen befo'. He made me let 'im in, Missy. I didn't want to, but he made me."

Millie frowned. "Offer them tea, and tell them I will be with them shortly. And, Tiera, shut the door to the sitting room when you return." Tiera nodded and turned to leave. Millie sipped her tea. She had warned him, yet he had still come. But she was glad. She had papers she wanted him to see.

"Will you accompany me?" Millie asked.

"Of course. Where are the papers from New York?" Matthew got up and pulled back Millie's chair.

"In my study." They went down the hall, passing Tiera as she finished closing the door, a bitter look on her face. Like most slaves and freedmen who knew of Daniel Geery, she hated the man.

Millie retrieved the papers while Matthew put on his suit coat. He thought of shoving a revolver in his belt but pushed the thought aside. Surely Geery wasn't that much of a fool.

Millie joined him, papers in hand. Matthew opened the door, and they entered the sitting room. She smiled as Geery turned to face them, a sour look evident. Geery's attorney was standing next to the fireplace warming his hands, and Millie greeted him, noticing that a third man stood near the window. She did not recognize him, and he did not move when they entered, making her uneasy.

"This is business, Millicent," Geery said flatly. "This gent can wait in the other room."

"This is my fiancé, and he's here at my invitation. And if you forget you're in *my* house, Mr. Geery, I'll drive you out of here with a whip."

Geery sneered. "Ah, Mr. Alexander, aide to Secretary Benjamin, formerly of New Orleans, a student at West Point before the war. Yes, I know who you are." The tone was anything but one of admiration.

Matthew showed no emotion at Geery's knowledge of him. "Mr. Geery."

"Daniel, why have you come?" Millie asked firmly.

Geery waved the third man forward, and the thin form emerged from the shadows. "Russell Gainer. You may have heard of him," Geery said.

Matthew had never been around a man in whose presence he felt the depth of darkness that he felt with Geery. Though Millie had spoken of his temper and character, being in his presence explained why she feared and even despised the man. Matthew had also heard of Gainer. He owned a large slave-trading house in Richmond.

"Yes, he deals in inhumanity," Millie said coldly. "Why have you brought him here?"

"We've had a large number of slaves run away lately. It seems the Union's position on slaves being contraband is encouraging them to flee. Mr. Gainer has evidence that two of your slaves are helping others escape, most notably mine and those of your other neighbors. He's here to purchase the troublemakers in order to prevent further harm to the rest of us."

"Mr. Gainer's evidence is of no value to me," Millie said. "We have no slaves here, you know that."

"Ah, but you do," Geery said confidently. He glanced at his attorney, a cue to chime in.

Mr. Blunck was visibly sweating. Millie wondered why he would work for a man like Geery, but she supposed money was most of it. "As you know from my last visit Miss Atwater, the addendum to your contract states clearly that Mr. Geery must clear all sale of property and that any transaction made without his permission is null and void. I told you then that this would include the freeing of slaves and—"

"Do you have the addendum?" Millie interrupted.

Matthew worked hard to keep his face passive. He knew what Millie was about to do and applauded her strength, but he watched Geery. Of these men, he would be the most dangerous.

"Of course." He removed it from his valise and handed it to her. She looked at it carefully before handing it back. "Do you see any seal of filing on that document, Mr. Blunck?"

The attorney looked at the paper. "No, but that doesn't mean—"

"I am sorry you didn't notice earlier, Mr. Blunck, or that you decided to ignore the fact that no such seal is present. Law requires it. She handed him the papers from New York. "Those documents say that Mr. Geery never registered the addendum, and because it was not registered it's not legal. Therefore, Mr. Geery has no rights when it comes to the disposition of Beauchapel or its property, nor does he have first right of refusal on Beauchapel. Now, if you don't mind, Mr. Alexander and I were eating dinner and would like to return to it."

Geery flinched, and his face seemed to harden. "Is she right, Mr. Blunck?"

The attorney was scanning the sheets as quickly as he could and did not answer immediately.

"Mr. Blunck, *is she right?*"

"Y . . . yes, but I thought you said you filed the papers in Washington. This says there is no such record, and if there is not . . . but surely you did, and this is a mistake."

"I did, and whoever says different is lying," Geery said through tight lips.

Matthew spoke now. "If you had, there would be a seal of the city of Washington firmly stamped in the face of your document, Mr. Geery. It would also have the date and the signature of the city clerk on it. My friends in New York may be Yanks, but they are quite thorough. I suppose you could have your own verify their work. You do have attornies in the North, don't you, Mr. Geery?"

Geery was livid. "You did this!" he hissed through clenched teeth, his eyes glaring at Matthew. "I will break you for this."

"Break me?" Matthew smiled wryly. "It's quite clear you have attempted to cheat Miss Atwater out of her land. If you wish to push this further, I assure you it will be you who will be broken, Mr. Geery."

Geery took two steps and came toe-to-toe with Matthew. Before Matthew could prevent it, Geery had whipped a glove from a pocket and slapped his opponent across the cheek with it, causing Matthew's head to turn to one side with the power of the blow. He stiffened then gently touched his cheek.

"You have insulted my honor!" Geery said.

"You have no honor. That should be obvious to anyone here."

"I challenge you to—"

Matthew laughed. "A duel? We have moved out of archaic society, Mr. Geery."

The hand came up again, but Matthew caught it midair. He squeezed and forced the hand to open, removing the glove. He then used it to slap Geery hard across the face not once but twice. Geery stumbled back several steps grabbing his face, his nostrils flaring. Matthew saw Gainer reach for something in his jacket and wished he'd brought his revolver after all. Instead, Matthew jerked Geery around then shoved him directly into Gainer. Both men clattered in a mass of humanity onto the floor, and Gainer's gun fell on the rug. Matthew quickly scooped it up, unlocked the cylinder, and emptied the shells into the palm of his hand while Geery and Gainer struggled to be free of one another. He used his free arm to move Millie back a pace or two, her eyes alight with anger and a fireplace stoker in her hand.

"You gentlemen should leave before I let Miss Atwater loose on you," he said with a slight smile. "As you can see, you would leave the worse for it."

He waved the pistol toward the door, and the three men moved cautiously toward the front entrance. "Mr. Geery, Millie is my fiancée. If I hear of you coming on this property again, I will come here and take you up on your offer of a duel. But be warned I was first in my class at the Academy with a dueling pistol, and I *will* use that skill to end your miserable life if I have to."

Geery was livid, his body shaking with fury, his fists clinched tight, and his nostrils flaring in a face hardened by hate. "I will have this property! You'll see. No one will buy it! No one!"

"Not everyone in the South is afraid of you, but Millie does not intend to sell. You will have your money by the date due," Matthew said. "Now off with you, and do not show your face at Beauchapel again, or we will have you arrested." He looked at the attorney. "Is that understood from a legal point of view, Mr. Blunck?"

The attorney, pale and sobered, only nodded as he went through the door. Gainer went next, but Geery was still in a rage, his eyes glaring at both of them. "Mr. Geery, if you speak, it had better be in the form of an apology to Miss Atwater," Matthew threatened.

Geery forced himself to turn. He threw open the screen door with such force it banged against the wall and came directly back at him, hitting him and knocking him off his stride. He stumbled down the steps and climbed into the carriage just as Matthew threw the revolver to the carriage driver. "Return that to Mr. Gainer when you're off this property, no sooner."

The black driver gave him a grin with his reply. "Yas, suh!" With that he whipped the horses, and the carriage bolted down the lane toward the main road.

Millie sat down slowly in a nearby porch swing and dropped the poker, her hands shaking. Matthew waited until the carriage disappeared onto the main road before he eased himself into the swing next to her and put an arm around her shoulders.

She turned into him and began to cry. He held her close, giving her the best comfort he could.

But both of them knew it was still not over.

*   *   *

Lizzy saw the horses in the alley, but Elliott was not with them. She hurried up the back stairs, reached the room, and tried the door. It opened, and she quickly entered, closing it behind her. The room was dark except for the light coming from a few coals in the fireplace. "Elliott?"

"Hello, Elizabeth." The voice came from behind her, and she turned to see someone come out of the deeper shadow of a corner. The fire threw a glint off something in his hand, and Lizzy knew it was a revolver. She could not see his face clearly, but she did recognize the voice even though it was stiff, even unfriendly.

"Andrew. I thought you were in the East," she said.

"Put your revolver on the table, Lizzy." She removed it and placed it on the small reading table near the chairs. "I was until a few weeks ago." He paused long enough to turn up the gas lamp. "I saw Rand. I figured we might face one another again, so I asked to be transferred. Seems I only made things worse."

She eyed the revolver. "You can put that away, Andrew. I have no place to run."

He shoved it in his holster. "You were a fool to come here, Elizabeth."

She sensed a hint of frustration, even confusion. "I suppose that depends on you."

"I cannot let you leave here, you know that. You've seen too much."

"Then I'll stay."

"What?"

"That's the only other option, Andrew. I go or I stay. Whether I stay as a prisoner or as Susan Davis is your decision, but those are the options."

He cursed. "How could you do this?"

"I had no idea you were here. If I'd known, I would have stayed away from Bowling Green."

"But you still would have come to do your spying," he said stiffly.

"Of course. I am no less honorable in standing for what I believe than you are." She turned to the fireplace, threw several pieces of wood on the hot coals, and then punched at them with the stoker before leaning it back in its brass stand. "Neither of us thought it would ever come to this, but I suppose we should have. We cannot go to war on opposite sides and not hurt one another. The very fact that you are against me and I against you affects our feelings for one another. How could it be otherwise? Surely, I love you, Andrew, but I am your enemy as well and you are mine. I do not expect you to treat me as anything less. I knew what my fate might be if discovered. I do not expect you to treat me any different than if you were Buckner. If you let me go, I will run, and I will tell General Grant everything I have seen because I want to save my country from rebellious Southerners who have let their blind adherence to an inhuman treatment of blacks force them into a position of war." She took a deep breath. "You are the man I love, but you are also the rebel I hate, and I will fight you because you fight for them." She had moved close enough to the table that she was within reach of her revolver. She quickly picked it up and cocked it, pointing it at his midsection. "Now, I will leave you here, tied and gagged, or I can shoot you if you think it would be more in keeping with your Southern honor, but I am leaving, and if you try to stop me—"

His eyes flashed hot, and he took a step toward her and grabbed the gun to jerk it out of her hand when he went limp and fell to the floor. Elliott stood over him with a rifle, eyes wide. He went to one knee, checking for a pulse. "He's just unconscious. Rip up them sheets so's we can tie him up."

"Where on earth did you come from?"

"The armoir. I was waitin' fo' you when I heard him and the clerk outside the door. I hid myself. Now get movin', Lizzy Hudson, or I be tyin' you up and leavin' you both to settle this later!"

Lizzy threw the coverlets back and ripped several strands from the sheet, handing them to Elliott. "Thank you, Elliott," she said softly. "I couldn't have done it." She bit her lip, her hand stroking Andrew's forehead.

"Yes, I know's. But yo' voice made him think you was and made me think it too. He had fire in his eyes cause of it, didn't he? He would a made you do it, Missy, or he would have thrown you to the wolves. He say he loves you, but he loves them or his silly honor more. Simple as that." Lizzy got to her feet and sat on the edge of the bed mulling over his words. How *did* Andrew feel? She wasn't even sure about her own feelings anymore. Would she have shot him? And if she hadn't . . . ?

"Come along, Miss Elizabeth!" Elliott said. "We got no time t' lose if we want to get out of here with our skins." He went to the door, and Lizzy pushed herself off the bed, her eyes on Andrew. Elliott opened the door a crack then went out, and Lizzy looked one final time at Andrew before walking weakly to the steps as Elliott locked the door behind them. They reached the horses, mounted, and guided them into the still-busy streets, the sound of piano music, loud laughter, and chaos following them until they were on the outskirts of town. Elliott was quickly at a gallop then a full run, and Lizzy forced herself to drive her heels into the flanks of her own mount, tears rolling off her cheeks. They had to be far to the north by sunlight.

* * *

Andrew woke up as the door closed behind Elliott and Elizabeth. He struggled against the bonds for only a minute before he lay still, the impact of what had happened hitting him.

He'd been angry. He had reacted and could have actually hurt Elizabeth if someone hadn't stopped him. How could he have thought such a thing—or worse, acted on it? He turned onto his back and stared up at the silent ceiling. And Lizzy—she had a fire in her eyes he had never seen before. Would she have actually shot him? And if she hadn't, what would he have done to her? Imprisoned her? Or worse? No, he had only tried to disarm her. He wanted only to talk, to figure it all out, but then he'd been hit from behind. But by who?

What had this war already done to both of them? The chill climbed up his stomach into his throat.

He was struggling against his bonds when he heard a key in the lock and turned his head to see the door open, two men standing in it, guns drawn. They quickly holstered their weapons and knelt by his side. One drew a knife and cut his bonds while the other pulled the gag free of his mouth. It was then he noted that it was General Buckner and his aide.

"What happened, Captain? What are you doing here?"

Moorehead had gotten to his feet and lifted something in his hand. "Sir," he said. Buckner looked up at the brunette wig in his aide's hand. "Just as we thought."

Andrew bit his tongue, saying nothing, waiting. What did Moorehead mean? Had they learned of Lizzy's ruse?

Buckner saw the questions in Andrew's eyes. "We received a telegram from Susan Davis. She's still in California. She learned from a friend there that "Susan Davis" was performing for Confederate soldiers in Tennessee. She sent a telegram through Texas, but it took a couple of days for it to get here. Now, answer my question, Captain. What are you doing here?"

Andrew rubbed the back of his head and neck, his mind struggling for a way out, a story that might appease and still give him time to figure out how to protect Lizzy.

"When we saw her in the lobby, I thought I recognized her. I came to be sure. Her name is Elizabeth Hudson. She lives in St. Louis and is a sister to a friend from the Academy, Randolph Hudson. I met Elizabeth when on leave a few summers ago."

"Why didn't you say anything?"

"I wasn't sure and didn't want to offend Miss Davis if I was wrong. Question is who hit me? The last I remember I was staring at a brunette with Elizabeth Hudson's face," Andrew lied.

"Probably her servant; black fellow, called him Elliott."

Andrew nodded, getting to his feet. "We should get after her, sir. She didn't leave very long ago, and I . . . well, I'd like to lead my men in the chase, sir. I'll see that she's found and brought back."

"You've done enough, Captain. Return to your unit. Lieutenant Moorehead, send Colonel Forrest and fifty of his men. I want that woman found. Heaven only knows what kind of information she has."

Andrew felt his mouth go dry. Nathan Bedford Forrest was both ruthless and relentless, and he hated abolitionists. Lizzy barely had a head start.

"Yes, sir. Right away, sir." Moorehead left the room as Andrew retrieved his hat and his revolver.

"You had a chance to draw your weapon?" Buckner asked, an edge of suspicion in his voice.

"I tried, sir. That was when I was hit." He rubbed the back of his head again.

"You're dismissed, Captain. I'll stay, take a look around."

"Sir, I'd really like to go with Forrest. I feel responsible for Miss Hudson's escape."

Buckner eyed him carefully. "All right, Captain. Get moving."

Andrew left the hotel by the front entrance, found his mount, and rode quickly toward the area where Forrest and his men were camped. Elizabeth was in extreme danger, and he was tired of playing both ends against the middle. He should have gone with Rand that day, but he'd let his . . . his honor get in the way. He was sick of honor! Sick of what it was doing to him, of having to wake up every morning and convince himself he was doing the right thing. Well, he wasn't doing the right thing, and he wasn't going to do it anymore. This time he was done with the Confederacy.

But he must find Lizzy. If he lost her now . . .

He wouldn't. He would get her out. He must. And he'd go with her.

*　*　*

Lizzy and Elliott had left town in the direction of Russellville then cut north and back east toward Elizabethtown. The closest Union troops were at Louisville, but there were strong Confederate lines between Bowling Green and Louisville that they must avoid. If their ruse was discovered, the rebels would telegraph ahead and have pickets strengthened and watching for them. They had to stay away from Confederate strong points. That meant going directly north by the fastest possible route. Lizzy figured that meant a steamer.

They traveled through heavy forest until they reached the Green River. They then traveled north toward Morgantown. Lizzy had been to Morgantown years earlier. Rand had asked her to check out the viability of sending steamers up the Green River for commercial purposes. The waters on the Green were erratic and didn't lend themselves to year-round travel, and Lizzy had said so, but at this time of year there was plenty of water, and small steamship companies used Morgantown as a stop off. If she and Elliott could get there and get aboard a steamer heading north, they could be back to Cairo in four days.

Exhausted, they dismounted in a sheltered ravine and rounded up firewood. Elliott soon had it burning, and he walked to a small, clear stream to retrieve water for drinking while Elizabeth removed the saddles and tethered the horses. Though they would only rest an hour, the animals needed relief from their burdens and a chance to forage in the dried winter grass. She was warming her hands when Elliott returned and handed her the canteen.

"Do you think they'll come after us, Missy?"

She remembered Andrew's angry look, his determination, as she swallowed the last of her drink. "Yes, they'll come, but I think we covered our trail enough, and it's a big country they have to search," she said.

"But if'n dey get's ahead o' us, just waitin' . . ."

Lizzy nodded. As tired as they were they had to keep moving as soon as the horses were rested. "Try to get an hour of shut-eye, then we'll get moving again."

Lizzy curled up on her horse blanket and used her saddle as a pillow. Seconds later she was asleep.

*　*　*

"We'll never be able to track them," Forrest said to Andrew. "Even though she was seen heading in the direction of Russellville, I believe it is a deception. She is obviously a smart woman, and knowing we'd telegraph all the way to Hopkinsville, she would avoid that route."

"Even though Louisville is the closest Union stronghold?" Andrew asked.

Forrest nodded. "She'll avoid it for the same reasons. She will have an entire army looking for her and her freedman along those routes, so she'll pick another. He looked directly at Andrew as if measuring him. "She will go directly north but stay off the roads. That means we should search Morgantown then Hardford or Hardinsburg farther north. Don't you agree, Captain Clay?"

Andrew knew it was a hunch but a calculated one. He also knew Forrest was looking for his reaction. "Yes, I'm sure you are right."

"Good." Among the telegraphs he sent was one to the small unit of soldiers at Morgantown. It told them to be on the lookout. "We'll go to Russellville before turning north on the road to Morgantown. If we hurry we can get ahead of her." He spurred his horse and signalled his men to follow. Andrew hit his own mount in the flanks and rode alongside Colonel Forrest, his stomach tied in knots. He knew Lizzy well enough that he figured Forrest was right in his calculations, but he could do nothing but go along.

Andrew had been on patrol in the area only a few days earlier. They had run into Union troops. There had been a stiff skirmish, but they'd driven the federal troops out of the area, and Morgantown was presently in Confederate hands. Though only about fifty men were encamped there, it was enough to stop Lizzy if she wasn't cautious.

But he did get some comfort in knowing this was Elizabeth Hudson. She was no foreigner to clandestine escape or to rigors of hiding. She had good experience from her efforts to free runaways, and she was as smart and resourceful as anyone he had ever known, man or woman.

But she was also up against Colonel Nathan Bedford Forrest. Andrew had been on patrol with Forrest and knew no one with a more uncanny ability to find what he was looking for. Nor did he know anyone who knew central and southern Kentucky better. If anyone could bring Lizzy back, it would be Forrest.

They took a rest after ten miles of hard riding. Andrew walked to a small stream that fed the Green River to get a drink, and Forrest followed. They both knelt and scooped water into the palm of their hands to drink, a wary eye and ear on the terrain around them. They had run into Union patrols this far south of the Ohio before and were not about to be surprised by one now.

"Moorehead says you know this Hudson woman. She any relation to Randolph Hudson, Hudson Shipping?"

"His sister, why do you ask?"

"I used Hudson to ship cotton off my plantation. We would take it into Vicksburg, and he'd float it down to New Orleans. Used barges as well as steamers. Good businessman, shrewd, smart, top-notch." He paused, wiping his hands on his coat before sitting down on a fallen log. "Trouble is he was a dyed-in-the-wool abolitionist and even helped nigras escape by hiding 'em in his steamers. Lost two of mine while they were hauling cotton down to Vicksburg. Just disappeared. The locals said I should check Hudson's boat."

"And did you?"

Forrest nodded. "Hudson was aboard. Invited me on when I challenged him. Looked over that entire steamer; never found a thing."

He paused. "Except that the hold was smaller than it should be. I figure he had a secret room built down there, but neither me nor my overseer could find a way in." He spit into the water near Andrew. "I've hated the man ever since." There was a hard, hot look in Forrest's eyes. "I catch his sister, her freedman. I figure we can call it even."

"The woman is white, Forrest. You touch her, and I'll shoot you myself," Andrew warned.

Forrest smiled wickedly. "You can try, Captain Clay. You can try." He stood and went back toward the road, shouting a command to mount up. Andrew felt his hair standing on end. Standing and following, he removed his revolver from its holster, making sure it was both loaded and dry. He might need it.

*   *   *

Lizzy and Elliott arrived at a plantation a few miles south and west of Morgantown at about noon. They watched the place from hiding for nearly twenty minutes before Lizzy figured they might have an advantage.

It was a bright sunny morning, and the slaves were working around a large barn and other outbuildings, loading bundled dried tobacco leaves and bags of hemp fiber onto two large wagons.

"Where do you suppose they be goin' with them goods?" Elliott said.

"Probably to Morgantown, where they'll put them aboard a steamer and take them either upriver to Bowling Green then Nashville, or downstream to the Ohio. With the right papers someone in this part of Kentucky is still able to do either."

"Maybe we can catch a ride," Elliott said in some jest.

"No maybe's about it, but first I have to change my looks," Lizzy said.

Elliott looked at her. "What you mean?"

Lizzy smiled. "Elliott, this is one time when it might just pay to be black."

*   *   *

Andrew watched as Forrest met with the lieutenant responsible for the hundred men stationed at Morgantown. They were to picket at each road into town and the ones that may lead around it, checking the identity of everyone they met. He told Andrew to give a description of Elizabeth, and then Forrest told ten of his own men to go to the ferry landing and check everyone. The others he told to spread out around the main street itself and keep a wary eye. He said nothing about putting men near the steamship landing that was separated from the ferry landing by several hundred yards. But there were no steamships yet, and Forrest was using his men to best advantage.

He and Forrest sat on a bench outside a local mercantile store, each sipping a bottle of home-brewed sasparilla given to them by a merchantman. Both men were enjoying the refreshment while mostly ignoring one another.

Finally, Andrew got to his feet and stepped off the boardwalk into the street.

"Don't leave my sight, Captain," Forrest said with a hard edge.

"Wouldn't think of it, Colonel," Andrew replied. He wanted to add that he couldn't shoot Forrest if he couldn't see the man, but instead, Andrew just bit his tongue. Crossing the street, he sat down on the elevated boardwalk on the shady west side of the street. He was near exhaustion. He and his men had been on patrol for nearly a week, and he hadn't slept much. Then he saw Lizzy, and now he'd been up another entire night and day. It was finally wearing on him. He finished the last of his drink, set the bottle at his feet, then leaned his head against a post and lowered his hat over his eyes.

The town wasn't busy like Bowling Green or bigger cities. The street had occasional wagons, carriages, horsemen, and even a few children playing in it, but it was a lazy town by most standards, and he was quickly dozing.

Then he heard the ruckus at the end of the street and quickly pushed his hat back and blinked the sleep dust out of his eyes. He stood and headed toward the clamor to find the pickets arguing with a black man sitting in a wagon, reins in his hands, and a dozen other black folks standing or sitting about, waiting. He arrived at the wagons at the same moment as Forrest, who asked the private what was the problem.

"These folks are delivering this stuff to the steamer. I told 'em there ain't no steamer and they should go on home," the private answered.

"Steamer's a comin'," said the black man in a deep, husky voice.

"Well it ain't here, and we got an escaped—"

"Never mind, private," Forrest interrupted. "Get down, nigra," he said coldly.

The black fellow tied the reins around the tie post and got down from the tall wagon. Just as he did, the sound of a steamer whistle came from the river. Everyone looked that direction to see a small rear-paddle carrier coming up the river and about to slip into shore at the bottom of the road.

"Told ya steamah's comin'," said the black man without smiling. "Headed noth, suh. Massa, he done sold this tobacco and hemp months ago, and he won't appreciate us not gettin' dees here bundles an' sacks loaded. No suh. Steamah only comes once a week, an' if'n we misses it . . . he whip us sure, and den he come lookin' fo' answers, yas suh. That what he do." He shook his head as it hung down, then he pulled some papers from his pocket. "Dees here de papers, suh. See, day says we can send dis up noth, yas, suh."

Forrest stiffened. "Your master a Union man, or a does he support the Confederacy?"

The black man seemed to think a moment, rubbing his thick black beard. "Cain't rightly say, suh. I know's he feeds yo' men quite reg'lar like, but he don't say nuthin' to us nigras. We ain't smart nuf to know 'bout such things, yo' knows dat, suh."

"You have a smart master," Forrest said coldly. "Get moving."

The black fellow climbed back in his perch, and the others gathered about and either climbed up to sit on the tail of the wagon or walked beside it. Andrew watched them as they went by. Forrest ignored them. Most slavers wouldn't give a black man the time of day, let alone a good look, and Forrest was no different.

"That's a Northern steamer, Captain," Forrest said, with a wry smile. "She'll be on it when it leaves. At least she'll try." He paused. "Don't know why the Confederate government doesn't let us shut trade down. Don't help anyone but the North." The wagons passed by, and Forrest and Andrew both followed, more interested in the steamer than in the slaves. The boat rammed into shore and slid up the slope a bit before several workmen lowered a ramp by use of pulleys. The black workers backed the wagons up to the ramp and began unloading the wagons and carrying the sacks aboard. Andrew noted that other wagons soon came down the street with similar loads and formed a line to deposit their products aboard the vessel. The day wore on, and the sun was a dozen feet above the hills when the last of the wagons pulled away.

"It seems she must have gone another way," Andrew said.

"She's here, just waiting for the steamer to set off; I can feel it. I want you to take five men, get aboard. Take your horses and go to the next stop. We'll go overland, meet you there."

"I'll be out of your sight, Colonel," Andrew pointed out.

"You'll take Sergeant Hookings. He'll keep an eye on you, and he wants that woman just as bad as I do, maybe worse. Seems he was lookin' forward to Miss Davis's performance."

"Thanks for the trust, Colonel," Andrew said.

"I don't trust anyone, Captain, especially not friends of Randolph Hudson." He walked away leaving Andrew sick to his stomach, but he ordered five men to grab their mounts and follow him. He led them down to the steamer, where he was confronted by a captain with an overloaded ship.

"Can't take no more soldiers," he said.

"You don't have a choice." He led his horse directly past the captain and tied him to the railing along the side. The others completely filled the remaining space, and Andrew climbed a stack of hemp fiber and sat himself down as the ramp was pulled aboard and the steamer's rear paddle started to churn. He watched as the other soldiers tried to find places to sit as well and noted that Hookings was ordering an old black woman and a younger man to move from their sitting place between two stacks of bags holding dried tobacco leaves. They were slow, and Hookings started pushing them along then looked at his hand curiously.

"Hey!" Hookings yelled. Suddenly he was after them, and they were running up the steps to the second deck. The steamer was in the river and trying to turn about as Andrew jumped from the bags and followed the sergeant.

"Come back here!' Hookings yelled. The other four all noted the chase and immediately followed. Andrew beat them all to the steps and began climbing. When he reached the top, he saw no one. He turned around to face Sergeant Hookings.

"What's going on, Sergeant?"

Hookings showed him his fingers. "Shoe black, sir. That woman ain't anymore nigra than you and me!"

Andrew felt his mouth go dry. "All right. Spread out. Search the ship. I'll check the cabins and the captain's quarters."

"And I'm goin' with you," Hookings said coldly. "Colonel's orders."

"Very well, Sergeant," Andrew said, pulling his revolver and turning down the narrow walkway. The first cabin was only a few feet away, and Andrew stood to the side and knocked. No answer. Andrew tried the latch. It lifted, and the door fell open. They looked inside, but it didn't take long. Cabins aboard a steamer this size were usually nonexistent.

When they did exist, they were usually a bunk hanging on one wall with a small cabinet and washbasin at one end. There was no place to hide.

The next cabin was occupied, and the portly white man who came to the door said he had seen no one. They did a quick search anyway then moved on. It was then Andrew heard the scream. It was definitely Lizzy's voice, and he ran to the far end of the deck and around the corner to find her being manhandled by two soldiers. He ordered them to stop, but they ignored him so he fired his weapon in the air. One had a handful of Lizzy's dress and ripped it away as he stepped back, a scowl on his lips and lust in his eyes. Lizzy slapped him, and he was about to hit her when Andrew heard the shot. The offending soldier had a sudden look of shock cross his face, then he fell back against the wall and slid down it, leaving a trail of blood. His eyes were wide open. He felt something hard shoved into his back and stiffened.

"You killed him, Captain," Hookings said. "I'll take that gun."

Andrew looked down at his revolver, smoke still drifting from the barrel. He looked at Lizzy, her eyes wide, fearful and scared. If he dropped his gun, she would be defenseless and these men—

He whirled and fired at the same time. Hookings face went rigid with shock, and Andrew felt the impact of Hookings's weapon as the dying man's finger jerked and fired. He felt suddenly weak in the knees, and he heard two more shots before he hit the floor fighting for breath.

Elliott had surprised the third soldier from behind and knocked him cold. Lizzy grabbed Andrew's weapon and fired at the two others before they could get the weapons up. Both stumbled back and went over the side, landing motionless on the first deck as the captain of the vessel appeared. He immediately saw her weapon and raised his hands.

She looked at Andrew, handed the gun to Elliot, and knelt by Andrew's side, ripping his coat open, then his shirt. The bullet had gone directly through his stomach. She felt tears come to her eyes, felt them cascade down her cheeks. His hand went to her cheek, and she tried to blink the tears away, smile, give him some hope.

"You will be all right, my love. You will! Just hang on. Please, just hang on!"

"Shh," he said softly.

"No, Andrew! Oh, no, I am so sorry!"

He felt his feet go cold, but he forced a smile, rubbing her cheek with his hand. "It's all right, Liz. It's . . . I . . . I was going to leave, take you . . . go. I should have done it back . . . back at Bowl . . . Bowling Green." He grimaced in pain then gave a smile again, touching her cheek softly. "I'm sorry, Liz. I was a fool. I . . . you know I love you."

"Yes, darling, I know. You can't leave me, Andrew. Not now! Oh, I love you so much! Please . . ."

His eyes glazed over, and she felt death leave him limp in her arms. She bent her head down, kissing his face, crying out, sobbing. "No, no! Andrew! Please come back to me! Please! Oh, dear Father," she said, looking up at the skies. "Please no! Not this!" She shook him gently. "Andrew! Andrew! Please . . ." She cried, her heart broken and inconsolable. Elliott tried to get her up, but she shook his hand off and pulled Andrew against her, rocking back and forth, sobbing.

Finally, Elliott touched her gently on the shoulder again. "Miss Lizzy, them shots musta been heard back at that town. That other fella, he be after us real soon. We gotta get off this steamer and get goin', or we be caught fo' sho."

Lizzy fought to get control, laying Andrew's head carefully on the deck then getting to her feet. She wiped away the tears the best she could with the back of her hands, smearing the black on her water-streaked eyes and cheeks. She looked at the captain. "When you're out of sight of Morgantown, get us to the other side."

The captain nodded.

"And Captain, don't do anything foolish. I'm in no mood to be fooled with."

He shook his head and backed away then turned and moved quickly into the wheelhouse. Lizzy went to the side of the deck and looked back at the town. She saw men mounting horses in a hurry. It was chaos, but they were coming. She was glad she had seen the ferry was on the other side of the river. It would take at least an hour to get it back, so they would have a good head start. She turned to Elliott.

"There's a carriage in the hold. Tell its owner we will pay him for it, but we're taking it whether he likes it or not."

"And Mr. Andrew?"

"He died trying to stop us. They'll send him back to his parents a hero." It took all her energy to turn away and go inside the first empty cabin she could find. She found a pitcher of water, poured it in a basin, and washed as best as she could, trying to concentrate, but she couldn't, her heart breaking. Going to her knees she put her head in her hands and sobbed. Then began to pray.

For Andrew Clay, the war was over.

Chapter Twenty-Six

1862

MATTHEW ARRIVED BACK IN RICHMOND a week after Christmas. The troops on both sides were dug in for the holidays, and the city was filled with parties and festivities, even though the blockade was beginning to be felt in some areas. Matthew had gone to Beauchapel for the holidays, compiled his notes, and made sure everything he had seen was well marked on the map while attending several parties held by Millie's neighbors. Gratefully Daniel Geery was not present at any of them though Matthew had caught individuals following them and watching Millie's home. By the time he arrived back in Richmond, only a few days remained before the payment was due to Geery, and the expected bank draft had not come. But then, it wasn't easy getting money from north to south. Not easy at all.

He had sent word to Polanski of his need for the money. He didn't explain the reason or even mention Millie, but he said the money was needed to purchase a home in order to oil the wheels of deception. He hoped Polanski had enough influence to do the rest.

To complicate matters, Matthew had returned to his office to find that Judah Benjamin wanted to see him immediately and had chastised him for his treatment of Geery. Geery had apparently been hard at work over the holidays, and the entire department was whispering about what had happened. He had smoothed Benjamin's ruffled feathers but was left wondering just how much.

Matthew knew he hadn't heard the last of Geery. He and Millie were still being followed, and he still needed to get his information on rebel forces to Washington. To do so, he had to meet with Beth Van Lew.

Millie had come to Richmond with him to go house hunting. Matthew needed something in Richmond even if they did save Beauchapel, and now that they were getting married, he wanted Mille to be a part of the decision. While he went to the office that first morning, Millie sent a message to Beth Van Lew to arrange a meeting, and the courier returned with a note.

Their carriage pulled up in front of a house on Church Hill. Matthew helped Millie down, and under an umbrella, they ran up the walk then the steps to the covered front porch. The snow was wet and heavy and was piling up in feet rather than inches. The agent of the man selling the house greeted them then opened the door and ushered them inside, telling them he would wait in the sitting area while they took a tour and if they had any questions he would be available. The house was fully furnished, and the agent had a fire going in the living area, making that area most comfortable but leaving the rest of the house cold. It was obvious he wanted to stay put.

They looked at the dining area, kitchen, pantry, and back porch along with a study and library before going upstairs. Checking to make certain the agent was not following them, they went quickly to the master suite and closed the door behind them. Beth Van Lew sat in a chair near the fireplace dressed in shabby men's clothing.

"Matthew," she said, getting up from her chair and quickly greeting him with a hug and kiss on the cheek. "My, you do look good. Engagement has done wonders for you!" She pinched a cheek before turning to Millie. "Darling, you are beautiful as ever. Thank you for sending the message." She turned back to Matthew. "What have you learned, dear boy?"

Matthew pulled a map from his pocket and quickly went over it with her. "The James is nearly impregnable, and any attack of Richmond will require heavily armored ships in order for forces to get anywhere close. But look here. The defenses up the peninsula are weak. If federal forces could be landed at Fort Monroe and then attack up this line while the armored vessels go up the James, Richmond could be reached."

Beth nodded. "But surely some troops coming directly from the north through Manassas would be needed."

"Yes, and the rebel forces would be forced back to the battlements of Richmond as well. They would have to. The numbers in Richmond without them would be easily overrun. At that point either Richmond is taken or is under siege and will fall later."

Beth nodded. "And we know every emplacement, every battlement, its weaknesses and strengths. Only a fool could lose such a battle."

"We have those, even in the North," Millie said.

"But that's not all. I have seen the rebel's newest armored ironclad. It's called *The Virginia,* and it's formidable. Only one as strongly armored will defeat it. No frigate will overpower it. In fact they would be at great risk to try. We must tell them about *The Virginia,* and they must prevent her from getting into Chesapeake Bay. The rebels think that with her ability they can break the blockade of the James and even take Fort Monroe. If that's successful, we have no chance of hitting Richmond from the peninsula."

Beth Van Lew studied the map carefully, asking questions and getting clarifications. "This is a good deal of information."

"Can you get it to them?"

"This is too important to send through couriers. And don't forget, everything we send is in code, and to code this much . . . there is great danger of them missing something." She paused. "We need it delivered, Matthew. You'll have to make the delivery."

"But I can't leave now," he said. "I can continue to get this kind of information and—"

"You will return, of course," Beth said then smiled at Millie. "Every newly married couple deserves a honeymoon. You will have yours, but instead of holding up at Beauchapel, you, Matthew, will go north while Millie continues the deception."

"How exciting," Millie said, her voice etched with sarcasm.

"It's a sacrifice for both of you, but it must be done. Matthew has seen this ship and the fortifications. He alone can give them the detail they need."

Millie sighed, "Yes, well, as they say, for God and country." She paused. "There is one problem. Beauchapel might not be ours by then. My uncle has acquired a good deal of debt against my property, and Daniel Geery must be paid in the next few days."

Beth shook her head lightly. "You uncle has always been a greedy man, and Geery . . . I have never known a more powerful fool. It will do me a good deal of pleasure to deny him this attempt to destroy another. How much is the debt?"

"I need thirty thousand dollars more," Millie said with some embarrassment.

"I have sent for the money, Beth," Matthew said. "Though there's no guarantee . . ."

"There is no reason to delay," Beth said. "I have the money, and we must protect Millie and Beauchapel. Consider it a loan against future profits, if you like, or consider us partners. Either way, that's what your father would want, and I intend to do my best to protect his daughter."

Millie gave her a big hug. "Oh, Beth, I . . . I don't know what to say. I . . ."

"There is nothing to say, dear girl, but once you are free of debt it would be wise to consider selling anyway. Not to Geery, heaven forbid, but to someone else. Beauchapel is in line of the march Matthew has outlined, and the war could take it even more completely than Geery. Sell, protect your money, start somewhere else—that's my advice. But you can talk about such things later. For now we must concentrate on getting you married. The wedding must take place as soon as possible, but you do need time to spread the word and invite friends. It must be a very big affair because Millie's parents would want her to have such a wedding and because it will give you an even stronger cover."

"And how shall I travel north?"

"Something for us to ponder." She glanced at the door while refolding the map. "The agent is waiting." She handed the map back to Matthew. "Keep it and your notes safe, Matthew. We shall meet soon, but I shall come to you." She hugged Millie. "Buy the house. It is a most sound structure, has beautiful furnishings, and it sits only a block from my own. If we continue this ruse, it will be very convenient. Now, off with you both."

Matthew put his papers in his valise, and they left the room closing the door behind them. They found the agent pacing the floor at the bottom of the stairs.

Matthew extended his hand. "Sorry, we had a good deal to talk about. But you have a sale if the owner is willing to take a thousand less. It does have several issues that need repair and—"

"He, uh . . . has gone north. I'm sure he will accept. I'll draw up the papers and meet you at your attorney's office when they are ready." He smiled.

"Good. My attorney is Henry Hyde. Set it up with him, will you?"

"Of course." He bowed slightly, blew out the lanterns, and ushered them out into the storm before locking the door. He didn't notice the set of footprints that came down the drive and turned west up the street, nor did Russell Gainer, who had drifted off to sleep in his carriage a hundred feet further on. He awakened only as an old woman in ragged clothes begged him for a few coins, her greasy paw shoved through his window.

He swore at his driver and told him to get moving, leaving the old woman yelling at him and calling him names as she stood on the side of the street.

A chuckling Beth Van Lew watched him go. Then she waved her hand, and a carriage quickly pulled up in front of her. She climbed in and told the driver to go to the bank. Geery would be paid before the end of the week.

* * *

Lizzy sat in Ann's sitting room, her Book of Mormon in hand. It was their early morning study together, and she was listening to Benjamin Connelly teach about the sacrament from 3 Nephi. His insights on the use of the word *remember* as it was used there and in the book of Helaman were intriguing. She had never thought the promise made to remember Christ in all things would include daily prayer and scripture reading. It simply wasn't enough to remember Him in the moment but to *always* remember Him.

Lizzy and Elliott had kept ahead of the rebels sent to find them and had finally reached Owensboro, where they paid the owner of a small three-man skiff with a steam engine to carry them across the river to Rome, Ohio. By the time they arrived in Rome, her tears were all spent, and though she longed for home, it had to be delayed.

Instead, she and Elliott took a steamer to Cairo, where they met with General Grant and delivered their notes and those of John Fairfield.

Grant immediately began making plans for a march against Forts Henry and Donelson but was thwarted by Fremont, who was dragging his feet on every front, including this one. Lizzy returned to St. Louis and did not leave home for nearly two weeks. Frank Blair showed up on her doorstep just before Christmas carrying a present from Rand and Ann.

Lizzy asked Frank why Fremont wouldn't give the order to move into central Kentucky. Frank said that it was because of just such idiocy that Lincoln was trying to get rid of Fremont. Nothing as important as a drive through Kentucky would occur until that was completed. He hoped it would happen in the next few weeks.

Lizzy let it alone, too despondent and depressed to do otherwise. The days seemed long, nearly eternal, and though she thought her tear ducts had surely dried up, at unexpected times they opened and poured out more.

Finally, she decided she must leave St. Louis. She longed to talk to Rand, to tell him what happened, and to hear that everything would be all right. She packed, but Ann's mother wouldn't hear of Lizzy going alone, so the two women set out for Washington just after Christmas.

As they traveled up the Ohio, Lizzy had come upon a newspaper dated in November that outlined the wonderful arrival and performance of Susan Davis at Fort Donelson and in Russellville but claimed her performance at Bowling Green had been cancelled due to the serious illness of a family member. The rebels were covering their error.

After she arrived in Washington, she, Rand, and Ann had spent an entire night discussing what had happened. They had cried together, tried to make sense of it together, and even studied and prayed together. She had finally come to peace with all of it, but it had changed her, and she wasn't sure she would ever be the same again.

Ben closed his remarks, and those in the room added their amens before Rand asked everyone to kneel and then gave a prayer, ending their evening.

After her arrival, Lizzy had been quick to notice how the war had changed Rand as well. He had always been of sober mind, but he seemed to be even more so now. He spent his days at the camp preparing, training, sending men on scouting trips toward Manassas. When he came home in the evening, he said little and studied constantly. Except for their evening talking about Andrew, only Ann seemed able to break through the shell, and Lizzy was gratified to hear them talking and even laughing after they retired to their own bedroom.

She and Ann talked often. Ann seemed comforted about the loss of the child, and though there was still an underlying feeling of sadness, she cheered everyone and still worked hard each day at the medical depot. She told Lizzy about being present at the Washington infirmary when it caught fire. She'd helped carry more than a hundred men—soldiers and civilians—to safety. They had been taken to a nearby school that was also being used as a hospital, and since then Ann had added her voice to those of Dorthea Dix and Mary Lincoln, insisting that the government provide more qualified hospitals. Lizzy and Ann had even attended a rally at the offices of Congress where Dix had given a marvelous speech on the subject.

Malone's wife had come to Washington, stayed a month and returned to St. Louis, still in love with her husband. Isaac's wife had sent papers asking for a divorce. He had refused to sign them and said he never would. He hadn't heard from her since, but he'd heard from his business partner that she had moved south and was living with a brother in Vicksburg. Isaac said she could rot in Vicksburg.

The shadow of the war yet to come hung over everyone. There were endless entertainments in Washington, from circuses and magic shows to operas, bars, dance halls, and constant parties by the powerful and rich. It seemed the streets were filled with limitless ways to forget the war. Lizzy, Rand, and Ann saw the distractions for what they were and ignored them. In the end, there would be no escape. The fight, the bloodshed would come, and though they may try to make it disappear, it hung over every person like a thick cloud.

Lizzy had followed the news and had devoured every Southern newspaper that had somehow landed in the laps of soldiers or citizens. She had finally found one from Petersburg that listed the dead from the area but did not find Andrew's name. She wondered if his family had been told, if his body had been returned, and if they had learned of her role in it. How could they ever forgive her?

And the war hung on, relentless, stifling, depressing. Though Fremont had finally been replaced, the new commander of the army of the West, Henry Halleck, seemed intent on doing a little foot-dragging of his own. Lizzy knew at least some of her information would be outdated by now. Each day Andrew's death seemed more and more pointless.

But the larger Army of the Potomac, some hundred and fifty thousand strong, was even more paralyzed. At first, McClellan had blamed his lack of movement on a lack of preparation and training, then he blamed it on insufficient numbers. These excuses had allowed him to put off an attack long enough that winter could be used as another excuse. He had paralyzed an entire army while giving Richmond months to prepare for an attack. Rand did not swear often, nor did he gossip, but when it came to McClellan, he had cursed more than once, and his private denunciations were scathing. Hundreds, even thousands more would die because of McClellen's lack of action, and whether they were, as some thought, due to cowardice or, as others stated, a sympathy for the Southern cause, the result would be the same—great numbers of dead and a prolonged war.

But Lincoln's patience had finally run out. On January 27, he had issued General War Order No. 1. Because all of his generals seemed paralyzed and had not acted, he "ordered that the 22nd of February 1862 be the day for a general movement of the Land and Naval forces of the United States against the insurgent forces." He called for the movement of troops at Fort Monroe, the Army of the Potomac, the Army of West Virginia, the Army of Kentucky, Grant's force at Cairo, and the naval force in the Gulf of Mexico. These were to be in the field and on the attack by that day. Because McClellan stated the order was premature, Lincoln followed with another order four days later. The Army of the Potomac was ordered to seize and occupy a point upon the railroad south of Manassas Junction.

According to Rand, McClellan had thrown a fit but had given no orders to move the army, his attitude one of belligerence instead of compliance. Grant, on the other hand, had immediately approached Halleck and requested permission to attack Donelson. Permission had been given, and according to Rand, Grant was making every preparation.

There was a knock at the door, and Isaac Hooker and Brenden Malone came into the entry. It was an unusual occurrence, and Rand asked them what it was about.

"We've got orders to do some more reconnaissance," Isaac said. He glanced at Ann, smiled, then did the same for Lizzy.

"Ladies, he won't be late. Just need his trained eye for a look at where best to send Mr. Malone and me."

Rand retrieved his coat and hat then kissed Ann good-bye, and the three men left.

"What's that about?" Lizzy asked Ann.

Ann's face showed that she was as mystified as Lizzy, but she forced a smile and shrugged. "They send a small group south by horseback. Look over the Confederate line for changes and such. Rand's unit seems to get the assignment more often these days. Let's have breakfast before you and Ben leave."

They went into the dining room, where Ben, Amanda Alexander, Mose, and Lydijah waited. After sitting, Ann asked Mose to offer a blessing, and they started to eat.

Benjamin read several letters from friends in Salt Lake City. Though he wasn't in Washington all the time, he had returned on New Years in order to speak at the growing branch in Washington. It was at that meeting Lizzy had seen him for the first time since their adventure in Missouri. Rand had invited him for Sunday dinner afterward, and he had ridden home with Lizzy and Amanda Alexander. That evening they'd found themselves alone in the sitting room and had shared a laugh or two about their adventure in Missouri.

Lizzy didn't think she loved Benjamin. Even though he was of strong character, loved God and the gospel, and had an indispensable ability to make her feel that perhaps everything would be all right, she still felt a cold emptiness in her heart. How could she love another when her heart lay shattered in broken pieces?

"Well, I really must go, Elizabeth," Ben said. Ben preached in Lafayette Park when he was in the city and had invited Lizzy along.

"Are you sure you're ready for such an adventure?" Ann asked Lizzy with a smile. "I have witnessed what happens when Ben preaches."

"And exactly why I have asked her to come. The hecklers will not be so quick to accost me with a lady present," Ben said.

"Nor you so quick to accost them is my guess," Ann teased.

Mother Alexander and Lydijah said their good-byes and started clearing dishes as Lizzy and Ben went to the front hall and put on their coats.

Lizzy knew that Ann and her mother still hadn't heard from either of Ann's brothers, and it was a constant worry for both of them. The last they'd heard, Adam, the eldest, was now serving with the Seventh Louisiana and was somewhere near Manassas Junction. Rand had verified that the Seventh was there, but even as close as they were to Washington, no letters crossed lines, and no word of him had arrived.

Nor had they received anything from Matthew since he left the Academy. Lizzy heard that Rand had asked at general headquarters if there was any record of a Matthew Alexander in the federal army but had found none. Everyone assumed he had returned south and was serving the Confederacy, who knows where.

Lizzy had come to personally understand how the war separated family and loved ones. Without mail deliveries across lines, fathers, mothers, sweethearts, and friends heard little of one another. She supposed that if she and Andrew had been able to correspond, things might have been different at Bowling Green and Andrew might still be alive.

She shoved the thought aside as Ben held open her wool coat; she slipped inside it, and they left the house under blue skies with slowly drifting clouds. A slight breeze held promise of warmer temperatures. The weather was violent in its fluctuations lately, and it was nice to have a warm enough day that there was even a hint of early spring. As they began their walk she wished she had not dressed so warmly.

Couples strolled or sat on park benches while children played in the soft snow, everyone glad for a warmer day. As they approached Preachers' Corner, they noticed it was already well occupied, and Ben guided her to a nearby bench.

After a moment, he commented that the preacher to their left was probably Baptist and the one on the right a Methodist due to the emphasis in their preaching and the mention of past churchmen who had professed their principles. Lizzy thought they seemed like good preachers, well schooled in the scriptures, but people were paying little attention. Finally in discouragement, one stepped down from the block on which he stood and strolled away. Benjamin immediately got up and replaced him. He began by quoting Paul's famous statement to the men of Greece in which he challenged them about the unknown God whom they worshipped. Ben then declared that he, like Paul, had come to declare God to them. Several men left the Baptist preacher to listen to Ben's discourse on the Godhead and Their separate nature. After only a few minutes, a dozen people listened, several of them mothers holding children. Ben was a very good preacher, his voice strong but not overbearing, but it was the Spirit and confidence with which he spoke that was the most impressive. Lizzy noted that the Baptist preacher had lost his crowd and was certainly unhappy about it. He jumped down and walked adamantly into the crowd, pushing his way to the front and immediately challenging Ben's words.

"The scriptures declare the Godhead is one, and yet you, sir, declare Them separate. By what authority do you make such a declaration? Is this not blasphemy?"

"Good brother," Ben said, his eyes directly on his challenger. "As one who professes the Baptist faith, you are more familiar with the baptism of Christ than most. Do you not recollect that Christ stood in the water with John while God spoke from heaven declaring, 'This is my beloved

Son'? Surely we cannot think that Christ was a ventriloquist. Nor can we believe that when the Lord fell to His knees in Gethsemane and prayed for the cup to be removed that He was praying to Himself. If They are one in being, surely no such prayer would be needed. Christ could grant His own wish and have the pain removed. An unfortunate event to be sure, for our sins would still be upon our heads."

"But He also declared that He and the Father are one," cried out the preacher, raising his scriptures and shaking them at Benjamin.

"You are correct my friend; He does so declare in John 17, where He prays that we all might be one with the Father as He is one with the Father. But if the meaning is to be one in the flesh of His body, then God is surely a very large person. But that is not the meaning. Christ is speaking of us all being one with God as Christ was one with God in bringing about the salvation of His children. Yes, good brother, in this we should be one with God, and you and I should be brothers in that great work." He looked at the others, letting his words sink in. "The work of God is the saving of His children. He gave that work to Christ to do, and in this They are one. They work at it every day, and we must join in that work by coming to God and Christ, our Father and His Son, for our personal salvation. And that is my invitation to you. Come to the Father through the Son."

Lizzy felt the hair on her neck stand up as she both felt and heard the power of Ben's words, and she was not the only one. The Spirit was upon this small group, and they felt what she felt.

"But what is required for salvation?" asked a woman.

"Faith in the Lord then repentance. After these, baptism by proper authority and reception of the Holy Ghost. Then, good brother, we must endure to the end. We must keep His commandments and endure in our faith and our repentance," Ben replied.

"What do you mean, 'proper authority'?" asked the preacher.

"Paul teaches us that Christ was an high priest after the order of Melchizedek. This authority was given Him of the Father. Once He began His ministry, He shared that authority with His twelve Apostles and then with others He called the Seventy. Those with such authority are authorized to baptize in the name of Christ and to confer upon God's children the gift of the Holy Ghost. Thus, that authority binds us to God but also Him to us. Without such an authority, what is there to bind God to his promises?" He paused. "After He ordained the Apostles by the laying on of His hands, our Lord declared to them, 'He that receiveth you, receiveth me, and he that receiveth me receiveth him that sent me.' Thus it is and must be. We must be baptized by that authority, then we must receive the gift of the Holy Ghost under their hand. When we have found that same priesthood Paul declared the Savior had, then we have found our way to salvation."

"But surely all preachers have such authority," said one of the crowd.

Ben turned to the preacher. "Have you been ordained, good brother?"

The man stiffened. "My call came directly from God. It is He who has sent me to preach and baptize."

"I see. Forgive me, but do you have the same priesthood as Christ and His Apostles?"

"I have the priesthood of all believers. By His word to me He has given me authority," he declared adamantly.

Ben looked sadly at the crowd. "Well, brothers and sisters, it is for you to decide. If you feel this man has enough authority to baptize you, then I say follow him into the waters of the Potomac and let him act for Christ in your behalf. But if you think that authority must come, as Paul has taught, by one having authority given by the laying on of hands, then I suggest to you that you must keep looking." He paused. "But I do declare unto you that such authority has been restored by those who held it in ancient days, and if you wish to hear of it more fully, I hope you will join me this evening at 8:00 p.m. for a meeting at Kingsfield Hall. The Lord has not left us alone, brothers and sisters. He has once again spoken to us through prophets and has given us His authority by the same. Come, see the fulfillment of the Lord's prophecy through Isaiah that in the last days He will perform a marvelous work, even a marvelous work and wonder, among the children of men."

He waved at Lizzy, who stepped forward with the fliers and began handing them out. Even the preacher took one and walked away reading the information.

"My, that was exciting, but you never mentioned you were a Mormon," Lizzy observed.

"I'm not. I do not follow Mormon, Elizabeth. I follow Christ, as Mormon did. When they come tonight, we will introduce them to the restored Church of Jesus Christ, and they will learn of salvation through His restoration. They will see what Mormon taught. They will then know what 'Mormonism' is and can judge for themselves if what they feel and what rumors say of us are one and the same. Those seeking the truth will join us. Others will go their own way, but they will know what we believe and someday that knowledge will come to their rescue. Here, the next life." He shrugged. "It doesn't matter. We plant seeds, Elizabeth. Whether they grow or not is determined by the soil into which they fall." He picked up his bag, and they were about to leave the park when the woman who had asked the first question approached them.

"Sir," she said in a soft voice.

"Yes, sister, what can I do for you?" Benjamin asked.

She looked about, some reluctance on her face. "My . . . my husband is away. He . . . he fights for the South." She looked down. "My father, he says . . ." She bit her lip against tears.

"That your husband has lost his soul?" Benjamin said, gently completing the sentence.

She nodded.

Benjamin gave her a pleasant smile then looked at Lizzy. "Sister Hudson, would you like to answer this good sister's question?"

Lizzy smiled. "When it comes to salvation, God is our judge, not man. Don't worry, sister. Your husband will have every opportunity the Lord can give him to receive salvation, in this life or the next." Lizzy had to bite her lip against her own tears. She and Rand had discussed this very issue the night she had arrived in Washington. It had given her a great deal of peace, especially as they talked of those days in Nauvoo when Joseph taught the work for the dead. It provided peace regarding Andrew, and she had decided as soon as she could to see that Andrew received his baptism, but that would take permission from Salt Lake. She had written requesting it.

The woman's face showed immediate relief, and she nodded her thanks.

"Come tonight if you can," Benjamin said.

The woman nodded again and walked away, a greater lightness in her step.

Lizzy put the fliers in her bag as Ben watched. "You've changed," he said.

Her head tilted to one side, revealing her curiosity at the statement.

"I didn't think you held any mercy for Southerners," he said.

She chuckled. "It's true. I've seen slavers and what they have done, and it seemed hell would be too good for some of them."

"But you have hope for some now, is that it?"

"For all of them. Some may have to pass through hell to get to heaven, but salvation is available, isn't it?" They started walking. "The question isn't *if* they will be saved but *where*."

"The different kingdoms."

She nodded, and they walked toward home without speaking, both in their own thoughts. Finally, Ben spoke again. "We have nearly three hundred members ready to go west this spring. I will lead them to Florence in two weeks to build wagons and prepare them to go to the valley."

"So soon?" Her disappointment was guarded.

He nodded. "We will be the ones to make ready for the several thousand to follow from Europe." He paused. "You expressed a desire to come to Salt Lake once."

She nodded. "It's been my dream since childhood, but it will have to wait until Rand is free to run Hudson Shipping again."

"When are you returning to St. Louis?"

"In a few days," Lizzy said. "I assume you will go directly from New York to Florence."

He nodded. "Some of our branch here will go with me, but most live north of here so New York is the best route."

Lizzy felt some sadness but didn't feel to show it. She just wasn't ready.

"Ben, someday I'll come to Salt Lake. I just can't come now."

He nodded as they reached the front steps of Ann's home. She started up the steps when he turned her about and looked up into her eyes. His were both sad and tender, yet there was also reluctance and a bit of confusion as well. He seemed to be debating about what to say, *how* to say it, but finally he spoke.

"I loved you the moment I saw you; you know that, don't you?" he said.

The words felt warm, but she could not let them do more. Instead she simply stepped down and held him close until she could find the words. "Ben, give me time. Please. I need time."

With that she went quickly up the steps and into the house, directly upstairs to her room, closing the door behind her. She lay on her bed, put her face in her pillow, and cried. There was simply nothing else she could do.

Chapter Twenty-Seven

MILLIE WAS ABOUT READY WHEN she remembered her shoes and quickly went upstairs to retrieve them. As she returned downstairs, she looked about the house, making sure everything was ready. They had cleaned and scrubbed, washed and laundered for three days to make sure that the house would be ready for her and Matthew. Thanks to Beth Van Lew, Beauchapel was theirs now. They would return to it after the wedding. She had never been so happy.

"Missy, we must be goin' if'n we's t' catch de train," said Tiera.

Tiera was going with her. Mr. Dix and the workers would take care of things here until Millie returned. She joined Tiera at the door, closing it behind them before they both climbed into the carriage for the ride to Petersburg.

After the purchase of their Richmond home, Millie had begun getting a few additional pieces of furniture while Matthew saw to the placement of the announcement of their engagement and wedding date in Richmond's newspapers. A printer was hired to create invitations, which were delivered to the homes of the city's most prominent families a week later. With just two weeks until the wedding, it was no small feat to get everything planned and ready. Millie had stayed in Richmond as long as she could to make sure it all happened on schedule. Beth Van Lew could be of little help because they had to maintain their distance in order for Matthew's cover to remain untainted, so Millie had hired a professional wedding planner to make sure everything was ready. At the last possible moment, she had returned to Beauchapel to ready it for their honeymoon. There she retrieved her mother's wedding gown, altered it a bit, and made sure it was cleaned.

"Is the dress . . ."

"Yes, Missy, in the trunk. You relax now. We done got it all."

Millie had posted workers at the gates of Beauchapel after Geery's last visit, and one of them flung them open as the carriage approached; all the workers had gathered along the lane and were applauding as the carraige approached. She leaned out the window and shook every hand, getting congratulations and giving thanks, as they passed by. They were soon on the main road and hurrying toward Petersburg, and Millie used a hanky to dry her eyes.

The day was bright and warmer than usual, but the roads were still muddy from nearly two weeks of constant wet, cold weather. Millie rolled up the window cover and let the gentle warmth flow over her as she leaned back against the soft leather seat. She hadn't seen Daniel Geery since the night Matthew had chased him off, but she had seen Gainer and several others who seemed determined to continue their watch on her and Beauchapel. She didn't like being spied upon and had finally asked Mr. Huggins to get an order that it be stopped. Since then, she had seen no one lurking near Beauchapel, but she still felt like they were there, watching, waiting.

But Beauchapel was hers now and would soon be hers and Matthew's. Matthew's bank draft had arrived from the North via the Bank of England, and Beth Van Lew had been repaid and the house in Richmond purchased. Only Millie and Matthew knew the source to be the United States government. Even the letter that accompanied the bank draft said it was receipts for the sale of property in New York, and no one was in a position to question otherwise.

Millie drifted off to sleep and awoke only when they arrived at the depot in Petersburg. The trunk and suitcases were unloaded and sent to the baggage car while Millie and Tiera climbed the steps of the train car and located their compartment. Millie removed her bonnet and placed it in the overhead before unfolding the blanket that lay on one of two seats, stretching out, and covering herself. Closing her eyes, she was quickly asleep, and Tiera soon nodded off herself.

*   *   *

Daniel Geery's carriage pulled up to a nondescript building along the waterfront of the James River in Manchester, a town across from Richmond. Geery got out and went inside. He found Russell Gainer sitting with his feet on a table reading a newspaper. Another small, almost fragile man with facial features akin to that of a weasel was working at another table, pen in hand, his concentration complete. Gainer let the chair down and stood as Geery approached.

"How do they look?"

"He's the best. No one will know the difference."

The small man looked over the top of his glasses at the two of them, some irritation on his face. He did not like being distracted. Geery didn't care and walked over to the table, bent over, and inspected the documents carefully. "Yes, these will do. When will they be ready?"

"This evening," the small man said in a squeaky voice filled with cynicism. "Unless, of course, you continue to drool over them like some lapdog who has found a bone."

Geery controlled his desire to knock the little weasel across the room. He needed the documents now and had no time to find another forger. "Very good. Mr. Gainer, please come with me."

He started for the door, and when they were outside he spoke while putting on his gloves. "I don't want any loose ends, Mr. Gainer. Is that understood?"

Gainer nodded then went back inside as Geery got back into his carriage. The wedding was tomorrow.

Thanks to Matthew Alexander, Daniel had lost Beauchapel and had been made to look the fool in his relationship with Millie. He had been watching Alexander since, looked for something that would allow his revenge; he had even gone to powerful friends to sully Alexander's reputation, but it had been to no avail, forcing him to come up with some other way to get his pound of flesh. The documents would be ready just in time.

Millie would need him then. Turn to him. Everyone would see her grovel in an attempt to save Alexander; then they would see who was in control. She would sell him Beauchapel. It would be his price. And she would pay it.

*   *   *

Rand returned home earlier than usual. Ann did not hear him enter, nor did Lizzy. Both were busy helping Lydijah in the kitchen. Ben had left for New York. Ann had been surprised at his sudden departure, but when she saw Lizzy's red eyes, she decided one had at least a little to do with the other.

"Ladies," Rand said from the kitchen door.

The three looked up from their tasks, and Ann, pleasantly shocked, quickly rose and gave him a long hug and a kiss. "What are you doing home so early, darling?" she asked.

Lizzy was drying dishes and leaned against the counter, waiting for an answer. Lydijah sat motionless over a pan that she was mixing bread in.

"Oh, nothing. Just needed to see the most important ladies in my life, that's all," he answered, a tease in his eyes.

"Randolph, yo has always bin dee most ter'ble liar," Lydijah said. "Dis time ain't no exception neither."

Rand chuckled. "I suppose that's a compliment," he said. "Actually, our unit is being transferred west. It seems General Grant needs some support for a push down the Cumberland into Kentucky and Tennessee."

"Oh my. Is that good news?" Ann asked.

"In my book it is," Rand responded. "You know I can't stomach McClellan anymore. The man is creating a condition for eternal war, but if Grant can cut the Confederacy in half, we can end this thing much more quickly."

"But why you? Why the Missouri boys?"

"Because we *are* from Missouri. We're close to home, and some of our fighting will probably be in Missouri. It's our homes, our cities that they threaten." He paused. "We were sent here short term, Ann. We both knew that when you decided to come. They have plenty of troops here now, and we're needed there. It's that simple."

"But isn't it more dangerous with Grant?" Ann asked.

"By the time we get our men to Kentucky, he'll be well on his way. Sherman is in charge at Cairo, and we will be going there, at least at first. My guess is we'll stay there, hold things down and act as support."

Lizzy bit her tongue. She knew Grant. He would have every available man in the fight and that would include Rand, and Rand knew it as well. But he was trying to make Ann comfortable, and it would do no good to worry her with facts she could not change.

"But if we're here, and you . . ."

"I want you to go back to St. Louis as soon as you can. You need to be home, Ann; so do Lizzy and your mother. And Lydijah and Mose—all of you."

"But we have just gotten settled, and there is so much more to do here." Ann was clearly upset, her world suddenly turned upside down. "Oh, Rand, why didn't you talk to me about this?"

"Ann, you act as if I had a choice. I don't. We have been ordered to go west, and frankly I'm grateful. I thought you'd be overjoyed to get back to St. Louis."

Ann saw his frustration and immediately hugged him, her head against his shoulder. "Yes, yes, of course. I do miss our home, but it's all so sudden and overwhelming. There are so many things to bring to an end, so much to prepare for. I—"

"Take your time. Lizzy can go before you and make preparations. The rest of you can follow when you're ready."

Rand looked to Lizzy as if pleading for support, and she scrambled to gather her wits. "General Grant is a fine commander, Ann. Rand will be safer with him than with a bumbler like McClellan. You've felt for some time that your work here has reached its peak. Jane Terpo can handle the depot, and though the ladies of Washington will surely miss you, I cannot say that I shall miss them. They spend more time in tea and gossip than in accomplishing any real progress. We can do more in St. Louis. Don't forget that the war is just as real there as it is here, and hospitals and other facilities are just as in need of change. Besides I miss you, and Elliott and his family miss Lydijah and Mose. It's time to go home."

"And I does miss my gran'babies," Lydijah said. "I sure does."

Ann nodded, her head still against Rand's shoulder. "Yes, of course. You're both right. We knew it was only temporary, didn't we." She pushed away, a forced smile on her face. "Well then, we must begin to make plans. Are you home for the day, or do you have to go back?"

"I have the night. After that I'll be at camp preparing for transfer."

She went a bit pale, but a look of strength replaced it quickly. "Then we must get your clothes all washed and pressed. I'll not have you leaving this house looking like a pauper. Lydijah, please heat water. Lots of it. He'll need a bath as well and then dinner. We must have a fine dinner. We will send word for Isaac and Malone to join us. They can come, can't they Rand? Of course they can. You're their commander. You can make them come." She was already directing him down the hall toward the front of the house, and Lizzy watched them go. Ann was putting on quite a show—a cover for her worried heart. Deep down, Ann was glad McClellan was a foot dragger. It kept Rand out of battle, and now that had all changed and Rand was suddenly at risk again. It worried Lizzy too, but there really was nothing else to be done.

She stood then noticed Mose standing near the door, his brow wrinkled in deep thought. "What is it, Mose?" she asked.

He snapped out of it, forcing a smile. "Nothin', Miss Lizzy. I'll see to mo' wood." He turned and left.

Mose went out to the woodshed where Maple was splitting wood. He started to gather up sections, his mind mulling over his options.

"I heard what dey's plannin'," Maple said. "I guess I be outa work." Maple slammed the axe into another log, splitting it without difficulty.

"I be stayin' fo' a time, Mapes. You doan worry none." Mose headed back to the house with his arms full. He knew what he must do.

*   *   *

Geery walked into Judah Benjamin's office and was greeted kindly and offered a seat.

Benjamin knew who he was and asked what it was he could do for his visitor. Geery removed the papers from his valise and placed them on Judah's desk. "You have a spy in your department, Mr. Benjamin. If I were you, I would be rid of him." He sat down, a contented smile on his lips as Benjamin looked at the papers and then paled. Matthew Alexander was about to lose everything.

Chapter Twenty-Eight

BETH VAN LEW APPEARED AT the prison with her usual panache, demanding entrance. Because her papers were signed by Christopher Memminger, treasury secretary of the Confederacy, the jailer begrudgingly let her in the front door, made sure she wasn't carrying anything but books and basic medical supplies, then used his key to let her in the main cooking area of the jail. Some Union soldiers came to their feet as best they could, while others remained seated, too weak to move. Conditions at the prison had become deplorable, and as much as she had tried to get Confederate leaders to do more, she had failed. It made her stomach wrench as the soldiers stood, tring to smile and greet her. The commanding officer exchanged his book for another, then each of the other officers did the same. Inside the old ones would be letters punched out in order to describe Confederate troop movements as noted by the most recent prisoners brought in.

"How is Mr. Curtis, Lieutenant?" she asked. Curtis had caught typhoid and had been taken to the nearby makeshift hospital several weeks earlier. He had managed to get well enough by rebel measurement that he was returned to the prison. Beth Van Lew had seen others returned prematurely, and most had either returned to the hospital or had died. Since the prisoners had first come, she had seen more than a hundred die.

"Back in the hospital," the lieutenant said.

She winced then opened her basket and revealed the medicines she was allowed to bring. Mostly creams for wounds, sores, and rat bites; none were for pain or for serious illness. She fumed at her helplessness as she looked at those sitting about the room, the putrid smell of waste pots, rancid sores, fetid breath, and sweat nearly overpowering. Even animals should not be put in such horrid conditions.

"Miss?" The voice was weak and came from the frail form lying on a ragged blanket a few feet away. She went to him and knelt by his side, taking his extended hand even though she knew it was dangerous.

"Yes?"

"Can . . . can you get a letter to my . . . my mother. She . . ." He licked his lips as best as he could, his head falling to one side for lack of strength, but she still felt pressure from his hand.

"Yes, I'll try," Beth answered. She saw the envelope. It was addressed, and she noticed it was meant for somewhere in Pennsylvania. The jailers didn't allow her to take letters out of the jail, but they had not searched her person since the first time when she'd made them feel like idiots for trying. She quickly shoved this one down her neck, stood, and took a few others that were handed to her. She could hide only so many, even in her ample bosom, and they knew it, but she stuffed as many down her dress as she could without having obvious points of disclosure.

Each man nodded their thanks as she turned back to the lieutenant.

"Is Mr. Daines still with us?" she asked trying to push her anger aside.

"He's able to eat most everything now."

She paused, sadness in her eyes. "His friend Cyril died at Libby two days ago. Let him know, will you?"

The lieutenant nodded. "Newton says he would like to meet you soon."

Her heart quickened its pace. "Then his efforts are paying off," she said quietly, glancing at the small window in the heavy prison door.

"He says he'll see sunshine in another day."

She touched the lieutenant's arm, hopeful. She had tried incessantly to be allowed to see him, but the jailer had been adamant. It seemed Mr. Daines had committed an unforgiveable sin in the eyes of the rebels. "Tomorrow?"

"Yes, ma'am." The lieutenant smiled. "I took him his dinner. Talked to him personally. In the field south of us." He glanced at the small window again. "They've cut his food ration again. He's weak, and he knows that he won't get another chance."

Beth Van Lew nodded. The rebels thought they saw his end when he got typhoid, but he survived and won the sympathy of the old jailer, who improved his rations at least slightly. The new one, however, was a friend of the lieutenant who had brought Daines from Manassas and sworn vengeance upon him.

"Tell him we'll be ready," Beth said.

"Any news about exchange?" he asked. Most prisoners held on to the hope that the two governments would start doing exchanges, but neither had budged.

"Nothing."

The lieutenant only nodded. "Then we best start trying harder to get ourselves out of here."

"We'll be ready for you, Lieutenant. I promise," she answered.

Beth turned to the door, knocked, and waited for it to be opened. The soldiers in the room who could get up did so, humbly thankful for even these small favors. "I will see you in a week. God bless you all."

The door opened, and she walked through it, immediately confronting the jailer. "It's worse! You say it will get better, but it never does! It is always worse!"

He shrugged, an evil smile on his face. "It's beyond my ability to do anything about. If I have no food to give them . . ." He shrugged again.

"You have it, and you sell it! I learned of it just this morning, and I will tell others!"

His expression changed little. "They don't listen to you! You're a fool, a sympathizer! They put up with you, no more! Tell them! Go ahead!" His face grew hard. "And I will throw these dogs even less! Now get on with you. I have to let you in, but I don't have to listen to you! Go!" He pushed her toward the door, the other guards smiling. She turned on the jailer and slapped his face, hard. "We shall see! I still have friends, and one of them will visit your prison. I swear it. And when he does, he will kick your big behind onto the front lines, and the Yankees will shoot you. How could they miss? A house would be a smaller target! You're a pig, Burns. It's probably you who eats the prisoners' food."

He raised a hand to hit her back, and she stood defiant. Another man grabbed his arm to prevent it then ordered two of the guards to help Miss Van Lew leave the building. She was escorted roughly to the front door. Jerking her arms free, she stormed out. She climbed into her carriage, and it moved forward. Angry as she was, she had the presence of mind to note the field south of the prison. Tomorrow night she would send others, and Mr. Burns would lose his first prisoner. She would make sure of it.

* * *

Matthew had stayed at the hotel the night before the wedding in order to hold to the tradition that a man did not see his bride the day of his marriage. It was nearly ten in the morning when he left the hotel with Henry Hyde at his side, climbed into a carriage, and started for the church. The reception would be later in the afternoon at Henry's home, and the list of guests was long and prominent. A fact that was discouraging. All Matthew wanted to do was get married and take his bride back to their home.

"Well, dear boy, you've done it now," Henry said with a grin.

"Yes, and isn't it wonderful."

"She's a fine woman, but then I married what I thought was a fine woman. Unfortunately, mine has come to think more of society than of our marriage."

Henry's wife was a lovely woman but seemed constantly concerned about how prominent they were instead of how happy Henry was. It was fortunate that he was rich enough to afford her considerable wants but also unfortunate because his wealth had ruined her.

"Sometimes I wish the Yanks would come and take it all away, Matthew," Henry said. "At least then I would have my wife back."

Matthew wanted to reply but decided against it as they arrived at the church. They were stepping from the carriage when several soldiers approached, rifles in their hands. Matthew knew none of them and had the feeling something was very wrong.

"Mr. Alexander, Mr. Hyde," one of them said. "We are to escort you to the rectory. Mr. Benjamin is waiting."

Henry looked at Matthew for some sign of explanation, but all Matthew could do was shrug. They were immediately surrounded then directed around the side of the church. Matthew noted several curious faces watching from the steps, whispers passing between them. He wondered where Millie was and had a sudden fear for her.

Entering the rectory, Matthew was separated from Henry and searched.

Henry protested. "What are you doing? This man is a member of Secretary Benjamin's staff. You have no right—" He was practically carried from the room, and Matthew was roughly pushed through a door into a study. Benjamin was standing near the fireplace, and Daniel Geery was at the window, a sneer on his mean face. Matthew felt sick to his stomach but kept his face passive.

"What is this about, Mr. Benjamin?" Matthew asked as calmly as he could.

Benjamin looked up from the fireplace, a paleness in his face. His dark eyes searched Matthew's, then he looked down at the fire again. "Mr. Geery has documents that he says belong to you."

Matthew saw the papers in Geery's hands.

"A loan payment for Beauchapel? But why would such a document require this sort of treatment?"

Geery stepped forward, a defiant, haughty look of victory on his face. "Maps showing troop emplacements, giving numbers of soldiers in and around Richmond, and even information from your last trip down the James to Norfolk." He threw the papers on the table. "You are a traitor, Mr. Alexander. These documents prove it."

Matthew had a dozen thoughts go through his mind at once. He had such documents, but these were not them. How did Geery—Then it dawned on him.

"These are not mine," Matthew said firmly.

"It's your handwriting; they were found in your house," Geery said.

"You are a liar, Mr. Geery. This is about revenge, nothing more."

"Mr. Geery came to me this morning," Benjamin said. "He said he had proof you were a spy. He asked for soldiers to search your home, and these were found. Your fiancée was present at the time and is under house arrest next door in the church."

Matthew felt like throwing up but maintained his calm. There were no documents at the Richmond house. He had taken most of them to Beauchapel a week ago, and any small notes he had made since were mental in nature and hardly discoverable.

"Then he planted the documents before Millie came to the city. These are not mine, Judah, and if you will investigate further, you will find I am telling the truth and Mr. Geery is lying."

Geery threw another document on the table. "You deny that this is your handwriting?"

Matthew looked at the letter. It was familiar. He picked it up and looked at it more carefully. "I do not deny it. It is a letter sent to Millie only a few days ago. But what are you doing with my personal mail, Mr. Geery? This is certainly unseemly, if not entirely illegal!"

"The writing is exactly the same on those . . . those maps and drawings!" Geery screamed defiantly.

"No, it is not, and you know it. Those are forgeries." He picked them up, looking at them carefully. Knowing they were forgeries gave him an advantage. They were certainly good forgeries, but even good ones had mistakes. "Very good ones, but forgeries just the same." He went to Judah Benjamin and pointed to the word *Richmond.* "Note, Judah. The flair to the leg of the *R.* I have no such flair in my writing. Also note, the *i.* It is connected to the *c.* Something I never do. And here, these drawings and the abbreviations. The period is right next to the letter. In my abbreviation here, in this letter, is it the same?"

Benjamin squinted, and Matthew noted that Geery's eyes seemed suddenly wary, doubtful. He was questioning the ability of his forger, unsure now of his position.

"No, it's not the same," Benjamin said softly. He looked at Geery with less supportive eyes.

"I will accompany your guards to any prison you like, Judah, if you will call in an expert to look at these documents. Once that is done, Mr. Geery should be arrested. If he is not, I will accept his earlier challenge to a duel and shoot him myself. Anyone who attempts to perpetrate such a fraud on both myself and you deserves only the severest of punishments."

"He challenged you to a duel?"

"He did. He tried similar chicanery with Millie in an attempt to defraud her of her property. I foiled his attempt, and he insisted on a duel. I rejected his offer and warned him to never step foot on Millie's property again or I would accept his challenge. Apparently, this . . . this poor attempt at accusing me of being a traitor is his answer to my threat."

"Is this correct, Mr. Geery," Benjamin asked with a stern voice.

"No, yes, I mean . . . I did challenge him to a duel, but I didn't attempt to defraud—"

"Millie's uncle and Mr. Geery's attorney can both verify what Mr. Geery attempted to do," Matthew said.

Geery was sweating. "It's true, we've had our differences, but that doesn't mean these documents should be discounted as forgeries. A few minor differences do not clear this traitor."

"What led you to determine I was a spy? What evidence did you have that caused you to visit Mr. Benjamin and have my house searched?"

Geery's eyes darted about. "Your family—your sister is married to a Union soldier and abolitionist . . . and your fiancée, she is friends with Elizabeth Van Lew."

"Mr. Benjamin was aware of my sister's relationship with Randolph Hudson. He did business with Hudson Shipping and has met him. So I do not see how it discredits me in the least unless, of course, you believe it discredits Secretary Benjamin. And Millie's relationship with the Van Lews goes back to her childhood and friendships between their parents. Hardly enough to warrant an accusation of this nature unless, of course, you had every confidence that evidence would be discovered."

Judah Benjamin's face was red with apparent anger. "Mr. Geery, I will have these documents verified. If they are forgeries, I will have charges made against you. Do you understand? Or, I can burn them, here, now, and this will be the end of it. What is your wish?"

Geery's face hardened, his eyes filled with hate and fixed on Matthew. "You think you have won, but I will have—" He stopped, his eyes darting to Benjamin as he realized he was about to confess. "Do what you like with them!" he said angrily. "But I'm not finished with you, Alexander! You'll see!" He hissed the last words, angrily strode to the door, and left. Matthew felt his blood run cold. The man was insane.

"Matthew, I apologize, and if I were you, I would be wary of that man. He wants you dead." He picked up the papers and was about to toss them in the fire when Matthew stopped him.

"Don't destroy these, Judah. If Geery persists, it would be good to have this as evidence of his inept stupidity at such blackmail."

"Yes, I see what you mean."

"I thank you for being willing to hear me out, Judah. Others might have simply had me arrested and deposited in a dark cell to rot."

"It is what he encouraged," Benjamin said. He shook his head. "How such a man lives with himself is beyond understanding." He took a deep breath. "But come, your fiancée must be beside herself with worry. I feel horrible and must apologize. Dear Lord of heaven, what a fool I have been!" He took Matthew's arm and directed him toward the door as Matthew felt guilt trickle down his spine. While Geery's evidence was false, his accusation was not.

They left the rectory and walked to the church together. Benjamin removed an envelope and handed it to Matthew. "A little something for you and Millicent. I do wish you both the best, Matthew." He sighed. "If only Ninette were waiting in there for you."

"Ninette will be much happier with a prince than pauper, Judah. We both know that."

Benjamin chuckled. "Yes, I suppose you're right." They climbed the steps and met an angry Henry, who was still steaming from the way he was treated. Benjamin apologized profusely while moving both of them to the room where Millie waited.

"Judah, possibly it would be better if I . . . Well, she'll be upset, and possibly your apology could come later. I'll explain everything, and—"

"Yes, yes," Benjamin said. "I see what you mean, but you must convey my sincerest sorrow and ask her to forgive me. You must."

"Of course," Matthew said.

Judah nodded then went back to the large doors and disappeared.

"Shall I sue them both?" Henry asked stiffly.

"Geery, maybe, but we'll talk later. Right now I just need to see Millie."

Henry pointed. "Of course. In there. She's quite distraught and with good reason. What a fool." He opened the door and let Matthew in. "See you in a few minutes. I will calm the restless natives."

Millie stood near a window and ran to him the moment she saw him. "Matthew!"

He held her close, stroking her hair. Then they kissed before he quickly explained what had happened. Finally, her hand went to her mouth.

"Oh my! He was so close, and—"

He put a finger to her lips then held her tight again. "Never mind. The man is a fool. To think he would not be challenged on such a . . . The epitomy of vanity! But we'll have a good laugh about it later. Right now I want to get married. Still willing?"

"Even though I know the truth about you?" She smiled. "Yes, still willing."

"Then I shall meet you at the front of the church." He kissed her one last time, hurried from the room, shut the door, then leaned against it, catching his breath. The worst part was that had he been caught, he would have lost her. He took a deep breath, humbled, still frightened. Nothing would be more horrible.

*   *   *

Geery paced, his anger boiling in his stomach, the hate like fire in his mind. Nothing around him mattered, nothing. All he could see was Alexander's face, the smile, the look in his eye at what he had done to

Daniel Geery! He could not let him get away with it. He must not! He paced longer, deciding his next action. A moment later he strode from the alley, walking to the church steps then up them and inside, adamant, determined. He wasn't finished with them yet.

* * *

Straightening his suit and wiping a bit of lip rouge from his face, Matthew joined Henry at the back door of the chapel for their entrance to the front. Once in position, they heard the organ begin playing the wedding march. Millie appeared at the door to begin her walk down the aisle. It was the first time Matthew noticed the number of people filling a dozen rows. He knew few of them, but it didn't matter. The only one he cared about was half way down the aisle.

Matthew was contented, at peace, excited all at once, his eyes firmly on Millie's. So much so that he did not see the shadow appear at the base of one of the columns, raise a pistol, and aim. The sound of the weapon was loud in the room of endless wood and stone, and everyone jumped. Everyone but Millie.

He watched as if in slow motion as the look of shock came over her face. He saw the red appear on the front of her dress. Her head tipped back as she fell to the floor like a rag doll. The place was suddenly chaos as two more shots were fired, and Matthew tried to get past the panicked crowd to Millie. He felt the hard impact in his side, felt himself knocked into others, felt the sharp, hot, burning pain as his strength suddenly left him. He stumbled, grabbed hold of Henry then anyone and anything, kept moving, saw Millie sprawled out on the strand of carpet that ran down the aisle. He went to his knees at her side, lifted her head, tried to get her to open her eyes. Then he felt himself give up, felt the sudden relief from pain, felt the darkness encircle him as he toppled over next to her, the sound of more gunfire in the distant background. Then he felt nothing at all.

Daniel Geery had his revenge.

* * *

Newton waited for hours after dark fell before slithering through the short tunnel under the prison wall and standing up in the tunnel he had dug. The soil was soaked through and was nothing more than dripping, watery mud. But he took a deep breath, grabbed roots, and jerked down.

The last four inches of sludge broke free and fell down his ragged, filthy shirt into the hole; a refreshing dark rainy sky overhead greeted his eyes and nostrils. He dug the toes of his shoes into the sides of the hole and pushed himself upward, grabbing the edges of the hole and trying to lift himself out. He slipped once, twice, then a third time before he caught hold of a large root and pulled himself slowly up and into the night.

The hole was against the dark wall of the prison, and he lay flat against its cold surface, giving himself time to get his bearings. The easy path lay toward the street but the streetlamp would make him an easy target. Instead, he stayed in the dark and slithered through the dried winter grass toward the river. There, he eased himself into the chilly water before floating a good half mile and finally pulling himself out. He lay shivering and weak, catching his breath before pushing himself up and running toward a narrow space between two buildings. He felt a firm grip on his shoulder and tried to break free but was too weak.

"'Tis a friend, Mr. Daines," the voice said. Newton felt the hand grab his then lift and support him. "Miss Van Lew sent me. Come along. We'll get you someplace safe."

Newton used the man's strength, and they quickly walked another block before climbing into a carriage, where a blanket was thrown over his shaking shoulders. "How did you know where to find me?"

"We watch all along these streets. I seen you get outa that river, and I come after you." He helped Newton into the carriage then signaled for the driver to get moving.

Moments later the carriage turned into a drive, went up a slight incline, and then stopped. The man helped him from the carriage and to a cellar door before knocking. Newton heard the latch turn and saw the door lift. A shadowy figure emerged, took him by the shoulders, and led him down the stairs, closing the door behind them. He heard the horses' hooves pounding on cobblestone and regretted not having had the presence of mind to thank his good Samaritans. He was guided to a chair, trying to catch his breath while a lantern was lit, revealing a middle-aged women, concern and sadness in her eyes.

"Get undressed, wash yourself"—she pointed to a bucket of steaming water then at some clothes and a towel—"and get into warm clothes, then come up to the kitchen."

"Wha' if we were followed?"

"You weren't," she said with a smile.

"I . . . I need to be thankin' 'em fer their kindness," he said weakly.

"They know, Mr. Daines. We have a hiding place until we can get you out of Richmond." She started up the steps. "Don't be long."

Beth Van Lew entered the kitchen by the basement door and sat down, her mother staring at her. They were both despondent. Word had come of the shooting at the wedding, which they hadn't attended in order to keep their distance from Matthew. Both were in the hospital with serious wounds. The only positive note was that Daniel Geery had been shot and killed leaving the church.

"Does he look strong enough?" her mother asked.

"No. It will take some time. See that he is fed and then gets some rest. I must try and see Millie and Matthew."

Her mother nodded. She couldn't stop Beth, didn't wish to stop her. They must know if their friends would survive. It was a horrible night.

She heard the carriage leave the yard as she stirred the stew in the kettle over the fire. As she ladled out a bowlful, she heard the door open slowly, a face appearing that looked more like a skeleton than a real human being. The eyes were tired, but there was a strength that gave her hope.

She pointed to the chair. "You're safe and you must eat, but do it slowly. Too much in your belly will kill you."

Newton sat, took a deep breath, and picked up a spoon, but he couldn't move it farther, the smell and hot steam from the bowel wafting into his face and mesmerizing him. Then, without warning, tears rolled from his eyes, and he began to cry then weep uncontrollably. Beth's mother stood by him and pulled his face into her stomach, stroking his wet hair and cheek and giving him the best comfort she could.

He was finally free.

*   *   *

Beth entered the hospital with the hood of her cape in place. She passed a small vacant office and walked down a dimly lit hall to a double door that entered a large room full of beds. Half the beds were filled. The lights were dim, and everyone seemed to be sleeping. There were no nurses or doctors, and she left the room to look elsewhere. She heard voices down a wide hall and followed the sound until she arrived at smaller rooms. She listened at one, heard voices, opened the door, and stepped inside. Those present turned to look at her, and she removed her hood and glared at them, daring even one of them to challenge her presence. She knew none of them and was grateful. When no one spoke, she stepped to the bed to see an unconscious Matthew Alexander.

"How bad are his wounds?" she asked, looking at a man she assumed was a nurse.

"The bullet entered his side and split into fragments, but it was of small caliber. The doctor believes he retrieved the pieces and that none of them reached vital organs, but he will not be sure for several more days." He looked at her. "Are you a relative?"

"A friend to both him and his fiancée. Where is she?" Beth asked.

"Across the hall. She's alive, but her wound is much worse and . . ."

Beth was already opening the door and stepped directly across the hall to where a doctor was listening to Millie's heart through a stethoscope. Tiera stood to one side, her face filled with worry and her eyes red from crying. She immediately came to Beth and wrapped her arms around the newcomer, seeking comfort.

"Oh, miss, she bad! What we gonna do, what we gonna do?" She started to cry again, and Beth stroked her head and spoke in soft tones. "She'll be all right, Tiera. God will see to it. We must trust in Him!" She forced a smiled as the doctor faced her.

"You're very young to be a doctor," Beth said.

"Do not let my age fool you, Miss . . ."

"Van Lew."

He nodded, extending his hand. "Arnold Carrigan. I studied in the best medical school in Europe and returned only a week ago. We learned a good deal about this sort of wound, and I have been careful to make sure it has been treated as it should be." He paused, and Beth smiled. He was obviously concerned about giving her a full description.

"Go on, Doctor. I am quite able to handle any details you can give."

He smiled. "The revolver was small, one of those pocket pistols that are good only at very close range, so it didn't cause the damage a bigger ball would. If it had been one of those, she wouldn't be with us now." He paused. "No organs were damaged, at least to our knowledge, but we shall see. If not, she should recover rather quickly."

"And did you do the same with Mr. Alexander?"

"Yes. Fortunately, I was here when they arrived."

"We'll stay the night if that is all right," Beth said to the doctor.

"Only one of you should be in the room at a time. The other should get some sleep. We don't want you sick because you do not take care of yourselves."

"Very well. Tiera, my carriage is just outside the hospital. You are to go home and report to my mother what has happened and then get some sleep. Tell the driver to bring you back in the morning."

"But—"

"No arguments. You'll see her tomorrow." She wrapped her arms around Tiera. "She's going to be fine, but we must remain strong for her. You cannot do so if you do not sleep."

"Yes'm. I needs to let mah family know . . . at Beauchapel, Miss Van Lew. I—"

"I will send a telegram in the morning."

"Yes'm," she answered, relieved. "I is so glad yo' come, Miss. I doan know what ah would do if'n yo' hadn't."

They hugged each other tight again, and Beth sent her on her way. "You're an uncommon woman, Miss Van Lew."

"In what way?" She had already stepped to a washbasin and rolled up her sleeves.

"Your treatment of a slave, your concern for Miss Atwater . . ."

"Miss Atwater has no slaves. Her workers are all freedmen. As for my feelings about Millie"—she looked at the frail girl lying unconscious in the bed—"I have not had the blessing of children, Doctor. I consider Millie the child I never had."

"Then we shall treat her as such." He smiled. "I must check on Mr. Alexander. Let the attendant know if you need anything."

He left, and Beth stepped closer to Millie. She was breathing evenly and seemed at rest, but Beth knew the worst was still ahead. Infection, sepsis, and fever could all weaken or kill Millie. Beth intended to do everything possible to see they didn't.

But she had another reason for coming, and she must not forget it. She didn't know where Matthew had put his notes and maps or if they were safe. She must make sure, secure them if need be. She didn't even know why this had happened. Why had Geery shot them? Was it rage, jealousy, or did he know about Matthew's work? It seemed impossible for Geery to know such a thing, but she must use all caution.

Millie groaned, moved, and Beth went to her side and held her hand.

After a few moments, the door opened, and Judah Benjamin walked in. He was not visibly surprised to see Beth in the room, and that was a bit of a shock to her.

"Mr. Benjamin," Beth said.

"Miss Van Lew. How is she?"

"If infection doesn't sit in, she'll be fine. What happened?"

Benjamin launched into an explanation, and Beth listened carefully, especially to Geery's failed attempt to accuse Matthew of being a spy. She thought it ironic and had to stifle relief and amazement. "Geery was a fool," Benjamin finished.

"A dead one, I was told," Beth said.

"Yes, the soldiers were still waiting outside. When he ran from the church, he fired at them. They returned fire. There was nothing else to be done."

"His family will want answers," Beth said.

"And they are easily given. Mr. Geery was jealous, vengeful, and went mad. What other explanation can there be?"

Beth only nodded, grateful Benjamin saw it as so black and white.

"Matthew is across the hall. I need to see him before I leave. Good night, Miss Van Lew. Please keep me informed on their progress if you can. I know you are close to her. Matthew explained it all, and if I can do anything . . ."

"I'll let you know."

He left the room, and Beth went to the chair and sat down, relieved. She supposed every cloud had a silver lining, and if this had one, it was that such an act had put Matthew and Millie above suspicion. If they survived that could only bode well for the future.

Chapter Twenty-Nine

RAND AND HIS MEN ARRIVED at Cairo two weeks later. While Isaac and Malone saw to their unloading and encampment, Rand went to headquarters and reported their arrival. He was immediately ushered into General Sherman's office, heartily welcomed, and then brought up to date on Grant's plans.

Grant was already moving down the Tennessee River toward Forts Henry and Heiman and would do battle within two days. From there, federal troops would move across land to Fort Donelson to lay siege and capture the place.

Sherman sat back in his chair. "When the general moves against Donelson, you and your men go directly down the Cumberland by steamer. You will off-load above the fort and then join General Grant's force."

Rand nodded. The weather was cold and waffled between snow and sleet. The rivers had ice chunks, and the wind was mostly from the north. It would be a battle against the elements as much as against the rebels.

"How is Ann?"

"Expecting again," Rand said with a smile. "She's on her way back to St. Louis by train along with her mother and Lizzy. Lydijah is with them as well. They should be in Chicago by now."

Sherman nodded. Rand had heard the general had taken himself out of the fight for two months, but he was back. He looked strong, seemed in good health and alert.

"I'm fine, Randolph," Sherman said, reading his thoughts.

"I have no doubt of that, General." He stood.

"After we take Donelson, the general intends to move south against the rail lines at Corinth. If we can capture those, we move against Vicksburg.

The navy is after New Orleans and should have it by then and be on their way to Memphis. By the end of the year we hope to have the Confederacy cut in half."

Rand only nodded as he stood. "We'll do our part, General."

Sherman also stood, and they shook hands. "Yes, I know. I won't be seeing you at Donelson. Ulysses wants me here so that I can move down the Tennessee to Corinth in force. I hope to see you there."

Rand nodded and gave a quick smile. "I don't intend to disappoint you, General." He turned to leave. "I've been down the Tennessee clear to Pittsburg Landing. Best place to camp would be at a place called Shiloh." He smiled, left the room, and walked out of the building. Mounting Samson, Rand headed back to the river, unaware of the pair of dark eyes half hidden under a wide-brimmed hat, watching him as he left; Rand was not alone.

*   *   *

Mose looked after Rand only a moment, his head down so that he wouldn't be seen, then went back to standing in a line of contrabands waiting to be given jobs for the day.

Once he had seen Miss Ann and the other women off to St. Louis, he had packed his own bags and headed west after the Missouri boys, leaving Maple in charge of crating the rest of the personal and household items for shipment. Maple would see to the house until the Hudsons decided what to do with it.

From Cincinnati, he'd been on one of the same steamers as the Missouri boys but had kept himself in the hold along with other blacks making the trip. He did not want Randolph discovering his presence just yet.

He reached the front of the line and faced the soldier at the table. "Contraband?"

"No, suh, freedman lookin' fo' work."

The soldier asked for his papers, and Mose showed them to him. "Yer a bit old fer such work, ain't you?" the soldier asked while looking over his papers.

"No, suh. Been workin' all my life. Ain't nothin' any harder about it now than there was when I was yer age."

The soldier smiled. "All right." He handed Mose back his papers. "Find an empty spot in any tent in the worker's camp then get on down to the docks. Help those boys unload supplies. If you ain't dead by mornin', come back fer another job."

"Yas, suh," Mose said. He picked up his bag and headed for the workers' camp. The docks would be a good place to be. That way he'd know if Rand's unit stayed put or went south. Whichever it was he intended to accompany them.

Mose had liked being a part of the war effort at the medical depot. It made him feel better, but it still wasn't enough. He intended to get in this war, one way or the other, and if Mr. Randolph Hudson was going where the fighting was then that's where Mose would be too. If Randolph stayed put then he'd do the same, but if he didn't . . . Well, Mose would find a way to tag along until some captain or colonel or general or even the president himself figured out blacks should be allowed. Then he'd be the first in line, old or not. If they turned him away 'cause he had graying hair, he'd slap them silly until they paid attention to his heart more than his hair color.

He found the camp and began asking about for a place to lay his bed roll; he finally found a spot in a tall teepee-looking tent. One of the workers was inside fiddling with a bedroll when Mose walked in. Mose looked about, and the boy caught on he was looking for a spot and pointed.

"Isn't a pleasant place in winter," the boy said. "Cold as sleeping outdoors, but at least it keeps some o' the rain off." He finished what he was doing and left. Mose put his gear down, removed his Book of Mormon from his pocket, and tried to shove it inside his pack, where it was usually kept. It jammed into something, and he reached in to see what it was. Lydijah's knitted gloves stared him in the face, and he smiled before sticking them in his pocket and his Book of Mormon into the pack.

Lyidjah would sure as daylight bend his ear good if she knew what he was up to, and if she had known . . . Well, he'd probably be minus both ears from her pulling on them. She was a strong-willed woman and had told him more than once that he was too old to get into such a fracas as this one was going to be. But he had to try. She would just have to understand that. He stood, pulled on the gloves, and felt their warmth immediately. Besides, it was her dream too.

He turned and left the tent, heading toward the docks. She had to understand he couldn't just stand by anymore. He must do what he could, get in the fight where they'd let him. It didn't matter what it was—digging trenches or hauling wood and water. He must do his part. There simply was no more leaving it to others.

*   *   *

Newton woke with a start, the light of a lantern nearly blinding him. He raised a hand to protect his eyes.

"Mr. Daines, good morning."

Newton knew the voice of the woman who had first welcomed him after his escape, knew it very well. It had called him to breakfast every day for two weeks.

"Miss Van Lew. 'Tis a bright light ya be carryin'. Might you shine it a bit away?" It was always the same. Instead of a simple knock on the hidden door, it was always the light—obnoxious, unnecessary. But he wasn't about to complain. He was alive, and her method of waking him each morning for breakfast was of little consequence when he considered the bigger picture.

The light moved away as she stood, a slight smile on her face. He threw aside the covers and slipped from the small hiding place into the larger upstairs bedroom. He was much stronger now, nearly ready for travel. "An' 'ow ere things in Richmond this dark and dreary mornin'?" He noted the heavy clouds and light snow outside.

"Full of news. As I told you, the Union has taken Roanoke Island. They're moving farther inland and are opening a back door to our fair city. President Davis is taking a beating in the papers this morning, and it seems Judah Benjamin, his secretary of war, may have to resign."

"Ah, 'tis a bright and pretty day then," Newton said.

They were standing near a table set with food enough for two. He sat in one chair after helping her sit in the other. She clasped her hands, lay them against her chin, and said grace. He took his hand off the toasted bread that he'd been inclined to devour the moment he sat, instead bowing his head. When she was finished, she poured coffee for both of them.

"I visited the jail again yesterday. They have a new jailer now. It seems the old one is being punished for your escape. Things are a bit better for the rest of the men, and they are pleased that you are safe and doing so well. They have begun to dig a tunnel of their own now, and we may have others escape soon." She added another half spoon of sugar. She would normally add more, but sugar was harder to find these days. A good sign the blockade was working. "They've moved every available man into battlements south and east of town near the canals, so they no longer have the men to keep hunting for you. Even I'm no longer being watched."

"Then 'tis time fer me t' be movin' on to Washington, is it?"

"We must still be very cautious, but if we don't move soon, I fear our information will not arrive in the hands of Mr. Lincoln in time, but you must be strong enough, Newton. I do not wish to put you at risk if you are not ready, no matter the need."

"An' the good soul who gathered wha' ya 'ave t' send north. Is 'e as well as I then?"

They had talked about Matthew's information without her giving his name. "Yes, he is doing much better."

"How do you expect t' be gettin' us ou' o' the city?"

"By boat, Mr. Daines, but you'll be carrying very incriminating evidence. If you're caught, you'll never see the inside of a prison. You'll be hung or shot."

"Ah, 'tis a joyful bi' o' news, Miss Van Lew. If I ever come close t' anuther rebel prison, I'll surely do the hangin' meself. I will nah sleep anuther night in such a place."

She looked carefully at him. He was no longer the gaunt man who had escaped Ligon Prison. His face had filled out well, accentuating his handsome features and bright eyes. His strength had returned, and she had watched him do a hundred pushups only yesterday then use the top of the doorjamb to lift himself up and down another hundred. He was ready. And she wished he wasn't. He'd been good company, and she had learned to enjoy his quick wit and conversation. Though she loved her mother, it was nice to have another to talk to, as ostracized as she'd become because of her Union sympathies.

Quickly standing, she cleared the empty dishes onto a tray but left him a full cup of coffee along with two additional pieces of toast and enough marmalade to cover them. "We'll leave tonight then." She went to the door. "A good day to you, Mr. Daines." She closed the door behind her, and Newton continued to sip his coffee. He was ready and had no desire to stay even until night. Richmond might be considered an elegant and sophisticated city, but what he'd seen of it made a rat's hole look pleasant.

He went to the drape-covered window and pulled back an edge slightly to look down on the yard, where a carriage with a team of fancy white horses was waiting. He saw Miss Van Lew get aboard, and the carriage left his view.

Miss Van Lew was a fine lady. Not a handsome woman, but there was something about her that intrigued and even quickened his heart a bit. Possibly it was her kindness and willingness to put herself at such risk.

He let the drape fall and went to the mirror hung over a dresser. His beard was thick, heavy, and streaked with a strand of gray, an unusual thing for a man of his age. He opened the drawer and found a straight razor, soaping cup, and brush. It was time he found the real Newton Daines again.

*   *   *

Beth Van Lew entered Millie's room to find Matthew sitting in his usual chair at her bedside, holding her hand, but today she was sitting up, her feet dangling over the edge of the bed. She was still a bit pale but obviously stronger.

"You've been for a walk again. How wonderful," Beth said.

Matthew turned around and gave her a smile. "A miracle, isn't she?" he said. Matthew was fully dressed, his face with good color, but his movements were measured, avoiding any sudden motion that would cause pain.

"Yes, very much so," Beth said. But she could see worry in both sets of eyes.

"What's wrong?" she asked.

Matthew glanced at Millie then spoke. "You heard Judah Benjamin is being replaced."

Beth nodded. "The loss of Roanoke. It was in the papers this morning. The article said Mr. Benjamin was to blame."

Matthew nodded. "Judah has put himself on the altar even though it was President Davis's decision not to reinforce the island. Just not enough manpower; but Davis doesn't want that fact known. It would make the Confederacy look weak. Davis would be forced to negotiate. He won't. He is blinded by his own will." He paused, standing and bringing Beth a chair. "But that isn't all. Months ago General Johnston asked for more men and money to shore up defenses at Fort Henry and Fort Donelson. Because of advice from myself and others in the department, Judah didn't act on their request." He smiled. "Fort Henry surrendered yesterday."

"But the papers said nothing of it this morning," Beth said.

"Judah just left here. It'll be in the afternoon papers. By nightfall, he will have been censured by the Confederate Congress for his bad decisions and will resign tomorrow." He returned to his seat. "The new secretary of war seems to think the problem runs deeper than just Judah, and he intends to replace anyone who might have been responsible. Though he does not know why I gave the advice I did, he sees that it was bad advice. In effect, I will be fired for incompetence."

Beth nodded, her brow wrinkled in thought. "Benjamin is one of their most talented and perceptive leaders. With him out of office it weakens the government."

Matthew smiled. "He won't be leaving anytime soon. It seems Davis means to repay Judah for his loyalty in taking the blame for these fiascos. He's making him secretary of state."

Millie spoke. "Benjamin has offered Matthew a position in the state department, but he'll no longer have access to the military secrets he has now. In fact, Mr. Benjamin wants to send us to the Caribbean to negotiate opening ports and new markets for the Confederacy."

Beth nodded. "Effectively taking you out of the war. How considerate."

"From his perspective it *is* considerate, very much so. Judah feels guilty for what happened at the wedding. It's his attempt to make amends by putting us out of harm's way."

"And what are you going to do?"

"Decline his offer but not yet. For now we'll say only that we wish to return to Beauchapel so that Millie and I can recuperate."

"That's sensible enough," Beth said.

"If Mr. Daines is ready, I intend to leave with him," Matthew said.

Beth stiffened, shocked by this revelation. "But how will you cover your disappearance?"

"We're recovering from serious wounds. We expect others to honor our desire for quiet and privacy," Millie said. "Our servants will help me carry on the illusion, and why should others doubt us? They're all quite aware of what happened, and most are very concerned for our well-being. I've received notes and flowers almost every day." She pointed to a stack of letters on a nearby table.

Beth looked at Matthew. "Are you strong enough? If you're discovered and have to run for your life . . ."

"Quite sound, I assure you," Matthew said. He winced as he pushed himself to his feet. "Just stiff, sore, but the wound is healed, and the doctor is very pleased.

Beth wasn't sure he was telling the truth but knew it would do no good to pursue it. "And when you return, what then?"

"We decline the assignment in Caribbean but ask to remain under Benjamin. The war department isn't the only place we can glean information," Matthew said.

"We can still do a good deal of damage," Millie added.

Beth thought a moment then nodded.

"Our biggest worry is that he won't be able to return. In that case, I'll find a way to join him when I'm strong enough." She squeezed Matthew's hand. "Besides, if the Union acts on the information Matthew has, they will capture Richmond by summer."

Beth only smiled. It was a big *if*. As slow as the Union was to act, one could only wonder at how effective they might be, especially since they had allowed time for Richmond to be so heavily fortified and defended. Fools usually followed one mistake with another.

The air seemed heavy, stifling, and Beth stood and went to the window. Millie was still too weak to go; Matthew must; it was as simple as that. If there was fallout, they would deal with it later. "You have discussed this a good deal. I can see you have your minds made up." She turned back. "Very well. We must get you all to Beauchapel today. A carriage will pick you up in a few hours and take you to the train station. I will get Mr. Daines there."

Matthew stood. "We need some things from our Richmond house. Coats, clothes, toiletries, and some blankets and pillows for Millie. Can you bring them?"

"Yes, of course. I'll send them with the carriage along with two servants to help you."

The door opened, and Tiera entered with a stranger at her side.

"Beth Van Lew, this is John Howland, minister at the Methodist church where we were to be married." Matthew smiled. "I think it's time we had that wedding."

Chapter Thirty

THE SUN WAS JUST SHOWING itself above the eastern hills when Matthew checked the steam gauge. The boiler had heated enough water to get them moving. Millie stood on the shore, watching as steam rolled off the cold water to a height of five to eight feet and making visibility at the surface difficult. She could hear another steam vessel but could only see an occasional wisp of its shape and form as it moved ghostlike across the water. It was a calm morning, no wind, the sky clear of even a hint of clouds. Another hour or two and the mist would disappear unless a winter storm moved in—an event that was just as likely to occur as not this time of year.

Beth handed Newton the basket she held then went to stand by Millie. They had only arrived at Beauchapel late last night, and even that journey had weakened her. Matthew had tried to get her to stay in bed, but she wouldn't hear of it. Now Beth had to put an arm around her to help her stand.

Matthew jumped from the small vessel and approached. Beth moved aside long enough for him to hold Millie close and give her a kiss. "I will see you in two weeks, I promise."

"Yes, I know. You will be careful, won't you?" she said, laying her head on his shoulder.

"Mr. Daines will make sure of it, won't you, Mr. Daines?" Matthew turned back to where Newton was standing at the dock holding the mooring rope.

"Tha' be me first an' only goal, Mrs. Alexander. He'll be comin' back t' ya real soon. I'll nah only 'ave ya t' answer to but the Hoodsuns as well if I doan't keep his precious soul safe and sound, and I ain't abou' t' mess wi' the lot a ya."

It hadn't taken Newton long to connect Matthew to his sister, Ann. Since arriving at Beauchapel, it had been an endless stream of stories about the Hudsons that made their short visit at Beauchapel a joyful one. Matthew longed to see Ann, but he wanted even more for Millie to meet her. He wanted for all of them to be together and even considered taking Millie with them, but that had all been put aside as Millie grew weaker on their journey to Beauchapel.

"Be gone, then," Millie said with the best smile she could muster. "The sooner you are on your way, the quicker you shall return."

Matthew kissed her one last time on the forehead then hugged Beth before climbing back into the small steamer. He waved, pushed on the lever that would engage the propeller, and got them moving as Newton jumped into the boat and waved as well. Millie and Beth both waved back and watched them pull away and head for the current at the middle of the river, disappearing into the mist as they did.

The winding James River was deep, muddy, and filled with debris sent down from recent storms; Newton scrambled to the front to give directions around any that might prove hazardous. They traveled warily at first, the sun getting warmer and the mist dissipating. It should be entirely gone by midmorning.

They were going to Carrollton, just west of the Confederate strongholds of Norfolk and Craney Island, where ships of the Confederate James River Squadron were stationed. Under cover of dark, the men would cross the river and land at Newport News. There, they'd take horses across land to Fort Monroe before catching a Union ship to Washington. If all went as planned, they would be in Washington in four days.

They traveled for several hours, and each removed their coats, the sun getting hot. It was near evening, and Newton had dozed off when he felt the boat slow and opened his eyes to find Matthew concentrating on something.

"'Tis the look of a hawk about to fly t' the kill, Matty boy. Wha' d' ya see?"

"Look," Matthew said. He'd spotted a ship up an inlet, and the form of it was disturbing.

Newton looked in that direction but didn't see the ship.

"Along shore, in the trees. Low profile, ironclad," Matthew said.

Newton nodded slightly to show he had laid eyes on the ship while Matthew turned the tiller to get a better look. The profile of the ship, though half hidden, was troublesome. In Matthew's visit to Norfolk a few weeks earlier, there had been no such ships, and the fact that she was hiding in an inlet half way up the James gave him pause as well. He worked the tiller feigning to dodge debris, his eyes on the ironclad's observation deck. Close enough now that he could see her profile more clearly, Matthew realized who she was.

"The *Blackhurst*," he said softly. "He turned the tiller downstream, his stomach churning. "How on earth did *she* get here?"

Newton was still eyeing the vessel and noted that she was pointed at both ends and clad with iron on her sloped sides. She had a long ramming boom sticking out like the tongue of a lizard and a smokestack midship that was puffing light smoke into the limbs overhanging the river where she was trying to hide. He saw five cannons sticking out of windows on her visible side and figured there were five more just like them on her reverse side. Landing boats hung above the cannons, and a half dozen sailors stood atop her flat top, two of them spying them with eyeglasses. Not more than fifty feet long and twenty feet wide at its widest, it was sleek and threatening; he quickly looked away.

"Ya seem t' know 'er," Newton said to Matthew.

Matthew nodded. "According to the papers, she was supposed to have been sunk in Albermarle Sound at the battle of Elizabeth City."

"'Tis lookin' nice 'n healthy t' me eyes," Newton said. "One blow from 'er cannons and we'll be swimmin' t' Monroe."

"Dahlgren rifles. Deadly accurate over miles."

"'ow did they ge' past th' blockade?"

"They probably came up the swamp canal from Elizabeth City before the Union cut them off." They were past the inlet, and the ship disappeared from view. "There were two others just like her at Elizabeth City, the *Raleigh* and the *Beaufort*. If they escaped as well . . . and if the *Virginia* is sea worthy . . ." He paused, thinking.

"The *Virginia*?"

"Another ironclad. Twice the armor, bigger guns. She'll make this class look naked in comparison, but when I saw her a few weeks ago at Norfolk, they were still having trouble with her maneuverability in shallow water. The weight of the iron requires a deep hull, and the variations in the bottom of the James give her trouble."

"She's built fer deep water then?"

Matthew nodded. "Her hull belonged to the USS *Merrimac*. When Virginia seceded, some fool ordered the federal navy to leave Norfolk and Portsmouth and burn the Gosport navy yard and any ships harbored there. The *Merrimac* was a deepwater commercial ship in for repairs. They burned her, but when the Confederates took over the port, they found her hull undamaged below the waterline and decided to build an ironclad on her they could use at sea." He took a deep breath. "You ever been down this way, Newton?"

Newton shook his head in the negative.

"Well, the end of this river turns to the north. In the bend of that turn lies Norfolk, a sheltered harbor controlled by the Confederacy. Portsmouth and the navy yard lie at the southern end inside that harbor. On the river's northern side, along a break work, stands Sewell's Point. It has fifty cannons that look down on the river. Just a half mile upstream is Craney Island. Another Confederate fortress sits there and overlooks the James as well. The rebels have a number of ships harbored at Craney that—along with her guns, those at Sewell's Point, and those on the ships harbored in those ports—keep the Union navy from coming up the James." He paused. "But just downriver and on the other side lies Fort Monroe, held by the Union. Next to it is Newport News, which sits almost directly across the mouth of the James from Sewell's Point. Monroe overlooks the confluence of the James into Chesapeake Bay. Under the protection of nearly a hundred cannons, Union warships wait for any Confederate ship that tries to get in or out of the James, effectively preventing it."

"So there be a standoff. The Union navy canah get up th' James t' Richmond, an' the Confederate navy canah ge' out o' the James inta th' ocean."

Andrew turned the tiller, taking them closer to the south shore. "Until three weeks ago, Richmond was getting supplies up the canal system from Elizabeth City, but when the Union took Roanoke Island and then Elizabeth City, they effectively shut off the flow of goods into Richmond. Some goods still come in by land, but it will never be enough to supply the population with what they need just to survive."

"Ya mean they coul' be starved into submission," Newton said, reflecting on his experience in jail. "Serve 'em righ', tha'."

"If Richmond starves, the Union wins the war. The Confederacy can't let that happen. They have to break the blockade. If the *Blackhurst* is here, in the James, it's a safe guess that the *Raleigh* and the *Beaufort* are here as well and that the rebels are keeping them upriver to prevent the Union knowing they're here until the *Virginia* is ready to leave

Norfolk harbor. Then all four, along with the rest of the James River Squadron, will try to break the blockade and get the *Virginia* into deeper water where she hasn't any equal. If that happens, the Union could lose Monroe and Newport News, and Richmond and the James would be open for commerce again."

"An' Richmon' woul' be saved," Newton said. Matthew watched as Newton, sitting in the front of the small steamer, suddenly became focused on something behind them. Matthew turned to look. A column of black smoke was rising over the treeline of the inlet where the *Blackhurst* was hidden.

"They be comin' out o' hidin' is me guess," Newton said.

Matthew nodded, turned around, and pushed on the lever that gave them more power. The small boat lurched forward toward the southern shore. He didn't know if it was coming after them, but he thought it best to give them a wide birth either way.

The *Blackhurst* quickly appeared, turned downriver, and drove forward into the current. When she reached the middle of the river, she kept coming and seemed to be headed directly for them.

"Well, Mr. Daines, I think we're about to discover if your forged papers will pass muster."

The *Blackhurst* was within a hundred feet, and a sailor used a megaphone to order them to come alongside and be boarded. Matthew waved agreement and moved the tiller to redirect the boat. Once close, he shut off the propeller and glided to the side of the ironclad. A sailor threw them a tethering line as a young midshipman came down from the top deck by way of a ladder and joined six other sailors that appeared around the central deck, rifles in hand. Matthew worked hard to keep himself calm, a smile on his face.

"Good afternoon, sailor," he said in a friendly voice. "What can we do for you?"

"Name and papers, Mr. . . . ."

"Alexander. Matthew Alexander. This is my associate Henry McConnell. My wife and I own Beauchapel, a plantation northeast of Petersburg, just upriver about five miles." He pulled out his pocket wallet and removed his papers. His were real; Newton's were forgeries provided by Beth. The permits to traverse the James for business purposes were also real. Millie had obtained them months earlier. It was how she'd managed to get most of her crop to market. He handed them to the midshipman, who looked them over carefully then handed them back.

"We're delivering this tobacco seed to the docks at Carrollton," Matthew said. "Are you going that way? We could try to keep up. The Union batteries at Newport News are a bit worrisome."

"Mah advise to y'all is to go back the way ya come," he said in a slow Southern drawl. "Mouth a this here river will be a might crowded bah the time y'all git t' Carrollton Harbor," the midshipman said. It was then that Matthew saw the commander come down the ladder and realized he knew the man, had met him weeks earlier on his trip to Norfolk.

"Lieutenant Gettings, nice to see you," Matthew said.

The lieutenant looked a bit shocked then recognized Matthew. "Mr. Alexander," he answered. "Y'all are a far pace from Richmond."

Matthew and the lieutenant had talked at length over dinner about what was happening at Norfolk. At the time, Gettings had no command but was serving as an aide to the commander of the Confederate navy at Norfolk. He was privy to a good deal of information that Matthew wanted. Gettings liked a good bottle of wine and spoke freely when greased with it. In fact, much of what the young lieutenant had told him was mentioned in the notes that lay hidden a few feet from Matthew.

"I'm on leave. You remember me telling you about my fiancée?"

"Miss Atwater. Yes, I remember. Y'all tied the knot, then?"

"A few days ago. She owns Beauchapel, a plantation upriver. This is her overseer, and I decided to accompany him on a delivery of tobacco seed to Carrollton and revisit Norfolk." He smiled feeling it best to change the subject. "I see you finally have your command. Congratulations. I'm glad my recommendation bore fruit." Matthew had promised Gettings he would put in a good word for him. He hadn't. It had all been a part of greasing Gettings ego in order to pump him for information. Andrew figured the same grease would come in handy now.

The lieutenant smiled. "Only temporary. The captain is down with the typhoid and mending back at Norfolk." His countenance changed. "I'm sorry, Mr. Alexander, but I am afraid y'all will have t' come with us."

Matthew feigned a shocked look. "Mr. Gettings, you know who I am. Surely you do not intend to detain me."

"Ah apologize, suh, but, well, them is mah orders, suh. No one is to git passed us for the next twenty fo' hours, suh. When we leave at dawn, we'll pu' y'all back on the rivah, but fo now, y'all can't go any futhah downrivah."

Matthew extended a hand to a sailor and was pulled aboard. He felt a bit of pain from his wound but hardly noticed. He pulled the lieutenant aside, his mind working fast on how to press further. "Then they're bringing out the *Virginia*." He said it softly enough only the lieutenant could hear.

Gettings's shocked look told Matthew he had guessed right, and he put an arm around the man's shoulders. "Lieutenant, you forget I work in the war department. The *Blackhurst* is here for one reason, and one only—to support the *Virginia* in its efforts to break the blockade. Your escape from Elizabeth City was hidden for a reason, and your orders to come downriver are well known to me. I just didn't know the day. I suppose that decision was made after I left Richmond." He paused for effect. "But now that we're here we'll do as you say until time for you to join the *Raleigh* and the *Beaufort*."

Another shocked look. "Ya know about them as well?"

"Would you prefer that a man in my position was left in the dark, Mr. Gettings?"

"Ah, no, suh, not at all, suh."

"You best get back to hiding, Mr. Gettings. Other boats may be on the river besides my own."

"No, suh. The docks at Richmond have been shut down and patrol boats were supposed to be on the water at dawn. I cain't understand how y'all managed . . ."

"We left in a heavy fog and must have just missed them." Matthew realized how lucky they'd been, and his mind scrambled for what to do next. "We appreciate your hospitality, but possibly Mr. McConnell and I should leave you to your work."

The lieutenant thought a moment, unsure of just what to do. "Ah . . . Ah guess since you're with the war department . . . but y'all can only go upriver, suh."

"Fine, fine. Jamestown is close by. We'll go there." Confederate William Allen owned Jamestown Island and raised troops at his own expense to defend it. The army then sent Catesby Jones, a lieutenant, to direct the building of batteries and conduct ordnance and armor tests for the *Virginia*. Matthew hadn't been able to cross the river to Jamestown but thought now was a good time.

"Yes, suh, I suppose so."

"Then we'll go there until tomorrow morning." He turned back to his steamer and nodded for Newton to get in the boat. "Good hunting to you, Mr. Gettings. The Confederacy is depending on your success tomorrow."

Before the lieutenant could disagree Matthew jumped in the steamer, removed the tether rope, and pushed them away from the *Blackhurst*. He sat at the tiller and pushed down on the handle; their small vessel churned into the current and back the way they had come. He didn't look back for fear Gettings would have second thoughts.

"Wha' now, Mr. Alexander?" Newton said with a sly smile.

"We find a way to destroy the *Blackhurst*, Mr. Daines. If we don't, the Confederacy will have an advantage the Union will not be able to overcome, and they'll break the blockade tomorrow."

"The destruction o' one vessel will nah tip the scales much, Matty, me friend. Nah much a' all."

"It'll put a wound in their side, Mr. Daines, and that will slow them down, if not cripple them."

Newton nodded. The *Blackhurst* was a deadly machine, and even if it sunk a single vessel, it would be too many. They had to act tonight.

*   *   *

Newton and Matthew docked at Jamestown and were welcomed by the town's commanding officer. Matthew showed them his papers, and they immediately offered lunch and a tour of the battery overlooking the river. Matthew noted each emplacement. They would be of little value in any real advance by a Union flotilla, but he commended the commander and flattered his ego. Along the way, they were shown the armory and powder room—unguarded but locked. Newton figured its explosives would be easily filched. There was a small coffee house in the village, and they spent the afternoon sipping coffee, deciding on a plan, and passing the time before dinner. They left the coffee house just after dark.

Matthew removed a wheelbarrow from a deserted work site and pushed it toward the armory, where Newton was already waiting, the door wide open.

"It seems you have a talent for lock picking," Matthew whispered.

"Laddie, in Ireland a lock coul' mean starvation. Wee boys learned how to breech a better lock 'n this un if they wished t' reach manhood."

They removed two fifty-pound barrels of powder, some fuse line, and waterproof tarpaulin. Putting it in the wheelbarrow, they closed the door behind them before pushing the barrow toward the steamer tied at the docks.

"Seems t' easy," Newton said.

As they reached the end of the dock, Matthew noted that a picket was sitting atop a bale of cotton, rifle in hand. "While you were spending your childhood learning to be a thief, did they also teach you how to use that skull buster?" Matthew asked.

"'Tis a shocking judgment ya make o' me, Matty boy. Thievan does nah necessarily lead t' breakin' heads, though it was a common malady fer the ones who were of little talent fer filchin.'"

"Do you or don't you know?" Matthew said.

"Keep yer little barrow on course, Matty boy. I'll be seein' t' the soldier."

Matthew rolled the barrow onto the dock, and the soldier immediately got to his feet and blocked the way. The fist came so quick and hard that he dropped the rifle and fell to the ground like a sack of rocks. Newton caught the rifle before it hit the dock and smiled. "See now, yer standin' there wastin' time. Move it, afore I 'ave to whip ya."

Matthew pushed the barrel as Newton pulled the soldier behind the bale and left him lying in a deep sleep. He reached the steamer just as Matthew loaded the second barrel and jumped aboard. The boiler was no longer hot and couldn't be used without drawing attention, so he quickly slid the oars out of their holding place and hooked them in their stays. Newton cast off the line and pushed them away from the dock as Matthew lowered the oars and dipped them into the muddy waters.

Newton sat down and did not speak until they were in the current and quickly moving south. "We finish this, and 'tis most likely they'll know t'was us," he said.

As the moon broke through the clouds, Matthew looked downriver in an effort to get his bearings. The light quickly disappeared, but he saw they were well away from shore and into the current. He pulled his coat tighter around his ears and pulled his wool hat down. The gloves Millie had given him were wool but wet and beginning to freeze.

"Ere ya listenin' to me, Matty boy?"

Matthew nodded.

"You'll nah be comin' back to live a life in the open, me fine friend. Ya best decide if this be worth the loss."

Matthew didn't answer. He had thought of the consequences most of the day, but he had no choice. He could not let the *Blackhurst* join the fight. It would cost too many lives, not to mention possibly break the blockade. This had to be done.

The clouds gave them cover for a few minutes, and Matthew used the time to get closer to shore. He would dock on the up side of land, out of view of the *Blackhurst.*

Newton had his own decision to make. The plan could work, but it would be dangerous to life and limb, the chances of them getting away precarious at best, deadly at worst. But it had to be done, and if he was caught in the process, he would not go back to a rebel prison. Not now, not ever.

They reached the shore and scooted into the shadows as the cloud cover disappeared and the moon glistened once again over the water. The finger of land blocked their view of the *Blackhurst.* Newton grabbed a branch, pulled the steamer to land, then stepped out and yanked it up on dry ground before disappearing into the woods while Matthew began preparing the fuses. Moments later Newton was back.

"She still be sittin' there," he said. "Several be on land, probably t' eat an' sleep. But 'tis enough smoke in 'er stack t' make me think she be leavin' afore long."

Matthew nodded. It was near midnight. The *Blackhurst* would have to leave by two to get downriver by dawn. "More wood. We want full steam."

Newton nodded and went to the fire door of the boiler. He opened it and began putting in quarters. Once he had a fire going, he looked out to the river as if someone might see the flames. The moon was out again and nothing but occasional debris floated on the river. He warmed his hands then went to the hidden compartment in the vessel's front bench and removed two rifles and like amount of revolvers along with powder and shot.

Matthew watched him, a slight smile on his face as he looked at the extra powder and shot. He figured they'd never have time to use them.

Chapter Thirty-One

NEWTON STOOD ON THE CREST of the hill again and blew into his hands, his eyes trying to look through the rain and darkness. The clouds had finally pushed against one another, filled the sky, and then thundered their disapproval at humankind before dumping a heavy rain as proof they meant business. Newton could see lanterns moving about on the deck of the *Blackhurst* and on the land behind it and figured they were breaking camp. He went downhill toward their boat, slipping and sliding on wet, slushy ground. He was shivering as he reached the vessel and found Matthew just finishing putting up the waterproof tarpaulin. Steam rolled out of the stack, and the fire that blazed behind the vented door of the boiler's fire pit welcomed him to warm his hands.

"They be leavin'," he said as he thrust his hands toward the fire door.

Matthew got out and shoved the boat into the river then hopped aboard and sat under the tarpaulin at the tiller. He eased the lever, and the propeller churned against the muddy water. He kept it next to shore, and as they came around the point of land, he saw the lanterns along the *Blackhurst*'s decks and noted she was moving away from shore. Newton positioned himself in the front of the steamer, the tarpaulin keeping him and his weapons dry. He lifted a revolver and tossed it to Matthew then stuck the other in his own belt before grabbing a rifle and preparing to shoot.

Matthew felt the rush of adrenalin as he lit the fuse, pushed the lever to full throttle, and directed the tiller into a collision course with the *Blackhurst*. The rain and clouds gave them good cover while also annoying the men aboard the *Blackhurst* and preventing them from vigilance. They were a hundred feet away when the *Blackhurst* hesitated in the water. He heard voices, screams, just as the first bullet struck their small steamer.

They were only fifty feet away when Newton fired. A black form holding a lantern aloft was suddenly thrown backward and disappeared over the side as the ship lurched forward in an attempt to escape the collision. Bullets whizzed past Matthew's ear, and Newton picked up the second rifle, aimed at the man on the top deck, and fired. The steamer was within twenty feet as Matthew yelled, "NOW!" He and Newton flung themselves overboard.

Their little steamer hit the *Blackhurst* just in front of her gun deck and near the boiler room, skipped over her low, unrailed side and onto her flat deck. It lay there like a beached whale and was still sitting there when Matthew bobbed to the surface of the river. For a moment he thought the fuse had gone out or the powder had been drenched, but then his small steamer ignited into a burst of powder and flame and came apart in every direction. The impact of the small vessel's iron fire pit rammed into the ironclad's metal plating with such force that a hole was blown through it and into the *Blackhurst*'s boilers. The second explosion was horrific. It lifted the *Blackhurst* off the water and split her in two. Matthew cringed as men and parts were flung into the air helter-skelter and debris slammed onto the water. He saw a large piece of the gun deck coming toward him, and he submersed himself and drove down as it hit. The impact nearly broke his eardrums, but he swam hard and reemerged ten feet away, where he was struck in the head by a piece of debris, momentarily stunning him. He shook it off, forcing himself to swim in the general direction of shore while watching the burning, topless hull of the *Blackhurst* float downstream.

He reached the shore in near exhaustion but managed to pull himself onto the muddy bank, where he lay shivering and somewhat paralyzed. He felt hands grab his drenched shirt, pull him to his feet, then all but carry him stumbling up the bank and into the woods. There was a piece of the deck burning in a semi-open spot, and he was deposited next to it where he lay trying to catch his breath. Then he heard the click of a revolver's hammer and opened his eyes to find Gettings standing over him, his eyes cold with rage, the gun shaking like a leaf on a windy day.

"Lieutenant," Matthew said, too tired to even care if the trigger were pulled.

The gun went off, and Matthew felt the sharp sting of the bullet as it grazed his cheek. Gettings was cocking the hammer once more with shaking hands when someone slammed into him, and he suddenly disappeared. A moment later, the sound of a second shot caused Matthew to jump. He forced himself to roll over and get to his knees, his eyes on the two men who lay on the wet winter grass a few feet away. The piece of deck was still burning but beginning to flicker as the rain soaked its surface, but by its dim light, Matthew crawled to where Newton and Gettings lay side by side. He looked down at them both. Gettings's eyes were locked on the heavens, and Newton was struggling to push himself up on his elbows.

"Well now, Matty, me boy, it seems yer little ploy was a success, tho ya near got yerself killed at least twice as I seen it."

Matthew couldn't help the smile. "Seems your own luck is holding out, Mr. Daines"—he noted a deep gash in Newton's arm—"though you are also a bit worse for wear and tear."

Newton looked at the cut and shrugged. "A bit o' flesh wound bu' nuthin' so serious as to think a joinin' Mr. Gettings."

Matthew looked through the trees at the debris and wondered if there were any other survivors. They best not wait around to see. He pushed himself to his feet then offered Newton a hand while wiping the blood away from the wound on his cheek. "Come on, Mr. Daines. We have a ways to go to find shelter."

"If it's survivors ya be worried abou', ya should nah. They're all dead, and this one needs to join 'em in the river. Better chance of 'em deciding it was an accident if they doan find him wi' a bullet in 'is chest."

Matthew nodded, and the two of them each grabbed an arm and drug Gettings back down the hill to the river and watched him float away. Matthew saw the bodies of others floating about in the backwash along the shore. He found one half ashore, a rifle still in his hands, his powder and ball bag hung around his neck. There were no visible wounds, and Matthew figured the impact killed him. He took the weapon and bag then shoved the man on his way before climbing back up the shore, the light of the last burning piece of ship allowing him to see his way. The cold was penetrating his skin; they needed to get warm more than they needed to escape. He stepped to a piece of still-burning debris and stooped to warm himself when Newton joined him and threw him a wet coat. "The owner's in no need of it at present," he said. He was holding one of his own near the flames to dry, and Matthew handed off his then tried to find some dry wood. He found a few pieces of semidry chips under a deadfall and pulled it out before returning to their fire and throwing it on. The wood steamed then dried, and the flame grew. Steam floated heavenward from their soaked clothes. Matthew noticed the rain had stopped. At least drying out was no longer a losing battle.

Matthew pulled the waterproofed bag from under his shirt and checked to make sure it was safe. Finding the papers still dry, he put them back inside the bag before laying it down. The two of them shivered but slowly warmed, neither speaking for a long time.

"'Tis a funny thing 'ow killin' seems right before God in time o' war," Newton said.

The words made Matthew shiver even worse as he realized what they'd done. Some of the men aboard the *Blackhurst* probably had wives, children; most would have had parents praying for their safety. Now they were gone, and he and Newton had made it so. He suddenly felt extreme sickness in his stomach and ran to the water's edge to throw up. He stood there, bent over, aching and shivering from toes to head, when he heard the sound of a motor. He looked across the water and saw a lantern then the outline of small ship.

"'Tis company we'll be havin', Matty boy. We best be on our way." He grabbed the rifle, Matthew grabbed his bag, and they scrambled up the side of the bank into the trees. The moon had once more appeared and gave them light as they ran. They were still a long way from Union lines.

Chapter Thirty-Two

"WELL?"

Isaac had his head down, his Book of Mormon in his hand. "I told you baptism won't make a bit a difference. Ya go in dirty, ya come out dirty; simple as that."

"Tha's true enough, Randolph," Malone chimed in. "A man who 'as sinned like ol' Hooker ain't got a prayer of comin' clean in a little water."

Isaac frowned. "Why thank ya, Mr. Malone. Nobody like the Irish for makin' a man feel worse fer his sins."

The wind howled outside, and the rain and sleet were a loud patter against the tent, but the three of them hardly noticed. They had finally caught up to Grant and were camped just west of Fort Donelson, but the weather had put a hard stop to any action. Rand wasn't sure when Grant would order them to move. Instead, the army had hunkered down, hoping the weather would give them a chance in the morning.

"Baptism has nothing to do with getting clean," Rand said. "The Atonement does that, and you both know it. You haven't murdered anyone, Isaac, and neither has your Irish tormentor, though he does slaughter the English language a good deal. There isn't a sin you might have committed that a broken heart and the Lord won't fix, and you know it as well as I do."

"'Tis nah hard t' get i' done, Isaac; jus' step ou' in this weather, an' you'll be baptized fer ya can count t' ten," Malone said with a grin.

"Sprinklin' don't count," Rand said after a chuckle. "Baptism is not about the past, Isaac; it is about the future." He paused. "You said you asked for forgiveness and have been every night since your blessing. I can't see you asking without meaning it, so it's done. He accepts a broken heart, and He takes your sins. Baptism is about committing to

Him about the future. It's about promising to obey more and sin less. It's about giving that broken heart to Him and meaning it—no hypocrisy and no deception. If you aren't ready to do that, then stay out of the water. But I'll tell you this: sin will hang onto you like a mean dog on your pant leg if you don't take the next step. You need the gift of the Holy Ghost to avoid falling back into sin, and you don't get that without a good dunking as a sign of a willing heart."

It was quiet for a moment. "'e's right, Hooker. Ya come this far. Ya best get i' done. No 'alfway on this one," Malone said.

"And what about you, Malone?" Isaac said.

Malone shrugged and smiled. "I started later than you. Give it a little time."

"Remember Alma's words, Malone. Don't procrastinate the day of your repentance. You're a bigger foot dragger than McClellan."

"I am cu' t' the core, Randolph." He grinned then sobered. "I'm close laddies, really, bu' me heart isn't quite ready fer bein' a Mormon. Isaac now, he kin do it without so much as a pause fer air, but . . ."

He was leaning back in his chair, and Isaac used a foot to sweep the legs out from under him. Malone landed on his backside, bringing a sudden halt to his excuses.

Hooker stood. "All right, Rand. I'm ready, but we'll be doin' it now. Grant will have us in battle before sunup, and they'll be no time tomorrow." He grabbed his coat, undid the flaps at the front of the tent, and was gone. Malone scrambled to his feet, grabbed his own coat, and followed Rand out. They found Isaac staring up at a cloudless sky and a bright moon.

"Seems the good Lord wants to be watchin' ya, Mr. Hooker," Malone said.

They went through the trees and toward the river and were soon on its shore. Removing their coats and hats then their boots, pants, and shirts, Rand and Isaac slipped down an embankment where there was a small piece of land jutting into the water. In the light of the moon, Rand could see a gradual step down and went into the water until he was nearly waist deep. Isaac joined him, and Rand showed him how to grab his arm before telling him what to do. Isaac simply nodded then looked at Rand. "Baptism or not, try t' drown me, and I'll shoot you."

Rand chuckled. "Yeah, I know."

He raised his arm to the square, said the words, then let Isaac back into the cold water. He pushed him down enough to know even Isaac's long hair would be submerged then pulled him out. Isaac stood there, a wide grin on his face. He swept his hair back and wiped the water out of his eyes then blinked and looked up then over at Rand. "Makes you tingle, don't it?" he said with a grin.

"Yeah, it does."

Isaac wrapped his arms around Rand, and they hugged for a long minute as Isaac thanked him. He had never felt so warm, so clean in all his life, and Rand had never felt more thankful for his friend.

"Thank you, Randolph. I ain't never felt better in my whole life."

"Hey, what's goin' on?" They looked at the shore to see a pickett standing there in the moonlight. Trouble was, he was wearing a rebel uniform. "Nothin', son. Just getting baptized," Isaac said.

"Sir, are you Union or Confederate?"

"Don't rightly consider myself either right now, boy," Isaac said. "And if you'd like to join us and have my friend here baptize you, you'll see what I mean."

"No sir, been baptized," the pickett said. "But if y'all be Union, I'll have to shoot ya."

"Then shoot," Isaac said as he walked to shore, Rand behind him. "But at least let me get my boots on afore ya do. No sense dyin' without I have 'em on." He sat down and started to put on his boots. The boy seemed a bit nervous.

"We're going to have a confirmation if you would like to join us," Rand said.

"A what?"

"A confirmation, boy," Isaac said. "You know, where the gift of the Holy Ghost is given to the confirmee."

The boy lowered the rifle, deep in thought. "Is that like a christenin'?"

"Not hardly. I already got a name, son. What I need's the gift of the Spirit. Now you sit down there and pay attention, and you'll see what it all means."

Malone had eased his revolver from his holster and was about to pull back on the hammer when Rand signaled for him to put it away. Malone hesitated then shrugged and let it slip out of sight at his side. Rand stepped to Isaac, laid his hands on his head, and confirmed him then gave him a blessing. When he was finished, he slowly lifted his hands and sensed a quiet he had not sensed before.

No one spoke until the boy did. "Never felt nothing like that before," he said softly.

"No, me neither," Isaac agreed. He stood, and he and Rand hugged again, then Malone got to his feet as Rand and Isaac picked up their clothes.

"You have a nice evening, son," Isaac said to the pickett. "And don't be comin' in the line of fire tomorrow. I don't want to have to shoot you."

They started back toward Union lines, and the boy just stood there until they disappeared in the trees, thinking maybe there was a God after all.

* * *

Newton and Matthew walked all night. They found the Confederate lines at Williamsburgh, presented their papers, and were relieved to be let through to Yorktown. Apparently their role in the sinking of the *Blackhurst* had not been discovered, but both knew it would only be a matter of time. Renting two horses at Yorktown, they rode east toward Bethel. There were patrols to deal with—they avoided two but were surprised by a third. Still their papers got them through. As they approached Bethel, they turned south toward Newport News and ran directly into a skirmish between Confederate and Union patrols. They hid in a barn while the two sides tested one another and by nightfall were able to slip past the rebel position and directly into the hands of Union soldiers. They were arrested and sent into the strongly fortified walls of Newport News, where they slept the night then met with the commander the next morning. A telegram was sent to Monroe then to Washington, verifying Matthew's identity, and by afternoon they were on the road to Fort Monroe, passing through the burned-out city of Hampton.

Matthew knew that Confederate raiders had burned the town, raiders made up of men who owned the homes and businesses. They didn't like their domiciles being used to house contraband slaves or federal soldiers, so they had laid waste to the town at their own great expense. It was an eerie feeling passing through with nothing but brick chimneys and fallen walls, but Matthew feared it was a sign of things to come.

They reported their intelligence to the commanders at Fort Monroe. They'd heard rumors of the *Virginia* and had seen the *Raleigh* but were not aware of the arrival of the *Beaufort* and the *Blackhurst.* Stunned by this news, they immediately moved their wooden frigates to spots covered by Forts Monroe and Newport News for protection, then sent wires to Washington. Apparently, the Union had developed an ironclad of their own, and it was ordered to leave its harbor immediately for the James in order to even the odds. The return telegram bore bad news. The Union ironclad was not fully ready for sea and would not arrive for another ten days. Though the *Virginia* hadn't come out of Norfolk Harbor that day, Matthew knew it was only a matter of time. He only hoped this new Union ship, the *Monitor*, would arrive first.

The next morning, he and Newton boarded a ship for Washington and arrived there the next day. They were met at the docks by half a dozen men; Matthew introduced Newton to Allan Pinkerton and Joe Polanski. Newton spent the next twenty-four hours waiting as Matthew explained what he'd learned to President Lincoln and a dozen others. It was the first time Newton had seen General McClellan, and when asked to tell about his experience, Newton took the opportunity to tell the good general what the folks of Richmond thought of him. He thought the little general would surely bust a gasket but hoped it would get him off dead center before it was too late. At midnight, the exhausted travelers had gone to soft beds at a hotel.

The next morning they went immediately to Georgetown and the Hudson home only to find a stable boy the sole remaining occupant. Newton learned that his Missouri boys had already gone west.

Disappointed, they took the carriage to the telegraph office and sent word to St. Louis that they were both in Washington, safe and sound. Matthew promised a letter later that would explain everything.

"Wha' now, Matty boy?" Newton asked.

"I'm due at the war department. You?"

Matthew had been told to stay put. Plans for a drive up the peninsula from Fort Monroe were already being discussed, and they needed him there.

"I'm off t' Cairo t' catch up t' me unit. Ya can jus' drop me a' the station, an' I'll be on me way."

They had both been given money last night. It was enough for clothes, food, and a ticket west. Newton had no time or desire to shop and would wear what he had on his back.

Matthew leaned out the window of their carriage and gave the instructions to the driver. They rode in silence, both deep in thought about what would come next.

They soon arrived at the train station, and Newton extended a hand to shake. "Bring yer lovely wife to St. Lou, and we'll all celebrate the end o' this here catastrophy t'gether. Shoul' nah be long."

Matthew only nodded. He had seen McClellan's reaction last night. It didn't give him a preponderance of hope in the Union's chances of a quick end.

They shook and Newton climbed down. "'Twas goo' t' fight by yer side, Mr. Alexander. Yer a true-blooded American, and I'm glad t' call ya me friend."

Matthew stuck his head out the window. "You are a man of strong heart, Mr. Daines. Stay alive until we meet again."

Newton grinned as the carriage pulled away.

Chapter Thirty-Three

THE WEATHER HAD TURNED EVEN colder by morning, but the long drum roll called everyone to get up and prepare for battle at 3:00 a.m. They could hear the Confederate response in the distance. No one was sleeping on either side of the line.

Rand and his company had been assigned to General C. F. Smith's brigade and were on the far left. Donelson and the town of Dover were now encircled by more than twenty-five thousand Union troops on the west and blocked by the Cumberland River on the east. By 5:00 a.m., his Missouri boys had moved into position behind the lines and were shivering as the first light shone through the mist of a cold, crisp morning. They would be in reserve and must be ready to move to any position in a moment's time. For now they must wait.

* * *

Mose sat in the seat of the altered wagon, a black named Charles at his side. The rear of the wagon had been enclosed with doors at its back—a makeshift ambulance. Five other such wagons waited in the rear for the battle to begin. Mose had volunteered for this duty just like the other black men involved. They all wanted in, all wanted to do their part, and for now, Mose knew this was as close as any of them would get to a real battle.

Charlie wiped his mouth with the back of his sleeve. He was shivering, part due to nerves, part to fear, and part to inadequate clothing. "Yo' scared, Mose?"

"I'd be a fool not t' be." He looked at the soldiers moving down the road at double time then turning into the woods and forming the battle line. "Ain't nuthin' t' what they's feelin' though. Guaranteed."

He leaned out and looked back down the road. He had driven
his wagon past Rand's camp as they were getting ready for the march.
Now they stood quiet, seemingly calm, waiting as the *thump, thump* of
thousands of feet moved to war. He closed his eyes and said a silent prayer
for Mr. Rand and his men. Then he heard the distant muffled sound of
thunder and knew it wasn't thunder at all. The rebs were ready to fight.

*   *   *

Mounted on Samson, Rand heard the first cannon fire a little after
dawn. From his position at the foot of the slope leading up to the fort,
he couldn't see the shells landing, but he heard the impact and knew
McClernand's brigade, positioned south of Dover and the fort, was
getting hit with everything the rebels had.

Isaac's horse stamped the ground, his head down, the sound of
gunfire igniting both his fear and desire to get on the move. Isaac
stroked its neck as he spoke. "McClernand will be hard-pressed to hold."
He was using his binoculars, scanning the rebel entrenchments directly
in front of them. "They moved men out during the night. If we hit 'em
now, we could take those battlements."

Rand took the offered binoculars and scanned the entrenchments
then the fort itself. "They're trying to break through McClernand's
position. We need to get our boys closer to that end. That's where we'll
be needed, and it won't be long."

As if in answer to Rand's speculation, a horsemen burst out of the
woods behind them and told Rand to get his men around to the right
and support McClernand. It was worse than they thought.

Isaac was already giving the order, and the Missouri boys began a
quick triple-time pace, passing the battlements of General Lew Wallace's
artillery, who were pummeling rebel entrenchments up the hill. As they
turned east along the southern Union line, Rand saw that Union troops
taking cover in the embankment along Wynn's Ferry Road were taking
heavy fire and were not on the attack but holding their own against
rebels coming straight at them. The field was covered with a heavy, damp
smoke, and even though they were a hundred feet behind the lines and
half hidden by a row of trees, Rand could taste the gunpowder. But
he pushed his men hard in the direction of the main battle. He saw
McClernand on top of a distant knoll but was distracted as cannon fire
shattered trees and crashed into the ground twenty feet away. His men

hesitated, but Isaac and Malone screamed at them to be steady and keep moving. The line straightened and drove forward.

As they reached the edge of a cleared field within eyesight of Dover, Rand saw that the Union line was already beginning to break, and rebel infantry were careening down the slope in an all-out attack. He reined his mount in, letting his men catch up while he carefully took measure of the situation. Isaac came up next to him, then Malone did.

"Our right is breaking," Isaac observed. "The rebs have a path through if we don't get in there."

"Malone," Rand instructed, "drive straight in here with A Company. Your goal is that battlement jutting out on that small hill. Then slam into the rebel right and pinch off their attack." Rand looked at the Union line along the road. They were beginning to creep backward, away from the fight, about ready to break as Malone yelled for A Company and gave the order. A Company immediately peeled out and formed the attack behind the Union line. "Hooker, take B Company and form on Malone's left. Head straight at them up the hill. Get to those trenches!" He pointed a hundred yards up the hill. "I'll take C Company and shore up the weak point at the crossroads. Move!"

Isaac gave his orders, and B Company formed as A Company was off with a yell. The startled Union soldiers trying to hold their line saw the attack and were quickly on their feet and joining in. Rand noted that some went down the moment they rose, noted that some of his men were hit and falling, but he immediately ordered C Company to follow him as Isaac and B Company ran forward. Once more the Union line felt the fervor and came to their feet to join the attack.

The road now clear of its defense, Rand had C Company in a run toward the crossroads. They hit the battle there like a battering ram and immediately cut the rebel attempt in two with direct fire at short range. Rand rode Samson into the fray and used both sword and revolver to drive shocked rebels before him. Suddenly, the rebel attack came to a halt, hesitated, then turned in opposite directions, the rebels retreating in chaos and the Union retaking their position and firing at rebel backs. Rand felt something slice at his leg, felt the pain but ignored it. He whipped around and used his sword to slice at whoever had come at him, hitting the man's hand and nearly amputating it. Rand finished him with the last bullet in his revolver. He quickly slid from the saddle, picked up the fallen soldier's pistol, and fired at an oncoming rebel, throwing him onto his back motionless. Another came at him screaming, bloodlust in his eyes. Rand used the pistol as a club and hit the man to the side of the head, sending him to the ground. He struggled to get up, but Rand pushed his sword through the rebel's chest then pulled it free. He shot another only a few feet away then another at a greater distance.

They reached the first trenches of the Confederates and went in. Rand ordered the men to fire, and they poured out a horrible fusillade that cut the Confederate retreat to pieces.

It was then he saw the row of cannons. It was not aimed for distance but directly at his men in the trenches. He heard the boom, saw the smoke, and dove for the ground, screaming at his men to get down. But his yell was too late.

*   *   *

Mose and Charlie jumped from the wagon as it came to a halt at the tree line. They opened the rear doors, grabbed two stretchers, and stumbled toward the wounded along the road. The smoke was thick across the field, the sounds of the battle horrible as cannonballs whistled, exploded, and punished the Union line. The pop of rifle fire was incessant, a solid sound of constant destruction. Mose kept low and ran for a soldier who lay moaning along the road. Mose reached him just in time to see him breathe his last. Sweat was rolling down his face as he raced to another, Charlie just behind him. They lay out the stretcher, lifted the wounded man onto it, and picked it up. As they stood to carry the soldier to the ambulance, Charlie was struck between the shoulder blades, dropped the stretcher, and fell to the ground. Mose ducked as bullets whistled around his ears.

He pulled the wounded man back to the cover at the road bank only to find his patient no longer alive. Mose huddled against the bank, his eyes on Charlie. He didn't move. A cannonball exploded nearby, and Mose covered his head. Union soldiers came out of trees and hurried past him and up the hill into the battle. He got to his knees and looked over the edge of the bank. He saw some fall and tumble back; others paused to fire.

Mose watched as one soldier loaded his weapon, raised it but didn't pull the trigger, and started loading again, jamming more powder down the barrel. If he fired it with two rounds . . . Mose launched himself up the hill just as the soldier aimed the gun. He fired before Mose could reach him, and the gun exploded in his hands and blew up in his face. He was dead when Mose reached him. In his fear, he had loaded twice but only fired once.

Mose felt a bullet graze the top of his shoulder, and he dove for cover behind another soldier's lifeless body. He saw a rifle. It was primed. He grabbed it, stood, and raised it to his shoulder. The field was suddenly in slow motion. He could see it all, could see each fight, each soldier. He looked for the enemy, put the sight to his eye, and pulled the trigger. As the man was thrown back, Mose grabbed the dead soldier's ball and powder bag and began to reload. When he was finished, he stood and ran forward.

*　*　*

Some had heard Rand's scream, but some did not. As the cannon fired its grapeshot, Rand hit the bottom of the trench. The deadly fire cut men in half, leaving a horrible path of destruction directly through his line. When he lifted his head and stared at the slaughter, his blood ran hot with anger, and he stood, clawed his way up the embankment, and charged the cannon emplacement, screaming. Others surrounded him, rushing forward like a wave, reaching the emplacement, and overrunning it just as the fuse was lit. Rand threw all his weight into the cannon's barrel and drove it left as it exploded. His ears were ringing, and he was disoriented as he struggled back to his feet to find Hooker at his side, fighting three men armed with knives. Rand shot one of them; Hooker threw one over his shoulder and stuck the third with a bowie knife. He stood there, large and violent, staring at Rand, a slight smile on his face, then the smile disappeared and blood appeared on his shirt. He tumbled over, the smile turning to shocked wonder as he stared at the heavens.

Rand grabbed him by the collar and quickly pulled him into a nearby trench, out of harm's way. He knelt by his friend. Hooker blinked, a slight smile on his face. No, not Hooker. Hooker was invincible.

"Well now, seems you dunked me just in time," Hooker said. He coughed lightly as Rand tore open his friend's shirt only to find a sickening hole in his chest. Rand tried desperately to stanch the blood. Hooker gently grabbed his arm. "Too late, Randolph. Too late. You take care a Ann now, ya hear, an—" He coughed again, and blood drenched his lips. Then his eyes glazed over, and he was gone.

Rand put his friend's head down, tears filling his eyes when
something hit him hard and flung him headlong into the mud of the
trench. When he turned over, he was staring up into the mad eyes of a
rebel soldier, his face bloodied and his hand clentching the bayonet that
was about to end Rand's life. Then a rifle butt slammed into the rebel's
head, and he toppled over into the trench facedown. Rand scrambled to
his feet as someone grabbed his arm and pulled him up out of the trench
and behind an outcropping of rocks. Union guns fired all around him,
and mini-balls from the rebels splashed in the mud on both sides.

"Massa Rand."

Rand heard the voice but was in shock and didn't respond.

"Massa Rand!" The man shook him, and Rand looked into the blood-
and mud-splattered face and thought he was seeing things.

"Yo' stay down, Massa Rand," Mose said. He turned, aimed his rifle,
and fired.

"Mose! What . . . ?!"

"Dey's comin'," Mose said as he calmly reloaded. "Yo' bes' start usin'
dat pistol, Massa Rand, or we's both dead men!"

Rand forced himself to turn and look around the side of the outcrop.
The rebels were coming. He quickly looked behind them. The Union
line was still coming forward. He started to scramble out from behind
the outcrop when Mose grabbed him and pulled him back. "Wait fo'
t'thuthers," he said calmly. "Just shoot."

Rand nodded slowly, the shock disorienting him. He tried to shove
it aside, aimed, and fired angrily at the oncoming rebels. He emptied his
cylinder, quickly removed it, put in a fully loaded one, and fired again
and again and again. Hooker was dead! They'd killed Hooker.

Mose grabbed his hand. "Massa Rand, ain't nothin' gonna bring
back Mr. Issac, and just shootin' all dem bullets without thinkin' doan
do us no good. Now you take a deep breath and aim jus' right 'fore they
overrun us."

Rand blinked, nodded, then took a deep breath, and was about to
fire when more Union soldiers joined them at the outcropping or dove
into the trench where Hooker lay. The nearest looked at Mose, his
mouth agape, then at Rand with wonder.

"Ain't you never seen a black man afore?" Mose said with some
irritation.

The soldier looked at Rand. "Sir, this here ain't no place for no black . . ."

"Never mind, soldier,' Rand said. "Concentrate on the enemy. *He's up there.*" He pointed with his gun. The soldier hesitated a look of confusion in his eyes as he stepped past Mose to face Rand directly. "He's black, an' I ain't fightin' with no *black* no matter . . ."

Rand saw the rebels pop up out a trench to his left saw one raise his revolver to fire at the belligerent soldier. Then a hand grabbed at and jerked the soldier back, tossing him away just as the bullet slammed into the outcrop where he'd been standing. He saw Mose fire his rifle, killing the reb, then begin to reload. The belligerent soldier's mouth was agape as Rand gave him a cold smile. "It's good for you that this *black* isn't as particular as you are." He said flatly. He looked at the rest of the men.

"Boys," Rand said. "Let's get 'em!"

Rand started from behind the outcrop, and the men followed. More came out of the trench behind them with a yell and scrambled after him. Their sudden appearance startled the rebels and they hesitated, fumbled with their reload, then began to turn tail as Rand and his men charged. Rand no longer had his sword but grabbed for his knife, fired his revolver, and drove forward. He saw the panic in rebel eyes, saw the line break, saw them retreat in panic. He went to one knee and fired the rest of his cylinder at fleeing backs. As he replaced it with another, more Union soldiers joined on his left and pressed hard against the rebels.

As the confederates ran back the way they'd come, they were hit with the mini balls from a hundred rifles, decimating their numbers. The Union soldiers charged—shooting, stabbing, killing. Then they suddenly disappeared as Confederate cannons fired directly into them. He felt the the shrapnel rip into him and throw him back. He tried to get up but couldn't. His left side . . . What had happened? Why couldn't he get up? Pain shot through his body, and he looked at where his arm should be only to find a limp, torn, and bloddied sleeve. His mind seemed to go grey, then black. He fought to stay conscious . . . tried to lift himself, get to his men. Then there was darkness and he felt nothing at all.

*   *   *

Mose saw Rand fall and quickly went back down the hill to his side as more Union soldiers ran past him and into battle. Mose saw the blood and knew the injury was bad. He tossed his rifle aside then used what strength he still had to lift Rand over one shoulder. He must get his friend to the ambulance. They started down the hill. Mose slipped, fell, but didn't drop his precious cargo. He forced himself back to his feet and started again. Then he felt something hit him in the side with such force it knocked him off blance, and he fell again. This time he couldn't hold Rand, and his friend fell into the mud and began to slide down the hill until he lodged against a small tree.

Mose tried to get up, but his legs didn't seem to work. Desperate to get to Rand, he pulled himself through the mud and grass as his mind became clouded with pain. He shook it off and pulled with all his strength. He must get Rand to safety. He finally reached Rand, and with the last bit of strength he could muster, Mose reached out and took his hand. "It be alright Massa Rand," He whsipered. Some . . . somebody come soon. You . . . you be all . . . alright."

"Mose," Rand said softly. "Tell Ann . . ."

"You ain't gonna die, Massa Rand," Mose said softly but firmly. "You hold on now. You has t' jus' hold on. Miss Ann need you, and tha' . . . tha' chil', he be . . . he be . . ." His voice was soft, tired. He swallowed hard against the pain.

"Why, Mose? Why did you . . ."

"Ah had t' do mah part, Randolph. I had to. Ain't right you fightin' for us folks alone. Just ain't right." He coughed, fighting for another moment. "Tell Lydijah . . . tell her not t' fret none 'bout what I done." He squeezed Rand's hand briefly with the last of his strength. "Tell her . . . tell her I loves her an . . . an we be seein' . . . I be waitin' with yo' ma and pa. Tell her . . ." Mose coughed again, and it is was all he could do to take another breath. Then it just went out of him. He thought to fight it for a moment, but then knew he couldn't. It was time. He closed his eyes.

Rand felt the stillness. "Mose?" he said weakly. He squeezed Mose's hand. Nothing. Rand felt the ache in his heart, felt to scream at his friend, wake him, but couldn't. His mind slowly clouded over, and he felt cold. He hung onto Mose's hand, the strength oozing out of his body as quickly as the blood that stained the ground beneath him. Then he felt another presence, but it was all a blur now and he felt cold. He could hear someone speaking, saying his name, but all he could do was hang onto Mose's hand, try to fight the blacknes. Someone lifted him, broke his grip on Mose. He tried to cry out, but the words just wouldn't come as darkness crept into his mind then smothered him.

* * *

Malone stared down at his friend wondering if he could live long enough to get him help. His arm was surely mangled, nearly gone. Malone had thrown a otrnizuet on it att the armpit, stanching the flow but still…

"Sir," a soldier said to Malone.

Malone turned a bit so he could face the soldier who spoke. As he did he noted that the battle was now far up the hill and that Union soldiers finally had the upper hand. He also noted the hundreds of dead or wounded scattered about like stones on a rocky slope. The cost of taking Fort Donelson would be very high. He turned back and started walking again.

"I'll bring the black, sir," the soldier called after him. "He . . . he saved my life," The soldier said.

Malone only nodded, then hurried away from the battle. He had to get help for Rand.

*   *   *

The soldier looked down at the lifeless body. The battle seemed far away now, far less deadly. Though gun and cannon smoke hung heavy on the muddy hillside, the Confederates were surrendering, throwing their guns out. They had been beaten.

An approaching soldier looked at Mose then kicked at the body. "What's a filthy darkie doin' out here?" he said with obvious distaste. He was about to spit in Mose's general direction when a fist caught him under the chin, lifted him off the ground, and planted him flat on his back. When the stars cleared away, he looked at the first soldier with anger. "What'd ya go and do that fer?" he said, grabbing his jaw. "Darkies ain't supposed—"

"Well, this one was and thank goodness fer it or I'd be dead as the rest of these boys, and if'n we had a few thousand more just like him, them cussed rebs would be done fer." With that he turned down hill and started walking. The second soldier got to his feet nursing a nearly broken jaw with his fingers. He'd never seen a white man defend a black like that. Never.

The first soldier reached the road and found a wagon that was being used to haul the dead and wounded. He started to put Mose into the back of it when the man driving the wagon cursed him. "You ain't puttin' no black—"

The soldier put him in the wagon anyway, and the driver came down off it in a flurry of harsh swear words. A moment later he was lying on his back wondering what hit him as the soldier climbed aboard the driver's seat, and whipped the horses into a quick trot. This time nobody tried to stop him.

Chapter Thirty-Four

Five Months Later

MILLIE STARED INTO THE DARKNESS, her ears pricked to listen. The boat should come at anytime.

Judah Benjamin and Henry Hyde had both appeared at her door a week after Matthew's departure. She had let them in and listened to their questions and their ranting, offering the answers she and Matthew had decided on before he left. They went away thinking she had been duped even more thoroughly then they, but both left angry, Benjamin far more so than Henry. His last statement was that he should have listened to Geery. Millie only smiled, thinking it ironic. If Geery hadn't gone mad, he actually might have lived long enough to have enjoyed at least some of his revenge.

From the conversation, Millie had learned just what Matthew had done and what it had cost the Confederacy. The sudden demise of the *Blackhurst* had thrown the James River Squadron into disarray and sparked fear that their entire plans had been discovered and may come unraveled. Instead of attacking at the appointed time, they had delayed. Though they finally did bring the *Virginia* out of Norfolk and attacked the federal fleet with a good deal of success, they were not able to break the blockade. Having the *Blackhurst* might have made all the difference.

A week later, Beth Van Lew had visited Beauchapel with a friend and Mrs. Tuck. The friend had offered Millie a handsome sum for her plantation, and they had arranged to have the money sent to the Bank of England. Word had come only two days ago that the money had arrived.

Tuck had received a message via the couriers from Washington, and she had brought it to Beauchapel herself: Matthew was safe in the North and would come for her as soon as he could. But Tuck had a better idea. It was too dangerous to wait, both for Millie and for Matthew. Tuck had arranged for Millie's escape.

"Should be comin' soon," Tuck said.

Millie looked at the moving shadows around her. Even at night, the bright white hair of Mr. Dix shone in the darkness, and the children were having a horrible time keeping quiet, but she didn't mind. They were safe here. They had made it to Union lines.

Since the battle on the *Monitor* and the *Merrimac*, the upper James had been heavily patrolled, and Millie and her workers had escaped over land, using Underground Railroad stops well known to Amberline Tuck, who had been helping blacks escape for more than ten years.

Tuck had hid them in broad daylight. She shackled the blacks in two wagons then had several friends ride shotgun. Millie rode in a carriage behind the group and played the role of the devilish owner who was taking her runaways back to her plantation in the Shenandoah. Rebels bought it, and as soon as their group wound its way through the difficult roads in western Virginia's mountains, they raced for their point of rendezvous. It was a small town Tuck had lived in once and knew well. It was on the Union line, and they'd sent word of the plan by courier to Matthew.

Their escape had been aided by McClellan's drive up the peninsula toward Richmond. With the need for more troops there, the Confederates had withdrawn many of their forces from Front Royal to Manassas Junction. Though McClellan had bogged down just east of the Chickahominy River, near the Clays' plantation, the Confederate force between Washington and Fredericksburg was stretched and porous. Matthew had sent word it would be and of how to get through it. Though there had been frightening moments and close calls, they had finally wiggled their way through the lines to safety.

"I has t' be goin', Millie," Tuck said. "You tell your beau hello for me."

Tuck intended to use all the darkness she could to get her and her men past nervous rebel patrols. They had traded their wagons in for horses, and the four of them were itching to get moving.

"I will." She hugged Tuck tight, thanking her. "Be safe, Tuck, and if you have to run—"

"Ain't no reb driving me outa Virginy," Tuck said as she mounted. "I'll fight 'em first." She shoved her pipe in between her ragged row of teeth.

"Now, you doan worry none about me; you just be makin' babies with that thar husband a yorn. We need more good Yanks in this here world."

She grinned then turned her horse as the men each tipped their hats and followed. Millie waved and thanked them one last time before they disappeared in the darkness.

"Mrs. Alexander."

Millie turned to the soldier in front of her. "Yes, Lieutenant Mackson?"

"They're just up the road, ma'am. If you'll bring these folks along, we'll get you where you can join them."

Millie called to the others and told them to come along. They quickly followed the soldier. They reached the federal camp but skirted it, the glowing fires and shared laughter giving her a warmth she didn't expect. Matthew appeared out of the darkness, and she dropped her bag and ran, jumping into his arms when she reached him. He whirled her around, kissing her, laughing, kissing her again as her workers gathered around clapping and singing.

An older woman slowly approached the couple. Matthew stood back, still holding Mille's hands in his own, and directed his wife's attention to the other woman. "Millie, this is my mother. She came all the way from St. Louis to see you."

Millie hugged Amanda tight, and Amanda beamed. "Oh my, my, how wonderful! And such a pretty girl, Matthew. More than you deserve; I can see it even now."

Matthew bowed slightly, smiling. "Why, thank you, Mother." Millie returned to his arms as Mackson approached.

"Mr. Alexander, we have to get you moving," the lieutenant said. "It'll be light soon."

The troops camped around them would march early. It seemed there had been a raid during the night by Tom Jackson's forces. He was doing a good job keeping the Union busy here so they couldn't send more troops east to Richmond.

Matthew and Millie walked arm and arm to the wagons, quickly loaded the workers, then climbed into the seat of the first wagon. She hung tightly to his arm as he whipped the reins on the horses' rumps and got them moving. She didn't care about the war now. She was safe. Matthew was safe.

And that was all that mattered.

* * *

Ben saw the horse and rider coming down the street of Florence, the sun behind them. He put a hand up to get a better look at the familiar frame sitting in the saddle. He smiled as the horse came to a halt next to him.

"I understand you're the man to talk to if a woman wants to go west," Lizzy said with a smile.

Ben felt his heart begin to pound faster, but he forced a frown. "That depends."

Lizzy gave him a quizzical look. "Depends?"

"On whether you can take orders," Ben said.

Lizzy slipped from the saddle, removed her hat, and slapped it against her hand to knock off the dust. "I'm not used to taking orders."

"Yes, I know," Ben smiled. "How are you, Elizabeth?"

"Anxious to see Salt Lake."

Ben feigned concern, his eyes going to the holstered revolver at her side. "I'm not sure the sisters of the Relief Society are ready for you, Elizabeth."

Lizzy chuckled. "I won't shoot any of 'em, Ben. I promise."

He laughed lightly. "No, I don't suppose you will." He took the reins from her hand, and they started walking, Cruz behind him. Lizzy put her arm through his. He put his hand on hers and felt its warmth. "You'll need supplies," Ben said.

Lizzy glanced over her shoulder, put two fingers in her mouth, and gave a sharp whistle. Ben looked back to see two wagons appear out of a side street. There were two large Belgian workhorses pulling each. He saw a man and a woman riding in the seat of the first, the man handling the team. In the second, there was an older black woman, a white fellow at her side driving the team. They caught up, and Ben smiled at the couple in the first wagon.

"Mr. and Mrs. Hudson, nice to see you." He hadn't seen Ann or Rand in some time and was surprised to note that Rand was missing an arm.

"And you, Ben," Rand said with a smile. Ann had one hand on her stomach, the jostling causing her some difficulty, but she had a wide smile. "Mr. Connelly, nice to see you again."

"And you," Ben said.

"Jacob said you might have room for us in your group," Rand said.

"We always have room for Saints, Randolph," Ben replied.

"Good." Rand nodded once. The reins lay in his remaining hand, and he slapped them against the horses' rumps. They continued moving forward. The second wagon passed by, and the man tipped his hat to them as Lydijah smiled and spoke.

"Massa Ben, how is you?" she asked with a smile.

"Ah, Lydijah. I haven't eaten well since leaving your kitchen! Will you cook for us tonight?" he asked.

Lydijah laughed. "It would be mah pleasure, sho nuf. Sho nuf! But it be costin' yo'!"

"Anything, dear girl! If I have to eat another of my own meals, I will simply die."

"Yo' be takin' us to Salt Lake, and ah cook fo' you ever day, I will."

"It's a deal." He reached up and took her hand then looked at the man whom he did not recognize. "And you, sir, I . . ."

"Daines. Newton Daines. 'Tis a pleasure to be meetin' ya, Mr. Connelly. We'll have to talkin' about your Irish name when we have the time. Miss Lizzy says a goo' deal abou' ya but nah enough. An' you'll nah be eyein' 'er aofre we have our little talk. Me life is dedicated to her wellbein,' an' I ain' abou' t' see ya lookin' on 'er fer marryin' withou' knowin' ya better." Newton grinned, and Lizzy went a bright shade of red. A rare color for her.

Ben smiled. "We'll be talkin', then."

Newton tipped his hat and whipped the reins over the horses, and they began again. Ben watched them go. "A rival is my guess."

Lizzy chuckled. "A champion boxer. Beat Kernlin of St. Louis, if you know the name."

"Indeed. All the Irish know of Mr. Kernlin. Shall I shapren my skills at the art of fist of cuffs then?"

"Time will tell, Mr. Connelly."

Ben paused. "Isn't he your friend who was imprisoned in Richmond?"

"Yes. He escaped." When she finished telling him an abbreviated version of the story, they had arrived at the staging area just outside the town. "Newton arrived at Fort Doneslon just after its surrender. He found Rand in the hospital, near death, Malone at his side. He sent word to us, and Ann and I went there and eventually brought Rand home.

Malone and Newton went on with Grant to the Battle of Shiloh. Malone was killed there, and Newton was hit in the leg, shattering the bone. He doesn't have much use of it now, but he hopes to mend enough to return to the war. I hope it's over before then. We've lost enough friends already."

He glanced at her. There was still a good deal of hurt and loss in her eyes. Andrew Clay had made a deep mark.

"Have you heard from Andrew's family?"

She nodded. "Matthew Alexander was able to get my letter to them through a Mrs. Tuck. I received a return letter from Andrew's father just a few days ago. They were grateful to know what had happened. The Confederate army said only that he had died defending Bowling Green. Horatio said he was grateful it was in defending something far more important to Andrew than the honor of the Confederacy." She paused. "The body was returned to their plantation for burial." She forced a smile. "Horatio freed his slaves but most of them decided to stay and work for him. It was Andrew's wish."

They walked in silence to where Rand and Newton had pulled the wagons under the shade of some trees. He and Newton were unhooking the horses.

"I wish it had worked out differently, Elizabeth. I . . ." Ben couldn't finish the words.

Lizzy faced him and placed a finger against his lips. "Andrew will always be a part of my life, Ben, just as your wife will always be a part of yours. Neither of us will forget them, and that is as it should be. But I believe they would want us to be happy, don't you?"

He nodded, a slight smile on his face. "Yes, I suppose they would." It was then he heard the sound of axe against wood and turned to see Newton chopping up some dried timber.

"Mr. Daines, you'll not be needing that wood. You have time only for a little cold food before we pull out."

Rand looked up, and Newton gave an amiable smile. Ann poked her head around the corner of wagon cover, and Lydijah stopped removing pots from the back of the wagon.

"Tonight?" Lizzy asked, "But . . ."

"We have several hours of daylight left. We want to be at our first camp by dark." He started to walk away. "You'll be the last of fifty wagons, Mr. Hudson," he called back. "Those Belgians are fine animals, but they won't last as long as oxen. If I were you"—he pointed back toward Florence—"I would trade them and quickly." With that, he turned back and began giving orders to other wagons to get ready to leave. The camp turned into a bustle of activity. Rand shrugged at Newton, who picked up the axe, limped to the wagon, and put it in its place. He limped back to help Rand prepare the Belgians to be lead to Florence while Lydijah and Ann began putting things back in the wagon.

Lizzy stood there for long minutes watching Ben Connelly, a smile on her face. After a moment she turned, picked up Cruz's reins, then mounted. When Rand had the four animals hooked together, she took the lead rope and started back to Florence. It was going to be an interesting trip to Salt Lake. An interesting trip indeed.

About the Author

ROBERT MARCUM IS A RETIRED professor of religion. He taught seminary and institute for seventeen years before being hired at Ricks College and BYU-Idaho, where he taught until retirement in 2008. He has a bachelors degree in history from BYU with a minor in art, and a masters degree from Idaho State University.

His interest in writing began at a young age, but it was in 1989, after taking a creative writing class from a fellow professor at Ricks College, that he created his first manuscript for publication. Since then he has written twelve novels in both the action-adventure and historical fiction genres for the LDS market.

His wife, Janene, an English teacher by trade, does her best to correct his grammar and strengthen his stories with her tireless edits and counsel while his eight children and many of their twenty grandchildren are among his most avid cheerleaders. Robert loves history and has traveled extensively to Europe, the Middle East, and around the United States in an effort to enhance his novels with the important detail that only visual presence can offer.

In preparing for the Nation Divided series, he has read more than twenty books on the Civil War, including personal journals of those who participated, in order to give readers the most vivid and personal view of the events surrounding this period of American history.